ABOUT THE AUTHOR

One of the most neglected American writers and also one of the best
loved, Nelson Algren wrote once that "literature is made upon any
occasion that a challenge is put to the legal apparatus by conscience
in touch with humanity." His writings always lived up to that defini-
tion. He was born March 28, 1909 in Detroit and lived mostly in
Chicago. His first short fiction was published in *Story* magazine in
1933. In 1935 he published his first novel, *Somebody in Boots*. In early
1942, Algren put the finishing touches on a second novel and joined
the war as an enlisted man. By 1945, he still had not made the grade
of Private first class, but the novel *Never Come Morning* was widely
praised and eventually sold over a million copies. Jean-Paul Sartre
translated the French-language edition. In 1947 came *The Neon
Wilderness*, his famous short story collection which would permanently
establish his place in American letters. *The Man with the Golden Arm*,
winner of the first National Book Award, appeared in 1949. Then
came *Chicago: City on the Make* (1951), a prose poem and *A Walk on the
Wild Side* (1956), possibly his greatest novel. Algren also published two
travel books, *Who Lost an American?* and *Notes from a Sea Voyage. The
Last Carousel*, a collection of short fiction and nonfiction, appeared in
1973. He died on May 9, 1981, within days of his appointment as a fellow of the American Academy and Institute of Arts and Letters. His
last novel, *The Devil's Stocking*, based on the life of Hurricane Carter,
and *Nonconformity: Writing on Writing*, a 1952 essay on the art of writing, were published posthumously in 1983 and 1996 respectively.

THE LAST CAROUSEL

NELSON ALGREN

SEVEN STORIES PRESS
new york

Copyright © 1973 by Nelson Algren
All rights reserved.
First Seven Stories Press edition, 1997

Seven Stories Press
632 Broadway, 7th Floor
New York, N.Y. 10012

In the U.K.:
Turnaround Publisher Services Ltd., Unit 3, Olympia Trading Estate, Coburg Road, Wood Green, London N22 6TZ U.K.

In Canada:
Hushion House, 36 Northline Road, Toronto, Ontario M4B 3E2, Canada

Library of Congress Cataloging-in-Publication Data

Algren, Nelson, 1909-1981
        The last carousel/Nelson Algren—1st Seven Stories Press edition
        p.   cm.
        ISBN: 1-888363-45-2
        I. Title.
[PS3501.L4625L3 1997]
813'.52—dc21   96-48583
                                                            CIP

Printed in the USA

10 9 8 7 6 5 4 3 2 1

For Kay Boyle

BY THE SAME AUTHOR

Somebody in Boots
Never Come Morning
The Neon Wilderness
The Man with the Golden Arm
Chicago: City on the Make
A Walk on the Wild Side
Who Lost an American?
The Book of Lonesome Monsters (EDITED BY NELSON ALGREN)
Conversations with Nelson Algren: (WITH H. E. F. DONOGHUE)
Notes from a Sea Diary
The Last Carousel
Nonconformity: Writing on Writing

CONTENTS

ACKNOWLEDGMENTS

"Dark Came Early in That Country" was first published in *Atlantic*, August, 1968, under the title "Home to Shawneetown." Revised.

"Could World War I Have Been a Mistake" was first published in *Audience*, Vol. I, No. 1, under the title "Swan Lake Re-swum." Revised.

"Otto Preminger's Strange Suspenjers" was first published in *Focus/media*, 1972.

"I Never Hollered Cheezit the Cops" was first published in *Atlantic*, October, 1972. Revised.

"The Mad Laundress of Dingdong-Daddyland" was first published in *Commentary*, September, 1969, under the title "Decline and Fall of Ding-Dong Daddyland."

"The Leak That Defied the Books" was first published in *The Dude*, 1961, under the title "God Bless the Lonesome Gas Man." Revised.

"Tinkle Hinkle and the Footnote King" was first published in *Dial*, fall 1959, under the title "Ding-Ding, Tinkle Hinkle, the Finkified Lasagna and the Footnote King." Revised.

"Brave Bulls of Sidi Yahya" was first published in *Playboy*, December, 1972, under the title "The Way to Médenine."

"I Know They'll Like Me in Saigon" was first published in *The Critic*, February-March, 1969. Revised.

"Airy Persiflage on the Heaving Deep, *or* Sam, You Made the Ship too Short" first appeared in *Works in Progress*, No. 1 (issued by the Literary Guild of America).

"No Cumshaw No Rickshaw" was first published in *Holiday*, November, 1971.

"Letter from Saigon" was first published in two parts in the March-April and April-May, 1969, issues of *The Critic* under the title "That Was No Albatross."

"Police and Mama-sans Get It All" was first published in *Rolling Stone*, May 27, 1971, under the title "White Mice and Mama-sans Get It All."

"Poor Girls of Kowloon" was first published in *The Critic*, November-December, 1969, under the title "They Don't Belong to Us."

"After the Buffalo" first appeared as the introduction to *The True Story of Bonnie and Clyde*, New American Library, 1968.

"The House of the Hundred Grassfires" constitutes the material deleted before publication from *A Walk on the Wild Side* and first appeared in the anthology *Nelson Algren's Book of Lonesome Monsters*, Lancer Books, 1962. Reissued by Bernard Geis Associates, 1963.

"Previous Days" was first published in the *Chicago Sunday Tribune*, April 30, 1972, under the title "Blanche Sweet Under the Tapioca."

"Merry Christmas Mr. Mark" was first published in the *Chicago Sunday Tribune*, December 4, 1949.

"I Guess You Fellas Just Don't Want Me" was first published in *Audience*, November-December, 1971, under the title "Ipso Facto."

"Everything Inside Is a Penny" was first published in *Playboy*, July, 1962 under the title "The Father & Son Cigar."

"Go! Go! Go! Forty Years Ago," a reminiscence of the Chicago White Sox of 1919, was written for the *Chicago Sun-Times* during the 1959 World Series.

"A Ticket on Skoronski" was first published in the *Saturday Evening Post*, November 5, 1966. Revised.

"Ode to an Absconding Bookie" was first published in the *Chicago Sunday Tribune*, October 9, 1972.

"Bullring of the Summer Night" was first published in *Playboy*, June, 1970, under the title "Get All the Money." Revised.

"Moon of the Arfy Darfy" was first published in the *Saturday Evening Post*, May 7, 1964. Revised.

"Watch Out for Daddy," the middle section of this piece was first published in *Playboy*, April, 1957, under the title "All Through the Night."

"The Last Carousel" was first published in *Playboy*, February, 1972. Revised.

"Epitaph: The Man with the Golden Arm" was first published in *Poetry: A Magazine of Verse*, August, 1947.

THE LAST CAROUSEL

DARK CAME EARLY
IN THAT COUNTRY

"WE'LL fight you on condition you don't knock Reno out in the first two rounds," DeLillo's manager told me, "after two it's every man for hisself."

"Honor Word?" I asked him.

"A hundred dollars and you pay your own expenses to Chicago, Honor Word," he told me.

"Do we take it?" I asked Beth.

"We take it," she told me.

"I don't have the expenses," I told her.

Beth gave me the expenses.

We were the semi-windup. A place called Marigold.

During instructions I asked DeLillo where was he from. He didn't answer. I didn't expect him to. I just wanted him to think about where he was from while I was working the lace of my left glove loose.

I caught him light with the lace across the eye early in the round. He stepped back and complained to the ref. The ref tightened the lace and waggled his finger at me: naughty Roger. By the middle of the round DeLillo's eyelid had begun to swell. By the end of the round he couldn't see on that side. I could have reached over and belted him out but I didn't. I'd give my Honor Word.

In the second I got on his blindy side and clipped him under the ear. He sagged. I could have finished him off but I didn't. I danced him up and down till his ear stopped ringing. You see I'd give my Honor Word.

When we came out for the third I extended my gloves to him.

"It ain't the last round," DeLillo told me.

"It is for you," I told him, and reached over and knocked him cold. I always did have color.

I sent the hundred to Beth by money order. It got back to Shawneetown before I did. When I got there I still had some expenses.

"It shows I can fight a *little*, don't it?" I asked Beth.

"A little; but not much," Beth told me.

"Well, I know the *moves*, anyhow."

"You know the moves alright," Beth told me, "but you can't fight much."

Friday, that week, we caught the Fight of the Week. The room would have been warm enough without a fire, but Beth has to keep one going all year round because of my Pa. The old man was sitting in his overcoat, like he does all year round, helping us watch Pete Mathias, the middleweight titleholder. Being a fighter is a step up from the mines, to Pa.

Mathias was having trouble against an opponent no smarter than Reno DeLillo.

"He wouldn't be taking chances like that against *you*, Roger," Pa told me, "he wouldn't let hisself open against *you*."

We let the old man say what he wants so long as he don't complain. Pa don't have the right to complain anymore.

Around the eighth round I got the feeling I *could* whip Mathias. I got the feeling so strong I switched the fight off. Beth smiled just as if she understood.

Beth always smiles like she understands everything about everything. Maybe she does. The idea of my quitting the ring and opening a diner was hers. She found one for sale, too. Two thousand dollars. In Carriers Mills. But we were no nearer buying it than we were four years ago when we first got engaged. Maybe she don't really understand anything.

My hundred-dollar kayo at the Marigold wasn't featured by *Ring Magazine* and I greatly doubt it will be listed in *Boxing Year Book* under *Great Battles of All Time*. When I got into San Antonio I had forty dollars left and I had to fight some fellow Sweetmouth Jenkins at the Army Post there. He got a white manager.

A couple hours before fight time there was a polite rap at my hotel door. The door wasn't locked. I didn't bother getting off the bed.

"I'm Jenkins' manager," a little man in white seersucker, holding his hat in his hand, told me. I still didn't get off the bed. I'd never seen a fight manager holding his hat before. It was my first time.

"My boy is a nice boy with a wife and family," this Polite Manager let me know. "Ah hope you don't bust him up *unnecessarily*, Roger. I'm not asking you not to beat him. Just don't bust him up. His wife is hardly more than a girl, Roger."

"Am I fighting Jenkins or his family?" I asked this Polite Manager.

"His wife will be down front, Roger. She's expecting."

I got off the bed.

"My name isn't 'Roger,' " I told the man, "it's 'Holly.' Now what *is* this anyhow? Would your boy take it easy on *me* if I had a wife expecting?"

"Ah purely regret having brought the matter up, Mr. Holly," he told me; and left just as if I were letting him down. " 'Holly' is my *last* name!" I hollered after him.

But he kept on walking like he didn't hear.

Mr. Sweetmouth Jenkins, sitting across the ring from me, had a mouth like a tribal drum. And here he comes at me with his piano-key teeth sticking out too far. I can feint him with my shoulders. I can feint him with my feet. I can feint him with my eyes or hands. But Mr. Sweetmouth is so busy doing everything wrong he don't even know I'm feinting him. How can I take a man out I can't set up? He got away from me six times in the first two rounds and in the third he begun looking good. I could almost hear Mrs. Jenkins saying, "Daddy, you looked *wonderful* the first three rounds." Daddy wouldn't be able to answer because his jaw would be wired. I *decided* that. I went out for the fourth to nail that tribal drum.

I couldn't nail it. He was too strong. He kept grabbing my arms in the clinches and squeezing the muscle. He made me ache all over with his chopping and butting and scratching my face and chest with his head full of wire bristles. Nigger fighters know how to use that patch against you. I made up my mind: "I got to start outthinking this cat."

I outthought him from the sixth round straight through to the final bell. And all the while I was outthinking him he was chopping me from one side of the ring to the other till my arms were paralyzed and I was swallowing blood.

"By unanimous decision, Sweetmouth Jenkins!" the announcer made it, "over Roger Holly!"

I got a scattering of applause for having two front names.

But Sweetmouth Jenkins hadn't beat me. His manager had. It's what you get for not making yourself hostile right from the go. I can still beat Mr. Sweetmouth Jenkins.

But when you're thirty-two and have been at this trade thirteen years you've pretty well used up your hostility. I caught a midnight bus to Galveston. I had to fight somebody there I didn't even know his name.

After the bus lights dimmed and the other riders were sleeping, I tried to get to sleep by remembering the names of men I'd fought. I couldn't remember more than two or three. I remembered the fights. It was just the names I couldn't remember.

So I remembered the names of the places I'd fought in. I did better on those. I remembered the Camden Convention Hall in South Jersey and the Grotto Auditorium in San Antonio and the Moose Temple in Detroit and the Marigold in Chicago and the New Broadway in Philly and the Norristown Auditorium and the Arcadia Ballroom in Providence.

And that week at Presque Isle near the St. John River, with potato pickers being trucked in from all over the country, and Evergreen Shows put up a canvas with a sixteen foot ring, on a platform two feet high in the center, and billed me as The Penobscot Strongboy—"Don't be afraid, folks, he is only a little man and his hands are gloved."

They were gloved alright. Right after supper the merry-go-round electrician bandaged my hands and I soaked them in a bucket of salt brine to toughen the bandages till they were like rocks. I had to keep my hands in my pockets when I strolled the midway with the early evening crowd.

Dark came early in that country. We used old carbon lights to light up the banner, strung between two poles in front of the tent, showing two boxers squaring off. It would already be dark, and the carbon lights flaring, when the electrician would bang on an iron ring, the barker would get up on the bally with a big horn and holler "Ladies and gentlemen! We are bringing you here tonight and every night this week, meeting all comers, the Penobscot Strongboy, undefeated in the State of Maine! This show will pay twenty silver dollars to any man who will last three rounds with him! Mind you, gentlemen—*you don't have to win! Just stay three rounds!* He is only a little man and his hands are gloved."

That was when I'd step up on the bally wearing a bathrobe over my fighting trunks. I was eighteen then and weighed 142 pounds.

"Ladies and gentlemen, the best carnival fighter ever seen in this part of the country, The Penobscot Strongboy!"

He'd keep talking until he'd get some smalltown fighter, only half-willing yet ashamed to back down in front of friends, to step up. Even if he *could* fight a little, I could do a little more. But he'd always tell the fellow, in front of the crowd, that he couldn't hold the show liable if he got hurt in the ring.

On the third night we ran out of heel-walkers. I had to slip the electrician ten dollars to fake three rounds with me just to get a crowd watching. It worked. For the second show gave a big hand to a rough-looking redhead around 175 pounds. The crowd knew him and liked him. I began smelling money. The show manager came in and told me, "Roger, we got a full house out there and four nights to go. You know what to do."

I knew what to do alright. If you had a full house, and a man wasn't dangerous, you let him stay and win twenty silver dollars. Because the crowd would file out and pay again for the next show. So I whipped a light right high to Red's head to get up his guard, then shot a jab low on his belt—*very* light—just low enough to get the crowd to hating me. Then he hit me a solid punch and began carrying the fight to me. Red wasn't simply trying to stay—and he *had* a good right. But his left was just good enough to fill his coat sleeve.

Toward the end of the third round I began throwing wild rights, like I was desperate to knock him out so as to save twenty dollars. I made sure I missed every one. To make it look even better I went down on one knee as if he'd hit me really solid. Even Red thought he'd hurt me.

When the bell rang ending the third round the crowd was screaming, "Kill him, Red! Kill him! He's no good!"

"Ladies and gentlemen!"—The manager came out—"The Penobscot Strongboy admits your man is a very good man, and that he would *rather* fight somebody else. But *our* man is a sport, he is going to give *your* man another chance. We will now pay *your* man twenty silver dollars—But"—pause—"if *he* is as good a sport as *our* man, he will let the twenty ride and this show will now pay him *fifty* silver dollars if he stays the second three rounds! If he fails to stay the show owes him nothing."

The crowd, of course, was all for it. So was Red. Those two hundred and fifty fools rushed out and bought tickets and were back in the tent in no time at all. The ticket agent had to stop selling because we couldn't get any more into the tent.

I felt sorry for Red but it couldn't be helped. When he rushed out at the bell I slid along the ropes, threw a terrific right to his gut that doubled him over, shifted for leverage and threw a left hook that had everything I owned behind it. Red rolled under the bottom rope onto the edge of the ring. He was out almost two minutes.

I still remember that manager ballying the crowd as they filed out, one by one and not one saying a word—"Don't be afraid, folks, he's only a little man and his hands are gloved!"

And the Rainbow Garden in Little Rock and the Garden Palace in Passaic and the Armory A.C. in Wilkes-Barre and the Fenwick Club in Cincinnati and Antler's Auditorium in Lorain, Ohio. I went back to Detroit and remembered the Grand River Gym and the old Tuxedo A.C. on Monroe Avenue.

Just before I fell asleep I knew those were the names of the places where I'd used up my hostility.

It was getting light across that Gulf Road land between the Gulf Road towns when I woke up. I'd made this scene before. The land looked to me the way beds do in cheap hotels where you don't get clean sheets unless you pay a week in advance.

Bed after bed.

I got a room like that in Galveston. Then I went to look for a corner man. I had to fight somebody calls hisself Indian Mickey Walker.

It isn't always easy to find somebody to work your corner in these east Texas towns. Sometimes you can find an out-of-work fruit-picker to carry your bucket. If you're lucky you'll find an old-timey fighter, fight-manager, or fight-follower to handle you. Them kind are the ones who don't take money off you. Yes, I've carried my own bucket. Into rings where the ropes were unpadded.

At the Ocean Athletic Club I found a skinny little hustler from New Jersey, calls hisself Dominoes because he's been hustling domino parlors in the Rio Grande Valley. He'd kept one hand in his pocket so long one shoulder was higher than the other. I bought him a meal. Then I took him back to my room and emptied my little green-and-white Ozark Air bag on the bed: cotton swabs, surgical scissors, carpenter's wax, liquid adrenalin, smelling salts, Spirits of Ammonia, iodine, Monsel's Solution, Vaseline, adrenalin chloride, and half a pint of brandy. I showed him what everything was for except the brandy. Dominoes already knew what brandy was for.

I asked him did he know anything about some clown calls hisself Indian Mickey Walker.

"Strictly an opponent," Dominoes told me, "I seen him fight a prelim at the Garden when he come up from the bushes; but he come up too fast. Went down even faster."

"All the same he done better than I done," I had to admit. "Closest I've got to the Garden was McArthur Stadium in Brooklyn."

"Never been there."

"McArthur Stadium or Brooklyn?"

"Neither," he told me, "but I'll tell you what I think. I think you need a manager."

"What for?" I asked the man, "I never needed somebody to tell me the best hand to hit an opponent with is the one closest to his jaw. I never needed somebody to teach me that when you clobber someone it's

6

a shrewd idea to duck. What can a manager do for me beside robbing me blind?''

"He might get you in at the Garden," Dominoes decided—"or wouldn't you like that?"

"There's people in hell would like ice water," I told him, "but that don't mean anyone's bringing the pitcher."

Indian Walker was a shoeshine fighter. Stands in the middle of the ring with his head down and flails both arms like he's shining shoes. Built like a weight lifter. More hair on his chest than I got on my head. Some Indian.

The ref was one of them Elks Club athletes who'd refereed so many fights he'd gotten punchy. He likes to show who's the boss by sticking his head between us and hollering "Break!" so you could hear him in the back of the hall.

He stuck his head in there once too often. The stupid Indian nails him and down goes the ref onto one knee. The whole house began counting him out. He made it up at eight. After that he stayed out from between us. But every time we clinched somebody would holler "Break!"

Indian Walker won seven of the eight rounds. One was about even. The ref give me the fight on points. I got the winner's end, a hundred dollars, for not knocking the referee down.

I hung around home a week or so. Then I got a call from Minneapolis.

Some businessmen up there had "discovered" a six-foot-five schoolboy and had bought him half a dozen fast knockouts. They offered me five hundred and expenses to fight him. The reason they wanted me, I guessed, was because nobody has ever had me off my feet in a ring. It would be a boost for the Schoolboy Giant if he should be the first. I told the men to send me a hundred for expenses in front, that I'd want the other five before I got in any ring with a Real Live Giant. Then I phoned Dominoes to meet me in St. Paul.

"It ought to be worth fifteen hundred," I told Dominoes. He understood what I meant. So did Beth. They *had* to want a tank job. Beth didn't say anything. She wanted that diner in Carriers Mills.

I took a look at the Schoolboy Giant working out. Some giant. It didn't seem possible that they were going to let me go after him. He was *all* schoolboy.

Yet nobody rapped my hotel door. Nobody stopped me on the street. Nobody phoned me for a meet. "Something funny is going on," I told

Dominoes. "Something funny *isn't* going on," Dominoes corrected me.

The weighing-in was in a downtown newspaper office. The room was full of bush sportswriters. The Giant was undressing in a corner. I began undressing too. I let him walk toward the scales first. He was about to step on the scale but I hollered right in his ear "Get off that scale!" and shoved him so hard he almost toppled. I pointed my finger right up at his nose—"Don't *ever* let me catch you trying to get on a scale in front of *me! Do you hear?"

After I'd weighed in I stepped down.

"You can weigh yourself now," I told him.

He weighed 232. I weighed 172. They billed me at 180.

It wasn't till after the instructions, waiting in my corner for the bell, that Dominoes whispered, "They're dropping him."

The Giant's people were betting against him.

Well, all right. So was I.

He came out into the middle of the ring, put his left foot into one bucket and his right foot into another, extended his left hand and poised his right exactly as he had been told to do. I walked right up on his big flat feet, worked the ball of my wrist into his right eye; then held. I stepped back at the break, missed deliberately with my right in order to catch his other eye with my elbow; then held.

He put both gloves across his eyes; so I walked up on his feet again and butted him in the mouth. He half-turned toward the referee and said, "He's walking on my feet," and I reached over and knocked him into a spin. He caught himself going down by his forearms.

I didn't go in on him. I waited till the ref got out from between us. The Giant put both arms around me and held me till the bell. I went back to my corner wobbling from his hug.

Sometimes you can feint a man into position for an uppercut. You can feint him with your hands, your head, your shoulders, your eyes or your feet. I was always best at feinting with my feet. I let the Giant work me into my own corner and feinted him into the ropes. Then I let him work me into his corner and feinted him the same way—this time he went sprawling.

I was just trying him out. Feinting isn't enough. The idea of feinting isn't to send a man sprawling. The idea of it is to get him just enough off balance so that when you hit him a shot at the same second you feint him, he goes down. If he feints you right back you go down. In the middle of the second round he spread those big flat feet again.

I walked right up on them and butted him in the mouth. He turned his head to the ref to complain and I hit him on the jaw again. This time he went to both knees. He got up on one with one eye shut, the other cut and his mouth bleeding. Yet he got up at nine and still seemed to be in his right mind. So I followed him and he smashed my nose in with a big right hand.

I grabbed his middle and held; just held. I'd never been hit that hard before in my life. And all the while he was weaving from side to side it was me weaving from side to side trying to keep the ref from getting me off him. I didn't let go until I was sure I wouldn't hit the floor.

Then I came up fast and skulled him in his bloody mouth and he skulled me back so hard I had to hold again. The Schoolboy Giant was catching on.

I felt Dominoes pressing my skull with his fingers as hard as he could. Then he used the liquid adrenalin. "It's a *bad* cut," I heard him tell me, "*real* bad."

A right uppercut is a sucker punch. If you don't time it exactly you leave yourself open to your opponent's cross or jab. You have to think ahead to land it, anticipate your man's moves. It's a good punch to throw at an opponent who fights a little lower than you. But if you're fighting one a full head higher, you have to bring him down to you. I went for the Schoolboy Giant's body. A right to the heart, a left to the solar plexus. He lowered his head, his arms crossed level with his heart; with my right glove almost touching the floor I pivoted on the ball of my left foot. And brought it up. He pitched face forward as if he'd been mugged with a crowbar.

I watched his legs while the ref counted him out. The doctor was working on him a full half-minute before his calves twitched. The last I saw of the Schoolboy Giant two handlers were dragging him to his corner with his toes scraping the canvas.

Dominoes gave me interference to the locker room. Some kid threw a handful of popcorn in my face on the way.

"Lock the door," I told Dominoes as soon as we got inside. I didn't get up on the rubbing table. I didn't take off my robe. I just looked at Dominoes a long time.

"Mister," I finally told him, "*never* tell me I got a bad cut. *Never* tell *anybody* he got a bad cut. Tell him it's nothing. Only a scratch." Then I began throwing up.

A postcard from Shawneetown was waiting for me at Boise. All it said was *Everyone Here Fine Don't Get Hurt.*

I read it sitting on a locker-room bench. After I'd read it I put it with Beth's other cards telling me Don't Get Hurt. Then I put on my trunks and went upstairs to the gym.

There was a poster next to the door. It said Cowboy Goldie Williams *vs*. Roger Holly. I began throwing my left into the heavy bag.

A good many people don't remember I began fighting as a left-hander. A good many people don't even remember I began fighting.

A lanky young fellow in blue jeans and Spanish boots stopped to watch me. I paid him no heed.

"You left-handed?" he finally asked me.

"No," I told him, "right-handed."

"Then *hit* it right-handed," he told me.

"I'm developing my left," I explained.

"*Developing?*" He looked like he couldn't believe his ears—"at your age you're *developing* something? Hell, you're old enough to be Cowboy's old man."

"Reckon I could be his old man," I admitted, "if I'd married when I was fourteen."

"Nobody gets married that young," he decided.

"But it don't make no difference," he filled *me* in—"Cowboy Williams is going to beat you silly. He's going to gouge you 'n' bust your eardrums, too. He's going to pound your kidneys. He's going to crack your ribs. He's going to bust your jaw. He'll give you con-*cussions!*"

"What do we do following *that?*" I asked him, "Play unnatural games?" and went back to the bag. I wondered who had sent him.

When I climbed into the ring that night I found out who'd sent him. The fellow who came down the aisle in a white satin robe was the same fellow. Cowboy Williams had sent hisself.

A fighter so keyed up as to play trick-or-treat before a fight is likely to start fast, I guessed.

I guessed just right. He came tearing across the ring and I caught him coming.

All I had to do was step aside to let him fall.

I kept an eye out for kids holding popcorn bags on the way to the locker.

While I was dressing the promoter came in and sat down on the bench.

"I can get you on at the Tulane Club," he told me, "five hundred and expenses."

"I'll take it," I told the man, "who do I have to kill?"

"Your worry will be how to keep from getting killed. You're fighting The Pride of New Orleans."

"Who's New Orleans proud of now?"

"Jesus St. James. *Stay in shape.*"

"I don't have to stay in shape to beat somebody named St. James," I told the man.

I stay in shape all the time. I don't drink or cat after women. If you stay out late on Monday you still feel it Friday in this trade.

I didn't find out till we got to New Orleans that Mr. James was unbeaten. Twenty-two professional fights, fourteen wins by kayo, six by decision, one no-decision and one draw. Mr. James could hit, it looked by the record.

He didn't look like he could hit in his corner. A college boy, no more than twenty, six foot high and not a mark on him. Carrying his left like he was just walking down the street. I'd have to watch that hand for certain. He also looked like he could move around. I didn't need anyone to tell me I wouldn't last ten rounds against this athlete. I went out and bought a pair of Sammy Frager five-ounce gloves, of which three ounces is in the wrists. I thought that just *maybe* I might get away with them. At the weigh-in I gave them to the referee. He looked like a doctor.

"Do me a small favor," I asked him, "let me use these tonight."

We were standing right next to a scale but he didn't put them on it.

"Beautiful gloves," he told me. "How much do we owe you?"

"Not a dime," I told him, "they're on the house."

He came into the dressing room that night and handed me the gloves and then left me and Dominoes *alone*. No deputy. Nobody. I'd never had anything like it happen to me before.

Dominoes pulled on white tape tight as I could stand it without stopping the circulation. Then he put black tape over the white. Then he put white tape over the black. I was loaded.

We'd hardly finished taping when someone knocked. Dominoes stepped out to see who. He stepped back in and shut the door behind him.

"There's a fellow out here wants to know if you'll take five hundred to let St. James go the distance," Dominoes told me.

"We take it," I told Dominoes. So out he steps again and steps back in and shuts the door and hands me five c-notes.

"I don't have pockets in my trunks," I told him, "you hold it."

All I did the first two minutes of the first round was to test myself to see how I felt. I felt kind of limber. So I go in and hit Mr. James with a left hook and he starts to go down. I grab him and we're still falling. We're both falling all around the ring, me trying to make it look like it's *me* that's out on his feet. I leaned him against the ropes with

11

my weight against him so he wouldn't slide onto the floor. And all the while the crowd hollering for *him* to finish *me!* I leaned on him till the referee pried me off. By that time the athlete had come around.

All I did the next two rounds was miss punches by the yard, dance Mr. James up and down, duck, bob, weave, clinch, and complain to the ref to keep this stinker going. The crowd didn't care for it.

"If you don't start fighting you're not getting paid," the ref told me at the end of the fourth.

"I got to get rid of this kid," I told Dominoes in the corner, "he's going to faint on me."

"Better not," Dominoes reminded me, touching the five bills in his shirt pocket.

The crowd had its blood up. They'd paid to see a fight. I hit the Pride of New Orleans with another left hook and he went out cold. Flat on his back and arms stiff at his sides.

Dominoes picked up the stool with its legs sticking out and ran interference again back to the dressing room. As soon as he'd locked the door someone began pounding on it.

"Coming under the door," I hollered; and slipped the five bills underneath it.

I'd beaten three unbeatables in a row all by kayo. So a magazine did a story on bush league fighters without managers and said I was the best of a bad lot.

"You're not in the bushes no more," Dominoes decided, "you got a manager now."

"Who?" I asked him.

"Me," he told me.

I didn't say anything. I just let him go ahead.

Oh, that Dominoes. He signed me up for three ten rounders in a single week: Monday night, Wednesday night and Saturday night.

"What are we doing Thursday?" I asked him.

Beth took it well. "I always knew you were a bad lot," she told me when she read that magazine piece, "but I never dreamed you were the *very best* of it. At least you fight a lot. And you do have color."

The poster said Sol Schatzer Proudly Presents—I couldn't read the rest because Dominoes was sitting with his head against it, pretending to be on the nod.

I read the contract in front of me through twice. Both times I stopped

12

where it said *In event challenger establishes legitimate claim to title, he herewith agrees to purchase managerial services of co-signer.*

"I can beat Pete Mathias without a manager," I told Schatzer.

"It's the customary contract," he told me, "I don't have all day. So sign."

I pushed it back to Schatzer.

"You know what you are, Roger?" Schatzer told me, "you're an Agony Fighter, *that's* what you are. You know what else you are, Roger? You're an Agony *Man, that's* what you *also* are. You can't fight and you won't let an opponent fight. You can't make money for yourself, and you won't let somebody who can make it for you. You don't *want* a manager? Has somebody been around here lately asking? Somebody phoning to ask could he manage Roger Holly? *Who* been asking? *Who* been phoning? I'll tell you who: *nobody. That's* who been phoning to manage Roger Holly."

"I just *got* me a manager," I told Schatzer and nodded toward Dominoes; on the nod under the poster of Pete Mathias.

"That's a *manager?"*

Schatzer jumped up, raced around his desk with the contract in his hand, and shook Dominoes like a half-empty sack. Dominoes opened one eye. Schatzer pushed the contract into his hand.

"Manager! Read a contract your fighter won't sign! *Read,* Manager!"

Dominoes tore the contract in two and let the halves fall to the floor.

"I don't know what you're getting so excited about, Roger," Schatzer told me when he'd caught his breath, "all I'm doing is protecting myself. If you should get lucky against Mathias, *I* lose *my* title. All the contract means is I manage you. Don't I have a right to protect my own interest?"

"How much does the co-signer take?" I asked Schatzer.

"Twenty-five percent, clown," Dominoes said like talking in his sleep.

"All right, Roger, I'll level with you," Schatzer began leveling. "Just for the sake of the argument, let's pretend you *do* have a chance against Mathias."

"I didn't say I had a *chance,* Mr. Schatzer," I told him in a respectful tone. "I said I *would,* I *can.* I *know* I'll beat Mathias."

"OK. So you *can* beat Mathias. So can Al Ostak. So can Vince Guerra. So can Lee Homan. So can Indian Walker—and every one of them can whip you and hold the title longer and draw better, too. Am I right or am I wrong?"

"I have a decision over Walker," was all I could think to say.

13

"I know about that decision," Schatzer found me out. "Indian Walker is a washed-up Has-Had-It-Has-Been. But he can still beat *you.*"

"Then why not offer *him* the fight? Why offer it to *me?*" I really wanted to know.

"Because then he'll get thirty percent of each man in a rematch," Dominoes cut in again, "and three guys he can get thirty-five percent out of."

"You stay out of this," Schatzer told Dominoes.

"I can whip Indian Walker," I told Schatzer.

"You can't even whip Sweetmouth Jenkins," Schatzer told me.

"I couldn't untrack myself that night."

"All right," Schatzer said, glancing at his watch, "go ahead and whip him. Whip anybody you want. Whip Mathias if you want to. How you're going to get into a ring with him without me is where *you* got a problem."

It was true that any one of those fighters could whip Mathias as easy as I could. It was true that there were just as many fighters who could take *me*. It was true that, if I got the title, I wouldn't be able to hold it long. It was true I never drew big.

And what was truest of all was that if I didn't get this chance, I'd never get another.

"Give me the damned paper," I told Schatzer, and signed it.

"I'm sorry I had to speak to you like I did, Roger," Schatzer told me. "I did so for your own good. Actually I have nothing but admiration for you."

Three days before the fight Schatzer sent for me. He came right to the point.

"I'm seeing you get five thousand dollars before the fight, Roger," he told me.

"I don't get it," I told him.

"In small bills. The day before the fight."

"I still don't get it."

"For not straining yourself to win, clown."

"Let me maul it over in my mind a couple days," I told Schatzer.

I didn't tell him I wasn't going to take the five thousand.

If I let him know I wasn't going to take it, he might have Mathias fake a training injury. If the fight were postponed, I'd never get another chance. Nobody would be demanding to know when these two tigers were going to do battle. It would just mean somebody else taking the title off Mathias, that was all.

I put Dominoes in the gym to watch Mathias.

14

"He don't have to fake no injury," Dominoes reported back; "when he cuts out of the gym, he puts on a pair of foggy-type magnifying glasses so he can tell a taxi from a police car. But he's going to go through with it all the same. Schatzer must have a fix with the Commission medics."

"He must need the money pretty bad," I told Dominoes, "he must need the money *real* bad."

It's never bothered me to climb into a ring first and wait in my corner until an opponent comes down the aisle and climbs through the ropes to the house's applause.

When Mathias came up the aisle everyone applauded; and half the house stood up to get a better look.

I could see him coming better than most, being higher up. He was in a flashy green silk robe. But the way he was coming, between two handlers, both of them half a head higher than he was, I saw what Dominoes meant. They kept him between their shoulders as they came to keep him walking straight. When they reached the ring they waited till he got a hand on the top rope. Then one kind of half-boosted him into the ring. Mathias raised his gloves over his head and held them there until one of the handlers shouldered him toward the corner. Then he just stood there until the other handler put a stool up.

"He don't see me," I whispered to Dominoes.

"Hell, he can't even see the stool," Dominoes whispered back.

What went through my mind was: This is going to be awful.

I didn't know how awful it was going to be.

Mathias kept his eyes on the floor during instructions. All I could see of his head was where he'd combed back a few strings of red hair to cover a bald spot; and a little pink horseshoe at the tip of his nose where the bone had been taken out. It must be filled with wax, I thought. When I tap him in the forehead the horseshoe will get red. When I hit him squash on it, it's going to *pour* blood. But something about the way he was standing made me think he wasn't listening to the referee. Then the crowd whooped and he didn't hear the whoop. Something more than his eyes was wrong with Pete Mathias. His handlers steered him back to his corner.

He came out of his corner and hit me in the mouth with his head. He slipped my lead and threw a right hand that near tore my head off at the neck. I moved back, mulling him to give my head a chance to clear. He caught the nape of my neck in his glove, jammed his iron jaw into my shoulder, and *whack-whack-whack-right-left-right*, I got hit by three house bricks from this deaf-blind tiger. *What has he got in his gloves* went through my mind, holding on hard. I stepped back to ask the ref to examine his gloves. What he hit me with I never felt. I came to in my corner feeling Dominoes' fingers pressing the skin above my right eye. "Did I go down?" I asked him. "No, you got back here by yourself," he told me. By the way he kept pressing I knew it was a deep cut.

"Is it bad?" I asked him. "Only a scratch," he told me. Mathias was standing in his corner waiting for the bell to spring upon me. I only hoped he'd wait until it rang.

"He's blind as a bat," Dominoes said.

"Then how does he know where I'm at?"

"He's *listening*."

"He can't hear neither."

"Stop scraping your shoes on the canvas. He's catching vibrations. Get up on your toes—*if he can't hear you he can't find you.*"

And the bell.

I came out tippy-toe, stuck a glove in Mathias' face, and tippy-toed quietly away. Mathias wheeled and went for the opposite corner.

"Other corner!" every fink in that house stood up hollering.

Talk about your informers! If there'd been a Stool Pigeon's Convention in town, every single delegate had come to help Pete Mathias find me.

Between rounds he didn't sit down. Just stood there boggling his head about trying to find out where I'd gone. Just before the bell his handler would whisper to him where I was hiding and push him. He'd come right over there. All I could hope was he wouldn't put his glasses on.

The way I lasted through that fight was by grabbing his left glove in both of my own and holding on to it for dear life for as long as the referee would let me. Once I stuck my head under his armpit to keep him from digging that iron chin into my shoulder and striking me. From this purely defensive position Mathias was so hampered he couldn't do anything but smash the wind out of my lungs, bang my ears till they rang, pound my kidneys to shreds, and rabbit-punch me at will—"you got him, Roger," someone hollered in the dark behind the press row, "you're gettin' your blood all over him!" I don't know whether Mathias heard this—but something suddenly got him *mad* at me. He got my lower lip in his glove in a clinch and gave it a twist that almost tore it off. I grabbed his adam's apple and sunk my teeth into the lobe of his left ear—the ref got my teeth out by pulling my head back by the hair—but I was still choking him to death. Then he split my right cheek wide open with the point of his elbow.

"I didn't *mean* to hurt him," I told the referee.

"If that's how you men want to fight it's alright with me," the referee gave us the go-ahead.

Mathias wasn't cute-dirty. He wasn't even scientific-dirty. He was temper-dirty. All I could do those last two rounds was grab his elbow, spin him, give him a choke job, chop him in the groin and try a butt on that tender nose now and then. Just to let him know I was in the fight, too.

And then on an old scarred bench was a swab stick, the cardboard core of a roll of gauze, the top of a Vaseline jar and half a bottle of liquid adrenalin.

That was what I had to show for getting my face punched in for fourteen years.

On the evening of the first day that we opened the diner at Carriers Mills, Beth switched on the Fight of the Week for our two customers.

It was Sweetmouth Jenkins, challenger, against Pete Mathias, titleholder. Jenkins kayoed old Pete in two minutes and eleven seconds of the first round. I switched the set off and went back to waiting on the two customers.

People around here say I never could fight much, I just knew the moves. Beth says I had color.

The Marigold in Chicago and the Armory A.C. in Wilkes-Barre and the Valley Arena at Holyoke and Joe Chap's Gym in Brooklyn and The Grotto in Jersey City and The Casino at Fall River and Provenzano A.C. in Rochester and the St. Cloud Music Hall and Antlers Auditorium in Lorain and Billow Abraham's Gym in Wilkes-Barre and Conforto's Gym on Canal Street and Sportsman's Bar in Covington and the Council Bluffs Ballpark and the Hesterly Arena in Tampa and the Tacoma Ice Palace and the Great Lakes Club in Buffalo and the Century A.C. in Baltimore and the Paterson Square Garden and the Coliseum Bowl in Frisco.

If just people didn't keep running so fast these days, backwards sometimes.

You never can be sure what they might do to you by mistake.

COULD WORLD WAR I
HAVE BEEN A MISTAKE?

THE *Premier Danseur* of the Imperial Russian Ballet, Vaslav Nijinsky, had a pair of feet, I'm assured, that you'd have had to see to believe. For the base of his toes and his heels were equidistant from his ankles. Nothing with feet like that had ever been seen outside of Australia.

When Sergei Diaghilev, that great impresario, first saw Nijinsky's feet he revealed no emotion. "Upjump for me," was all he said.

Nijinsky went straight up five feet off the ground, completed an *entrechat-six,* and descended slowly.

"I see you're out of condition," the impresario observed.

The following afternoon, during a performance of *Les Sylphides,* Nijinsky accomplished an *entrechat-huit.* The applause was deafening. He awaited the impresario's congratulations with confidence.

"Have you tried coming down on one toe?" was all Diaghilev asked.

One week later, presenting *Le Pavillon d'Armide,* with Karsavina and Baldina, he achieved an *entrechat-douze.* Then, instead of walking off the stage, he leaped toward the wings, floated upward and disappeared. Nobody saw him land. Nobody even *heard* him land.

The house went as wild as though he'd performed a superhuman feat. Which, obviously, he had.

The applause went on so long, without the dancer reappearing, that Diaghilev went to look for him. He found Nijinsky at last, one hand pressing his heart and the other grasping a stage brace. He had only breath enough to ask Diaghilev—

"Now?"

"Why you come down so soon?" Diaghilev complained.

Nijinsky paled.

"Master," he asked coldly, "what is it you require of me?"

"Etonne-moi!" Diaghilev replied. "Astonish me!"

Upon which Nijinsky hit him across the face with a nine-pound mackerel he'd been holding behind his back.

"I *knew* he was going to say that," the *premier danseur* filled the press in later— "he used it on Cocteau last week. This time I was *ready*."

Diaghilev, thoughtfully picking mackerel bones out of his teeth, felt a dawning realization.

"I am going to transform the ballet from a chic but moribund art form into a superbly effective agency for the promotion of *avant-garde* values," he decided. "I will begin by convincing the fashionable *élite*—whom I shall seduce into financing my opulent productions—and end by winning over the general public! For although the average *mujik* refuses to spend a kopek to see a *premier danseur* do an *entrechat*," he convinced himself, "he will pay several roubles eagerly to see a great impresario get slapped in the teeth with a mackerel."

He immediately began building a new routine. Commissioning Picasso, Bonnard, Gris, Derain, di Chirico, Fokine, Nijinska, Matisse, Utrillo, Rouault, Miró and Braque as set designers; Massine and Balanchine as choreographers; Debussy, Ravel, Richard Strauss, Poulenc, Milhaud, Prokoviev, Stravinsky and Buffy St. Marie to write the musical score, they opened at last in Odessa. The Archduke Ferdinand of Austria attended.

Diaghilev, wearing a putty nose, an orange string tie down to his yellow shoetops, baggy pants tied with a rope and a battered stovepipe hat, had all the best lines. After Nijinsky had completed an *entrechat-six,* Diaghilev got to say: "Try going a little higher." And after Nijinsky had gone a little higher he got to say, "Why you come down so soon?" And, after Nijinsky asked, "Master, what do you require of me?" he got to say *"Etonne-moi!"*

Upon which Nijinsky got to hit him with a mackerel with unnecessary force.

The Archduke fell out of his box and was assisted back.

Fistfights broke out in the audience; dancers were unable to hear the orchestra above the uproar. The Archduke fell out of the box again. An usher helped him back.

Exercising great presence of mind, Diaghilev brought Nijinsky onto stage center and began harmonizing on *If I Can't Sell It I'll Keep Sittin' On It I Just Won't Give It Away.*

The house quieted slowly. When it became deathly still the Archduke fell out of the box again. This time nobody helped him back.

19

It was a *succès de scandale*. Diaghilev and Nijinsky were on their way to continental triumphs.

Their greatest successes, understandably, were in the seaports.

Yet with every triumph Nijinsky grew more irascible.

"Leave room when you pick teet'," he reproved Diaghilev.

The impresario refrained from reminding the dancer that it was mackerel bones he was picking out of his teeth. All he did was to suggest that perhaps, thereafter, they might use a foam-rubber fish.

Nijinsky became infuriated at the mere suggestion.

"*You! You! You!*" he cursed Diaghilev, "*You are a Portuguese oyster!*"

"I'm sorry I even brought it up," Diaghilev apologized. But Nijinsky was not to be pacified.

"I take orders only from the Gods!"—he let Diaghilev in on something he'd known for some time but hadn't wanted to let the press in on.

"Before I would use an artificial fish," he made it final, "I would abandon my art!"

"Have it your own way," Diaghilev gave in—"But let me remind you that, next week in Barcelona, it'll be *your* turn to say *Etonne-moi!*"

The act broke up in Barcelona.

Which simply goes to show you how much integrity in art depends upon who is swinging the mackerel.

And causes me to wonder whether, were the Archduke found to be alive and well today in Argentina—Wouldn't that make World War I a mistake?

OTTO PREMINGER'S
STRANGE SUSPENJERS

"I can't recall a single director in the history of movies who has turned out so many rotten pictures or been so continuously ridiculed by every critic with even the most rudimentary classroom knowledge of what films are all about," a film critic complained recently,* "somebody should do something about Otto Preminger. Like teaching the man how to make movies."

This cry from the heart recalled my own brief hour as a glass of fashion and a mold of form. And my fascinating fall.

It must have been about the time that Carol Channing was doing her unforgettable *Mehitabel* on Broadway. Who could then have foreseen the same actress, stripped to panties and bra, making love to Frankie Avalon in *Skidoo?* Or that Mr. Preminger's own star, then ascending, would peak with *Hurry Sundown?*

"I can't afford the rent," I told the studio agent who'd conducted me into a spacious and well-appointed apartment.

"Otto is taking care of it," he informed me in a whisper.

A fellow toting a case of scotch walked in. He had SUNSET LIQUORS stitched in gold across white coveralls.

"I didn't order that," I told him.

"Otto's taking care of it," the agent whispered again.

The SUNSET LIQUORS man returned with a case of beer and a bag of ice.

"I didn't order that either," I insisted.

"Otto will take care of it," the agent reassured me softly.

"What's the name of this place?" I asked him.

"Chateau-Marmont," he told me in the same hush-hush tone. I

*Rex Reed in *Home Furnishings Daily*.

couldn't tell whether he had a speech impediment or was just naturally secretive.

Two more strangers came in, carrying a floor-model television set. I looked at the agent.

"Set it down over there," I instructed them.

The following morning I answered a knock. Someone wearing a white jacket and carrying a medic's bag entered.

"Your barber," he announced himself.

"I cut my own hair," I told him.

"I was sent for," he explained.

"*I* didn't send for you," I decided, turned him about and eased him out.

"Somebody just sent someone to shave me," I later complained to the Whispering One.

"I don't know," he told me softly as ever, "but Otto would have paid for it."

"Why?"

"He *likes* you."

"Can't he even wait till me meets me?"

"He's going to pick you up at ten o'clock tomorrow morning."

I was waiting at the curb ten minutes before the hour. When you're making a movie there's not a moment to lose. Otto drove up in a Caddy so long he'd have to back up to turn the corner. I got in.

"Good morning," I greeted him.

Otto didn't bother with *that*.

"You like *donn?*" he asked instead—and the windows opened of their own volition!

"Or you like better *opp?*"—the windows closed automatically.

I be dog. I'd never in my whole life till now had *one* button do *three* things—up, down or stand still. By the way Otto was beaming, I judged he'd patented all three. Would he ever like me enough to let me blow the horn?

We wheeled past a golf course. Above the greens two large birds kept hovering.

"How you like apartment?"

"Comfortable," I acknowledged.

"Is Frankie's."

"Frankie?"

"Sinatra."

Then waited for me to cry, "Spit on me! I'm in the very front row!"

"Oh, I thought it was Bogie's," was all I could think to say. I judged the birds to be buzzards looking for dead golfers.

We began picking up helpers. One had two cameras slung around his neck. He plumped for *opp*. The next was carrying a makeup kit. He came out for *donn*. The third was a middle-aged fellow who lit up a pipe as much as to say he actually didn't give a damn, one way or another, opp, donn or sidewise. Otto caught his eye in the rearview mirror and you should have seen that fellow emptying the bowl of that pipe into the ashtray. He was still scanning the upholstery for traces of ashes when we reached the studio. Nobody was helping him to find them, either. If you want to make a movie you have to break the tobacco-habit first.

While the make-up man was pitty-pattying Otto's cheeks, I followed the camera-fellow around, plugging in extensions for him. I was happy to be on hand where history was in the making.

No sooner had the makeup man given Otto a fresh complexion than the photographer told him to smile pleasantly—then tripped the flash without delaying. He was working against time and he knew it.

The phone rang. Otto answered it without changing position.

"No *no*," he informed the caller, "for that we import entire cast," and hung up. "Everybody wants to be Mahatma Gandhi," he explained. I was learning something every minute.

After the makeup man and the photographer had completed their chores, Otto beckoned me to his desk. He gave something a nudge and its top rolled back, revealing an illuminated panel of push-buttons. He invited me to press one he indicated. I did. There was a low, whirring sound. An instant later a secretary entered.

"That's alright, dear," Otto excused her, "I was just demonstrating." I felt I should have gotten *some* credit.

He pressed another. The fellow who didn't care one way or another came in; with the bowl of his pipe still visible in his lapel pocket. This was more fun than making windows go up and down.

"You and pipe *bot'* oudt!" Otto gave him a direct order. The fellow wheeled back out of the door before it had closed behind him. When you're making a movie you have to stay on your toes every minute.

"*See?*" Otto asked me, "If you can turn on TV by remote control, why not send for people like so also?"

I couldn't think of a good reason not to. Provided they'd come.

"Why you write about such people you write about?" he wanted to know.

"They live around where I live."

"*Why* you live around such people?"

"Because when I live around other people they turn out to be such people, that I go back and live around just *such* people."

"What a lousy excuse," seemed to be Otto's thought.

"You *like* underdogs?"

"I like some people who are under, but not *because* they're under. Under is just where they happen to be. You like people just for happening to be on top?"

Being on top or being underneath wasn't just a happening to Otto, I judged. For he seemed to think I was putting him on: being on top was self-sufficing, it appeared: as being under spoke for itself. Opp. Donn.

The phone rang again. This time it was for me. The Whispering One.

"Be nice to Otto," he cooed; and hung up.

"That was my agent," I told Otto. "He *coos.*"

"What he *coo?*"

"I should be nice to you."

"You find that difficult?"

"Why force matters?"

"Don't you want people to *like* you?"

"Very few."

"I see you're not success-oriented. I'm very success-oriented myself," he assured me as if I could never have guessed. "I would like to be less success-oriented; but my standard of living prevented. Why can DeSica do on two hundred thousand what it takes us a million to make? Because DeSica wasn't born in a success-oriented society, that's why. I've made pictures myself that lost money! I've also made pictures that gave people enjoyment! What if it *wasn't* art? They lost money anyhow! Do you remember the camera work in *Great Expectations*? That wasn't mine either!"

He began wiping his makeup off with Kleenex.

"Why did L. B. Mayer object to making the *Red Badge of Courage* and it turned out he was right? *He* could pick up a phone and say 'Send me ten creative artists! I want ten creative artists!'—and he got them! *There* was a man who knew how to set people against each other! People say if he were alive today he wouldn't be as great as he was—I say he'd be even *greater!* One day to the next, nobody working under L. B. Mayer knew if he was going to get a raise or get fired. Today actors become producers because of tax problems. So everything costs too much.''

I wanted to push another button.

"That's why this is the free world—if everything didn't cost too much we'd stop being free! So what do reviewers expect of *me?* To go *against* society? Every time I make a movie I pay the price for being born into a success-oriented society as though it were *my* fault!''

I didn't know what society could do about it either. Unless there was a button somewhere somebody hadn't yet pushed.

"I don't even read reviews about myself," Otto went on, "if someone don't like me I take it to heart.''

I began to see that society had a responsibility, too. Come to think of it, if Otto hadn't been a really nice person to begin with he would be even rottener now than he already was. You have to see both sides of a question when you're making a movie.

"Now," he seemed to be coming in for a landing or at least to touch his wheels on the airstrip—"Now I begin doing things for others. How did *you* begin?''

"How did I begin what?''

"Doing things for others. So people *like* you.''

I tried to remember back to how I'd gotten my start in this field. "I'm not sure," I had to admit, "but I do remember running a little game we called 'peek' outside of Camp Twenty Grand near Rouen. We called it that so the fellows wouldn't think they were playing blackjack. Actually it *was* blackjack but with revised rules. Such as the house taking all ties and keeping the deck. But we still paid off double when a player hit twenty-one. It gave me a good warm feeling, like doing something for others, when one of the fellows got lucky like that. The good warm feeling I got was because I knew that the money he'd won would come back to the house automatically; because of the rule about taking all ties. Still, it *was* doing something for the other fellow all the same; even though only temporarily.''

Otto was looking at me as if he hadn't seen me until now. And was just beginning to make up his mind. It took him a couple minutes to put it all together.

"In *my* films," he decided aloud, "director directs *all*. I hire the writers. They work for *me*. I take the blame, I get the credit. But I am pleased to have met such *interesting person*.''

His congratulations were offered but not his hand.

The phone was ringing when I got back to the Chateau. You know who it was.

"Otto is upset. We *told* you not to discuss salary with him."

"We didn't get around to that. He told me about his personality, that was all. He's having trouble with it."

"He's upset about *something*."

A long pause followed, as though the man were just sitting there trying to figure something out all by himself. I held on until he'd figured it.

"You must have made him feel *insecure*," he finally decided.

"Not intentionally," I reassured him, "I just couldn't take him seriously."

"He felt it was the movie you didn't take seriously."

"Come to think of it," I had to admit, "I'm not sure that I do."

A curious change began transpiring at the Chateau. I noticed it first when the same two fellows who'd brought me a TV came in and took it away.

Then the fellow with SUNSET LIQUORS stitched in gold on his coveralls handed me a bill for the liquor he'd delivered.

"Mr. Preminger is taking care of this," I tried to argue.

"He must have had a change of plan," was SUNSET LIQUORS' guess. And waited until SUNSET was paid.

The next morning a rental notice was pushed under the door. I phoned the rental office.

"Mr. Preminger is taking care of this rental," I told the woman who answered.

"Mr. Preminger isn't exactly crazy," she informed me, "we can give you forty-eight hours and not an hour longer." And she hung up with *that* ultimatum.

Well I be *dawg*. Could it be that Otto didn't like me after all? Would my Hollywood career wither before it had blossomed? Would I be stigmatized with the spendthrift gentry? Would I have to admit to my friends in Indiana that I'd never even met Frank Sinatra? With only forty-seven rent-free hours remaining and the clock ticking away, I would have to do *something*. I phoned Otto's office. His secretary answered.

"May I have an appointment to see Mr. Preminger at 2:30 this afternoon?" I asked her humbly. Then waited while she checked that out with the illuminated panel.

"That will be satisfactory, Mr. Algren," she congratulated me.

"Then have Otto meet me at the Club House bar at Santa Anita," I filled her in. "Post time is 2:30."

It was *my* turn to hang up.

* * *

Otto wasn't at the bar at post time. When you're making a movie you can't always get to the track on time. Catching a small winner in the first race helped me to swallow my disappointment. Another winner in the fourth left me with so little to swallow that I rechecked the bar. I began teasing the olive in my martini pretending I was going to gobble her whole and then just taking the tiniest nibble. A jock-sized man loitering in the shadow of the bar's farthest corner kept watching me. It came to me that I knew him.

Max.

Nothing had changed about Max except that the left lens of his shades had been cracked. He was still in the same two-pairs-of-pants suit he'd been wearing the last time I'd seen him, two years before, in Chicago. And he still owed me three hundred and fifty-five dollars. I didn't rap to him because a man who has to follow horses through a cracked lens isn't about to pay off a two-year-old debt.

He hadn't been a total stranger to me when he'd hit on me, that afternoon at Sportsman's. I knew the same people Max knew. Some of them were even permitted on the premises. Letting Max inside had been the oversight of the track security office.

I'd showed him what I'd encircled on my program: *Scatterug.* I wanted to play the horse because I knew Scatterug had sound judgment. He'd once tried to bite me at Cahokia Downs.

The horse was 9-1 on the board.

"When he gets up to 10-1, I bet him," I'd assured Max just as the odds flashed to 11-1. I turned to make my bet. Max had followed me.

"If I can't stop you from playing it, how about giving me your action, Nels?" he'd asked me, "I pay track odds."

I gave him a fifty to put on the nose. It had saved me the trouble of going upstairs to the window.

Scatterug had come past the stands running fourth on the rail, with the rider having all he could do to keep the horse from moving up too fast. The horse had felt like running. The rider had let him move up to second on the far turn; and had held him to the rail until he'd made the turn for home. Then he'd let him out. When he'd come past me on the stretch, I glanced back to see where the other horses had gone; and they'd looked like they were standing still. $24.40. Max owed me six hundred and ten dollars.

"Nels!" he'd returned with a twitch in his neck and had begun accusing me—"Nels! The first time you give me action you hit!" He'd pocketed the fifty; that much was clear.

That had left me with a pair of alternatives: I could come in on him to the people he was holding out on and have them beat his head in; or I could carry him on the chance he'd get lucky himself. I didn't mind if people beat his head in: yet it wouldn't get me my six-hundred-ten.

Max hadn't taken it on the arfy-darfy, I'll give him *that*. He'd paid me off two hundred fifty. In pieces. The last time I'd had to loan him another five to pay off his cab. I'd told him next time take a bus. I hadn't seen him since. Now, as I finally put an end to the olive's anguish, he rapped to me to come over and share his shadow.

"Meet Big Bernard," he invited me.

I hadn't noticed, until then, that the shadow in which Max was loitering *was* Big Bernard. He was so big he blocked off the light of half the bar. Bernard was plainly the heavy in *this* road show.

"This was the guy I was tellin' you," Max explained to him, "the first time he give me some action he hit."

Big Bernard looked down at Max. Neither of *his* shades was cracked.

"That don't make him a bad guy, does it?" he asked Max.

"Where you stayin', Nels?" Max asked me.

"A place I'm getting thrown out of tomorrow."

"We got us a pretty good place," he invited me, "you could sleep on the couch in the front room. Would that be okay, Bernie?"

"You don't even know you're alive," Big Bernard decided with finality.

"It's alright with Bernie," Max translated.

Big Bernard removed his shades and looked down at Max for a long moment. He had the biggest, lightest, baby-greyest eyes I'd ever seen. They were the eyes of a man who's been shortsighted so long that nothing they'd seen had ever given his conscience the faintest twinge. They were the eyes of a man who could do anything.

"How can the man tell if he wants to sleep in our place when he never even seen it?" he finally asked Max, "How do you know he even *wants* to hang out with us? You better start breathin' or somebody's going to come along and bury you." He turned to me: "We'll run you out to our place. You can see for yourself." Everything Big Bernard said was *final*.

"I'm ready to leave when you fellows are," I told them.

"Now all you got to do to get heat on us is start jumpin' the lights," Big Bernard warned Max as he climbed into the back seat and let me share the front with Max, "I'll turn state's evidence on you."

"You want to drive yourself then?" Max asked him. But received no reply.

The first light Max jumped was a yellow. I thought it was accidental until I saw him smirking into the rearview mirror to watch Big Bernard's apprehension. The next one he jumped was another yellow—but this time he didn't smirk when he looked into the rearview. He turned sickly green. "Are you *clean?*" he had just time to ask—but I had no time to figure what he thought I might be holding. Motorbike Cop One curbed us on the left side and Motorbike Cop Two was leaning into my side.

"Let's see what you look like in the daylight," he told me. But as soon as I stepped out he became more interested in seeing what Max looked like. I had a fleeting hope that they wouldn't look in the back seat. But Cop One was already seeing what Big Bernard looked like.

"Take off them shades," Cop One told Big Bernard. Big Bernard took them off. "What's your name?"

"I wasn't driving," was Big Bernard's defense; which didn't come to much.

"I didn't ask you was you driving. I asked you who you was."

"Herbert Harris."

"Let's see some identification, Herbert."

Big Bernard extracted his wallet carefully, carefully selected a card from among several and handed it to the officer. Cop One looked over the card, turned it over, then asked, "Who's Philip Harris?"

"A standup comedian," I tried to help out; but nobody paid *me* any mind.

"*I'm* Philip Harris," Big Bernard testified.

"Then why'd you say Herbert Harris?"

"The full name is Philip Herbert Harris. I use the middle name because I don't want to be confused with the comedian." The officer handed back Mr. Harris' card.

"Now let me see the other names."

"It's the only card I got."

The officer just stood with his gloved hand out until Big Bernard handed him another. The officer took it but kept his hand out until Big Bernard had handed him three more.

"Which one of these is you?"

"They're all friends of mine," Big Bernard explained.

"We got a wrong passenger here," Cop One filled in Cop Two. "Do you make his buddy?"

"Not yet," Cop Two answered, "but we're getting around to it. Five ID cards so far."

Knowing they'd be getting around to me any minute, I offered my wallet to Cop One.

"Who asked you for *that?*" he wanted to know. I put it back in my pocket. Some cop.

He walked around to the car's locked trunk.

"Let's take a look in here."

"I lost the key," Max said quickly.

"We'll make a new one for you at the station," Cop One offered. "Do you want to open it here or there?"

"I just found the key," Max discovered.

The trunk was packed tight with record albums.

"Let's see a bill of sale."

Big Bernard looked over the trunk.

"I won 'em in a crap game," he confided to Cop Two, "I got lucky against a fellow he was in the record business. He didn't have enough cash to pay off. I didn't want to be hard on him; so I took records, poor fella."

"We better send for the detail," Cop One suggested to Cop Two, and Two agreed.

A small crowd gathered while we were waiting for the detail. Two moved them on. "Nothing happenin' here, folks, just a traffic violation." He took my arm like he'd never seen me before and told me to move on, but I held my ground. I wasn't a *folk:* I was a *suspect.* I went over and stood beside Big Bernard. He looked more dangerous than Max.

A squadrol pulled up. Two citizen-dress men got out.

"Get in the car," One told me. This was more like it. I'd give him my name, address and social-security number, nothing more. "I can't crack this one," he'd have to admit to the Chief of Detectives after the long grueling under the lights, "he don't have a nerve in his body."

I handed him my wallet.

"Did I ask you to show me that?"

I put the wallet back. Some citizen-dress man.

At the station Big Bernard and Max had to take off their jackets and stand with their hands above their heads while being frisked. I put my hands over my head, too.

Cop One pulled Big Bernard's suspenders back almost a yard —"Look! *Booster suspenjers!*" he chortled—and held them there long enough for everyone to see there was enough space down there to hold a record player and a couple transistors—then let them snap—*thwang!* —against Big Bernard's big belly, and everybody laughed. Even Max.

So Cop Two pulled Max's suspenders back and, sure enough—*they* were booster suspenjers, too! He pretended to be looking for loot down there for a minute—then snapped them—*thwang!*—against Max's belly.

Everybody laughed again except Max.

"Shall I take my jacket off, sir?" I asked. I could hardly wait to show them I was wearing a belt.

"No. But you can take your hands down from over your head."

This time *everybody* laughed. Including me.

"Where you from?"

"Indiana."

"Ever been arrested in Indiana?"

"They were all bum raps."

"Mug and print these boys," the desk man decided.

"All I'm wearing is a belt," I clued him in. But it was too late. They didn't care *what* I was wearing.

That was how I got to get locked up with Big Bernard and Max, to wait for the paddy wagon to take us down for mugging. Big Bernard took one bench of the cell and Max took the other. I stood up. They were both pretty tired, I could see. Both were sleeping when the lockup fellow let us out to take the ride downtown.

A double line of prisoners was waiting to take the ride. A paddy-cop manacled each pair before they climbed into the paddy. Big Bernard and Max got manacled together because they were friends. I was the last one in line and held out my wrists; but I didn't have a co-criminal to get manacled to. The paddy-cop just climbed into the wagon and waited for me to follow. When you work for the police department you shouldn't take chances like that.

The driver started wheeling, causing me to miss the first step up, then began circling the yard slowly, thinking he had a full load. The paddy-cop in the back held the door open for me. But I had to chase the wagon a whole lap around the yard. On the second lap I made the step. The paddy-cop was very nice. He held out his hand to help me in.

"I see you made it," he congratulated me and closed the door. I hoped the other fellows wouldn't notice that I wasn't wearing manacles.

A Caddy has it all over a paddy for seeing L.A. Because windows don't go opp-donn in a paddy. The reason is that a paddy don't have windows. Which leads you to keep wondering how fast you're going when you're actually standing still; and why when you're standing still it feels like you're making time. But the ride was worth it to get printed and mugged.

"I ain't mad at you because the first time you give me your action you hit, Nels," Max told me when he came out of the wagon. "I was pretty salty at you for a while but I ain't salty no more. Take the key out of my jacket—the other side, that's it. The address is 9901 Manola

Way. Write it down so's you don't forget it. If we don't see you for a few days tell the landlady we went out of town on business. Make yourself at home."

That was all he had time to tell me. I was happy that Max wasn't mad at me any more. I was even happier to have the key to 9901 Manola Way.

But I was disappointed in not getting printed and mugged. All they gave me was a lady cop who said, "Roll up your sleeve."

"What for?" I asked her. I wasn't being defiant. Simply curious.

"To look at your vaccination," she explained.

"It isn't much to look at," I admitted modestly.

When I rolled up my sleeve I was puzzled to find there was no vaccination mark there at all.

"This is a real puzzler," I had to confess.

"Try the other sleeve."

I be dawg. There it *was!*

"What did they bring this one in for?" she asked as if nothing could have interested her less.

"To get printed and mugged," I told her hopefully.

"Who'd you kill recently?" she asked, looking at the lockup fellow and smiling instead of studying me. Then she just walked away. Some lady-cop.

The lockup fellow let me have a cell all to myself. I knew they'd put someone in there with me who'd start asking me questions like don't I get a bang out of playing with matches or would I like to buy some hot diamonds. But I wouldn't talk. He too would have to report back to the people who'd paid him, "That fellow don't have a nerve in his body."

Nobody showed up and it got sort of lonesome by myself. So I hung my belt on the bars where the screw would see I could hang myself any time I wanted.

He noticed it but all he said was, "Keep your pants on."

And he kept on walking.

After a while he opened the cell and I saw we were going back to the station. Just when I'd begun to like it where I was.

The paddy was waiting, and the prisoners were being manacled before they climbed in, just like before. I didn't see either Big Bernard or Max, but I didn't want to get left out again. So I pushed my way up the line a little and got manacled to a fellow who was dressed like *he'd* killed somebody very recently. By the time we got back to the station we'd become good friends.

32

The same officer was at the desk. I was glad to see him because he'd trusted me not to make a break for freedom.

"Why'd they bring you back *here?*" he asked me.

"I'd rather have stayed with my friends," I told him. "Can I wait for them here?"

"It's alright with me," he told me, "they'll be along in anywhere from four to six months."

The way Max was going about paying me off seemed a little odd to me.

"Why don't you just sign a twenty-five-dollar bond and go home?" the desk man asked me.

"I don't have twenty-five dollars."

"Then just sign the bond and send us your check."

Do you know that after I'd signed the bond, that fellow didn't even look up? I just kept moving toward the door, one step at a time—I think that dumb cop almost *wanted* me to make the street!

It had been a good day, all in all: Two winners, a ride in a paddy, and an apartment rent-free until the fifteenth of the month. I went back to the chateau, to get my clothes, in good spirits.

I was all packed when I got a knock.

There stood Otto accompanied by a small, frail, middle-aged fellow, wearing horn-rimmed glasses and holding his hat.

"This man is an old fan of yours," Otto explained.

"Are you Nelson Algren?" the hat-in-hand fellow asked as though hardly able to believe his good luck.

I acknowledged that I was. Why be coy?

"Would you read this for me?" he asked, handing me a rolled script.

"I'd be happy to," I assured him. I know how shy unpublished writers can be.

His manuscript had already been published after a fashion. It was a subpoena charging me with breach of contract. The Old Fan hurried away. Some fan.

As I hadn't signed any contract to breach, I wondered how much Otto had paid him to have the phoney drawn up and served. I'd known he had me figured for a mark; but now he was really going too far. Then, to top everything, he handed me a bottle of scotch.

It wasn't the first time that another man had threatened me. It wasn't the first time one had given me a bottle of whiskey. I'd also seen a man pleading on all fours. This was the first time I'd had one hand me a bottle of whiskey, go down on all fours—then shake his fist at me from a kneeling position.

I could recall being booted out of a joint by a foot that had spun me through an open doorway. Yet I hadn't been told that I was being kicked because I wasn't returning the kicker's love. It was my first time for that, too. Finding one of my hands unoccupied with any other task at the moment, I used it to take the proffered whiskey.

It was nicely gift-wrapped. I unwrapped it fast before he had a chance to take it back.

Otto began a lurching shuffle around the living room. All I could do, subpoena in one hand and bottle in the other, was to follow him with the same shuffle. We went two laps in this curious clockwise procession—until he pulled up and swung about so suddenly that, thinking he was going to snatch back his bottle, I turned and began lurching counterclockwise. Otto began following. When I finally pulled up he'd sunk into a chair on the other side of the room; looking more than ever in need of a makeup man. So I collapsed in another chair.

"I am nice man!" he announced abruptly. *"Why you make me act like ass?"*

The least I could do, to make it all up to him, was to open *our* bottle. Or read our subpoena.

"I am success-oriented," he began that weary tune once more—"But *you—you* are a *free spirit! You* have compassion! *You* are sensitive. You are *kind* man. *You* are for underdog. *You* are creative."

I sensed the danger.

"I fight it," I interrupted him, trying to get my defenses up in time—"I never let compassion interfere where I see a chance to make a fast buck. I figure I'd better wait to start doing something for my fellow-man until I'm richer than he is. Meanwhile he'll have to get along without my help."

"No! No! No!" Otto protested—"What am *I? Nothing!* What can *I* do? *Nothing!* Not without creative man like you!" He was crowding me.

"A producer can be a highly creative man," I insisted while trying to think of one.

"No, no—a producer is a businessman, nothing more."

"What good would an artist's work be without a creative businessman to bring it to the world on film?" I asked hopefully.

"Good! So now you can write screen treatment for me about suffering of drug addicts—but not too *much* suffering. Because how can a movie be creative if only a few people say it's any good? What we want is something creative that *everybody* wants to see!"

How I'd gotten so far from home I couldn't clearly recall. All I remember was that I'd decided to jump ship and pan for gold. And here

I was in a push-button fantasy listening to its proprietor. I noticed that the glass in my hand was empty; but I didn't remember drinking it.

So was Otto's. I refilled his and refilled my own.

When Otto took his leave he was wearing an expression too benign. I attributed this more to the whiskey than to anything I'd said. He was assuming, apparently, that the combination of the gift bottle, restoration of the floor-model TV and a rent-free apartment, plus the threat of a phoney subpoena, would suffice to keep me on his payroll.

Because, when he took his leave, still beaming, he offered me his hand.

That was the moment when I had the fleeting hallucination that Otto was wearing booster suspenders. And I knew that, if I extended my hand, I'd try to snap them—*thwang!* But I couldn't snap them because I was holding the subpoena. Any more than I could shake his hand. All I could do was to put the subpoena in it.

Big Bernard's and Max's quarters on Manola Way were comfortable. I lived in them until the rent was due.

But I didn't want to leave L.A. without saying goodbye to Otto. I knew it was no use trying to walk in on him to say so-long. Otto didn't operate informally. I'd leave a message with his secretary. If he didn't call back—as I was certain he would not—I would at least have made the civilized gesture.

When Otto answered the phone himself I was surprised.

"I'm leaving town, Mr. Preminger," I explained, "I only phoned to wish you the best of luck with the picture you're planning of the book I wrote."

"Who this *is?*"

"Algren."

The next voice was that of his secretary.

"Messages to Mr. Preminger have to go through his secretary, sir."

"How come he took his call himself then?"

"Because Mr. Preminger likes to check on who's calling *me.*"

"You mean I have to go through Mr. Preminger in order to reach his secretary in order to reach Mr. Preminger?"

"That is our *modus operandi*, sir."

"Otto keeps a tight little store, doesn't he?"

But she'd already hung up.

Poor Carol Channing. Preminger required her to perch atop an electrically-operated bed, in Lover Avalon's apartment during the screening of *Skidoo*, while it was lowered beneath the floor. Miss Channing, distrustful of all mechanical contraptions, thought she'd rather not. In

35

order to reassure her, Otto sat on the bed and commanded it to be lowered. Only moments after Otto and the bed had disappeared there was an ominous *thump:* the machinery had gone haywire and Otto was trapped under the floor.

Curiously, no immediate effort was made to rescue Otto. The actors looked at one another with faint smiles; the stagehands' eyes took on a glaze. And everybody just stood around exchanging glances.

All good things, of course, must come to an end. The bed was finally brought up; with Otto still atop it. And work was resumed on a picture that would have been the worst of all time had not Otto himself later made others even worse.

One of them was the picture Otto made of the novel I'd written. The sequences were so mechanical that it left me with the impression that I'd seen a series of stills instead of a moving picture.

And I understood how Miss Channing must have felt when she saw herself, in panties and bra, making love to Frankie Avalon.

I NEVER HOLLERED
CHEEZIT THE COPS

YOU don't have to sneak around a grandstand booking bets to become a "Known Hoodlum" at a racetrack. You don't have to pick a pocket or forge a check. You don't have to get caught with a piece of sponge that would fit nicely into a nostril of a short-price horse. You don't have to collect somebody else's bad debt with a Little League baseball bat. All *I* ever done to become one was to be an agent for race-riders—and that ain't even illegal. Until I handled Rusty de John I never had a trouble; neither with riders or owners.

How he got a name like that I have no idea, as he couldn't read English; far less French. When he had to write his folks in New Iberia, Louisiana, he'd send a postcard saying "Come" or "don't" and get somebody else to address it. Believe me when I tell you, when that boy said "Howdy" he'd already told you everything he knew.

He *could* ride. I give him that. If he saw a hole he could get a horse's nose through, he'd pull the whole horse through it. And he could make a hole in the wind.

Then he brought in something called Popcorn Bummy, off at 23 to 1, and as soon as the number went up the inquiry sign begun flashing: stewards' inquiry. They hadn't even waited for a rider to protest; they'd entered the claim of foul theirselves. Down comes the number and the horse is placed last.

The next morning I had to fetch Rusty to the projection room so he could see for himself what he'd done. And to give him a chance to defend himself against suspension.

"Now, if you'll just keep your mouth shut," I warned the boy, "you won't get more than five days. Tell them you realize your mistake and you're sorry. Then promise that, in the future, you're going to be more careful. *Whatever* they give you, *don't argue.*"

He nodded as though he understood.

The stewards sat up in front of the screen. Rusty and I sat in the back. The film began with the horses in the gate and the flag up. Then they broke and Rusty, big as life on Number 6, cut diagonally across the field, block-and-tackling the whole pack, bumping the Number 5 into the flank of the Number 4 till he had the rail and then began pulling away. The film cut off.

"You're a dirty liar!" Rusty stands up shouting at the screen, "a dirty liar! I never done it!"

"The boy hasn't had much education," I pleaded privately with the stewards. "Riding racehorses is the only way he has of making a living. Give the kid a break."

"Will you take thirty days?" the Chief Steward asks me, just as if I had a choice.

"Yes, sir," I thanked him. "Thank you, sir." I was glad he hadn't made it sixty.

"I got you off with thirty days," I reported to Rusty.

"You sonofabitch," he jumped right at me, "if you'd kept your big mouth shut they wouldn't of give me a day!"

"Rusty," I made up my mind, "I can't handle you. You're too ignorant. Just pay me the twenty you borrowed off me last week and we'll call it quits. No hard feelings."

"Pay you twenty bucks after you get me a thirty-day suspension?" —he stuck that little pug mug of his, more like that of a Pekinese than that of a man, so close to mine that it came right up to my shoulder—*"that's ut-rage-us!"*

"If you want to beat me out of twenty," I told him, "just beat me. Don't use your suspension as an excuse."

"Ut-rage-us!" he repeated.

"Rusty," I said, "if you were the size of a man I'd knock you onto your ignorant ass right here."

As soon as I'd said it I was sorry I had. I'm a full head higher and sixty pounds heavier than Rusty. Yet he didn't back off an inch.

"Here?" he asks me, "and get me *anothern* suspension when I'm on track parole? No, *sir*—but you just step behind that tote board with me, where we'll be out of sight, and we'll settle this man to man. We'll *see* who's *ignorant.*"

I just turned and walked off. But he followed right at my elbow—"I *knew* you'd lose your nerve, I *knew* you'd show yellow!"

So I swung right through the gate toward the tote board to pretend I really was going to take him on man to man. He came right behind me, shadowboxing and slamming his little fists together.

"O, *boy!*" he begins hollering, "I can hardly wait!" And starts spitting on his fists.

That was too much. I turned about and shot him a short jolt to the jaw just hard enough to set him down in the dust. He just sat there glinting up at me.

"Alright," he told me at last, "now you got me down, take my money. Take *all* my money."

"I don't want all your money," I told him, "I only want the money you owe me."

"It's all out on bets," he told me.

"You lie from a sitting position."

He got up and dusted himself off. "When you call a de John a liar," he let me know, "you call the whole de John family liars. Don't blame me for what happens now. You brought it on yourself."

And he turned and walked off with my twenty still in his pocket.

I didn't see him for several days. I figured he'd gone back to New Iberia to wait out his suspension for thirty days. If he didn't come back for thirty years that was fine with me.

On Sunday morning I came around a corner of a shed-row and run right into him and two little helpers. Both approximately four foot eleven and looking more like Pekingese than people. They couldn't be anything but a brother and a father. I judged Dad to weigh in at ninety-nine pounds; and Brother couldn't have gone over ninety-six.

"Don't take fright," Dad told me, "us-uns ain't goin' to jump you all three. Us-uns don't fight thataway. But you'll have to take us-uns on one at a time."

"Where?" I asked; not wanting to take that long walk out to the tote board.

"Right *heah!*" Brother stepped up; so I knocked him down with the same hand I'd knocked down Rusty. He just sat there looking up at his pa.

"Your turn, Dad," he tells him. So I reached over and knocked the old man down.

"Where's your mother?" I asked Rusty; and knocked him down too.

Then I waited till the whole family got to its feet. The old man gave me his hand. "The better man won," he told me, and I took it. Then I shook Brother's hand.

"Now that we got that settled satisfactorily," Rusty decided, "you can come back to work for me anytime." And offers me his hand also.

I didn't take it. "Not till you pay me the thirty you owe me," I told him.

"*Thirty?*"—he starts getting hot all over again—"all I took off you was twenty!"

"You owe me an extra ten for the embarrassment you've caused me in having to knock down your whole family," I explained.

Rusty grabbed his wallet and took out three tens. "*Here,* you cheap bastard," he tells me, "but I'll tell you *this* much—from now on you're my *swore enemy!* I'll never borrow another nickel off you as long as I live!"

I took the money.

Three nights later I was leaning on the grandstand rail, waiting for the horses to come out on the track, when I saw him coming. But he wasn't coming like a Swore Enemy.

He was wearing slacks, jacket, and half-boots zipped on the side, all very sharp and all of it right out of the store. I began marking my programs so he could take me by surprise.

"Got anything good, old buddy?" he asks, leaning over my program.

I took no note of his sharp frame. I just encircled Number 10. Popcorn Bummy.

Rusty leaped straight up in the air waving his hands like he's flagging down a train.

"Sam! I won't let you bet that lame dog! I won't let you go to the window! I won't let you throw your money away!"

He was protecting me from myself.

Actually I hadn't made up my mind to bet Popcorn Bummy until that moment. When people try to tout me off a horse, I bet it just to show them.

"Nobody, but *nobody* is going to talk me off Popcorn," I filled the boy in; although I hadn't even looked at the *Form.* And he saw I meant it because he quieted down.

"If you're going to throw your money away, Sam," he strangely changed his tune.

"I didn't know you were running bets," I told him.

"Just till they lift my suspension."

"If you run a bet for a security man, your suspension will be for life."

"No danger, Sam," he assured me. "I know every security man around this bullring."

"You can't know them all," I warned him, "they keep changing.

They send them to other tracks where they aren't known and the ones from other tracks come here."

"I don't have to know the man's *face*, for God's sake," he told me irritably. "Don't you think I can tell a cop just by the way he *looks?*"

"Don't get overconfident," I tried warning him once more.

"Look, Sam," he reproached me, "if you don't want to give me your action it's all right with me. But just tell me so to my face instead of beating around the bush. Or are you scared I'll book the bet myself?"

"I know the people you're running bets for, Rusty," I let him know, "and as ignorant as you are, I don't think you're *that* ignorant."

And I handed him a fifty.

"On the nose," I told him.

He looked at the fifty with some surprise, but he was no more surprised than I was. All I'd been considering, when he'd come up, was a six-dollar across-the-board bet. Let's say I overreacted and let it go at that.

Popcorn Bummy was off at 11 to 1. He broke in front of the field, held a three-length lead into the turn for home; and was so far in front at the wire that the other horses thought he'd run off and hid somewhere. He paid $24.60. Rusty owed me six hundred and fifteen dollars, American.

His left eyebrow was doing a curious twitch when he came up and he kept pulling on a fresh cigar he'd forgotten to light. I'd never heard him stammer before but he was stammering now.

"B-buddy. The f-f-first t-time you g-give me ac-action—"

I took a guess that he'd booked the bet himself. I guessed right.

"I'm tired of knocking you down myself," I told him. "I'm going to let the people you're running for take a turn."

Actually I wouldn't have gotten the boy smashed up. Not even for six hundred and fifteen dollars. Besides, how would that get me the money? At the same time I didn't want him to think he could run out on me that easy.

"Give me till tomorrow to get it up, old buddy," he pleaded.

"I'll be waiting for you right here at post time," I warned him as sternly as I was able, "and that don't mean a down payment. I want it *all*." And I walked away.

I saw him later, at the bar across the highway, with a pair of his new buddies. I didn't go near them; I stay away from those groups. But, by the way they were buying, one on either side of him, it hadn't yet entered their minds that he might be double-crossing them. Rusty was so confident that he was smarter than anybody, while all the time he was dumber than anybody, it made me feel just a little sorry for him.

I didn't stay even a little sorry long. When he met me at the rail the following evening he really began getting to me.

"If you don't have the bread don't give me a story," I told him the moment he came up.

"Sam, it's *not* a story. It's the truth, so help me."

"I don't want to hear it."

"It don't have anything to do with Popcorn," he promised, "it's about hot stuff."

"Is that a horse?" I made the mistake of asking.

"No, it's plaid stamps—a *thousernd dollars worth!* The man is lettin' me have 'em for only *two-hunderd-fifty!* 'n' I got a buyer ready to buy fer *six-hunderd-fifty!*"

"You can't lose money that way," I perceived. Then we just stood looking at one another. He seemed to be expecting something from me.

"Sam!" he finally lost patience with me—"Don't you *see?* I clear *four hunderd!* 'n' turn it right over to you! Then you 'n' me are buddies again!"

"Count me out," I cut him short.

"Count you *out?*"—those Pekingese eyes stared up at me in utter amazement—"count you *out?* Man, you're *in.* I already told the man you were letting me have the cash. You *can't* let me down *now!*"

"Out," I repeated. "Out. That's spelled O-U-T. It means not In. That's spelled I-N."

Rusty just didn't seem able to take it in. He shook his head incredulously.

"I'll *never* understand you, Sam. Try as I may. And Lord knows I *hev* tried. Here I am doin' everything in my power to pay off an honorable debt and what do *you* do?" He stuck a finger in my chest. He *dug* it in. "What do *you* do?" He jumped back and began that arm-waving routine. "I'll *tell* you what *you* do!"

"I appreciate your trying to pay me off, Rusty," I told him quietly to calm him down. "Pay me off when you get lucky. I'll wait."

"All right," he suddenly resigned himself to my view, "and I really appreciate your going along with me. Now just let me have a few bucks so I can get started again."

Even while I was reaching for my wallet everything in me was telling me to stop. Everything in me kept saying don't and yet I didn't know *how* to stop. All I had the strength for was to leave the twenty inside, take out a fiver and four singles, and then to palm the five.

Rusty just stood looking at the four singles: he couldn't believe it.

"Is that *all?*" he asked incredulously.

I unpalmed the five and said weakly, "Yes, that's all."

"Sam," he told me in a voice too sorrowful to believe, and making no move to take the bills, "Sam, I always knew you were cheap. But when other people said so I always defended you. I never dreamed, until this minute, that everything everybody ever said about you was true. You really *are* cheap, Sam. It hurts me to say it. But when a man shortchanges his best friend, what else *is* there to say?"

Then he took the bills, stuffed them in his pocket; and walked slowly away.

There was no use telling myself he'd conned me out of being his creditor into being his debtor. I *realized* that. But I felt awful all the same.

So awful that I stayed away from the grandstand rail so he couldn't find me. I just couldn't go through another one of his mindless deals.

How he knew where I was I'll never know. But he spent a dollar-fifty to get into the clubhouse so he must have been sure. Between the 5th and 6th races I was in the Clubhouse Bar; and that was where he found me. And sat down beside me with the kind of look only a dog whose master has given him a bone and then snatched it out of his mouth can give.

"Have a drink, Rusty?" I asked him resignedly.

"You think I'd have a drink with my Swore Enemy?" he put it to me. "Don't you think I have any pride at *all*?"

"If you have any pride at all, Rusty," I filled him in, "you'll pay me off the bet you booked."

"Sam"—he was using his confessional tone—"Sam, if you only knew the lengths you've forced me to in hitting that bet."

I waited.

"Sam"—and suddenly he looked genuinely frightened—"Sam, I'm in trouble. I need your advice." And he drew three C-notes out of his lapel pocket as though he were afraid of them.

"Booked a big one, I see," was all I could say.

"A hundred across on the Number 4—and it's off at 11 to 1, same as Popcorn. What do I *do*, Sam? Tell me, what do I *do*?"

I glanced at the tote board. The number 4 had jumped to 14 to 1. The horses were out on the track.

"Simple," I told him, "you've got ten minutes to get to the hundred-dollar window and put the man's bet down. Or you can play it straight and give it to your own man and let *him* worry."

"Either way *I* wind up with nothing," he complained.

"Rusty," I tried to explain, "if the horse even gets up for show money, you're through. You'll be lucky to get back to New Iberia alive, for God's sake. Don't you see you've got more riding than *money*? You got your *livelihood* riding, man."

He saw it at last. He just sat there looking so young, yet so old, I realized I'd never seen anyone look that frightened.

"Bet it for me, Sam," he asked me like a child, "I can't make it to the window."

"Have a drink while I'm gone," I told him and took the bills. I was going through the door with the bills in my hand when the two security men came through; and then they weren't in my hand at all. The one was blocking the door, and I heard Rusty cry out "Cheezit the cops!" and start racing blindly around the bar. The other security man didn't even chase him. He just waited for him at the door.

That was a long walk down to the Security Office. I was afraid that Rusty would make a run for it and I'd be part of his scene. The security man must have had a firm grip on him. But he didn't let it show; and the one who'd taken me in charge didn't put a hand on me. But it was all over before we got to the office. The bills were marked, of course. And they had been in my hand.

Rusty, I was not surprised, tried to get out of it the same way that he'd tried to get out of a suspension: by jumping up and hollering at me, "You're a dirty liar!"

It didn't do him any good. But it didn't do me any good either. I didn't even mention the bet he'd booked for me. What good would *that* have done either of us?

Leave it to Rusty. *He* brought it up!

What could I say? Even though I'd somehow been able to prove that I hadn't booked that hundred-across-the-board bet, it remained that I *had* placed a fifty-dollar bet with an off-the-track bookie.

"Tell me one thing, Rusty," the Chief of Security wanted to know out of nothing but simple curiosity, "what made you holler 'Cheezit the cops'?"

"I never hollered 'Cheezit the cops.' " Rusty flatly denied the charge. "What I said was, 'Gentlemen, the law is present.' "

Of all the ways there are to become a "Known Hoodlum"—just look at the route *I* took.

THE MAD LAUNDRESS
OF DINGDONG-DADDYLAND

FOLDING a copy of *Playboy* in his left hand while holding his pants up with his right, the old man slipper-sloppered through the old flat dark and narrow—

Don't throw bouquets at me—he cajoled a world that had long dishonored him—

Don't laugh at my jokes too much—he asked a world that had never thought him a comic—

People will think we're in love—although he'd always found people detestable and people had found him a horror.

Coughing, hawking, phlegming, one shoulder higher than the other from working with penitentiary rubber, he lurched lopsidedly with one suspender dragging. Through rooms appointed with fixtures of another day.

There were many doors to pass in Dingdong-Daddyland before one reached the kitchen: a kitchen which served as a forge—or a forge that served as a kitchen. Where a pair of sexless wrecks—two long-ruined heroin-heads—were drying contraceptives on a shoe-rack hung above a gas stove.

Odors of paint, paint-cleaner, turpentine and glue, mixed with that of gas flames burning too evenly. And a reddish dust lay over everything.

Attended by two ancient junkified finks, this kitchen-forge was the capital of a curious kingdom which rose, a long decade past, four stories above the blaze and clang of West Congress Street. And endured, through one whole summer, fall, winter, and spring: then jackhammers began breaking stone a mile away.

Kitchen and kingdom, forge and finks, fell in a single night.

That summer was one of such steady heat that the heroin-heads dried the *Dingdong Daddies* on the back-porch clothesline.

"How much cost your little sausages up there?" a neighbor-woman once called up from the alley. The innocence of the question had made it the family joke of Daddyland.

"How much your little sausages?" the old man now greeted his serfs to ask how they were feeling. "How much your little sausages?" he retorted dryly when Vivi-V tried pumping him about where he hid the heroin with which he paid them.

And, sometimes, when Vivi-V asked it, it meant, "What difference does *anything* make?"

Through a flashflood spring, when pipes backed up, this head—the one who wore specs—threatened the old man with exposure if he didn't increase her morning fixes: then bickered with the other head over who was to put the feathers on the *Ticklish Tessies*. Yet she poured the rubber to fit the forms, stretched the latex and brushed it with glue; painted the casings and hung them with care.

And dreamed of a huge cache of H hidden somewhere in the walls of the old dark-walled flat.

They hung *Barney Googles* and *Cupid's Arrows*. They worked with rubber and gas and glue. They soldered bright tufts upon *Feathered Friends*. They painted the casings and burned the culls.

Yet neither went dancing down below.

This curious commune, whose Sovereign Lord was the crazed ex-con calling himself Dingdong Daddy—

> *I'm a dingdong daddy from Duma*
> *'N you oughta see me do my stuff*

—was a single-crop country. The sexless wrecks packaged latex fantasies like cornflakes. While he boxed blue films in his bedroom. And shipped the lot in cartons labelled *Educational Matter*.

Don't-Care girls and Won't-Care girls, Can't-Care girls and Why-Care girls; girls so fresh the dew still lay upon them; others so hardened they looked retreaded; girls from small towns looking flattered and girls from the city looking wronged—all, all had been trapped *flagrante delicto*. To show the world what Dingdong meant when he said: "I know what women do. What they *really* do."

In Daddyland there was no jazz. There was no music cool or hot. No Diners' Cards nor income-tax hangups. No one spoke of money and no one spoke of love. Its currency was a fine white dust; and the fine white dust was its one love. Nor did it matter, in Daddyland, whether the world went with a bang or a whimper. The sooner the better was how all Dingdong-Daddylanders felt.

For though Beulah seemed content enough with just enough heroin to keep from getting sick, that Vivi-V was a regular little pig about the stuff. If Beulah let her scrape a couple grains of dust off her own deck, that wasn't enough for Vivi-V. No, she wanted to cook herself up a soup-ladle fix that could kill a milkman's horse. (What would kill a horse would never kill Vivi-V.)

Beulah would have liked to find out, too. But she let Vivi-V do the searching.

The old man himself had no habit at all. Unless you care to call cartooning an addiction. For, while working with rubber had become his craft, cartooning had become his obsession. A chaplain had given him a child's drawing-book in which he had worked with crayons. Then he had begun tracing comic-strip characters—Barney Google, Moon Mullins, Captain Katzenjammer, and Little Orphan Annie. He'd stuck to it as if he got something out of his crude imitations.

The stuff was brought to him by the Mumbling Man, a piece of psychotic refuse dressed in a dark brown suit a size too large. Whoever he was, whatever he was, he never spoke to anyone but Dingdong—and that only in a side-of-the-mouth mumble. Dingdong would take him into the bedroom and shut the door. A few minutes later the Mumbling Man would shuffle out. Then the women knew they'd have enough H to keep them from getting sick another week.

Once, when Vivi-V had tried to get more out of Dingdong Daddy by getting too sick to work, he had cut her off altogether.

"No work no stuff," was how he'd put it; and had let her go blind, throwing her arms about and drooling saliva, before he'd bring her back to the world of the living.

"That's the last time she'll try *that,*" he'd assured Beulah, and it *had* been the last.

Of these three sixty-year-old juvenile delinquents, the old man alone had had no love life. None at all. Both women had been hookers in their day. But he'd been a virginal youth when he'd become a number; and had come out over the hill.

Those passions, which in his youth had burned, though now hardened by rubber and made fast by glue, had yet flickered like smudgefires for four iron decades: and had not yet turned to ash when his parole had come through at last.

He brought out with him a facility for working with rubber, a copy of *Playboy;* and a terrible deprivation of the heart.

Moreover, he brought his walls with him: he could not go down to the street. The years behind bars were done; yet unseen bars remained.

Playboy, to the old man, was the most erotic magazine he'd ever read. No wet sex dream of his adolescence had ever been so sexy nor so wet as the dream this magazine aroused in him. The pages of his ancient copy were warped and stained by the prison hours in which he'd fingered and thumbed them.

Yet the foldout child in the middle was untouched. His eyeballs glanced off nudes. He'd never finished a *Playboy* story. But ah—those ads for color TV, those watches in oyster cases carved out of 18-karat gold—"If you were racing here tomorrow you'd wear a Rolex"; "Creative Playthings—something wonderful stays with your child"; "Are you a member of the Jaeger Club?"; "Days of sun, salt-air, sea-nights beneath the Southern Cross"; "The Escape Game as Played Only on a 27-Day Carnival-in-Rio Cruise"; "Waiting for your Footprints in the Sands of Kauai Surf"; "What if someone calls you in the middle of the music?" Pause selectors, automatic turntables, Polaroid cameras, projectors guaranteed against focus-drift with both remote and automatic slide-changing—"Sit anywhere near Zenith's unique circle of sounds with exciting Fm/Am/Stereo!"

Oh, to *acquire,* to *get,* to *accumulate,* to *have everything*—that was *it*: two-door refrigerators, meerschaum pipes, and watches that told the date as well as the hour—*merchandise—that* was what aroused lust in a man! Ashen passions, chilled by the lovelessness of his iron years, were rekindled in dreams of commodities.

For the heart knows its deprivation; and takes its own measures.

"Not a number in the joint but wasn't there on some woman's trick-ery," Dingdong now accounted for all convictions, federal, state, or municipal. "I *know* what women do. I know what they *really* do."

How else could the old man think? If women were, actually, man's great blessing—but no—it had all been too hard to believe *that.* It had all been too long.

Dingdong was one of those extremely rare long-termers capable of making a penitentiary passion come true. His was a latex fantasy of liver-ish yellow tipped with firehouse red; then tufted by a feather soft as down. In purple, gold, or beige. That sold for a dollar each.

And had honored himself by naming it the *Dingdong Daddy.*

Since the world had done him no honor at all.

For he himself had devised the mold whereon Earth's first *Dingdong Daddy* had been forged. *Ticklish Tessies, Feathered Friends, Cupid's Arrows,* and *Barney Googles* were merely variations on the master's grand theme: *The Condom of Tomorrow.*

* * *

In air made thick by paint, paint thinner, and turpentine, Beulah perfected the piecework; while Vivi-V had to stir the rubber. Because Beulah had seniority.

And, since stirring rubber was no more difficult than stirring oatmeal, and no more interesting, Vivi-V watched Beulah's artistic touch with an envious eye. And Beulah, sensing she was being envied, would take exquisite pains in painting a bulbous nose on a *Barney Google*.

She would step back from her work, her finely-tufted brush in hand, cock her head and measure perspectives until Vivi-V could scarcely bear it.

"A condom's a condom," she would comment, "it don't matter *whose* face you paint on it."

Beulah wouldn't so much as glance at her lest she lose perspective.

"I just don't *know* why I'm so creative," she would marvel aloud, "I suppose it's because I'm a natural-born *specialist*. The layman, of course, doesn't understand these things."

"Specialist my careworn ass," Vivi-V snapped, "as though sticking a feather onto a condom can be considered in the same class as being a *vocalist*."

"I'm sure you sang very well in your day, dear," Beulah assured her, "you could hardly have been sounding like a baby buffalo with an arrow through its lung *all* your life."

"Let me know when you're having an exhibition," Vivi-V asked dryly.

"There's a *trick* to my work," Beulah bragged.

"If there's a trick to it you're the party to turn it," Vivi-V observed.

A faint flush pleasured Beulah's flesh. Like a touch of pink on broken calcimine.

"That's the nicest thing anyone has said to me in years," she thanked Vivi-V without irony.

Suddenly Vivi-V remembered something: "Once I used to eat bennies like popcorn when you let me hold the bag. Blue-heavens, red-birds, yellow-jackets—I was a barbiturate cat. Nembutal, Luminol, Amytal, Trional, Try-'Em-All. I was a goof-ball cat. Then I hit the *real* thing."

"I *could* have been a typist," Beulah assured herself aloud, "but my fingernails were too long."

"I thought morphine sulphate was the real thing because it had that big *smash*—like your head was coming apart." Vivi-V stopped bobbing her pink bow over the liquid rubber for a moment. "It wasn't the *really* real thing. Not at all."

"I could of been somebody's secretary," Beulah reflected, "but I had all the wrong clothes. I could have been a copper's old lady one time. But I just can't *bear* a nab."

"The *real* thing was nothing but a low, slow glow," Vivi-V remembered her own bittersweet sorrow, "like little flowers burning and everyone talking whispery, saying something smooth yet frantic. No bang, no smash, just a leveling off of everything. And when everything is leveled everything is God. Junk makes a place in your heart you can't ever forget. You *know* you got to give up everything for it. You *know* you have to be punished in the end. It *must* be God—How could anyone find his punishment without it?"

"I *could* have been an airplane stewardess 'n flown around," Beulah decided, "except things were geared one way and I was geared another. I could have had a rich, happy life."

"What good would that have done you," Vivi-V wanted to know, "if you were dead the whole while?"

"I could have been—" Beulah began again, but Vivi-V interrupted her, "When you start hitting toward fifty," she bobbed her pink bow so rapidly that she didn't notice Dingdong standing in the door, "you feel like you want to go down to the graveyard and wait for your Maker beside your stone."

"Had she gone down there when she was sixty-five," the old man announced himself by addressing Beulah, "she would have been waiting for her maker for some time now."

"Goggly-Eye-Owl you!" Vivi-V welcomed him—"*you* don't even have a maker! The warden found you in somebody's pants after they hung him!"

"Never should've hung him," the old man reported, "should've hung you instead."

"*Look* who's talkin'," Vivi-V challenged him directly. "By how far did *you* miss the rope, Goggly-Eye-Owl?"

The old man merely inspected the rack. Sure enough, he found a *Barney Google* on the top-most rack, reserved for nothing save *Dingdong Daddies*. "Bedbugs won't bite you!" he accused her—and flung it at Vivi-V, who caught it and swung it within an inch of his nose. Beulah stepped between them, took the casing out of Vivi-V's hand and placed it on its proper rack.

"Don't you be so hard on her, you *hear?*" she reproached Dingdong quietly yet firmly. Then, turning on Vivi-V, "And don't *you* be so hard on *him.*"

"Put his mind in a cat," Vivi-V told herself softly, "and what you got?" And answered herself just as softly, "A crazy cat, *that's* what."

"Bedbugs don't bite her," the old man repeated.

It was true: Vivi-V had so much heroin in her, bedbugs fled the beds she lay in.

"You make one more funny move around here," the old man issued a final warning, "you're one one-hundred-year-old flapper whose ass is going to be back on the street, ribbon-bow and all!"

"When my ass goes back on the street, Goggly-Eye-Owl you," Vivi-V retaliated, "back to the joint *your* ass goes."

"I don't *have* to toss you back on the street," Dingdong changed his mind at the very thought of doing more time, "I can rough you up right *here!*"

"You *try* roughing *me* up," Vivi-V challenged him, "you motherless penitentiary toad from Fink Row, you best get your best hold. You'll never get a second!"

Beulah urged him to the table; where he sat like a huge unclean child with yesterday's eggstain on his chin.

"Wash off the egg," she ordered him.

He rose reluctantly and washed at the sink's single spigot, making the faucet squeal spitefully. Then dried his face on a towel Vivi-V reserved for her own private use. But since neither gesture succeeded in irritating Vivi-V, he began banging his baggedy knees together while crisscrossing his palms on them and croaking—

Why don't you do-do-do
What you done-done-done before.

Beulah let him finish Charlestoning. Nor did either woman pay him any heed while he clattered his spoon against the rim of his cup.

Neither paid him the slightest heed. So he crumbled dry bread about the table; then brushed the crumbs, as if accidentally, to the floor.

Yet provoked no reproach.

"I am in the happy position," he announced like a man running for office, "of becoming a living legend in my own time! I have everything I ever wanted! Success in business! Identity as an individual! And the love of many friends."

Then he spat high against the wall and left them alone at last.

"I've cried till I couldn't cry," Vivi-V remembered, "I've cried till I won't cry again. But when he says that about bedbugs—"

"He don't mean everything he says, dear," Beulah assured her.

"Oh, he means it alright," Vivi-V felt certain; then added, "I could kill him in the alley. I could kill him in the House of God. I could kill him under a Christmas tree. I could kill him in the street. I could kill him in his sleep.''

"He *does* have his good side," Beulah yet defended the old man, "he *does* give happiness to people. And he's helping to keep us ahead of the Russians.''

"He hasn't done a thing for *me,*" Vivi-V complained. And Beulah forebore reminding her that, when Dingdong had taken her off the street, she'd jumped three bail bonds in a month and had a fugitive warrant pursuing her.

As she also forebore reminding the old man that either Vivi-V or herself could put him back in the pen by testifying in court against him.

What deterred her wasn't distaste for playing a treacherous part: treachery was Beulah's trade. "But where would you go then, poor thing?" she'd asked herself more than once. "Where would you score for enough stuff to keep yourself from getting dead-sick on the open street?"

And as for Vivi-V, *she* was such a little pig about the stuff that she wouldn't make it till midnight on the street though she slept all day.

Were they his prisoners or was he theirs?

The lives of all three were in the hands of each.

One dead of winter dawn Vivi-V dreamed she was standing trial in a courtroom in another town.

"What in God's name is she *on?*" His Honor asked someone unseen.

"Your Honor," she'd heard Beulah's voice defending her, "nobody *knows* what this woman is on."

"What are you on, Sis?" the Judge had then asked her gently. That his features were those of a white teacher whom she'd had, briefly, as a grade-school child, she did not wonder about.

"I'm not allowed to say in open court, Your Honor," she'd answered.

"Come into chambers," the Judge decided. And now she'd found herself standing in a spacious chamber lit by a great gas-burning chandelier casting a curious blue-green light.

"*Now,* young woman," he had demanded sternly, "what *is* this stuff? Liquid cocaine?"

"Greater than cocaine, Your Honor," she had answered.

"Morphine sulphate?"

"Greater than morphine sulphate, Your Honor."

"Heroin?"

"Greater, Your Honor."

"Come around here, Sis." The Judge had instructed her to come around to his side of the desk, and had opened a drawer: she'd seen a hundred different kinds of powders and pills; and a set of sixteen-gauge hypodermic needles.

"Any of *these*, Sis?"

"None of these, Your Honor," she'd tried to explain. "What I'm on is the Daddy of them All." Then the blue-green light of the great chandelier went down; and came up again in a dark red glow.

So she came to her red-lit wakening. The red nightbulb of the narrow hall was casting shadows across her wall.

After such a dream, Vivi-V would lie talking softly to herself; or would sing very low so as not to waken the house:

> *All the good times are past 'n gone*
> *All the good times are o' er*

Her memory was a spiral stairwell whereon disasters came tumbling like sorrowing clowns. How long had it been since she'd sung—a slender Sixty-third street chick with hair and fingernails dyed platinum blonde —in front of a microphone raised like a chromium cross.

> *Good morning heartache*
> *Here we go again—*

above a soiled bar? How long had it been since she'd been billed as "a girl who was popular when she was here once before—I give you the Inimitable Vivienne Vincent."

The *Inimitable Vivi-V*. Who'd refused to sing like Sarah Vaughan; nor even like Her Nibs Miss Georgia Gibbs. Who'd let Miss Patti Page go her own way while *she* went her own, proudly belting lyrics out in night-blue dives till dawn. And belting each so inimitably that once a barfly had lifted his head and told a bartender, "I never heard anything like it"; and had put his head back on his hands.

Half-memories mixed with flash notions in her mind; remembering the same old soiled lyrics and the same old soiled bars. Little lacey fancies came, like kerchiefs on a line; turned and moved and wandered through her wandering mind. Small and silken fancies about singing for a living far beneath the traffic's cries.

Downward forever downward had been the route she'd gone; singing *Good Morning Heartache* to a thousand heartbroken dawns.

53

Until at last she'd cried out, to someone, toward morning, "I don't know what I'd do if I thought there wasn't any bottom"—and there had been no bottom. Only a falling without end.

She hadn't hit bottom yet.

Sometimes she would rise and begin gathering up soiled clothes, from the front room to the back—sheets, shirts, underclothes, towels, curtains, socks, stockings, drapes, aprons, skirts, brassieres, handkerchiefs—all would go into the old-fashioned bathtub. In a soapified mist Vivi-V would wash, scrub, dry, and hang clothes from the front of the old flat to the back.

"She's on her laundry kick again," Beulah would report to Dingdong, "you got any shoelaces you want ironed?"

Even when a clothesline went up over his easy chair in the front room, and underwear began to hang against the windows, Dingdong never interfered with Vivi-V's compulsion to launder everything in sight.

For one thing, it kept her out of searching the flat for a hidden cache. For another, it got his laundry done.

"She's going to look for the cache in the gas-meter," Beulah would fink to the old man while the water was running in the tub. And would wonder, even as she finked, whether the cache actually *was* in the meter.

Once Beulah had warned him that Vivi-V was planning on breaking into the back of his cuckoo-clock, hanging above his easy chair. He'd never used the clock for a cache. But after he'd discovered that Vivi-V had opened it, and found nothing, he'd kept a cache there for a month. Then he'd tipped off Beulah to the clock; and had taken the heroin to another hiding place.

Sure enough, the clock was broken into that same night.

That was why, as much as the old man and Vivi-V distrusted one another, both distrusted Beulah: Double-Fink, Counter-Counter Agent, Friendly Investigator, Perfidious Confidante, the most of all.

And why Beulah was so aware that, while she was keeping one eye on the old man for Vivi-V, and keeping the other on Vivi-V for him, and both were keeping an eye on each other, that each was keeping one eye on her.

"No one in my family was ever in politics, Emil," the cop, at the wheel of the car parked in the alley, assured his partner. "I had to break the ice entirely myself."

"Around five o'clock I begin to get tired," Emil recalled; for both were dead-weary of cruising.

"Leave the parking lights on, Stan," Emil suggested. "It looks better that way. Like we're just laying low for a culprit."

Stan wondered vaguely whether a culprit was a suspect who'd done time. He'd have to look it up.

"Sometimes I sleep overtime," he informed Emil; implying it might be best if one of them stayed awake.

"I got caught six times at Navy Pier," Emil boasted; just to let Stan know he hadn't yet been decorated for vigilance.

"I had a partner once who *never* wanted to sleep," Stan recalled dreamily.

"The fink," Emil sympathized.

His sympathy was lost. Stan was already snoring lightly. A moment later Emil was on the nod, too.

On the nod in a dead-end alley's depths; with a cardboard box over the flash. Law and Order was working quietly.

Four stories above them, Dingdong-Daddyland lay like a great refrigerator in which the light had gone out. The three outcasts slept among the broken-handled cups of hopes that had never come true. Their dreams, long dried, yet somehow still cherished, lay among crusts that had once been loaves.

The old con slept. Beulah slept. Only Vivi-V remained awake; waiting until Beulah's sleep grew deeper.

Then she unwound herself like a shadow from the sheets and moved, like a ghost of a ghost, into the bathroom. She locked herself in and raised the lid of the water-closet, peering in at the water-bulb. On its surface she could see no sign of any mark where the rubber might have been split; so she tried it with her eyes shut, letting her fingers explore the surface of the rubber: the fingers came to a slight indentation and held there. She adjusted her specs with one hand, keeping a finger in the indentation. Then, peering more closely, she saw, sure enough, that a small slit had been made in the rubber and vulcanized. Her fingers found the edge of the patch and pried it off. In her anxiety she tore the slit wide—and there it was: a paper, a full ounce of *something*.

She sniffed it. It wasn't heroin. No matter. She melted a few grains in a spoon over the gas flame, took her sixteen-gauge needle out of her pocket, placed the spoon carefully beside a chair, sat down and crossed her ankles. Then she hit herself in an ankle vein with whatever it was.

She sat that way a long minute. Then she began scratching her upper lip; then her stomach, then her ankles. When she had finished scratching, she rose.

Wellsprings of energy began flooding her: she had never felt so well since she'd been born.

Beulah was used to waking to find Vivi-V missing; and then, by listening, to follow her movement about the flat by small creakings and creaks and murmurings beneath the creeper's feet.

The sounds that wakened her now were not furtive: there was a clanging of pans and kettles and pots from the kitchen, and a high falsetto singing:

Blue Moon
You saw me standing alone

Beulah rose and saw every light in the house ablaze, and Vivi-V wearing not a stitch but a baby-blue apron tied behind her in a flowing bow matching her pink ribbon-bow. That bow looked now like the rainbowed halo of her junkified glow.

Vivi-V, racing near-naked between stove, pantry, and sink, then into the bathroom and back to the stove, forced Beulah to stand back against the kitchen wall to keep from getting knocked down.

"Is there something going on, dear?" Beulah asked.

"Oh, have *consideration, do* have consideration," Vivi-V scolded her on the run, "we're late with the chicken. Late with the roast! Not a clean tablecloth in the house! Somebody stole the best silver!"

"Why?" Beulah asked weakly. "Are we expecting somebody?"

"Oh for Heaven's sake, you know very well we're having guests—and there you stand not even offering to lend a hand!"

"I only thought it was early in the day to be making soup," Beulah explained.

"This isn't soup as you well know—it's hot water for the sheets and pillow-cases—oh, *have* consideration."

"If you're going to launder tonight, honey," Beulah asked calmly, "why heat water on the stove? Why not just turn on the faucets in the tub?"

Vivi-V stopped and thought that over: "Why, *of course,* how *silly* of me. Will you turn on the water in the tub for me, there's a good girl? I have to watch the soup."

When Beulah had the hot water drawn, she stood by to keep the mad laundress from plunging into the scalding tub herself. For she was piling tablecloths, sheets, pillow-cases, window shades, shoes, spoons, napkins, saltshakers, shirts, and a potted geranium—pot and all—into the tub. Then began stirring it wildly with the old man's umbrella.

56

"Can I help in any way?" Beulah asked again. Vivi-V couldn't hear her because of the roaring of the water. Because of the steam, Beulah could hardly see her.

"Needle and thread on the dresser, dear," Vivi-V instructed Beulah, "if you *really* want to help"—and one of Dingdong's socks came flying and dripping as it flew. Beulah caught it. And began a confused retreat.

Dingdong was sitting before the TV, that was still whirling blindly with sound turned down. Beulah entered quietly. She would say she was looking for needle and thread.

But the old man's head was sunk on his chest. He was snoring lightly. She watched him with her hand on the brass knob of the old-fashioned bedpost. And heard Vivi-V caroling—

> *Red sails in the sunset*
> *All day I've been blue—*

* * *

Emil sat up.

"What's the matter?" Stan asked.

"I heard someone walkin'."

"We better start cruising. It might be Task Force Tuf."

Emil ducked into the rain, took the box off the car's flash, and in its blood-colored beam he saw a woman seated on the sill, washing a window in a 3 A.M. rain.

"Up there! Up *there!*" he jabbed a finger toward the wall.

"If you want to go up and find out, I'll wait here," Stan told Emil.

"What *are* people thinking of anyhow," Emil marveled, "washing windows in the rain?"

Then he observed a puff of dark smoke blowing out the window past the woman on the sill. Well, he could just as easily have *not* seen *that.*

That same blood-red swing of light across his window had wakened Dingdong. He brushed his hand across his eyes, shook his great head, and shambled to the window.

He heard the beat of the rain against the pane, and peered down. A squadrol with a cop at the wheel and another cop coming around the end of the car!

He raced to the front room where the blue films were stacked, hauling madly at twine he had knotted too taut. Stumbling into the bathroom, trailing the twine behind him, and didn't pause because the tub was full of steaming laundry. He heaped the film on top of the clothes, and raced back to the front room for more. Then for matches.

"They're on the way up! Don't let them in without a warrant!" he cried warning to Beulah, and hauled her by one arm to the front and shoved her into the bathroom. The film on top of the laundry blazed up.

Beulah began heaping cardboard cartons onto the fire, and the smell of burning rubber made a perfectly terrible stink.

While Vivi-V, enraptured by window washing, went endlessly washing and rewashing the rain-soaked pane.

Dingdong lurched and heaved and coughed and spat and choked and phlegmed from the front room to the back, heaping more cardboard cartons of *Dingdong Daddies* onto the fire; till smoke darkened the ceiling and made the lights burn like lights in an eclipse of the sun.

But Stan and Emil were merrily wheeling, already miles away; relieved to be out of the jurisdiction of the Chicago Fire Department.

Until Vivi-V finally slipped back into the kitchen, caroling as she came—

I know there's room for me
Upon your knee

Dingdong, looking out the window, saw that the squadrol was gone. He sank into a chair, blue film dangling from his hands. Beulah sank onto a chair on the other side of the room.

Between them Vivi-V came in; looking done in. She was coming down fast. She looked like she wanted to say something; but the old man waved her off. She turned and went quietly. When Beulah followed her a few minutes after, she found Vivi-V sleeping the sleep of total exhaustion. The old man slept where he sat.

Toward nine he woke. Coughing and phlegming, in air black and odorous, spitting now and then, he moved through the flat assessing the useless damage.

Broken boxes, burned film, clothing and ruined sheets that had been both washed and scorched; a smoldering shoe: a pot of stew that had boiled over into the flooded forging-room—from front to back Daddyland looked like a land struck by a tornado, fire, and flood.

Yet a many-splendored line of *Feathered Friends* was still festooned above the stove; like a rainbow of hope in the smoldering air.

Would some neighbors report smoke? A fire inspector at the door would be as catastrophic as a policeman. All morning Vivi-V and Dingdong shared their common dread: kicking a habit cold turkey for her; dying in a cell for him. And in this common fear their feud was forgotten. There was no longer any point in threatening one another with prison; when prison for both was so near.

She opened windows, drove out the smoke, and cleaned up the litter. He helped as best he could.

"Beulah's sleeping late," he complained to Vivi-V.

"Let her sleep," Vivi-V decided.

Toward noon Vivi-V went into the bedroom to wake Beulah. She came out looking so bleak that the old man guessed before she'd said a word.

"Gone?"

"*Gone.*"

Beulah had crept downstairs in the night like a bug in flight.

Where had she gotten the courage to leave? The old man looked in the bulb of the water-closet. Finding it split and the stuff he'd hidden there gone, he assumed that had been where she'd found the courage. When he checked his bedroom, however, and found she'd missed his big cache, he felt gratified that she'd taken such a minute prize. He never learned that she had gone without taking any drug at all: that she had simply fled in dread of the police. To take her own chances on the street.

Dingdong seemed to accept Beulah's flight with resignation. But after Vivi-V had cleaned up the kitchen, flushed the last condom down the drain, and the last bit of evidence against the old man's enterprise had been destroyed, he rose and fumbled about until he found a piece of chalk. He ran a rag across a section of the wall to serve as a blackboard. Then, with his tongue between his teeth, and Vivi-V sleeping, he went to work.

Sometimes on tiptoe and sometimes flatfooted, pausing now and again to spit, scratch himself, or lean back to gain perspective, he completed his letter to the world. Then the chalk dropped from his hand, and he went to his bed; weary to his very bones.

Later, Vivi-V saw a rude caricature of a woman with a neck like a turkey-hen's, the belly bloated and the knees badly knocked, the breasts lactated like empty hot-water bottles, the whole figure stippled by disfiguring hair; and flies buzzing about the figure everywhere. Below the old man had scrawled his final conviction:

WOMIN DRAW FLIES

"A once great mind has snapped," Vivi-V commented aloud—and wiped the figure out with two swipes of a damp cloth.

* * *

Though the lives of all three had been in the hands of each, the balance of power shifted with one of the three gone.

With Beulah at hand, Vivi-V had been the most imperiled of the lot; because the old man could open the gates of a terrible sickness upon her any moment he chose.

Now he *had* to keep her well. For there was nobody now but her to shop and cook and wash and help him make it from day to day.

The Mumbling Man never came any longer. Yet every morning Vivi-V found a pinch of heroin beside a spoon on his dresser. Every noon there was another pinch. And at night there was another pinch for her to sleep on.

She searched that bedroom high and low—even when she knew he was only feigning sleep. She raised his pillow when he raised his head; there was nothing under his pillow.

When she swept under the bed she examined the bedsprings; nothing was hidden there. She looked behind the mirror; in the light fixture and along the walls. It *had* to be in his bedroom. He hadn't been out of it in days. Yet she never found a single pinch.

Meanwhile she shaved him, washed him, humored him; brought him tea and toast and little candies to suck on. She changed his sheets and listened to his rambling accounts of merry penitentiary times.

So it was that, in his final hours, the old man drew some small ironic measure of contentment from a woman at last.

Once, toward evening, he looked up at her as though he had never seen her before.

"What I said about bedbugs—you know—" he faltered—"was just in fun."

"What I told you was in fun, too," Vivi-V assured him.

The old man's face flopped about: he was trying to smile.

Vivi-V opened his window every morning; so he could hear the jackhammers breaking stone half a mile away.

Every morning they came nearer. One morning he asked her to open the window wider so that he could hear them. But, when she opened the window, he could not hear them at all.

"It's Sunday," she explained. But he didn't seem to understand why he couldn't hear jackhammers. Suddenly he asked, "How much your little sausages?"—and asked it urgently.

He died that evening just before the street lamps came on. When she came into his room with tea, he was sitting up; but the glaze was on

60

his eyes. She laid his head back on the pillow: understanding her dream at last.

"The kick greater than H," she told herself aloud; taking his wrist-watch and ring.

In her final search, all she found was a couple of twenties in his wallet and a few dimes on his dresser.

Yet once, as she looked about the bedroom, her hand rested, where Beulah's hand had: on the big brass knob of his bed. She had never noticed that the knobs of the bedposts could be unscrewed; nor that the posts were hollow. She never knew that, beneath her hand, was five pounds of pure heroin.

She left the door open behind her. And walked, in a light November rain, to the Desplaines Street station. She came in there looking like a ghost wearing a pink ribbon-bow.

"Vivienne Vincent," she told the officer at the desk, "there's a couple warrants out on me."

Half an hour later Stan and Emil were mounting the stairs. Sure enough, just like that old junkie had said, there *was* a stiff.

Some stiff. Wasn't even wearing a watch.

"Maybe the Fire Department was here already," Emil suggested.

Stan found a pair of pants that fit him, supported by a pair of suspenders with clips that said *Police Brace* on them. Emil found a woman's raincoat. A package of dry cereal and a bucket of hardened rubber was all their search for treasure yielded.

The few sticks of furniture weren't worth hauling down the stairs. The bed was such an old-fashioned heap it wasn't worth dragging down four flights.

"Besides, the stiff's still in it," Emil pointed out.

The dead-wagon came. A woman on her way to the supermarket with a shopping bag, the words VOTE FOR DALEY emblazoned on it in red, white, and blue, stopped to watch the dead-wagon boys lift a corpse into the dead-wagon.

"I'm glad it ain't me," she thought; and went her ways.

The Board of Health inspectors didn't bother cleaning out the flat because the building was coming down anyhow.

The first swing of the wrecking-ball buried the old bed under tons of bricks.

Before the bricks were hauled away, the year's earliest snow lay lightly above them. Then a contractor, using County Jail labor, hauled them away.

* * *

This was in that time of year when silver-paper bells hang by tinseled cords in the offices of all the loan companies. It was that time when Save-Your-Home-Loans holds Open-House-For-Money in offices lit by an aluminum Christmas Tree: one proudly bearing a shining six-foot papier-maché dollar-sign, hung with brightly-polished quarters, nickels, and dimes; all the while it keeps slowly revolving.

While poorer firms can offer no more than tidings of comfort and joy under a single unmoving star.

Then a winter of a single wind set in. Snow-shadows went tobogganing down the crumpled, yellowed, tattery-torn mattress that the old man had died upon. And at night a street lamp shone upon the bent and dented upside-down bedposts the old man had died between.

The midnight B-train passed overhead. And no one who rode the B-train knew that a hundred thousand dollars worth of fine white dust stayed dry in the deeps of those rusting posts.

All that winter smudgefires burned, both sides of West Congress, after the jackhammers had gone still.

Phantoms of old-time junkies passed and repassed between their wild and flickering flares.

Shadows of long-gone hepsters, phantoms of fools who never could learn, went by like shadows on old walls: forever trying to turn one more trick.

Nobody remembers where Beulah went. Nobody has heard of any woman calling herself *The Inimitable Vivi-V*. Where the old man is buried nobody knows.

The passion that, in him, had been transformed by fear of women into deep need of something to love *safely*—a paper doll or a girl wearing a bunny-tail—curiously overlapped that of lives equally barren yet more affluent.

His letter to the world was never mailed. In the world in which he lived there were no postal zones. Had it been read, even by chance, no one would have paid it any heed: the old con's spelling was so bad.

Yet had he made the connection, for which he was groping, he would have become the living legend that in fancy he felt himself sometimes to be.

For he shared a secret fury with the world: a hatred of all birth that comes from love of man for woman.

THE LEAK THAT DEFIED THE BOOKS

ROMAN-From-Metal-Finishing never expected more out of life than to be married to Selma-From-Endless-Belting. Selma-From-Endless never dreamed of any life other than one of being married to Roman-Metal-Finishing. Had anyone prophesied that a day would come when Roman would wear the proud blue and grey of Some People's Gas Company, who would have believed? Neither I nor the other children of Moorman Street.

For Some People's Gas is a mighty utility, owning miles of gas piping and gasified bookeepers keeping gasified books, to see that people who use Some People's Gas pay their gaseous bills. It employs gasified collectors who come to the doors of people who have not paid for their Some People's Gas. Nobody knows but that there might somewhere be ghastly courts where people who steal Some People's Gas are sentenced—quite properly—to gas-lit cells.

And this vast empire of gas tubing and gas meters, gas inspectors, gas collectors, gas directors, gas detectives and gas detectors, rulers of an underground city as extensive as the city above it, depends completely on the little hunk of snot and bone called: The Nose.

Down in the dark megalopolis where water drips between abandoned walls, a tiny leak in rusted tubing may blast innocent persons through their roofs in the middle of a summer afternoon. In the middle of a wintry night is better yet.

Selma and Roman were so serious about one another that one day she said to him, "Let's go down to Hubbard Street and get the free blood-test."

"I go where I'm needed most," Roman agreed.

Selma stood on one side of a screen and Roman on the other.

"Do you have good urine, honey?" she asked him. "Mine is fine."

"It was romantic-like," Selma told me, "it was like being in love."

The next week Roman received an induction notice.

"I'm needed there even more," he assured Selma.

The first time he lined up with his squad, a second lieutenant observed that Roman had more muscles than the army knew how to use.

"Keep this man off KP," the lieutenant instructed the first sergeant, "he's boxing material. Make that out in triplicate." Then he looked Roman over once more.

"See that this man gets a quart of milk a day while in training. Make that out in triplicate also."

For the remainder of his stateside army career Roman received three quarts of milk a day.

"How come you get three quarts for yourself when eight of us fellows have to divide two quarts?" an undernourished corporal wanted to know.

"Because I always go where I'm needed most."

Roman never minded hitting somebody with his fists if it was all right with the other fellow, and then the other fellow would hit Roman with his fists and Roman didn't mind that either. He had simply never thought of it as a profession.

Roman won his first four fights on knockouts as they were all fellows from Los Angeles. He had never been in a fight before where he had never been hit himself; it came as a complete surprise. This had it all over KP.

"There's a sergeant from Butte been pretty lucky so far," his First Sergeant told Roman. "If you can put him away you'll make Pfc."

"I don't know if I can handle the responsibility of office," Roman admitted candidly, "but I go where I'm needed most."

The fellow from Butte knocked Roman cold in twenty-two seconds of the first round.

"If you hadn't come out of your corner so slow," his first lieutenant reproached Roman, "he could have knocked you out in nineteen."

"I'll try to come out faster the next time, sir," Roman promised.

And he kept his word. After that Roman got himself knocked out so fast that other armies began sending in men to see him get it. One night eight German PWs, flanked by two MPs, walked in. His opponent broke Roman's nose as soon as they met in the middle of the ring. The eight Germans stood up in the front row and cheered with a single shout.

"You're raising morale all over the post," the first sergeant encouraged Roman, "keep it up."

Roman kept it up. How many times his nose was broken not even his HQ company knows to this day. Medical records, however, reveal that he was in the Ft. Bragg infirmary thirty-two times. Since medical records are made out in quadruplicate, this indicates that Roman's nose was broken eight times in defense of democracy.

On the day that Von Rundstedt began his great drive to the sea, Roman sneezed so hard in the Ardennes forest that he blew a bone fragment out of his right ear. Von Rundstedt kept coming all the same.

Selma was waiting for Roman at the gate when his turn to be discharged came up at Camp Grant. But Roman didn't come through the gate. His nose had been broken so often, it turned out, that he was no longer entitled to be a civilian.

Every time he sneezed, he was informed, he put innocent bystanders in danger of being struck by bone fragments.

Faced with the alternative of signing up for the regular army or of having his nose cleaned, Roman endured a night-long struggle to decide where he was needed most. In the end he tossed a coin. Heads he'd go for the operation and marry Selma; tails back to Germany. It came tails. He made it two out of three. Tails again.

When it got to the most out of 131, Selma won: 66-65.

The operation was so successful that now Roman could smell things he had never even known had a smell before. Passing a bakery, he could tell whether they were baking egg bread or potato bread or rye or pumpernickel. Passing a butcher shop he had only to sniff to tell whether the cut on which the butcher was cheating was liver, pork or steak.

And of all the smells he had never smelled that he now could smell, the sweetest smell of all was that of Selma-From-Endless.

Selma came to him now in waves of lilac, rose, pine and rhododendron. Roman didn't smell too bad to Selma either. They were married at St. John Cantius on a Sunday morning that smelled of incense and minute rice.

Their honeymoon was a whole Sunday afternoon in Nelson Brothers Rock Garden.

One morning shortly after their wedding Roman was smelling the difference between Old Fitz and Old Grandad in Sigmund's Whiskey-Tavern, when he smelled something which was neither Old Fitz nor Old Grandad; nor even Sigmund. He traced it around a corner of the bar and right under Sigmund's feet.

"Gas," he told Sigmund.

Sigmund couldn't smell it. The customers couldn't smell it. Nonetheless, Sigmund phoned Some People's Gas.

The Some People's Gas Detector couldn't smell anything either. But when he put the automatic gas-detector to where Roman's nose was pointing, the needle jumped.

"You ought to be workin' for Some People's yourself," the Smeller told Roman.

"I got a cousin works downtown there," Sigmund told Roman. "I'll bring him over. We'll talk to you and Selma about gettin' you on."

"*You* don't talk to no Selma," Roman told Sigmund. "*You* talk to *me*."

Some People's Gas put Roman on call as an apprentice smeller. Now, any hour of the day or night the phone might ring and Roman would jump into his gas company uniform, grab his Some People's Gas-Detecting Bag and wheel, walk, run, taxi or bus to the leak whether fast or slow.

"It's romantic, sort of," Selma told Sigmund, "like a doctor's wife almost. And in forty years he gets a pension."

Sometimes Roman had to creep beneath a sidewalk and sometimes he had to climb a chimney. Sometimes he had to break a hole in a roof and hang head down. Sometimes he had to get people out of bed and sometimes he had to fight off dogs; and sometimes he would answer a call from a woman with a slow leak.

One evening Selma put knoodle soup on the table. Roman took one spoonful and then poured the pot down the sink.

"Rotten soup by rotten cook," he told Selma, "tastes like gas."

"Take bat' before you come to bed," she told him later.

"Had bat' by afternoon."

"Take another. Wash under arms."

"I go where I'm needed most," Roman agreed, and took another bath, and went where he thought he was needed most: Their bedroom.

Selma had locked the door.

"Ain't knoodle soup smells by gas," she shouted from inside, "is Mister *you!*" and she began pounding on the walls.

After that Roman ate his meals in restaurants and slept on the front room couch. His blanket smelled of gas.

Among men who smelled of gas, Roman now felt more contented than among people who smelled of nothing but pink soap. He had always gone where he was needed most; but where he was most needed was now no longer Selma's bed.

And as there aren't any other places to go for men not wanted in a woman's bed, Roman worked as much overtime as he could; and spent the rest of his hours in Sigmund's Whiskey-Tavern.

One night the Jerry Lewis show was so bad that not even Roman, who could stand almost anything so long as it was televised, could take it.

"If that boy had a brain," he announced gravely, getting down off

66

the stool beneath the set on which Jerry was stomping somebody in traction, "he'd be dangerous. I'm going out to look for a leak."

In that ashen TV night Roman's face was that of a man who had fasted many days.

He hadn't been gone two minutes before Sigmund called to me, "Mind the bar!" and was out the door and down the street in the opposite direction to which Roman had gone.

"Where's *he* going in such a hurry?" someone wanted to know.

"Not to look for no gas-leak," someone answered.

Sigmund got back behind the bar a couple of minutes before Roman returned.

Roman looked much better than when he'd left.

"A leak!" he called out cheerfully, "under gas station where street-car bends the corner!" And he raced to the phone to report it to Some People's Gas.

By nine A.M. the following morning, a squad of drillers had blocked off traffic both ways down Moorman Street. The hole the drillers dug looked promising; yet the promise was unfulfilled. A detection squad worked under floodlights all that night.

A vapor-test machine showed nothing at all.

Four gasified historians, working with maps showing the paths of gaspipes, some put down by the city at the turn of the century, found no evidence of a gas pipe ever having been laid down within twenty feet of where Roman had smelled gas.

"There isn't any leak," the four gasified historians decided, "for the simple reason that there isn't any pipe there."

"I smelled gas," Roman insisted.

Thirteen new holes were dug. In every one of them a hose attached to a Davis Gas-Testing machine was lowered.

In one of the holes the needle of the machine jumped a couple of degrees, Roman's hopes jumped with it—then sank when the needle returned to zero.

"This leak defies the books," Roman had to concede.

"The leak don't defy *nothin'*," the foreman of the Gas-Detection Unit made up his mind, "for the simple reason there ain't no leak to defy."

The Gas-Detection Unit went home; the Vapor-Testers went home; the Davis Gas-Testing machine rolled away. The drillers left.

Roman came down to the loosely-filled hole in the middle of the night, flashlight on his knees. He went sniffing up the curb and down.

"I've found the spot," he phoned Some People's Gas at four A.M., "seven feet down and creeping."

"That case is closed," the Chief Gasified Historian informed Roman and hung up.

At 12:55 A.M. the following Sunday morning, while we were playing twenty-five-cent limit and Roman was watching a rerun of Joan Crawford in *Lingerie Party,* a fatal blast of fatal gas blew the fatal bed upon which Selma and Sigmund had been making fatal love, up through that fatal roof.

The same blast blew up the kitchen of the bungalow next door, in which the last celebrants of a wedding party were still celebrating instead of letting the groom take the bride to bed. Had they left when they were no longer welcome, the pair would have been able to have them back for wedding anniversaries for fifty years. As it was, the groom was blown to shreds and the bride was paralyzed, from the waist down, for the rest of her life.

The same blast blew the back porch off the house next door, dispatching an elderly grandmother to an elderly grave. Her husband, troubled by prostatitis, had left the porch a minute before the blast; thus saving his own life. Moreover, the shock of losing his wife of many years cured his prostatitis by giving him a coronary just in time to be buried beside her.

The family cat, long in the service of this elderly pair, had its right foreleg and left hindleg severed. Yet somehow it survived, hopping about in a most curious fashion, for some years. It was finally brought down by a rat who'd become embittered at having been deafened in one ear by the same blast.

Roman took our congratulations modestly.

"I owe everything to the army doctor who operated me," he assured us. "I give him full credit for everything."

Late last Saturday night I took the shortcut across the lot where Roman-From-Metal-Finishing once lived with Selma-From-Endless. Yellowed newspapers were caught, as always, among the weeds. And the weeds moved slightly as I passed; though there was no wind.

Then a scent of gas rose ever so faintly, from somewhere far under the arteried stone.

He went where he was needed most.

TINKLE HINKLE AND THE
FOOTNOTE KING

I was in New York recently for the skating at Rockefeller Plaza and was sharpening my skates at the Sherry-Netherlands when the telephone rang and a woman's voice informed me, "Mr. Kazin would like to have you for dinner."

"I don't blame him," I told the voice and was about to hang up when it struck me a fellow like that might use some advice. "Tell him to look for me in the lobby," I suggested, figuring that by putting it that way I could still make it hard for him to find me. When I realized he could scarcely eat me in plain view of a desk clerk, I went downstairs and there were two of them waiting, one a breathless blonde.

What caused her shortwindedness I have no notion, but she looked like a cross between a shrike and a barbed-wire fence. The fellow with her was built along the lines of Budd Schulberg but richer. I surmised he must be a CCNY poet so I asked, "How's business?"

When put to someone in the poetry line this is supposed to be a highly ironic question; but this one didn't take it that way. All he said was, "Slow. The holidays." And added, "Do you like Italian food?" He was going the flour-and-cheese route on me.

All the way to the restaurant they kept touting the cheesified lasagna that had made this place famous from coast to coast. So I told them of a cave crosstown that had got itself a very big name for its Frenchified toast; but for myself I was a meat-eating mouse and at the moment was so eager to get at a T-bone that I might not even wait till the brute had died.

Once at a table they both swung to a sort of finkified ravioli that looked like the dogs had had it under the house. I went for the oyster stew and the filet avec three champignons. That didn't make the conversation any gayer.

"What do *you* do?" I asked the lady shrike by way of breaking the ice.

"I work at Doubleday," she told me, "but I don't like it. Everyone around me is so *grim*. *Nobody* laughs at Doubleday." I could pretty well see how things might work out that way, but I wanted to be helpful. "They laugh at Random," I told her.

"I don't see anything in the least funny in *that*," she assured me.

"I don't think it's highly comical myself," I had to admit, "I just thought it was better than sitting around looking at each other. I often say comical things; sometimes I even tell comical stories. Like one time a friend of mine in Chicago, a little fellow but a very big man in his own narrow circle, got to be a judge. We always called him Ding-Ding before he was on the bench because he had once turned in a false fire-alarm. He had the hook-and-ladders swinging around corners all over the Westside, looking for something on fire. All of us reproached Ding-Ding for doing a thing like that, and he took it so to heart he promised never to pull another fire-box so long as he lived. And he stuck to his word so good that when there was a vacancy on the bench they picked Ding-Ding because he had by then become widely known as a man of his word. Even now when he is a judge and so has license to indulge himself a little now and then, he will turn his eyes the other way when passing a fire-box. And when he has to decide a case of someone accused of fooling with fire, he can be very stern indeed."

"I don't see anything funny in that either."

"Wait till I tell the whole story," I asked her, "you'll purely howl. Because even though he doesn't pull fire-boxes any more, Ding-Ding still thinks along hook-and-ladder lines. You just should have been there, the time he was holding a bench trial of a kid accused of setting fire to a church. 'We have to keep Chicago strong and America mighty!' Ding-Ding hollered, 'Hard labor! No parole! Take him away forever! Bury him! Twenty years!'

"But this boy jumped up and hollered, 'Your Honor! This case has been fixed!' and his lawyer knocked the boy down.

" 'What did he say? What did he say?' was all Ding-Ding could think to ask, he was that taken by surprise.

" 'Your Honor, he said he is only a kid from the sticks,' the lawyer explained.

" 'Why, then we recommend mercy, remand the case, suspend the sentence and adjourn this court,' Ding-Ding decided.

"But when the lawyer took this kid home and told his father what he'd jumped up and hollered, the kid's own father knocked him down.

"That same evening the bailiff dropped by and he talked to the boy like a father, too. But the boy felt very bitter about being knocked down publicly, so the bailiff said, 'Well, we're in private now,' and he hit the boy and knocked him down also.

"Ding-Ding came in later, wanting to know what the bailiff thought he was doing, trying to book a fix himself. The bailiff explained that, because of the nature of the charge, he was afraid Ding-Ding wouldn't stand for a fix and might even get a bailiff fired who arranged one.

" 'It isn't the man who sets an occasional fire who burns me,' Ding-Ding explained, 'it's the character who pulls a fire-box in cold passion when nothing is burning that I can't bear—Oh, these god*damned* false-alarm phonies!'—and he turned and belted that boy so clean the kid went out cold and when he came to, just lay there crying quietly. So you see, that little Ding-Ding, when it came around to *his* turn, he hit the kid harder than anyone."

I looked at my cheesified friends. The lady looked ready to eat her young and boredom was trickling out of Alfred's ears.

"I'm doing a critique on the Existentialism of Zen that will appear in *Capistrano: A Western Review,*" he told me, keeping his big surprise back for a moment: "And I'm thinking of including a footnote on you!"

This was going to happen whether the swallows came back on time or not, it looked like. "I'm real relieved to hear about this," I told him, although what I was really so relieved about was that I finally had a line on him. He was a one-book novelist who had swung to the footnote field, a subsidiary of the critic's trade: that is, I'm told, the coming thing in prose.

Conversation, after that, eddied around whether Theodore Dreiser was a *great* writer, a *great great* writer or just a good old sport. I maintained, and still do, that the pen is mightier than the sword. Then they began pitting Edgar Allan Poe against the fellow from Yoknapotawful County the way fight buffs like to match Ketchel against Robinson and all like that. I couldn't help noticing, with these fearless finks, that the best writer was always the one who'd been dead longest.

"I saw a play," I told them just to change the way the talk was tending, "it was by some fellow who served eight years in an English jail."

"I don't see anything to be proud of in being in jail," the shrike-lady told me.

I looked down at the last lonesome oyster in my stewless, drained and drying bowl, and the oyster looked back up at me baffled as could be. "Where did everyone go, Dad?" it wanted to know. When the waiter took him away I knew I'd lost my only friend around *that* table.

The footnote king was still cropping ravioli but he looked up for a moment, dried his chin and asked what the play I saw was about.

"Capital punishment," was the closest I could come. It was such short notice.

"O, this *killing, killing, killing,*" the footnote king mourned. *"O Castro—enough."* Coming from someone who liked dead writers better than live ones, that struck me as a little odd.

"I just can't see how anyone can still believe in capital punishment," the shrike-lady taxied in. "They used to hang eleven-year-olds for stealing sheep in England—but that didn't put a stop to sheep-stealing."

"A person's habits are pretty well formed by the time he's that age," I remembered. "If they'd strung up a couple of ten-year-olds just as a preventive measure it would have put a short quick stop to the mischief—and there'd be more sheep for the rest of us today. As it is there's hardly enough now to go around."

"I fail to see anything funny in that either," she assured me.

"They laugh at Random," I reminded her.

"You said that before."

"I know I did. But I forgot to tell you about Tinkle Hinkle."

"Another Chicago judge?"

"No, this was a convict fellow from East St. Louis, name of Hinkle, who could digest anything. He didn't like working in the prison machine-shop so he began eating bolts, nuts, washers, whatever he could pick up, in hope he'd be sent to the dispensary. He got so much junk inside him you could hear him tinkle when he walked, so the other cons named him Tinkle Hinkle. The warden heard him tinkle, too, so he had him put under the X-ray and there was so much ironware inside they had to operate. The operation was a success, because when it was done the warden said, 'We're transferring Hinkle to the mental ward—I said *mental* not *metal.*' I thought that was pretty good for a warden," I apologized.

Then I withdrew a malevolent little packet of toothpicks, of a breed possessing such tensile strength that I don't apply them to the teeth at all. I simply hold one parallel to the table and leap upon it, gnashing.

Shreds of filet began spewing to all sides. "Stop that!" the shrike-lady commanded me. "*Put* that thing away! Alfred! *Make* him stop!" But the toothpick and I were now as one and I wouldn't be stopped long as wood endured. One particularly juicy shred landed in the middle of a plate of spumoni owned and operated by a Zen Hipster five tables away; waiters came running, someone blew a whistle; I fled for the door without my coat and made it at the very moment my hosts tried coming through also: for one mad moment we were all three wedged. Then the wedge gave, they fell into a cab and wheeled away. Leaving me coatless, toothpickless, defrocked and bereft.

Somewhere down Sixth Avenue a fire siren wailed. Remembering Ding-Ding, I hoped it wasn't a false alarm.

I remained bemused after the siren, true or false, had died upon the wintry air. What was it that had lent my host an aura of such fraudulence?

He hadn't tried to sell me a hot watch. He hadn't implied that he had powerful influence with the Carnegie, Guggenheim and Rockefeller Foundations. He hadn't divulged intimacies from the lives of the Spendthrift Gentry.

He'd done nothing more than reveal a mind better fitted for measuring meat than literature, that was all. And, as butchers go, he was honest as any. Weighing Saul Bellow, he felt obliged to retract a couple thumbs of praise; lest he'd tipped the scale in favor of a writer he admired. As, when weighing Norman Mailer, a writer of whom he disapproves, he would feel obliged to put in a couple phrases expressing respect; if not esteem. You have to hit it right in the middle when you're this kind of critic.

The difficulty here being that he was dealing with passion; not with hamburger. He'd been preoccupied his whole adult life with an art based upon passion; and his own emotional equipment was that of a man who could measure accurately but could feel little.

And so, like Tinkle Hinkle, he'd swallowed so much erudition that he clanked when he talked. And yet himself had never been capable of writing a single line of English prose worthy of recollection.

"Too timid to damn, too stingy to applaud," Joseph Heller summed up this critic in 1962.

There has been no occasion since for revising Heller's estimate.

HAND IN HAND THROUGH
THE GREENERY
with the grabstand clowns of arts and letters

"DEAR Mr. Algren," a young woman writes from Wheaton (Ill.) College, "I am a freshman and am standing on the threshold of a literary career. What is my next move?"

"Your next move, honey," I had to caution her, "is to take two careful steps backward, turn and run like hell. That isn't a threshold. It's a precipice."

The girl appears to feel that she is about to be welcomed through the gates of that enchanted land named "The Smiling Side of American Life" by William Dean Howells; later to be packaged by Richard Nixon as "Our Free Civilization"; then telecast as Marlboro Country.

A smiling image yet sustained, in air-conditioned stillnesses, when summer is the season. Then Creative Writers' Workshops, poetry seminars and Festivals of the Arts will materialize midst campus greenery. The Failure of Hemingway The Failure of Faulkner The Failure of Whitman The Failure of Melville The Failure of Crane The Failure of Twain The Failure of London and The Failure of Wolfe will be revealed by one-book novelists embittered by the failure of David Susskind to invite them to a party where they might have met George Plimpton or even Allen Funt. Just *anybody*.

Perpetual panelists will clobber perpetually rejected novelists with symbolisms concealed in the work of other perpetual panelists. Manuscripts will be returned bearing the instruction: *Insert more symbols.* This can happen anywhere but chances are better in Vermont.

There a kind of Sing-Along-With-Mitch picnic-king who can sing *For He's A Jolly Good Fellow*, impersonate Dylan Thomas and denounce Jacqueline Susann for commercialism while counting his own house, will welcome cash-customers to his lonely-hearts literary supermart in the hills of Vermont. DEPOSIT REQUIRED ON ALL CARTS.

The mock-up poet will himself assure Miss Wheaton that nothing stands between her unreadable novel and its publication except consultation with a publisher's representative; whose identity will remain undisclosed until she's coughed up tuition for a season of creative picnicking (including a pass to the company store). At so much *per diem.*

The company-store pass won't get her into Faculty Cottage because the Sing-Along Supervisor draws a sharp caste line between published and unpublished writers. Miss Wheaton won't make this elitist group because not only is she unpublished but she's not well-groomed enough to make up for it.

Well-groomed women, seeking sanctuary while a divorce-mill is grinding, will wheel up in Caddies. A Junior Editor, grown middle-aged in search of a self he'd loved and lost, will arrive by Mohawk Air bearing an initialed attaché case containing only a pinch-bottle of Haig & Haig and a signed copy of *Atlas Shrugged.* Poor girls from the Village will arrive in sandals, seeking a piece of the Establishment and higher heels. Pursued by studs, barefoot or finely shod; on the prowl for a piece of anything.

The authoress of one nonbook will explain how she made it in a man's world. The editor of *Seminal,* a quarterly financed by his mother-in-law, will not reveal how he made it in a woman's world. Then virgins budding between hard-covers, and paperback editors mildewing between soft, poor girls afoot and old girls a-wheeling, Discover-Me-And-I'll-Discover-You Faculty Wonders, a subscriber to The Famous Writers School who claims he wants Max Shulman's autograph (that *must* be a put-on), one-bookers, non-bookers, publishers' representatives, pinch-bottle vets, Miss Wheaton Supermart Dante and all, will spring hand-in-hand through the greenery and up and down the hall.

For one week or two or ten.

But after the grabstand clown has checked his holdings and counted all the carts in Vermont, Miss Wheaton will be left standing within the very door where she'd come in—to marvel at the emptiness of her own cart.

At so much per diem *per diem.*

Where had that "Publisher's Representative" gone? Could that quickie in the greenery have been with nothing more than one more unpublished poet? If Breadloaf hadn't been exactly a precipice it sure as hell hadn't been a threshold.

"Good writing thrives like corn in Iowa City," Miss Wheaton, still perplexed, reads in the *N.Y. Times,* "where 125 of the nation's most promising writing students just signed up for another semester of agony and ecstasy at what is generally considered the best author's course in the United States—the Iowa University Writing Workshop.''

A six-month deferment from the armed services or the chance to have a steady boyfriend free from parental supervision provides the ecstasy; the agony belongs to the parents footing the bills. For what is offered at Iowa is cover, concealment and sanctuary. Their parents' whole purpose having been to protect their young, out of their playpens and into their teens, from winds of economic weather, the kids who come to the Iowa Workshop have never even been rained on, poor things. Their strongest passion is watching Batman and their greatest hope that they will never get wet.

"The mere fact that the younger American literary generation has come to the schools instead of running away from them," Prof. Wallace Stegner of Stanford assures us, "is an indication of a soberer and less coltish spirit.''

Prof. Stegner says that exactly right. The younger literary generation has come on the run because it's cold out there. The sobriety, and lack of coltishness, constitute their qualifications for reporting fashions or sports; or teaching "Creative Writing" on another campus. They bespeak a readiness to be cowed in return for a stall in the Establishment barn; at whatever cost in originality. They will not buck. They will not roar. At times they may whimper a bit, softly and just to themselves; but even that they will do quietly. For what it lacks in creativity, the Iowa Creative Workshop makes up in quietivity.

"Are you one of the quiet ones who should be a writer?" The Famous Writers School asks the same question that the founder of the Iowa Workshop—himself a "Famous Writer"—is asking: "If you are reserved in a crowd you may be bottling up a talent that could change your life. If you've been keeping quiet about your talent, here's a wonderful chance to do something about it. The first step is to mail the coupon below for the free Writing Aptitude Test.''

The second step is to unbottle your money and send us some.

The University of Iowa is a good place to go if you want to become a journalist, a linguist, a zoologist, a jurist or a purist. Its Creative Writers Workshop is a good place to go to become a tourist. For it provides sanctuary from those very pressures in which creativity is forged. If you want to create something of your own, stay away.

For if the proper study of mankind is man, it follows that to report man one must himself first become one. How is one to create something who has not, himself, been created? How is one to *make* something without first having been made into something himself?

The style is the man: the personality that is unformed cannot create form; the young man or woman who is unintegrated himself cannot integrate wood, stone or language. Nobody can become *anybody* until life has pressured him into becoming *somebody*.

And as becoming somebody is a solitary process, not a group-venture, so art is a solitary process—not a field-trip in pleasant company.

Why has the Iowa Writers Workshop, in its thirty-five years of existence, not produced a single novel, poem or short story worth rereading? Because its offer of painless creativity is based on a self-deception. The student provides the deception and the school provides the group.

"Writers in groups are with few exceptions the most impotent and pernicious of tribes to infest the planet," the playwright Ed Bullins assures a *N.Y. Times* interviewer, "it would be healthier for a writer to socialize with drug addicts than with a claque of hacks."

Had the *Times* man gone to the kids, instead of playing patsy to the brass, he would have learned what they taught me:

"It's a respectable way of dropping out." "The longer I hang on here the longer I stay out of Vietnam." "I had to find a school where I wouldn't get kicked out for bad grades—either that or go to work for my old man." "It may lead to teaching creative writing somewhere else." "Too many squares around my home turf. I was getting conspicuous." "There isn't anything I really *want* to do—but hanging on here makes it look to my folks like I do." "My parents keep pushing me to get married but I want to have fun and games first." "I heard they were going to reevaluate the impact of literary naturalism on American writing and I want to get in on the ground floor."

"Iowa City," the *Times* man reveals the workshop's advantages to poets who teach there, "is the place where a poet can relax in the knowledge that a regular paycheck will come in no matter how badly the book goes." That it can go badly enough to embarrass readers, without stopping a paycheck, is demonstrated by the founder-poet's own odes to fried rice.

Of the eighty-odd students whose work I read at Iowa at least thirty were too disturbed, emotionally, to write coherently in any language. Only two used English lucidly; and neither of these was native-born.

This is not to put down summer extension courses in photo-journalism, science-fiction, writing whodunits, juveniles, or how to train your chihuahua to be an attack dog. Such workshops can prove commercially worthwhile as well as being fun; and campus rates are usually more reasonable than those prevailing at Fire Island or Aspen.

Therefore pay no heed, Miss Wheaton, to Festivals of the Arts in spring, poetry seminars in summer nor "Creative Workshops" in the fall. Avoid hootenanies in Vermont unless you're paid to appear or own a piece of the maypole. What "poet" would be peddling rides on a wooden carousel in the hills if he could bring a horse-and-rider alive on paper?

Nor pay any heed to the professional critic. He is not a man who has succeeded in literature but one who has been defeated by it. He knows everything about literature except how to enjoy it.

The relationship of the writer to the critic is comparable to that of the jockey to the chartwriter. After the horse has been ridden, and the risk taken, the chartwriter will analyze, for tomorrow's bettors, a race that, for the rider, is forever done. What the rider has yet to learn cannot be gained from anyone who has not had the living animal under him.

If God can't help him, both jockey and writer know, neither chartwriter nor critic can. For it is the imminence of the actual experience, whether riding a thoroughbred or enduring the shock of reality directly, at first-hand, that make the findings of the critic or chartwriter remote to the rider or the writer.

Imminence of death or prison also makes sharper the outcast sharpie's eye. His freedom being dependent upon distinguishing between fox and hare, he becomes both hare and fox. Fear of the pursuer and compassion for the pursued become quickened in him; as they become dulled in those who are neither hunter nor prey.

"Why shouldn't a cheat speak well sometimes," one of Gorki's thieves wants to know, "when decent people speak like cheats?"

Between the year that James Haggerty assured us that the moral of the U-2 incident was "Don't get caught," and the year the Pentagon Papers were leaked, we became increasingly aware that people in government must sometimes choose between losing their positions or speaking like cheats. It should come as no particular shock, therefore, that those whose hands control levers in the American literary establishment may become most outspoken for respectability when their own operations become disreputable.

"What this novelist wants to say," one lever-puller becomes suspicious of a novel wherein respectability does not depend upon private proprietorship, "is that we live in a society whose bums are better men and women than preachers and politicians and otherwise respectables (*sic*). This startling proposition . . ."

What's really so startling about preachers and politicians lying as fast as a dog can trot? Or of "bums" being better men and women than these same "otherwise respectables"? The designation of itself, by the

American middle-class, as "decent," and of the unpropertied as "bums," is demonstrated by this critic's aptitude for concealing that class's corruption while proclaiming its morality.

Why was it that nobody laughed when Malcolm X spoke; while multitudes chuckled when Hubert Humphrey wept on TV? Could it have been because, in racing his public-relations image from coast to coast, crying "You belong to *us!*" while clutching Lester Maddox's sleeve and, a week later, weeping stage-business tears over Martin Luther King's casket, that all Humphrey achieved was a demonstration of how weak and joyless a politician can appear while preaching strength through joy? Wasn't his failure to reach people due, at least in part, to the recollection of Malcolm X achieving strength through anguish?

"The strength of any nation lies in the children of its street-corners, its poolrooms and prisons and its alleys," Malcolm X had already forewarned us, "not in the power of its technology."

The direction Mr. Bullins points to young writers, out of the establishment and onto the street-corners, is therefore sounder than Prof. Stegner's confidence in campus sanctuaries.

Prof. Stegner is laboring under the illusion, common to academics, that a knowledge of the best that has been thought and said has a compassionating impact upon the human spirit: a premise of American criticism since the days of the Transcendentalists; who came up with their best ideas under a campus moon.

That a dedication to the printed word may conceal an indifference toward cruelty; and that understanding of justice and human dignity becomes enfeebled in proportion to one's sophistication should be obvious by now. Unless we've forgotten that it was scholars well-disciplined in Shakespeare, Hegel, Goethe, Freud, Marx, Dante and Darwin, who yet devised the cultural programs at Auschwitz.

For the most dangerous societies are not those whose tribesmen sacrifice a bear to appease their gods; nor whose gurus distinguish themselves by caking their skins with ocher-colored mud. More ominous are those foregatherings of begoggled PhD's, their skins caked by sun-dried erudition, most of them earless, who perform linguistics so magical that that which is unreal is made to seem real; that which is empty to appear full: that which is false to seem true. Sacrifices endured at such ancestral rituals prove bloodier, ultimately, than that of one stupid bear.

The secret of linguistic magic lies in forcing matter to fit the form; rather than permitting form to be shaped by the matter. Dr. S.I. Hayakawa's miraculous vision of the Chicago Police riot of 1968, as an unprovoked assault upon the just and well-restrained forces of law and order, is a classic example of a man editing reality to fit a personal ambition.

Dr. Jacques Barzun, pleading for retention of the death penalty upon the premise that Joan of Arc, given a choice of life imprisonment or of death by fire, would have chosen the fire, is thereby enabled to demonstrate that fire would have been *his* choice also. Which goes to show you how dependent intellectual integrity is upon who is handling the matches.

That a sane respect among men, one for another, has been preserved at all in this country is not owing to the Bomb-Em-Back-to-the Stone Age, Send-in-the-Marines Eye-For-An-Eye Otherwise Respectables, but by people speaking behind bars: Gene Debs, Cesar Chavez, Martin Luther King, Malcolm X and Phil and Dan Berrigan.

Jailbirds all.

That it has been Earth's dispossessed who have given Man his most abiding truths, from a conspiracy trial on the outskirts of Rome to the anguish of Solzhenitsyn, is an ancestral paradox now commonly accepted by writers, readers and critics alike. That outcasts may speak truth, however, still comes as disturbing news to the critic quoted above: one perpetually embattled in defense of mediocrity so long as it stays respectable.

A yearning for respectability, so tenacious as to be achieved only at the cost of sensibility, is revealed in a handbook for other churchmice working the Establishment while ostensibly preoccupied with the arts.*

"What then are the reasons for the connection between the study of literature and the contempt for success?" this critic inquires and answers himself: "The noblest of them is undoubtedly that the study of literature encourages a great respect for activity which is its own reward (whereas the ethos of success encourages activity for the sake of extrinsic reward) and a great respect for the thing-in-itself (as opposed to the ethos of success which encourages a nihilistically reproductive preoccupation with the 'cash value' of all things). To acquire even a small measure of independent judgment is to understand that 'successful' does not necessarily mean 'good' and that 'good' does not necessarily mean 'successful'. From there it is but a short step in the world to the ardent conclusion that the two can never go together, particularly in America and particularly in the arts."

Well, what would *you* do, given a choice of a nihilistically reproductive preoccupation of the ethos of success encouraging activity for the

Making It, by Norman Podhoretz, Bantam Books, 1969.

sake of extrinsic reward, or the thing-in-itself leading to an ardent conclusion? Wouldn't you rather watch Kukla, Fran and Ollie?

Laying out a dollar and a quarter for 262 pages done by a man who earns his living by the written word, then discovering that he has no stronger control of the English language than Richard Daley, is dismaying.

What, in God's name, is the man trying to tell us by splintering prose into such uneven planks? Simply that writers often pretend that the laws of supply and demand don't apply to themselves as rigidly as to businessmen. That's all.

While gentile kids were watching the Three Stooges, he reminds us, he himself was a Jewish boy who owned only one suit. Yet he made up his mind early that *he* was going to travel with the Fast Mensa Set, Jewish or *not!* And rode the subway all by himself to Manhattan. And walked right into the goy registrar's office and told him right out he was Jewish and had only one suit. And that after he made it he was still going to go home over weekends! Then he got right in there and practiced talking to gentiles until *he* got to meet George Plimpton, too.

And he *still* goes home over weekends!

Yet, how dreary to explain one's life in terms of the distance between names on mailboxes. Never giving us a glimmer of the faces and forms of the home of his youth: how soundless, odorless and colorless a life it appears: like watching TV on a night when the reception makes ghosts of the players.

And all merely to achieve the editorship of a magazine with less impact than *Women's Wear Daily!* Isn't the life of any precinct captain who succeeds, after years of struggle, in becoming Ward Committeeman, more meaningful? At least *his* life has had an impact upon the living.

The philosopher who thinks only for other philosophers has got to be lying. When he loses concern for those unconcerned with philosophy he is no longer a philosopher: he is an occupant with tenure.

The poet understood only by other poets is practicing a kind of pharmaceutics without a pestle: merely devising a certain distinction for himself by filling prescriptions and calling them cantos.

The revolutionary who revolutionizes his life-style but not his life has no closer connection with revolution than Tennessee Ernie Ford, singing *I Believe,* has with heaven.

Those who believe true change can be effected by meeting force with force may as well be riding with Hell's Angels. Changes will come from those most reluctant to straddle a bike: those willing to sacrifice power they already possess. Changing from a Harley to a Honda won't get it.

The artist who paints with one eye on the approval of those with the leisure to judge, the hands to applaud and the funds to buy, and no eye at all for those who'd rather go bowling than own a Van Gogh, may well gain approval. Then the light from the street strikes his masterpiece and all his colors wash out. He'd forgotten that Van Gogh didn't seek approval.

The literary critic, devising his thought from other thinkers, yet never consulting those who never think, may feel strangely uneasy about some clamor, coming to him faintly from beyond his shutters. He senses that a coherent literature, emerging from that clamor, would diminish him.

Are you still hanging around the edge of that precipice, Miss Wheaton? Still not convinced that it's *not* a threshold? Still bemused about what your next move ought to be?

One move you might make, I'd suggest, is to avoid sleeping with people whose troubles are worse than your own.

Another is to avoid drinking when you're feeling sorry for yourself. If you do you'll be finding yourself in need of a double-shot every time you consider what the world is doing to a nice person like yourself. And, since the world begins working on you early in the day, you'll have to get stoned to the bricks just in order to get out of bed.

Then you'll realize there's no longer any point in brooding about what your next move is going to be. Because you will already have made it.

Given a choice, never do anything anyone tells you you *ought* to do: unless you yourself want to do it. Given a choice, *always* do what you yourself want to do: even though everyone else tells you you *ought* not, you *should* not, you *better* not—and God won't like it if you do.

Watch out for what people tell you God wants you to do. Given a choice between your God and your life, save your life.

If your God is a God that tells you *He* comes first, he isn't any God.

If He's the kind of God who tells you to save your life, you'll never get another; pay attention.

If you can, believe in Him. If you wish, pray to Him. But bear in mind that your God is not mine.

Save your life. God can wait.

COME IN IF YOU LOVE MONEY

BUTTE, Montana, hasn't had a horse-wire for twenty-five years. The old horse-players are dying off and the young people won't take chances.

But the M & M Bar will book your bet if a race is being televised.

It was Derby Day, 1964, Northern Dancer was at the top of the M & M board at 4-5. Hill Rise was 2-1. Quadrangle was 4-1. The other entries didn't matter.

A redhaired youth, Stetson tilted, was dealing poker to half a dozen players. One was a middle-aged woman with a face ravaged yet virginal; like a debauched Joan of Arc. The others looked like storekeepers long wearied of waiting for customers. I took a seat.

"The game is draw poker, sir," Red warned me respectfully, "when you get caught bluffing you lose." He had a bag of salted peanuts and a Pepsi bottle beside his bank.

"What's the house cut?" I asked him.

"We use the joker for aces, straights and flushes, sir," he answered.

Eddie Arcaro materialized on the screen.

"It looks to me like every horse in this race has a chance," Eddie encouraged me to get a bet down. I gave the houseman five and five to put on Quadrangle.

"His name is Chiqueno," Joan of Arc promptly informed me. Had I asked her the man's name she would have told me what the house cut was. Montanans give direct replies only to questions you haven't asked.

"Isn't that the girl who was so drunk in here the other night before last?" Red asked nobody in particular. The players craned about to see and Red took a quarter from the pot for his pocket. Then he spilled peanuts into his palm, popped them into the Pepsi bottle and took a long drink.

"I never saw *that* done before," I observed, meaning the snatching of the quarter rather than the drink.

"It's a solution I worked out by myself," Red assured me, "the peanuts are too salty otherwise."

"I don't think that's the same girl," Joan decided, "she's part Mex."
Why a girl couldn't have been drunk the night before last because she was part Mexican, I didn't try figuring out. I was holding four diamonds. The fifth was a heart. I played the hand as a pat flush and won. It seemed too easy. Red slipped peanuts into the bottle and drank.

"Red was so drunk in here the other night it took three policemen to throw him out," Joan filled me in. "I think there's something else in that solution."

"How was I to know they were *policemen?*" Red defended himself, "they didn't have uniforms. When they grabbed me I thought they were just being friendly."

"You were too drunk to tell whether they had uniforms," Joan assured him.

"Well, what are you going to do if you can't dance?" Red asked me. "Stay sober?"

I could see how anyone, drunk or sober, might have trouble distinguishing between officer and citizen in Butte. I'd already been solicited, by schoolgirls, for a contribution toward uniforms for the local police force.

"Luck is going to play a part today," Arcaro prophesied, "it's all kind of historic, too."

Inside stuff.

Somebody wearing a green woolen jockey cap, with VFW threaded in white on its peak, took the chair beside me. I paid him no mind. Until the cards went around. Then the cap began revolving.

Beneath its peak I saw his eyebrows lifted in disbelief and his mouth rounded in astonishment—then both expressions jerked, in an instant, to bottomless despair. The fellow not only had some sort of palsy of his facial muscles, but he was also an extremely homely sapiens. I decided not to be distracted by the storms of emotion that passed perpetually over his ugly mug: all I would have to do was to keep looking at the TV screen.

"What's your story, Deadpan Jack?" Red asked him. Deadpan Jack made no reply.

The horses were coming out on the track, stepping lightly through a light drizzle.

"Distance will be decisive today," Eddie announced boldly. "But breeding is going to count too," he took it all back.

The left side of Deadpan Jack's face began quaking. His cap began revolving; first slowly then faster. I sensed he was holding a pat full house and threw in my pair.

"I pass," Deadpan Jack decided; and threw in his hand.

I can read a poker-faced player just by the *intensity* of his expressionlessness. But how do you read a man whose face expresses *everything?* I'd never before come up against such a situation. It was my first time.

The horses were in the gate. Before I could tell Red to deal me out, he dealt me the five of spades.

Ycaza broke Quadrangle out in the middle of the bunch and began saving ground. My second card was an eight of spades.

Orientalist was leading the pack, but I wasn't afraid of Orientalist. Quadrangle began moving up on him. All I had to fear was fear itself and Northern Dancer. My third card was the four of spades. I looked at Red to see what he had in mind.

Quadrangle got Orientalist behind him; but Hartack, on Northern Dancer, began making his move. He caught Quadrangle yet couldn't pass him. I looked at my last two cards. Ace of clubs and six of spades.

"How many?" Red asked me.

I threw away the ace.

"One."

Ycaza began pulling away from Hartack. Roman Brother passed Northern Dancer but couldn't catch Quadrangle. All Ycaza had to do was hold the horse straight and nobody could catch Ycaza now. He went under two full lengths in front of Roman Brother.

"How'd you pick that thing?" Red asked me.

"Arcaro gave him to me," I admitted.

"They'll bring you your money."

I looked at my last card. Joker. Straight flush. Deadpan checked his hand. He had a nose; had Deadpan Jack.

I risked a check because there were four bettors behind me. The second bet two dollars. That dropped the two behind him. Deadpan started to raise the pot ten dollars. Then, looking as though he were afraid he'd lose me, bet five instead. And began a slow revolution of his skull.

"Raises you three," Red announced.

I raised him five. His skull gained momentum as he raised me back five. I was as afraid of losing him as he was of losing me. I raised back five.

His skull came to a coasting pause, then went slowly into reverse. And as it began gathering momentum, fear following astonishment across his features; pursued by hope that was routed by despair; to be replaced by suspicion chased by undisguised delight: then bloomed with an infinite patience. Out of which canniness shone like a light.

If only he'd get bored, I thought, we could all get some rest.

He pushed all of his chips into the pot. Before Red had finished the count, Chiqueno came up and gave me forty-eight dollars and seventy-five cents. He waited until he realized he wasn't going to make seventy-five cents for himself.

"He raised you fifty-four dollars," Red told me. I shoved forty-eight into the pot.

"All in," Red told Deadpan Jack, and returned six dollars to him. Everyone waited for me to turn over my hand.

"I called *him*," I reminded Red.

Deadpan's hands couldn't handle his cards. Red turned them over for him.

Eight, Nine. Ten. Jack. Queen. All diamonds.

"How many did he draw?" I asked Red.

"Two," Joan answered for him.

"I think you were right about that solution," I told Joan as I rose to leave, "there *is* something else in it."

I didn't feel bitter. After all, I hadn't lost anything except the money I'd won on Quadrangle. And I'd saved six bits of that.

Butte, Montana, isn't merely a town where the cops don't have uniforms. It is also a place where The Company is too big to beat. Where the house cut is always too steep. And where victory, below ground or above it, consists in snatching a draw out of the jaws of certain defeat.

Butte is also a place where winds blow all day beneath the earth; where narrow rails cut through volcanic rock, bearing drivers, begoggled and gaunt, whose only light is borne by a battery attached to a helmet of steel.

Five thousand feet beneath the Butte Country Club, blood-colored streams stagnate between automatic ramps. A spatter of copper sulphate, in the ominous overhang, winks in the gloom like a handful of mischievous stars.

This gigantic fun-house has been tunnelled, picked, gouged, blasted, blown up, flooded, hammered and blasted for a hundred years in order to bring up two and a half million ounces of gold, three and a half million dollars worth of copper and six hundred and thirty-three million ounces of silver.

Which hasn't proved quite enough to buy benches for Main Street; a town mail carrier; nor uniforms for the police. In the times when gold came easy, in the days when flesh sold cheap, Butte's Chinatown ran two blocks wide and four blocks deep. Fifteen hundred whores were working three shifts in The District. And the odor of arsenic, off roasting ores, pervaded the dance halls. Where blue-green gas-flares, intermittently twisting, cast a pallor across the faces of fugitives, fire-ships and fly-by-nighties; all alike.

And a wind blew down off the tippled hills which withered blade, bush and tree for miles around. Birds fled Butte's side of The Continental Divide. Butte had the world's highest smokestack and fanciest whorehouse, deepest mine-shaft and longest ore-train, boldest thieves and crookedest judges, the most lynch-minded editors and bloody-minded mine-owners: and Stanley Ketchel fighting all comers at the Casino Theatre when he wasn't bulldogging drunks at the Copper Queen. But birds liked it better on the other side.

The city named itself The Richest Rock on Earth. And thousands thronged that golden gaslit town. Earth's finest players, sweetest singers, roughest fighters and chanciest gamblers made Butte their capitol. Butte had the loudest bands, the suddenest homicides, and the strongest miners' union ever organized.

In those days gold came easy; before the town settled for silver. Days when your life and your gold were one; before the town settled for copper.

The old Irishman in the cheap hotel room seemed, like the room's dull green walls and brown curtains, to be long drained of the colors of life.

And yet his memory was still brightly lit. His voice was still resonant and kept a touch of the brogue he had brought to Butte at the century's turn. Con Lowney, who'd survived the bloody mining wars by switching from mining to barbering, was ninety-one years old.

"I understand the animal," the old man remembered, "the unscroopulus industrials niver paused in their wicked gains. We were getting three-fifty a day and were trying for four bits more. Ryan was President of The Company at that time. But we'd elected our own man over The Company's man. Our man was Duffy. And ivery one of the ten men waiting for Ryan were Irish as well.

"When Ryan came in he walked up to Duffy as though they two were alone in the room. And took Duffy's two great hands into his own two small ones. 'Duffy,' he said, 'a man like you could be Governor of Montana' and I kicked Shannon, the man beside me. 'Watch this' I whispered to Shannon.

" 'Duffy,' Ryan went on, not once letting loose of Duffy's hand, 'the laboring people of this city are indeed blessed to have a union that protects their helpless little ones. And the union is double-blessed to have at its head a man of your high intelligence. *Is* there any telling how far a man like yourself might go? *'Could'* be governor of Montana did I say? *'Should'* be is what I ought to have said.' Duffy niver even *tried* to pull his hands out of Ryan's. When he sat down he was shaking."

"What happened to your four bits a day?"

"I knew we weren't going to get it when I kicked Shannon. Duffy voted with The Company because he wanted to be Governor of Montana"—Con Lowney permitted himself the flicker of a smile—"O, I understand the animal alright."

"What happened to him?"

"To Duffy? Indeed he didn't get to govern anything; not even himself. Ryan threw him back to us and we threw him out. He married a woman who owned a whorehouse. And he didn't even make Governor *there*. She put him to pimping to earn his keep and that was one trade Duffy drove naturally."

"Did you know Frank Little?"

"I knew Frank Little. A clean man and no double-crosser. He was half Indian and had but one good eye. We were on strike for better safety conditions, after the Spectacular Mine fire, when he came to Butte. The Company was waiting for him. He'd led the Free Speech fight in Missoula. They held a meeting on The Floor Next to Heaven—as we then called the sixth floor of the Anaconda offices—to decide what to do about the men organizing the miners. We knew The Company meant business when we found out that Roy Alley had chaired the meeting. I warned Frank to watch out. Doubtless others warned him as well. He spoke at the ball park in the afternoon, wearing a plaster cast on one leg, I don't know why. After the meeting he went back to his room. That was July 31, 1917."

There was a long pause. The old man looked exhausted. I rose to leave. He saw me to the door; yet held me there a minute.

"I was minding my own business in a restaurant once," he recalled—and whether he meant the day before or forty years ago wasn't clear—"and this young company lawyer came up to me and asked me, 'Lowney, do you believe in God?'

" 'Did *you* believe in Him the day you sent an innocent man, the father of four small children, to the penitentiary?' I asked him. He never spoke a word to me again.''

He held up his right hand with the fingers spread and asked me, "Do you beat The Company this way?'' and answered himself—"No.'' Then closed the hand into a fist that might yet knock a good man down. "You beat The Company like this. An injury to one is an injury to all.'' Then he closed the door.

Like closing a door on times before: when the gold had given out, yet flesh could still be bought. When copper was what the risks were for.

When fists were still what counted most but money counted more.

The sun behind the Butte Country Club was hurling bloodletting lavas skyward as it sank, casting a volcanic glow across the small bald cranium of the club's outgoing president.

When facing outward on life's tee—the Prez was declaiming—
What e'er may be my fate
God grant this one great boon to me:
That I may drive them straight!

And if my best be not enough
Then give me courage high
To jump right out there in the rough
And play them where they lie!

And when upon life's putting green
Others make the cup
If I do not may I come clean
And always be well up!

And when the greens of life are played
And my clubs are left aside
No matter what the score I've made:
May I have qualified!

"You *have* qualified, old buddy!'' someone cried out. And every man rose, in a standing ovation, to applaud as one. The Prez's eyes misted in receiving their tribute.

Introduced to him at the bar, I congratulated The Prez upon the sincerity of the poem he'd read. Not his own, he assured me modestly—just something he'd clipped out of a newspaper by an anonymous author.

"We've had some unfortunate experiences here," he added.

"I know," I advised him, "I read about the Spectacular Mine fire."

"I didn't mean *that*," The Prez explained, "I meant writers giving a poor picture of the city."

"O," I caught on at last, "you mean unpaved streets, silicosis, the police force not having uniforms, all of *that*."

"Not exactly," he told me, "I mean showing *respectable* people in an unflattering light."

"I don't have anything against respectable people," I assured The Prez, "but is it your opinion that emphysema is *not* an industrial disease?"

The question was indiscreet. Anaconda's doctors had just succeeded in pushing through legislation defining emphysema as a nonindustrial affliction, contracted by personal negligence; as one might contract gonorrhea. Thus releasing the company from financing medical assistance.

The Prez studied his scotch a long moment. Then he looked up.

"You *really* want to know my opinion?" he asked me directly.

I nodded.

"Turn the lock and throw away the key—that's *my* opinion—" and he walked away leaving a full scotch on the bar.

I drank it.

Locking them out and throwing away the key, like the poem he had declaimed, was something someone else had devised long before The Prez's time.

Like the banner headline the *Butte Daily Bulletin* ran, in an extra edition of April, 1920: SHOOT THE SONS OF BITCHES.

Since company guards had already wounded fourteen and killed one striker, the extra edition would appear to have been gratuitous.

All exits had been blocked, by concrete bulkheads, with no openings in them, when fire broke out on the 2400-foot level of the Spectacular Mine. One hundred sixty-four miners died of smoke suffocation.

Miners refused to return to work, after this disaster, until safety devices were installed. William Andrews Clark, an enraptured Puritan, refused to negotiate. He saw that the issue was not one of safety devices but of the right of miners to negotiate with management. He announced that he would flood the mines before he would negotiate.

As he had already proven himself indifferent to fire there was no reason to believe he would be troubled by water.

90

"I don't believe in lynching or violence," Clark had responded to the miners' protests, "unless it is absolutely necessary. Terrorism in this community must and shall cease."

On the morning of August 1, 1917, five cars, each containing four men and a driver, drove to Frank Little's boarding house. They dragged him out of bed in his underwear, looped a noose around his neck, tied him to a car and dragged him to a Milwaukee Railroad trestle; now known as Centennial Bridge. He must have been dead before they hanged him. They hanged him all the same.

FIRST AND LAST WARNING!

the note pinned on his ripped underwear read:

3-7-77
D-D-C-S-S-W

The initials were those of other union organizers then active in Butte. The figures specified the exact dimensions of their prospective graves. All made the depot.

None of the assassins were prosecuted. Most of them were rewarded with promotion to mine foremen and were later retired with pensions.

Six men drove up to his house at midnight
And woke the poor woman who kept it
And asked her, "Where is the man who spoke
Against war and insulted the army? . . .
I call you all to the bar of the dawn to give witness
If this is not what they do in America.*

Butte, Montana, has two sets of heroes. One is honored above ground, one below. One is memorialized by a plaque expressing his community's lasting gratitude:

William Andrews Clark
Pioneer, Prospector, Miner
Merchant, Banker, Railroad Builder
Benefactor of children
and
Philanthropist.

*From *When The Cock Crows*, by Arturo Giovanetti.

91

This memorial erected by
The Society of Montana and Other Friends
As a tribute to his great achievements
And to perpetuate his memory.

The other is remembered only by a faded photograph in the Miners Union Hall:

Fellow Worker Frank Little
Murdered August 1, 1917
By the Copper Trust
We never forget.

Times when gold came easy and yet men's flesh went cheap.
When fists were the thing that counted most.
But money counted more.

No light shines, either upstairs or down, from the old frame house on Wyoming Street. Within the iron fence before its door, uncut grasses make the house appear abandoned.

At the door one hears neither sound nor rumor of sound. Not until one presses the little white buzzer does it seem that people might be alive inside. Then a curtain parts, the door swings wide and laughter falls carelessly within a wealth of light.

This is the last of the golden brothels; where a great cut-glass chandelier still fragments the lights as it did in the days before gold became tainted by copper.

Velma, the gaunt and henna-haired madam, with a half-century of being a sporting-man's woman behind her, swings into the parlor to greet her guests—"What's the chicken doing for a living, boys?" Then calls down the hall—"Jo-Ann! LaVerne! Melanie! Parlor choice, girls! Parlor choice!"

Now cow-country whores, sorrowful as clowns, the girls who grew up in Meaderville, Seldom Seen, Flathead Lake, Big Arm or Logan Pass, come slouching in their party togs; to lean, weary with boredom, upon each others' arms. While the cow-country miners appraise them sheepishly. The embarrassment is all with the men. While the big juke booms—

I want to die for the Engine I love.
One hundred and forty-three.
* * *

92

One is a stout, housewifely bison in a dirndl. All she needs is a pink ribbon to look like a once-great mind had snapped. Beside her is a round and pouting creature, weakly abashed. The other two are tough blondes in black slips who appear to be sisters. One of the miners nods to The Bison and she shambles off down a hall of many doors. A couple boys dressed as cowboys, but who looked more like folksingers, follow the tough sisters. The pouting creature is left sniffing into a piece of colored kleenex until a shaggy old boy, his belly over his belt, gives her the nod. I wandered down a hall of many doors to see what was going on in the kitchen.

Velma was punching beer-cans there for the boys who'd already had it. The air smelled of beer mixed with disinfectant and perfume. Velma punched me a beer.

A poodle dyed pink raced in, yapping as though it were trying to herd the men into the bedrooms. Velma picked it up and told the brute, "*Quiet*, Heavensent." Then explained—"We call him Heavensent because Heaven sent him." She fussed with the baby-blue ribbon around the poodle's throat.

The only girl in the kitchen had a face too pale, like that of a child recovering from an illness, uninterested in anything except a menu from Hotel Finlen. By the smudges on it it looked as though many a *soup du jour* had grown cold since the *carte* had been abandoned here.

"Jo-Ann likes to pick out," Velma informed me. Like a child to whom a grownup has drawn attention, the girl put the menu aside.

"Are you from around here?" I asked her.

"I'm not from anywhere," she decided.

"Everybody's from somewhere."

"I'm from nowhere," she insisted.

"She's from Meaderville," Velma cut in.

The girl turned sharply on Velma. "How can I be from somewhere ain't even there?"

"Meaderville is gone," Velma explained, "wasn't but a few folks left there. The Company bought them out and bulldozed it."

"Even the high school I went to," Jo-Ann remembered, and picked up the menu to resume her "picking out."

Meaderville; Walkerville; Alder Gulch; Seldom Seen: all the old lost boom towns that died the first time when the gold gave out; then boomed once more when silver was found; and died again when silver thinned; and that then were bulldozed to get at the copper. Jo-Ann now feels as though, when the bulldozers came, they bulldozed her childhood along with her home.

"It ain't I don't know right from wrong," she tried to explain later, "but, ever since they bulldozed Meaderville, I don't seem to be able to get foot on the ground either way."

As I walked out on the night-streets of Montana, as I walked out in old Butte one foul night, I saw more dread-the-dawn dingbats looking for a doorway than I'd ever seen searching for a door around New York's Port Authority. More quivering, quaking, transfixed and trembling, catatonic, stoned and zonkified drunks looking for a park bench than I'd ever seen on Chicago's North Clark Street. I saw more pensionless and emphysemized voyeurs kibitzing the lightless corners than I'd ever seen on West Division Street.

Rain was sweeping the streets beyond the windows of the M&M at 4 A.M. Chiqueno, the houseman, had replaced Red in the dealer's slot. Of all the afternoon players only Joan-of-Arc, still trying to get even, sat on.

"Come in if you love money," Chiqueno greeted me. I sat beside a man whose face was still young under a thatch of snow-white hair.

"I'm Keith Kellar," he announced when I sat down, "everyone remembers me."

"I'm from out of town," I explained.

"*You* remember me," he assured Joan.

"I've heard of you," Joan told him noncommittally.

"There isn't a miner in Butte today who isn't better off because of me," he informed me. A minute later Joan caught him bluffing cold.

"Get everybody a drink," he announced as though his bluff had worked like a charm. Yet Joan was the only one who accepted a drink from him.

When the TV has long been darkened and the last North American drunk leans against the last abandoned bar, Butte doesn't feel like the richest rock on earth. It feels more like the loneliest hill in the U.S.A.

The bartender had tilted a chair against the wall and was on the nod; but had left his transistor murmuring among the bottles. The drunk, with one hand folded around an empty shot-glass, kept lifting it toward the murmuring in hope of another drink. Sometimes he slept; then woke to demand another drink; then slept once again.

In that long cavernous sanctuary the only light was the green-shaded lamp suspended eye-level above our hands. As its glow kept the cold and darkness out, so the cards, going around and around, kept everyone's loneliness at bay.

94

"If I'd drawn the joker I would have had a flush," Keith Kellar recalled his lost bluff.

"If that rabbit had had a pistol he would have shot the ass off the hound," Joan philosophized.

Then, out of the rain and into the light—here's Velma carrying Heavensent. I was really glad to see her hard old phizz. She sat at the empty table beside us and began drying the poodle with a towel.

"Does that dog talk, Velma?" Chiqueno asked her.

"He talks," Velma assured the dealer—"but he's promised not to tell."

"I thought you were leaving town," Joan challenged Velma.

"I am," Velma answered without taking notice of the hostility in Joan's voice.

"You've been saying you were leaving for fifteen years," Joan reminded her.

"This time it's for real," Velma assured her lightly, "I'm taking a position in Chicago."

"I've heard girls get fifty dollars a trick there," Keith Kellar put in.

"Good *Gawd!*" Chiqueno exclaimed in mock horror. "It would cost me a hundred and fifty dollars a day to live there!"

I'd never played poker with an experienced man, like Keith Kellar, who played poker so badly. He got caught bluffing so often it began to seem deliberate. Caught cold in one last attempt, he pushed his remaining chips to Chiqueno as a tip and left.

"Was he just bragging about being a big man for the miners?" I asked after he'd gone.

"He was," Chiqueno remembered, "then he got mixed up. Didn't know whose side he was on."

Having dried Heavensent and retied hi. baby-blue bow, Velma walked the pooch around the room as though it were a thoroughbred being led out of the paddock onto the track. Then, taking it into her arms, marched out into the rain.

As she passed through the door someone else came through it. I saw the green-wool cap, already slowly revolving, out of the corner of my eye.

I kept my eyes straight ahead.

Why did it always have to be the seat next to mine that was empty when *he* came in? I counted my chips: I was holding even. If I could beat Deadpan Jack out of one good hand, I'd leave this town with a sense of real achievement.

I won two small pots; then a heavier one. But Deadpan hadn't been involved in them. Outside the all-night rain had stopped, and a hazy smear of light against the door showed Butte would be here for one more day. I dragged the chips I'd just won into my bank without bothering to count them.

On the next hand I drew a pair of jacks, and discarded three cards. The first one I picked up was my third jack. A deuce of hearts was next. I squeezed the fifth card. It was the deuce of clubs.

Full house with jacks high.

Deadpan opened the pot for two dollars and I paid. All the other bettors dropped out except Joan. She raised the pot a dollar. The other bettors dropped. Deadpan rereaised her five dollars.

"Costs you six dollars," Chiqueno counted for me.

"Make it ten," I decided. Joan dropped. Deadpan raised the pot twenty. His one card draw had filled him up. And as he began that wavering motion, out of the corner of my eye I caught a flash: he was holding a full house with three tens.

I had him.

I began pushing my chips in. Then saw a card, pulled in from the last hand, among my chips:

Six cards! Dead hand.

There was no use trying to get rid of it: Chiqueno had spotted it. It was just a question of whether he called it or I called it on myself. I threw in my hand. Chiqueno understood.

"It was in the chips," he assured the other players, and turned up the five cards he'd dealt me.

"It would have been your pot," Joan told me as though I didn't know, "it was a misdeal."

"No misdeal in poker," I told her before Chiqueno could say it.

Deadpan's VFW cap was spinning by its own momentum while he stacked his chips.

Deadpan Jack murdered me and Deadpan Jack will murder you.

And Butte, Montana, is a town where everyone finds his own Deadpan Jack.

Since the times when gold came easy. And flesh was still not dear. When fists were the thing that mattered most.

Yet money mattered more.

BRAVE BULLS OF SIDI YAHYA

WHENEVER bread came within Simone de Beauvoir's reach, she crushed it to death between her palms. She'd crushed a hundred loaves between Marrakesh and Tunis, talking the whole while. She hadn't shut up since Casablanca and I hadn't had an unmangled slice since Fez. Why she had to turn fresh loaves into crumbs simply to turn Marx, Hegel and Freud into dry crusts, I understand no more today than I did in June of 1949. A Bedouin toiling between the shafts of a donkey cart, she assured me, was doing so because he could not afford to feed a donkey. For correcting my first impression that the man was Darryl Zanuck, I thanked her.

"When you see a woman forced to sell herself," she revealed after passing a whore in a doorway, "you know you are in a country suffering repression."

My defense, against Madame's sententiousness, thereafter was to load my camera every time we approached a woman waiting in a doorway. This simple action provoked such resentment in Madame that an intense passion for photography was awakened in me: a passion so pure that I would aim and click my camera even when it held no film. Women in doorways didn't care for this move either.

"For your being a citizen of a nation of exploiters you are not to be held altogether to blame," Madame allowed, "but to walk about deliberately pointing a machine at the very objects of that exploitation is more than merely adding insult to injury. It is collaboration with the makers of the camera."

"The people doing the exploiting around here are citizens of France," I had to remind her. "When we get to Guatemala, you take the camera."

Now we were sitting in the dining room of the Hotel Tunisia Palace. Bottles along the bar were still shadowed by the night just done. Bored beggars waited beyond the door. Overhead a ceiling fan kept rising a decibel in hope; then descending in a clattering fall as though disappointed in everything.

We had to go to Matmata because troglodytes lived there. Had no one ever heard of a troglodyte anywhere near Matmata, there would have been no excuse for anyone's ever going there. Since an entire colony had been surviving there, beneath the surface of the earth for immemorial African ages, that seemed all the more reason for staying away.

A portly young Arab wearing a GI fatigue cap sat at the bar; but he wasn't drinking. He was either sizing us up or thinking of turning in his cap for a fez.

"The absurdity of demanding fidelity in a relationship reducible to a physiochemical reaction has now become clear," Madame shifted from colonialism to sex without interrupting herself, "therefore, complete fidelity can be experienced only by those who impose it upon themselves as a mutilation. Women who are faithful can only compensate themselves by sublimation or by drink."

"Sweeping the floor might help," I suggested; but since Madame had never held a broom, the concept remained existential.

"Many couples conclude more or less the same pact as Sartre and myself, but Sartre and I have been more ambitious," she continued congratulating herself. "We seek to maintain through all deviations a certain fidelity.

"Recent experiments in parthenogenesis have disclosed that the egg may be penetrated by an ordinary safety pin and artificially fertilized. The male gamete is not necessary for reproduction."

That'll be the day.

Where had we gone wrong? The original understanding had been that she could make long speeches if she'd let me find the bars. I'd make the jokes if she'd pick up the tabs. I'd look the other way while she was destroying bread if she'd only let me photograph camels. Arabs wouldn't interfere so long as you stuck to aiming at camels. But the man atop the camel would let you know that *he* wasn't to be photographed.

This wasn't a superstitious fear that you were going to catch his soul in a little black box and stick pins in it. It was a religious conviction: "Ye shall make you no idols, neither shall ye rear you up a graven image." God commanded it and man is made in the image of God. There you have it. And if it sounds like Jehovah and *Leviticus* to you, it sounds more like Allah and Mohammed to the camel driver.

I spent one whole morning photographing camels only to discover that the camera had held no film. I was certain I had loaded it and suspected foul play. I immediately began eating all the bread in sight. Madame began paring the skin off her forearms with her fingernails. I gave her back the bread. She had stopped laughing at the jokes but was still picking up the tabs.

I might have attributed this to the fact that she had no sense of humor. On the other hand the jokes weren't funny. The real difficulty, it struck me, was that her sense of personal responsibility for the world had overwhelmed her responses to it.

The fate of the Western world, she assumed, hung upon the decisions of Jean-Paul Sartre. But since Sartre himself made no such assumption, the full responsibility not only for that world but for Sartre as well, had devolved upon herself.

For Sartre perceived the world as a clown show in which his own pratfalls appeared as absurd as those of everyone else. The more profound his judgments the more lightly he held them.

It never crossed Madame's mind that her love life might not be a matter of global concern. Sartre took for granted the world's indifference to his love life. Judging by some of the women he slept with, he was indifferent to it as well.

"A hero of the Resistance is thinking of cutting in on us," I gave Madame warning; but the overhead fan set up such a clatter that she didn't hear. Although she wouldn't have heard even had the fan come to a dead stop.

"Of course," she pointed out, "it is always possible that one of the new partners, or *allies,* may prefer a new attachment to the old. But this presents no difficulty as long as neither ally permits the new one to become permanent."

She was trying to tell me something.

"Or is it *your* point of view," she charged in hope of an argument, "that freedom can come through fidelity?"

"Heaven forbid!" I disclaimed the accusation, "I was only wondering what would happen if only *one* ally proved unfaithful. Would that mean they'd *both* have to stay drunk all day?"

"Every effort to free oneself entails risk," she warned me, "so let not my words be taken to imply more than they say."

It came to me then that she wasn't going to be able to sever our relationship simply. She would have to excommunicate me.

I was relieved to see that the Arab was finally making his move. He approached with a grave, deliberate mien, touched his cap to Madame, then turned his back upon her; and handed me a snapshot of a French soldier holding a telephone to his ear.

"Hassine Ameur Djemail," he introduced himself in French-accented English, "making long-distance call Paris-Tunis. Hassine Ameur

Djemail"—he exchanged photographs—"owner of Citroën. Hassine before garage of fastest automobile in Djerba. Two suits in garage." He changed photographs once more.

"Hassine Ameur Djemail before *Tour Eiffel*"—he paused courteously to give me a chance to top that. Then accepted the chair I offered him. Madame drew a big bright map of Tunisia from her purse and became oblivious of everyone.

"Of what government?" Hassine asked me.

"American."

"Of what government in America?"

"Of Chicago."

"Do you have oil for cooking in Chicago?"

"We have oil for cooking in Chicago."

"Do you have flour in Chicago?"

"We have flour in Chicago."

"Do you have eggs in Chicago?"

"We have eggs in Chicago."

"Then we are rich! You will write to the governor of Chicago that Hassine comes to make *brik*." He slapped me heartily on the shoulder. "I will sell this car and use yours to carry the Chicago eggs, the Chicago flour and the Chicago cooking oil to the Chicago cooking pot!"

I caught a fast flash of myself stirring a caldron of simmering oil in the lobby of the Civic Theater while Hassine passed among opera buffs, during an intermission of *Tosca*, peddling pastries wrapped in palm leaves.

"I have no car," I tried to weasel out of the deal.

"Are you not American?"

"I am an American who has no car."

"One must have a car to do business."

"I am an American who does no business."

Now he *knew* I was putting him on; and changed his tone.

"Do you have an enemy in Chicago?" he asked slyly.

"In Chicago everyone has enemies."

"I will have him killed in Tunis for five hundred dollars," he promised, "you are my brother." He turned to Madame.

She was drawing a red line down from Tunis to the desert's edge, encircling the places she intended to see. The red line bypassed Djerba.

"In Paris," Hassine tried to get her attention, "Hassine touched ice with his hands."

She encircled Carthage, Kairouan, Matmata, Gabés and Médenine.

"In Paris," Hassine tried again, "Hassine went to Folies Bergère."

No response.

"Hassine fought bravely for the French," he played his trump card. "In Paris Hassine was in hospital."

He turned to me, unbuttoned his shirt until his right shoulder was exposed. The scar extended from shoulder to elbow. He buttoned the shirt and raised his left trouser leg: A red seam zigzagged from ankle to knee. Shrapnel. He dropped the trouser leg.

"Although Hassine fought bravely for the French," he filled me in, "yet now they do not let him fight the Jews."

Madame glanced up from her map.

"What do you want to fight Jews for? Did Jews give you your wounds?"

"*My* wounds are no matter, Madame," Hassine explained heroically, "I wish to fight the Jews because they offend God."

"How can God's chosen people offend Him?"

"If Jews are God's chosen people," Hassine wanted to know, "why did He not pick *them* to conquer all North Africa and Spain instead of the Arabs?"

"If God chose the Arabs to conquer Spain, why didn't He let them keep it?"

"If He did not, why did He let them keep it a thousand years?"

"Would God now be letting the Jews hold the road to Tel Aviv, against Arab armies, had they offended Him?"

"A battle lost is not a war lost," Hassine answered promptly. "Had God meant Jews to win, He would have given them a flag. Now they make their own flag. God does not wish people to make their own flag. He does not wish people to *begin*. It is God's will that Arabs have an army because Arabs have always had an army. If Jews begin to have an army, then Bedouins will want one also. Even the people who live in the ground in Matmata will come to live on top of it. If God had wished them to live on top of the earth, He would not have put them to live beneath it. They too will want a flag."

"Why *shouldn't* they have a flag?" Madame persisted.

"Because they are only Bedouins who live underground."

"We will see Bedouins who live underground for ourselves," Madame decided, turning the map toward Hassine.

"It is not necessary to stop here, Madame," Hassine told her confidently, touching Carthage. "There is nothing here but old rocks. In Djerba is the most beautiful beach for bathing in the world."

"We do not wish to bathe. We wish to see old rocks."

Hassine smiled patronizingly: "In Djerba, Madame, are the world's sweetest figs."

"We do not wish for figs. Either to see or to eat."

Hassine shook his head sadly.

"In Kairouan, Madame, are nothing but old walls."

"We wish to see old walls."

"In Gabès," he kept trying, "are only women who are not serious. But in Djerba one may buy the finest pottery for only a few francs. In Djerba are the world's finest racing camels."

"Do you wish to see racing camels?" Madame asked me.

"I should like to see camels who are not serious," I assured her.

Madame customarily had so little concern for money that I wasn't even certain she could count. From her clanging French dialogue with Hassine, which now ensued, I was pleasantly surprised to observe not only that she could count but that she was driving him back across the sands.

While they were occupied, I snatched the remains of the loaf Madame had been working on. By the time they reached an understanding I had it consumed.

The understanding was that we were to leave the following morning at six; to avoid driving in the heat of the day.

"God willing," was Hassine's parting shot, "we will have tea in Djerba tomorrow evening."

"We aren't going to Djerba," Madame corrected him. But he was already gone.

Hassine Ameur Djemail was as deft as Madame herself at turning a deaf ear.

We began waiting for Hassine Ameur Djemail at 5:45 A.M.

The heat of the day, trapped all night between the walls, made the hotel lobby stifling. But the night clerk told me he could not switch on the overhead fan until the heat of the new day had begun. Wandering around the lobby looking for a switch, I marveled that he could tell how much heat belonged to yesterday and how much to this morning.

Madame dozed in an armchair. A wind from the desert paused in the street just beyond the door, saw that it was too hot inside our lobby and moved on down the street. Madame roused herself, shredded a copy of *Algérie Républicaine* and returned to sleep.

I asked the night clerk how he could tell the difference between yesterday's heat and this morning's, and he said he could not; that the decision was made by the day clerk, who came on at nine. I wondered whose responsibility it was to decide whether the streets were light or still dark.

I put a few shreds of the *Algérie Républicaine* together and pretended to read them until I fell asleep in the hotel's other armchair.

A touch on my shoulder woke me. It took me a moment to recognize Hassine, now wearing a white jellaba. He'd traded his GI cap for a fez.

"How are we to have tea this evening in Djerba if you are to sleep the whole morning in Tunis?" he demanded.

"We've been waiting since before six," I informed him. The clock above the bar showed half past nine; the day clerk was on duty, the overhead fan just beginning to turn.

"God was unwilling we leave so early," Hassine explained easily. "Against His strength we are helpless. You are my brother." That was just how he put it: I was his brother.

He gave his brother the front seat—the seat of honor—beside himself. He gave Madame barely time to scramble into the back seat. A minute slower and she would have been left behind. My being his brother didn't make Madame his sister.

"If we are to stop to look at rocks all the way to the desert, Madame," he reproved her, looking terribly put upon, "I will have no time to visit my mother's grave."

Hassine waited sullenly at the wheel while Madame and I walked among the rocks; where once the invincible city stood.

This was the point at which Dido, navigating by night instead of beaching her ship every sundown, disembarked. At her first dig she exhumed a cow's skull, presaging a city that would live enslaved. So she tried again farther west and brought up a horse's skull: adumbrating a city warlike and powerful. And she named it *Qart Hadasht*: New Town. The Romans pronounced it "Carthage."

The sea was still bearing tribute: waterlogged melons, Coke bottles and dead fish. It looked like the good times were gone. The New Towner had had his day.

And what a hard, hard time he gave everybody; especially the Roman. In battle as well as in business.

Right from the start the New Towner looked all wrong to the Roman businessman. He not only looked wrong but he *smelled* wrong. His ankle-length robe and his heavy perfume in themselves were offensive. Worse was his habit of prostrating himself before the European before talking business.

It wasn't until later—after the Roman shook off that cloying scent and went to the baths—that he realized he'd been jobbed. Again.

A nation of such effeminate hustlers should be a pushover in warfare, the Roman concluded. And found himself jobbed yet again.

The New Towners drove as ferociously in battle as they did in trade; and their boldness in both was matched by their enterprise on the high seas. Two thousand years before Columbus, the Carthaginian Hanno led sixty ships of fifty oars each down the west coast of Africa. Hanno presented his city with the skins of three African females who'd fought him so fiercely at Fernando Po that they'd had to be killed. The skins were of female gorillas. This remains the earliest recorded instance of a movement for the liberation of women.

"Hassine has not seen his mother's grave for two years," he began again as soon as we were back on the road, "but if Madame and Monsieur enjoy standing on rocks, that is no matter. Hassine's mother is nothing. *Madame's* pleasure comes first."

"If you had come to the hotel at the time you gave your word," Madame phrased her retort neatly, "we would have had time to see *my* mother's grave. Now *neither* of us will visit graves."

"*Madame,*" Hassine cautioned her as though she were being immodest, "you are only a woman."

"*Now* we go to Médenine," Madame ended the discussion.

There weren't many curves in that road from Tunis to Médenine and that was just as well, because the road was narrow and Hassine drove fast; and never troubled to use his klaxon except to summon the attention of Bedouins on donkeys going the other way. Hassine Ameur Djemail, Owner of Citroën with Two Suits in Garage, was passing! Attention must be paid to this man.

We drove between mountain and land, half scrub and half sand. At times I felt we were tilting downward into some sort of green-white hell. Madame dozed in the back seat and I dozed in the seat of honor. I was between sleep and waking when I sensed something pass and came full awake.

"A camel!" I announced triumphantly, craning my neck into the dust behind us. "I just saw a camel!"

"God willing, we shall see many camels," Hassine assured me, "and yet greater wonders. In Djerba—"

"*This* camel was hauling a cart," I finally put it together. "I didn't know camels pulled carts."

Hassine beamed at me. "An old saying of the desert," he counseled me gently, "three things cannot be made to pull a cart: the cat, the lion and the camel."

There'd be a hell of a row if they *did* get all three between the shafts, I realized. But somewhere in Tunisia a camel *was* pulling a cart—all by himself. Or herself. I kept my eyes on the road.

There was always a dust cloud approaching with something in its middle. Some turned out to be camels and some turned out to be carts; but never the one hitched to the other.

Hassine saw a Bedouin sleeping beside the road and gave the horn such a blast that the Bedouin leaped out of the blanket and into the brush. It was a woman.

"Why do you frighten these harmless people?" Madame came awake to ask.

"To keep them from thinking they too should have a flag," he answered immediately.

Between a sky too white and hovels too black we saw the last Jews on earth who earn their livings by driving camels.

This was the ghetto of Médenine. And again we had to leave Hassine waiting. Jews had exactly as much appeal to him as had the rocks of Carthage.

But Madame had an impassioned curiosity about all peoples; and I had my camera.

We found ourselves in a treeless square where camels made the only shadows. Like knock-kneed kings shorn of their powers, some standing and some kneeling, they formed a square within the treeless square. Because of the light, it took me a minute to discern that, in the shadow of each brute, a driver waited.

Their eyes, I sensed, were all on us. And to them we were even more alien than Arabs. Yet I sensed no hostility. It wasn't till my eyes adjusted to the light that I saw they were all boys.

One, robed in black, with a great shock of black hair and light-blue eyes, led his camel up to us. While the camel stretched its neck over our heads, the boy looked up at us, smiling as though expecting something. He was inviting me to ride his camel.

"Tell him I have a fear of heights," I asked Madame.

"He speaks no French," she informed me, "and I don't know how to say cowardice in Hebrew."

I tried to make a deal: "Will you take my picture if I get on top of it?"

She wanted no part of that camera; but the camel boy waved to a friend to act as photographer. The kid caught on to its mechanism immediately. The problem now was how to get on top of the brute.

You don't *swing* aboard as you would a horse. You *climb* it. Even when it's kneeling, you still have to climb.

I hauled myself to its top and very nearly went off the other side. I finally got into a sitting posture, with one hand canted toward the sun to get my face in profile; as I had seen Lawrence of Arabia doing in a photograph.

Then I looked down. I was *high*. Really *high*. I motioned to the kid with the camera to get out of the sun, and the gesture started the camel *moving!* I hadn't counted on its moving and I had to hold on to its neck to avoid being pitched off. The driver took the reins and began leading me around the square as if he'd captured something.

I couldn't catch the rhythm of the camel's walk. When I leaned forward it lurched, throwing me back; when I leaned backward it developed a new lurch and threw me forward. Camel boys came leaping all around the square, making merriment of my plight. I suspected Madame was enjoying the scene as well.

The would-be photographer ran beside the camel, trying to get me into focus. When that didn't work, he stopped and knelt to get a sight-line on me. But just as he'd focus I'd lurch, either forward or back, and he'd have to take off after the camel and rider again. At last he decided his best move was to get in front of the beast and catch us coming head on. When this didn't work, he began leaping straight up off the ground and snapping the camera in midair.

To be leading one's camel around the square in that tiny ancestral ghetto, with an American astride it, was plainly a distinction: The shock-haired boy was positively strutting. He made a complete turn of the square, bringing me back to where I had boarded. And then I knew I had a problem: how to get off.

I accomplished this by sliding down the brute's neck and then dangling. Had the driver not persuaded it to kneel, I'd be dangling yet. Madame apparently detected something humorous in this peril-fraught scene; but I overlooked this demonstration of bad taste on her part. It was one thing for a gang of camel rowdies to jump with glee but quite another for a supposedly sophisticated woman to join them. After she paid the camel driver and the cameraman, both accompanied us to the ghetto gate.

As soon as we returned to Hassine it was clear that we'd wasted the better part of his day. But before he could go into his complaint about spending time looking at rocks, walls, Jews or Bedouins—time that would have been better spent looking at Djerba—Madame gave the orders of the day: Rue Sidi Yahya.

I didn't know what she was up to and didn't ask, figuring I'd find out soon enough.

The entrance to the Rue Sidi Yahya was guarded by two French sol-

106

diers, checking the passes of soldiers looking for women. Sidi Yahya was reserved for black or Jewish whores and the common soldiery. Officers had access to the preferred brothels of white Moslem women.

My camera was loaded. I was *ready*.

I knew we were in the wrong neighborhood as soon as we passed the guards. It would have been no more than awkward, and in bad taste, for a respectable white Christian woman to come to look at women who'd been cast out, black and Jewish at that. But to have her followed by an American with a camera, and he followed by a fat Arab—and none of the three of them looking as though he were going to spend a franc —was a soundproof insult.

The shadow of a whore in one doorway met the base of the building directly across the Sidi Yahya: The street was that narrow. I speculated on the possibility of being confronted by a 6'7'' Senegalese pimp wearing a single earring and wanting to know just what I had in mind. That the street came to a dead end half a city block away was not reassuring. The girls were packed in there pretty tightly.

The Jewish women wore European dress. The tribal women, on the other hand, stood stripped to the waist, some with cicatrices of purple and indigo seaming their cheeks. Madame paused to speak to one; but the woman only fixed her gaze beyond Madame as though Madame didn't exist. When a woman needs a soldier with his pay in his pocket, there isn't much percentage in telling your story to a *madame sociologue*. She had no better luck with the Jewish women. Even though they weren't able to throw us out, they still didn't have to act as if they'd sent for us.

But after she passed one sandy-haired child, a girl no more than eighteen, I caught the suggestion of a smile from the girl. She looked to be both Jewish and French; and since French soldiers have been exploring the wilds of the Rue Sidi Yahya for a hundred years, she might well have been. Which would have made her *persona non grata* to the Christian and Moslem communities as well as the Jewish. I hesitated. She pointed to my camera, then to her face.

"*Foto?*" she asked shyly. "*Foto?*"

I was only too pleased to oblige. When I asked her to move just a bit to the side, out of the direct glare of the sun, she smiled pleasantly and snatched the camera out of my hands. Then she stood, still smiling pleasantly, yet with a shadow of menace on her face, the box held behind her, in her own doorway.

We were only having a bit of a joke between us, of course. So I held out a 100-franc note to keep it that way. She shook her head no: A hundred francs wasn't enough to keep it a joke. It might be for her; but there were now three other girls, all white, on either side and behind me.

All I had, besides the 100-franc note, was a 500- and a 1000-franc note. We could get by if I gave up the 500, but we really needed the 1000-franc one.

"*Ficky?* You *ficky?*" one of the girls demanded, slapping derisively at my fly. I came up with the 500. The sandy-haired one shook her head: No. Just as if she *knew* what I was holding. Then the two on either side began pushing and the one behind started acting funny too. I glanced toward the gate, where the guards were watching. They too were smiling. I came up with the 1000-franc note but held on to it until I got a grip on the camera. She didn't let it go until she got a grip on the bill. Then we both let go at once. She had the note and I had the camera. I looked around for Madame.

There was such a crowd of women around her, all jeering, that I couldn't see her. I looked around for Hassine. He was standing his ground but wasn't planning to advance. I moved reluctantly toward the small mob just as Madame broke free, coming fast on her flat-heeled shoes, the dozen whores strung out, pretending to chase her, some actually running a few steps behind her to keep her running. Hassine turned and fled toward the gate.

I gathered whatever shreds of my dignity remained, simply to wait until Madame had passed me in her flight. It just wouldn't look right, I told myself, to get to the gate before she did. I walked on hurriedly behind her to give the impression, to whoever was watching this wretched demonstration of cowardice, that I was the lesser coward.

Then, just as we'd almost reached the gate, the sandy-haired girl ducked in front of me, raised Madame's dress to her waist and ran behind her, holding the dress up with one hand and pointing with the other, jeering, "*See! She has one too! She has one too!*"

If the soldiers at the gate had laughed outright I would have liked it better than the tight little smiles I felt in passing; smiles that said we'd gotten no worse than we'd deserved. They were right, as Madame was the first to acknowledge—as soon as we were safely back in the Citroën and on the road.

Hassine kept his silence. He was abashed at his own cowardice, I surmised. But I overestimated Hassine. He wasn't in the least abashed: He was *affronted*. He had *warned* us not to look at Jews, he had *warned* us not to look at women who were not serious. We had insisted; with the consequent loss of Hassine's dignity.

"In Djerba there are no women who are not serious," he began *that* again. "In Djerba, we shall drink the world's finest tea. In Djerba—" "In Djerba," I interrupted him, "we would do better to smoke The Terrible Turkish Hubble-Bubble, also known as hashish, kat or *kif* "; my chief idea being that if I could get a water pipe into his mouth, it would keep him from trying to sell us Djerba.

"We are not going to Djerba," Madame decided from the back seat; and I was glad to hear it.

As dusk came up from the desert, a low wind stirred the sands. "That feels like rain," I told Hassine.

"I am of Djerba, a Man of His Word," he came through without hesitation, "it will not rain this night between Cairo and Damascus." He softened the blow with that benign smile and the assurance, "You are my brother."

We drove in silence after that. Once Madame laughed at something, all to herself in the back seat. Hassine looked at me curiously.

"She laughs in her sleep," I told him. I suspected she was reviewing the recent flight of the Frenchwoman and the American man on the Rue Sidi Yahya.

We drove until very late. I roused myself now and again when I sensed something passing us from the other direction. But when it was a camel, there was no cart. And when there was a cart, there was always some fool of a donkey pulling it. The air grew cooler and a slanting rain touched the windshield. I glanced at Hassine. He was ready.

"It is not rain," he explained, "only a few drops of water falling from the sky."

Once, our headlights caught a camel resting under a date palm. Its rear was pointing toward a cart. The cart was unhitched; but I felt close to elation.

"Close, wasn't it?" I asked Hassine.

"Three things—" he began.

"I know, I *know*," I interrupted him, "a cat, a lion and a camel."

The rain that was not rain touched the windshield; a wind that was not wind touched the dust. I was half asleep when, bright in the headlights' glow, came a camel that was not a camel.

It was pulling a cart. The driver was walking alongside.

Hassine watched the camel and cart go by: I watched Hassine. I kept my silence long after we had passed the group. It was growing light before Hassine spoke.

"That was not a camel"—he gave me his forgiving smile—"it was a dromedary. A beast that will do *anything.*"

Madame murmured something; then laughed, very lightly; more in sleep than in waking.

The day we returned to the Hotel Tunisia Palace I took a dozen rolls of film to a shop for developing. Later, when I called for them, the owner shook his head sadly and showed me a dozen rolls of blackened film.

"Camera *malade,*" he explained politely, and declined payment.

An old saying of the desert: *Three things cannot be made to pull a cart: a sick camera; a fat Arab; and a humorless woman.*

I KNOW THEY'LL LIKE ME IN SAIGON

San Francisco
1 Nov. 1968

Mr. Joel Wells
The Critic
180 N. Wabash Ave.
Chicago, Ill.

Dear Joel Wells,

I'm here in San Francisco waiting to board the *Oriental Jade*, a Republic of China cargoliner bound for Southeast Asia, because I always go where I'm needed most.

I know they'll like me in Saigon: Emmett Dedmon has just told me so in the *Chicago Sunday Sun-Times*. Emmett discovered, during his recent tour of Southeast Asia, that the South Vietnamese have added gratitude to their natural affection for Americans, because we are helping them to preserve their democracy. In the Mekong Delta Emmett had to talk a village chief out of forming an Emmett Dedmon Fan Club. And he was only able to tear himself away by promising the people solemnly that, if they'd let him go, he'd send them more Americans just like himself. I can hardly wait to get there. I'd board the *Oriental Jade* today if I had my passport.

I sent it to the Embassy of the Republic of Vietnam in September, along with an application for a visa to that country and a five-dollar check. The application was received there but the passport and the check disappeared themselves.

I obtained another passport, sent it by registered mail, received a receipt and a telephone assurance that everything was now in order, and the visaed passport was being sent to my Chicago address by airmail special delivery—with profuse apologies.

That was eleven days ago and it hasn't arrived yet. Slow as the U.S. mails may be, they aren't *that* slow. I have now just a little over twenty-four hours to get yet another passport. Needless to say, I won't entrust this one to the Embassy of the Republic of Vietnam. I asked Kay Boyle her opinion of *L'affaire du Passeport*. "American shenanigans," was her comment.

My father was born in this city a hundred years ago. I think it would have been bright of him to have stayed right here. I don't know whether that would have made me better looking; but I'm sure I would have had more fun.

The Chicagoan born in Chicago becomes an expatriate without moving off his own street. The San Franciscan becomes a tourist without leaving town. This is because Chicago streets are laid out simply to provide a means of getting to the nearest bank without using a machete. But San Francisco's streets were laid out to provide corners for San Franciscans to stand on while watching other San Franciscans passing by.

And they pass by all the time, mostly going up and down on cablecars; and looking out to see who's standing on the corners to watch them going up and down. The ride up and down hill on the Grant Street cable car is only fifteen cents and has more gaiety than the ferris wheel at Riverview Park ever had because everybody is heaped into the same basket; with the happiest cats those hanging on for dear life on the outside.

Saturday afternoon there was a mob—enough to fill four cars —waiting to board at the Grant Street dock. One block north they can take the bus; but the women shoppers prefer the cable car because the chances of getting jostled are better.

After those cold blank faces of the Saturday buses in Chicago, what a happy change! It takes two *big* men to run this thing: one to control that big iron machine—a *very* strong man's job—and the other to collect fares and cheer up his colleague who does the heavy work. "Ring that thing!" he commands the driver, "Santa Claus is in the next car."

I thought he was making it up about Santa Claus; but he wasn't. The driver began banging on his bell like mad, trying to get *Jingle Bells* out of it and coming pretty close; because *here come Santa Claus!*

That's right. About twenty of the prettiest chicks you ever saw, dressed in red and white miniskirts, were stopping traffic by sending up huge green, yellow and orange balloons and carrying signs, "Santa is coming!" Then, right behind them, an old-fashioned fire engine, also full of chicks with balloons, and its driver banging crazily on a steam calliope playing "Dreaming of a White Christmas"—this is on a hot, white, summery sunny day—and all directed by a clown-cop. Maybe he *was* a cop, I don't know; but he was wearing shades, had a beard, and was sporting some kind of zebra-striped hippie cloak. I never saw anything like it—no chance of anyone getting through *that* traffic; and nobody seeming to mind in the least.

Sitting on one of those dirt-filled boxes out of which a tree is trying to grow, a teen-age girl with a face like an unfed Pekingese catches my eye and asks me something. She says it so low I can't hear her—but I've already made up my mind I'm not buying *The Berkeley Barb*. She's not selling: "Can you spare some change?"

"Change? How much? What *for?*" I was startled.

"To eat, of course."

To *eat?* I'd already had breakfast! Then I realized *she* wanted breakfast, too! I gave her a quarter and waited for my change.

The little devil dashed into a restaurant with the whole quarter—and there wasn't a cop in sight! God, what I would have given in that moment for four of Daley's Boys in Blue to give her a faceful of mace, eighteen stitches in her skull and a couple of teeth knocked out so they'd know her the next time they saw her. "WANTED: *May be armed*; white, female, seventeen, solicits funds on the open street and keeps the change; attended classes in Berkeley and is suspected of being a flower-child and illegal sexual activity." These are things that make a man homesick for his home town.

Another transportation curiosity here: the drivers on the buses don't carry change. You have exact fare or you lose, that's all. How I found out was that I put a quarter in the slot (the fare is fifteen cents) and the driver just laughed—"the dime is for charity." Again there wasn't a cop in sight.

Bay Meadows has the best paddock I've ever seen at a racetrack. It's under the clubhouse and is circular, like a circus ring. The whole atmosphere of the track, like the city, is circus-like.

Had a good day: four straight winners, then a miss, then another winner. Then I skipped a race, threw away *The Form* and asked the girl I was with, who'd never been at a track before nor seen a *Form*, to tell me what her ESP was whispering. She felt it was Abighai's Nugget, in the eleventh post position and off at 45-1. I put fifty dollars of *their* money on Abighai to win and twenty more—also theirs—to place. The horse broke second and held it, continued to hold it, and before my mind's eye, as they came into the turn for home, a line of figures began crossing like a line of Rock Island box-car numbers —2,440.80/668.20. The rider lost ground on the turn. The horse came in fourth.

I leaned my head on the rail until the box-car figures disappeared themselves. When I recovered a bit of self-control I looked up at the girl. She was studying me apprehensively, like a child who thinks she's done something wrong but doesn't know what.

"I'm sorry," she apologized, "I was only guessing."

"You guessed just right," I had to reassure her—"the rider let the horse out too soon. If he'd held him until the turn—let's forget it and have a drink."

The moral being that when in San Francisco, throw away your *Form*. This has something to do with the climate, because the city don't work by the rules. Not only do people operate more on ESP than on logic here, but so do the horses.

Columnists whose impact goes beyond their city limits are rare as albino rhinos. After Finley Peter Dunne's *Mr. Dooley* passed in Chicago, it was fifty years before Mike Royko showed up there. New York hasn't had anyone like Heywood Broun since Heywood Broun. Ralph Gleason, operating out of San Francisco, struck a national chord with youth from coast to coast, through literature and jazz, in the fifties. He revealed the humbuggery of describing performers like Al Jolson as "Jazzmen." His discernment, always based on feeling instead of tradition, caught suburban as well as slum kids. After twenty years he still has the touch.

He bears a physical resemblance to Jimmy Gleason. If you don't know who Jimmy Gleason was, forget it. If you don't know who Kid Gleason was, forget that, too. If you know who Jackie Gleason is, it doesn't matter; because Ralph doesn't resemble him either.

Meanwhile back at the Embassy of the Republic of Vietnam, I am reassured by phone, that my passport and visa have been sent by registered airmail, special delivery to my Chicago address.

But when I phoned a friendly neighbor, who has been on the hawks for it, she assured me that it hasn't arrived. There's no use applying for another passport because they simply wouldn't believe that I'm not selling them as fast as they can issue them.

I want to go to Japan because I know they belong to us. I have 48 rolls of film but I have no intention of wasting as much as a single roll on countries that don't belong to us.

Or even on countries that do, but don't want to. There are three or four of those. Emmett didn't name them but he implied that there *are* countries that aren't as sound as South Vietnam. Thailand is okay but there's something funny going on in Cambodia, which doesn't seem to want to belong to *anybody!*

If they don't want to belong to anybody, they won't get pictures taken of them, that's all. And that goes for North Vietnam; because *it* belongs to *them*.

My camera is made in Japan and is described, in the directions for its use, as foolproof. With forty-eight rolls of film I should be able to get snapshots of half the fools in Asia.

I can't help feeling pleased with myself for getting away from Chicago's dangerous streets and finding myself a peaceful sanctuary in a small Asian city where a long tradition of nonviolence has been elevated by a hundred years of French culture. There is a Chinese suburb —Cholon—in which I plan to find a quiet set of rooms at a fantastically low rental; including maid service.

I *know* they'll like me in Cholon.

How I figure it is that since Chicago Caucasians, by and large, love me so little, Chinese Buddhists *must* love me a lot. Don't you think so? Especially if I give autographs, free, to their little ones? I think I'll begin by winning the hearts and minds of the children and then work up to the adults.

Yet something tells me I'm not going in the right direction. It's getting harder to tell where one's responsibility lies. If I had it to do all over again I'd settle for reporting the border crisis between Liechtenstein and Switzerland, which is going imperialistic; as is plain to see. On the other hand, countries that don't belong to us have a tendency to practice genocide—and that goes for those rotten Liechtensteiners, too! Isn't it interesting that the genocide-practicers—like Liechtenstein, Biafra, Guatemala, Iceland, Laos and Tanzania—belong to *them?* While the non-violent regimes—Salazar's, Franco's, Vorster's, Duvalier's and the Greek Junta's—belong to *us?*

I'll make the *Oriental Jade*. Less than eight hours before sailing-time, the passport arrived, special delivery, in the hotel lobby.

The Embassy of the Republic of South Vietnam had sent it airmail special delivery, just as I'd been assured. But had mailed it to Ames, Iowa.

Ames? Iowa?

I've never been in Ames, know nobody there, have no relatives or friends who ever went there.

How the passport found its way into the hotel lobby here I'll never know. I think I have my friendly neighbor to thank.

Certainly not the Embassy of the Republic of Vietnam.

If the South Vietnamese are running a war the way they're handling their mail, Uncle Ho don't need to send soldiers: the Saigon Government will collapse of its own incompetence.

I keep thinking of that San Francisco cop directing impossible traffic in an impossible getup—a clownified yippie purporting to represent law and order. Could it be that the accusation that the U.S.A. is trying to be the policeman of the world would be more accurate if the accusation was that he's a clown armed to the teeth? I don't know. I'm only asking.

AIRY PERSIFLAGE ON THE HEAVING DEEP

or

Sam, you made the ship too short

THIS is a Chiang-Kai-shekified cargo-tub whose crew is largely out of Taiwan; ferrying sixty-odd Caucasoids largely out of Lingering Death, Nevada. We share a saltwater swimming pool five feet deep and just wide enough to accommodate four Nevadans or seven Asians. When all eleven make it together you can fancy the jostling for position. Particularly since the pool is bone dry.

Well, so is Nevada.

We sailed out of San Francisco in a pelting rain and, two days out, it's pelting yet. "We guess weatha will cwear wain," the purser, Mr. Ho, announced on the PA system this morning. She tilts, then she plunges and albatrosses follow in the rain.

The bullies draped us in orange life preservers (stenciled *S.S. Moon of the Orient*) this morning. Then brought us out on deck sick or well. Where we had to watch them drag a length of leaky hose down the deck merely to exhibit Mysterious Oriental Skill. If the captain's hose don't hold water how am I to depend upon his life preserver? Even a Caucasoid can have enemies.

When they began sprinkling water into the sea, we all cheered dutifully. I hadn't realized we were passing a shallow place in the Pacific: We owe our lives to these brave fellows.

She pitches as she sways as she rolls. Is the captain doing it on purpose? A man who'll provide leaky life preservers is capable of anything. Even a paranoid Caucasoid can have enemies.

"We guess the wain cwears the weatha." Mr. Ho keeps working at it.

As she tilts as she lurches and buckles in every beam. There'll be faces missing at breakfast. If some are still missing at lunch it's all right with me.

If the captain *isn't* doing this on purpose, then they made the ship too short. That, or they made the waves too long.

"Now guess choppy weatha." I'll say this much for Mr. Ho: *He* admits he's guessing. That's more than can be said of the captain. *That* one goes around the deck telling tax-paying Americans, "That bird are *arbatross.*" *More* guesswork: If all they are are albatrosses, why do they keep swinging down over the deck looking for seasick passengers? I don't mind his guesswork on seagoing buzzards; but, with our destination in his hands, I want him to start using *instruments*. Even a seasick paranoid Caucasoid can have enemies.

After the heady excitements of fire drill and the tour of the engine room, I doubt my nerves will be up to tonight's showing of *Kim Novak at the Tokyo Olympics*. I've worked too long to gain the upper hand of my emotions to have them set ablaze, at this late hour, by The Passion-flower of Albany Park.

As she glides as she slides as she rides. For the sun is out, Mr. Ho is being fêted at the bar for his wonderful guesswork, the shuffleboard players totter and tilt; there is merriment in the Mandarin Lounge and the pool is asplash. I swam strongly the full eleven-foot length of the pool and then swam back again. Although breathing heavily, I was *not* exhausted. But I had to get out because someone else was waiting to get in.

The albatrosses drift and wheel and the blue waters roll.

In the deck chair next to mine, a woman studying a paperback on astrology removed her shades. In a sun too bright, in a face too white, green eye-shadow made her face look both young and ravaged. A lot of mileage for a run so brief.

"Are you making the round trip?" she asked.

"No. I'm getting off in Yokohama."

"Are you going to live in Japan?"

"No. I'm going to Saigon."

"Will you feel *safe* there?"

"Safe as where I'm coming from. At least I'll be able to walk around the parks. I'm from Chicago."

"Are your parks so dangerous?"

"It's not too bad in the daytime, provided you stay inside the lion-and-leopard building. We can even sit on the grass. But we have to get out after dark. Chicago parks are privately owned."

Her eyes were a fading hazel and her voice kept dying off. Her bikini, once scarlet, was washed to a sickly rose. She was pregnant yet she seemed to be traveling alone.

"What day were you born?" she asked.

"March 28th."

"You'll be all right," she decided, "that's Aries."

"Where are you from?" I only thought I'd ask.

"Pisces."

I hadn't known the sun was that strong.

I'm flanked, in the dining room, by a wisp of a blue-eyed Lancashire woman of seventy named Kathryn; and by the astrology bug from Pisces. Behind the centerpiece is a Mr. Earl D'Xavier, a gardenia gone bamboo. He was born in East St. Louis, Illinois, and now makes his home in Hong Kong.

"I *adore* the Taiwanese," Earl assured the breakfast board, "I adore the Thais too. I adore the Chinese because they make Silver-Fungus soup."

"I like Water-Dyaks best of any," I tried my best to be agreeable. "They eat mushed fish with a double-pronged spoon." And reached for the maple syrup.

"I *adore* maple syrup," he purred in his tenderest key, peeking around the centerpiece at me.

I couldn't see whether his ears were pierced but I let the griddle cake lay.

As his adorations are infinite and tastes exquisite, his years are indefinite and his manners execrable.

"May I ask you one question, Mrs. Adams?" he addressed Kathryn politely. "Exactly how old *are* you?"

Earl made a sharp move when he left East St. Louis.

"Mrs. Adams is thirty-nine," I decided.

He claims to be fifty-five yet can't be past forty. Why the reverse Jack Benny gimmick? Just to gain the assurance of strangers that he looks *marvelously* youthful for a man in his fifties? I've seen some cats of curious stripe; but this one's stripes have stripes. At his present pace he'll make a nursing home when he's forty-four just to be the youngest thing in a wheelchair.

The complaints of these Don't-Bomb-'Em-Back-to-the-Stone-Age-till-I've-Shopped-in-Hong-Kong Americans are continuous. Mrs. Lionel ("Ginger") Schlepker, of Los Angeles, has beefed to the purser that the girl who set her hair charged her two dollars and fifty cents and didn't set it right. She emphasizes the necessity of having an ashtray beside her plate, when she comes in to dinner, by waggling her finger under the nose of her waiter, Mr. Koo.

Mr. Koo says, "Yis, yis, *yis.*"

But the ashtray never gets there until Ginger begins using the centerpiece. Mr. Koo earns seventy-five dollars a month.

Mr. Lionel Schlepker, also of Los Angeles, won two bottles of scotch playing bingo last night. "I don't *want* Johnny Walker, I want Cutty Sark," he beefed to Mr. Ho.

Lionel got Cutty Sark.

"I don't *want* apple turnover, I want *ice cream,*" Mrs. Schlepker got on Mr. Koo again at lunch; although the menu didn't mention ice cream.

"Yis, yis, *yis.*" Mr. Koo brought ice cream.

"I don't *want* vanilla. I want *chocolate.*"

Ginger got chocolate.

Lionel placed a three-inch plastic cockroach beside the astrology bug's toast this morning. I let it lay because I appreciate sharp wit. Then she reached for the toast.

Her face turned the hue of her eye-shadow and she headed for the deck rail. Whether she made it or not I'll never know. If she did, it might have come as an early-morning surprise to anyone resting, with his face turned toward an open porthole, on A-Deck just below.

"I never thought an Aries would do a thing like *that,*" she reproached me on her return.

"It wasn't me." I refused firmly to take the rap.

"Then it was—I know who." She guessed right. "He's a Leo."

"I don't know if he's a Leo," I assured her, "but he's definitely an XYY."

The next time I saw the XYY joker he was watching Johnny Weissmuller on Japanese TV at the bar. A Japanese-speaking baboon was warning Tarzan of the approach of the Blackstone Rangers.

"What's he *saying* for God's *sake?*" XYY demanded to know. Why he thinks it the bartender's job to translate Japanified Baboonese I'm not sure I can't tell. The bartender just shrugged.

"Don't you people have anything more up-to-date than Tarzan?" XYY accused the bartender, who is Chinese, "*Switch it!*"

The bartender switched to a taped film of the San Francisco Seals playing the Tokyo Giants.

"Japs can't hit," XYY informed me. "They can field but they can't hit."

You don't *have* to have acne to be an XYY.

The one thing the captain *isn't* guessing about is his take on the fifty-cents-a-chance lottery sixty passengers purchased to estimate the ship's mileage per diem. With his martinis marked up to thirty cents at the bar and Benson & Hedges out of reach of the average buyer at fifteen cents per pack, it's no wonder he isn't in any hurry to get to port. But I noticed a clock in the engine room that can be swung to DEAD STOP. All I'd have to do would be to get past the HIGH VOLTAGE warning around midnight and then flash any receipt for an estimate of mileage lower than any other bidder. There must be *some* way of past-posting the captain.

As she strains as she creaks as she goes.

Kathryn Adams doesn't know what to make of American women.

"My *Lord*," she confided in me after lunch, "they *do* shovel it in, don't they? I haven't heard one word from one of them about anything except their digestive tracts."

"Then you missed it," I told her, "Mr. Schlepker outlined his system of rotating his clothes yesterday in the lounge. I'm sorry you didn't get in on it."

"O, *that* one," she recalled the XYY Life of the Party. "I *say*, I'm not sure he's stamped on every link, is he?"

"Stamped on every link?"

"When a bracelet is pure gold it's stamped on every link. It means that a person is genuine, that's all. You know, when one has *stature*."

"I wouldn't say Mr. Schlepker doesn't have *some* stature," I conceded, "but he could still walk under the rung of that deck chair on tiptoe without touching his head."

"Fo'cas' cwoudy weatha," Mr. Ho announced—and before he'd gone off the air the sea fogs began rolling in. He must have seen one coming.

But the astrology bug and I are friends again. I'd hardly sat down to dinner before she began giving me the benefit of any previous doubts about my charm as a table companion.

"Where *are* you from?" she wanted to know; just as if I hadn't already answered that one on the deck. Does she think, every time we meet, it's a Brand New Me?

"Lake Oswego, Oregon," I accommodated her by *being* a Brand New Me.

"*Oregon!*" she exclaimed with an elation so sudden I felt that Lake Oswego must be where I really *was* from. "Isn't that the *one* state where they still have good old country family life?"

"Only during the carp season,"—I tried to see whether there was room for two in her most recent hallucination—"most of the Gypsies have left the reservation."

Mr. D'Xavier peeked around the centerpiece.

"Are you going to stay in Japan?" he inquired.

"No, I'm going to Saigon," I answered.

"O, the Chinese are behind all *that,*" the astrology bug decided, "we ought to pull our boys out and let the Japanese hold them."

A once great mind had snapped.

"Are you going to write something about it?" she wanted to know.

"No," I tried to cut dinner short, "I'm just going there for a rest."

I felt her studying me.

"*You* have a personal problem," she concluded.

I shook my head, yes. I didn't add that it was one that could be solved if a typhoon hit her side of the ship.

She wasn't quite satisfied.

"You can tell *me* about it," she confided quietly, "*I don't talk.*"

"May *I* ask you one question?"—this was the East St. Louis gardenia doing some sniffing—he was that sort of gardenia. If you didn't sniff *him* he sniffed *you.* Or maybe what I'm thinking of isn't a gardenia; but I let him come ahead all the same.

"Don't you *love* our country?"

He really wanted to know.

"*Airy persiflage,*" Kathryn Adams put in just then.

That seemed to cover both the gardenia and the bug.

My first ocean passage was in 1943, aboard an English luxury liner converted to a troop ship moving in convoy. We never saw the ships behind us nor before. Fogs of the North Atlantic veiled them. One of the sub-chasers guarding us would come rocking through a swell, like a grey dolphin, now and then. That was all we saw, on the ocean sea, for twenty-one days.

We reached Southampton on the first of November. At thirteen hundred hours First Sergeant Bernard Weintraub, of New York, New York, assembled us for a word of caution about the way the English stevedores were handling the unloading of our engineering equipment.

"If you *have* to watch the Limeys work," he warned us, "wear your helmets. They handle that stuff careless."

At eighteen hundred hours Weintraub was lying dead on the deck. He'd been watching the unloading bareheaded.

Breakfast aboard the S. S. *America,* traveling first class in 1960, lacked nothing but a good French wine. With kumquats under cream, eggs under oath and something moving under the toast, why not? If it moves, fondle it. Why not Pinot? Indeed, why not champagne? So I sent for *that*. Why travel steerage on the *Titanic*?

The catch was that first-class service-people outnumbered first-class passengers and they wouldn't go downstairs unless the passengers went first. And the passengers couldn't go downstairs because the escape route to TOURIST, where everyone was having fun, was barred.

I was tailed up-deck and down by some creep armed with a Butane lighter: I had only to reach for a cigarette and he would come at me in a silent wolf-lope, lighter blazing.

Sometimes he kept a respectful distance behind me. But once he lapped me by making the deck, counterclockwise, and unbeknownst to me, was waiting with his back flattened against the door of a cabin. Just as I passed the door I drew my handkerchief and he set it afire. Even a survivor of Kim Novak's elocution-school acting can be immolated.

He tried to make up for his *faux pas* by stepping up his personal attention. Every time I left my cabin he'd duck inside and leave me a cornucopia of figs, dates, apples, oranges, apricots, peaches, pomegranates, grapes, and bananas, topped by kumquats; all paid for out of his own pocket.

When the stuff started rotting I'd heave it down to the second-class rabble and let them scramble for it. But the first-class passengers, at sea or on the beach, have looked like kumquats to me ever since.

Bound for ancestral Asia aboard the *Malaysia Mail* in 1962, I was the only passenger. But I couldn't stand the responsibility. All the Wisdom of the Ancient East which I acquired, I later incorporated as *Algren's Primary Law of The Ocean Deeps; or Never Play Lowball With The Crew of an American Cargo-Liner.*

This startling concept was later expanded by tours of Singapore, Cebu City, Pusan, and Kowloon into two subsidiary principals: *Never Sleep With Anyone Whose Troubles Are Worse Than Your Own; and Never Eat at a Place With Sliding Doors Unless You're Crazy About Raw Fish.*

Through rolling fogs and deepening mists, memories of earlier passages move in perpetual convoy yet.

One is of a dead soldier's face so darkened by blood that I failed at first to recognize it as our first sergeant's.

Another is of a woman with golden earrings who told me, "Americans think they go to moon. Americans crazy. Moon is not *place*. Moon is *Great Light*."

And all night long in voluptuous gravity she slept.

I was talking to Kathryn Adams when Mr. Ho's voice came on.

"Ladies and gent'men, light on sta'board are light of ship destination."

Sure enough, through the rain, the low lights of a great city began shimmering as though tethered in the water.

"Yokohama," Kathryn Adams assured me.

"If it isn't, Mrs. Adams," I cautioned her, "we've *discovered* something!"

"Airy persiflage," she answered, and tapped my hand lightly, "but you *may* call me Kitty."

I felt honored.

NO CUMSHAW NO RICKSHAW

A facility for the decorative is one of the minor satisfactions of being a Japanese person; when he's made a plate of fried mush appear to be baked Alaska, he feels he's accomplished something even though he has to eat it himself. He'd rather sell you a dried octopus wrapped to look like a chocolate Easter egg than have you hand him a hundred yen for nothing and walk off leaving him with an unwrapped squid.

A Parisienne doing up a black lace chemise for Françoise Sagan isn't in it with a Japanese counter-girl who's just sold a box of cashew nuts to a total stranger. Just when she gets to the final tassel and Total Stranger thinks "IT'S MINE! MINE! ALL MINE!" she goes for her little scissors and begins fraying each tassel. After the tassels have been individually frayed, each individual fray must be individually curled. And when she looks up to find Total Stranger has fled, she'll track him down on the Ginza and present him with his prize publicly—*arigato gozaimasu* and give my best wishes to your father.

One consequence being that I'm stuck with—in addition to the dried octopus—a kilo of something resembling candy corn. It was purchased during an intermission at the Japanese National Theater, intended as a gift to my companion, Miss Keiko Kanno, and has now begun to give off a faintly bittersweet scent like that of a medicinal herb. I'll be able to analyze it better after I've found a pipe.

That the Asiatic eye is slanted and the Western eye is round is one delusion which has sustained the East-Is-East-West-Is-West myth. Both are round.

The variation is in the lid. And while Western cosmeticians are turning a pretty penny making Caucasian birds look like Madame Nu, plastic cosmeticians here are doing a landoffice business touching up eyelids. Japanese chicks are now making the street looking like Bette Davis after Paul Henreid began lighting her cigarettes and blowing the smoke in her face.

125

The Asiatic eye has clearer vision; of that I'm convinced. Because Miss Kanno was able to detect, the moment she opened my second gift box, that what I'd presented her with was fish eggs; not candied pineapple. She was gracious enough to accept them, claiming fish eggs have it all over glazed pineapple.

Another advantage the Oriental eye has is that through it you can see better where you're going. Look at the Hairy Ainu, blue-eyed, round-eyed and hairy as hell, freezing to death up there on Japan's bleakest tundra. Common sense tells us that had they been able to see where they were going, they would have stayed in downtown Danzig. A fat lot of good the Caucasian eye did *them*.

The reason I keep showering Miss Kanno with delicacies is to reward her for her services as an interpreter. I wanted to find out what Shuji Terayama was talking about all the time. Whatever it was, he kept punctuating it with a right cross. Miss Kanno observed him quietly, from a short distance, then told me that he seemed to be describing some sort of game. By this time Terayama was circling the lobby of the Dai-Ichi Hotel with one shoulder slightly higher than the other.

"Now he riding horse," Miss Kanno explained.

The fact that Miss Kanno knows nothing whatsoever about either fighters or horses didn't help her interpreting. But she overcame this handicap simply by letting her hands fly to her pretty mouth every time Terayama said something. When she recovered I'd say something and she'd take another spell. I was pleased to see her enjoying herself.

Terayama, whose novels have been translated into French (but not yet into English) and whose underground theater has made him the voice of Tokyo youth, is the son of a farmer of the North who was killed in World War II. He is thirty-three and owns a mare which—he alleges—has won four times at Nayakama Park.

There were 80,000 horse degenerates crowding paddock and rail the Sunday he took Miss Kanno and me to see his speedy horse.

The horses break out of a gate—at Nayakama Park about half the size of the American barrier—onto a course a mile and a half around. But as they run counterclockwise, it seems like two miles.

As Terayama is a form player and Miss Kanno is a novice, I disdained his hot tips and went on her ESP. Miss Kanno and I had three winners. Terayama lost every race and his own horse ran out. He looked as if it had been claimed. Miss Kanno and I remained cheerful. When we offered to take him to dinner he appeared consoled.

Japanese horseplayers play to win it all or go broke, and most of them do. Stands selling secondhand goods line Okera Road, where losers and winners alike go milling when the last race has been run. The stands are the last chance for the losers to make subway fare home; raincoats, watches, jewelry, shirts, shoes and even pants, bought cheap off the *nabikai*—literally, the "weepers"—are on sale here for winners. The only thing you can't buy is a hat. Japanese men don't wear them. Not even winners.

But winners and losers alike seem cheerful. Although Terayama feels that the contentment common to the Japanese face is something of a put-on.

"Most lives in Tokyo are sad," Terayama feels.

"Bored," Miss Kanno corrected him.

"Same thing," Terayama insisted.

"Not mutually exclusive," I decided.

That the *pachinko* parlors are crowded, from morning till night, attests to a pervasive boredom. There are thousands of such pinball parlors here, where more men than women, and more young men than old, feed small steel balls into an upright pinball game more complex than the American version. Martial music blares, lights flash off and on, a clatter of small steel balls falls into a cup where a winner has hit—and promptly feeds them back into the machine. He tries to see how long he can play before going broke: spiritual hara-kiri.

"*Pachinko* is a monologue," Terayama observed, feeding small steel balls into a machine to redeem his losses at Nayakama Park.

Under the heading ABOLISH THE EMPEROR MOVEMENT, the *Saigon Daily News* of 4 January 1969 reports that a forty-six-year-old Tokyo factory worker had fired a *pachinko* ball, from a slingshot, towards Emperor Hirohito when the emperor appeared on his palace balcony to receive New Year *banzais* from thousands of Japanese.

"The man was arrested and identified as Kenzo Okuzaki, a factory worker who had been sentenced to ten years imprisonment on a murder charge thirteen years ago.

"Okuzaki's action marked the first time in postwar years that anyone has attempted to assassinate Hirohito."

The police took Mr. Okuzaki's *pachinko* ball away from him.

"When one has no one to talk to," Miss Kanno observed, "one talks to a machine."

I've never seen a sumo match and I hope I never see one.

It was my good fortune, on the evening that Terayama took Miss

127

Kanno and myself to Kuramae Kogukian, the sumo wrestling stadium, that the hall was being used to decide the junior welterweight boxing title of the world. Takishi Paul Fuji, a Japanese out of Hawaii, was defending against an Argentine, Nicolino Locche.

From the heights of Kuramae Kogukian, portraits of the bellies of the grand champions of sumo look down. Attached to these heroic stomachs are mighty arms and Herculean thighs.

Which is as it ought to be. Because the sumo champion's vast pride, his ferocity and implacable honor, his capacity for enduring pain and his dedication to his country are more clearly expressed by his belly than by his features; which are lost in fat.

Akashi Shiga-nosuke stood well over eight feet and weighed four hundred pounds. Ume-ga-tani was only five-six yet weighed three hundred thirty-five. Nomi-nosukne stood seven-ten and Big Sky Ozora seven-foot-three.

The main floor of this arena is partitioned into frames capable of seating several sumo fans, teapots and all. There are seats in the galleries and folding chairs ringside, for boxing. Now the main floor was filled by fight fans who sat cross-legged; not one had brought a teapot.

The pageantry of sumo derives from imperial tournaments, held in temple compounds and witnessed only by kings, courtiers and high priests. The gods, whose favors ancient giants sought, show up today in boxing rings as commercial sponsors, blessing all contenders. The ancestral ceremonialism has rubbed off onto modern Japanese boxing.

Tasseled banners, once borne by priestly corner-men assuaging The East Wind as well as The West, are now admen presenting gift boxes accompanied by a plug for the company. I had a hunch that the goody in Nicolino Locche's box was a nicer goody than the one Takishi Paul Fuji would open before the night was done.

This hunch had been provoked by the *Japan Times, Mainichi Daily News,* the *Ashai Evening News* and the *Honolulu Advertiser,* all of which agreed that Fuji was a lead-pipe cinch to knock Locche out within five rounds. One writer did concede that, if, by chance or luck, Locche should last eight rounds, he'd have an outside chance of still being on his feet at the end of fifteen. They were trying to reassure Fuji was what it sounded like. It sounded as though they were worried about Fuji and that Fuji was worried about Locche. It sounded like the buildup Chicago papers gave Chuck Davey the week before he had to go into the same ring as Kid Gavilan.

Everyone present who'd been born in the United States and had had his hands inside a pair of boxing gloves, had to be introduced before the main event. I was glad that none of *them* were given boxes. That accomplished, a gallery group began chanting *"Fuji Fuji Fuji!"*

There were about twenty of these enthusiasts, each draped in a white robe with a rising sun emblazoned on the breast, and a cheerleader, equally draped and emblazoned, to keep them from charging. I hadn't known the national honor was going on the main event.

But it convinced me. I asked Terayama, who knows everybody, to get me down for ten thousand yen—twenty-eight dollars American—on Locche.

"Betting irregal in Japan," he assured me.

"Betting also irregal in Chicago," I assured him.

He got me down at one-four. And when Fuji came out and threw a right hand, intended to end the fight right there, I had a moment of apprehension.

If Locche felt a wind go by, he gave no indication. He simply stuck a short left into Fuji's face, moved to the right, stuck it in again and then let the wind go. He let Fuji bull him into the ropes until he felt the top strand against the small of his back. He tested its leverage lightly while counting the house. The crowd began shouting to Fuji to go in and finish him, but Fuji sensed the danger; he didn't go in. Locche stuck the left in Fuji's face and walked away. The fight was in his hands.

He never let it get away from him. That was the whole fight: Fuji throwing those big rights and lefts, sending the gallery group into the perpetual chant of *"Fuji Fuji Fuji!"* —the crowd coming to its feet wondering how Locche could take such punishment, and Locche letting everything bounce off his elbows and shoulders. The crowd saw it as Fuji driving Locche into the ropes. It looked to me like Locche was suckering him in there. Locche looked, to me, more dangerous in that corner. Fuji acted like it struck him the same way. Locche began looking more and more like Willie Pep, the way he kept sliding Fuji's blows. And the way Fuji began punching himself out, *he* looked more and more like Don Hayakawa.

That's how it looked to the Argentine radio announcer, too, who was trying to drown out the cries of *"Fuji Fuji Fuji!"* by shouting *"Locche Locche Locche!"* into the mike. He got help from a small group off the pampas.

By the eighth round Fuji was so wearied out that he put his head down against Locche's chest and wearily flailed the air. While the gallery group continued their chant that now sounded like "Onward Christian Soldiers/Marching as to War."

"Fuji isn't going to last," I told Terayama in the middle of the eighth as though he couldn't see it for himself.

"Why you against Fuji?" Miss Kanno asked suspiciously.

"Because he's a bum," I had to tell her.

The seat cushions, tangerines and half-eaten sandwiches that showered the ring, when the referee held Locche's hand up before the bell for the tenth, weren't protesting Locche's triumph. The goodies were all for Fuji. It was the first time a Japanese titleholder had surrendered his title in the middle of a fight. And a world title is much more important to a defeated nation than to a victorious one. It took a cordon of police to protect Fuji from being mobbed.

"Surrender" was also the word the Japanese press employed the following morning. Fuji lost more than his title to Locche.

Fuji's dressing-room comment, "I quit because my face started getting red," left him wide open to let the press redden it more. "Surrender" has a more bitter sound in Tokyo, Vicksburg or Berlin than in London or Chicago.

Yet Fuji had his defenders.

"Locche win *only* because he fight *Western* style," Miss Kanno perceived. Fuji should have kicked Locche in the teeth was what she meant.

The day after the fight an old man sat down, cross-legged, in front of the Shinjuku Station with a sign around his neck:

Please talk to me

A man of the middle class begging, not for money, but for words.

He sat there three days. Of all the multitudes that hurried past, not one stopped to speak one word.

On the third a young man sat down, cross-legged, across the street from the old man, wearing a sign which said:

You say something first

What words can one say to a stranger? How is your father? Do we have mutual friends? Remember me to your mother?

The old man got up and went home.

Arigato gozaimasu.

LETTER FROM SAIGON

Mr. Joel Wells
The Critic/ Chicago, Ill.

Dear Joel Wells:

Living on Saigon's Milwaukee Avenue—the Tran Hung-Dao—at the point where Saigon becomes Cholon, is to live with one foot in Vietnam and one foot in China. Cholon is the Chinese ghetto, whose government is run by black-marketeers. Saigon is run by the old French *élite*, the Vietnamese whose training and schooling is French. Cholon's first language is Chinese; Vietnamese its second. Saigon's first language is Vietnamese; its second language French. English is spoken nowhere; not even among GIs.

There *is* a third tongue common to Cholon, Saigon, Thai, Filipino, Korean, Taiwanese, Australian, New Zealanders, and American soldiers —the one by which most business in this Babel is conducted. I myself have mastered it so you see it is fairly simple. It goes like this:

> What nem you? You speak me how much? Five hundred P? You Numba Ten, me give one hundred P. No swat. Two hundred P. Okay, you Numba One. You !ike nice gel, twelve-year old, Numba One? Me bring by your hou'. No swat. Sorry 'bout that.

Anyone who is unsure, for a moment, whether he is speaking to a Vietnamese or a Chinese, won't have to wait long to be certain. If the other's eyes are curiously dull, if he has a listless, dispirited air, fingers your watch and asks "What tam?" or pats your wallet pocket, he is Vietnamese. If the other person responds naturally, seems to know you're an individual like himself and doesn't seem to have some mischief in mind, he is Chinese.

If he rubs his stomach, puts his finger in his mouth to indicate hunger

131

(even though he has a toothpick sticking in his teeth as he pleads), he is Vietnamese. If he puffs an imaginary cigarette, simulates drinking a soft drink or lays his palm open and says "kendy?" he is likewise Vietnamese. (I'm not speaking of children, cripples, or professional beggars, but only of your man-and-woman-in-the street.) But if he acts like he knows who he is and has some class about *being* who he is, he is Chinese.

The Vietnamese vision seems to be normal, but they don't seem able to *visualize*. I've watched a motorbike rider making 60 mph down a street that curves blindly into oncoming traffic; he makes the turn without slowing down a fraction and meets another bike-rider, doing 65, whose vision is also okay; but he didn't visualize anyone coming around that curve at the same speed as his own, either. The traffic speeds on around the two tangled bikes—one rider with his head nearly decapitated in the spokes; the other lying doubled up where he's been thrown—until a policeman or soldier strolls over, studies the damage for a few minutes and ambles to a telephone. After a while an ambulance comes and scrapes them up. The traffic moves on. If one of the riders survives, the first thing he'll do will be to get another bike and make the same curve at the same speed. I don't think the Vietnamese are fast learners.

There must be fifty thousand motorbikes racing down the Tran Hung-Dao at any hour between ten and ten. It is the only big city in the world without public transportation. There is a cop for every bike. And every cop watching for Americans riding in a taxi with a Vietnamese woman. That, like dancing in public, is a civil offense here.

It's easier now for a civilian to shop in the army commissary (where goodies are varied and prices are lower) than for soldiers. The Embassy people dislike having to wait in line behind a queue of GIs to get canned milk-shakes, colored Kleenex, Zippo lighters and chocolate macaroons vacuum-packed in Brooklyn. So the GIs are now barred from the Cholon PX.

There are still a lot of soldiers barring my view of the Johnny Cash record selection, however: the Thai, Filipino, Korean and Australian soldiers *still* get in. It makes a patriot like myself wonder, having dedicated six months of my life to seeing that Salem cigarettes get into the hands of the poor people of Saigon, whether I'm *really* appreciated back home.

Another disturbing aspect of life here is the reluctance of American GIs to salute me. My ID card very clearly states that my status is equivalent to that of a major, yet not one of those rifle-carrying bums stands up when I go into a mess hall! They just go on *eating*.

So I just say "At ease, men," and let them go on eating.

It was different in *my* time, I can tell *you*. When I was a private, at Fort Bragg and Camp Maxey, *we* jumped to attention when an officer entered the barracks. First thing you know they'll be billeting the Negroes with US. I thought you ought to know this.

Another thing you ought to know is that I've had it in this slobbovia, namely Saigon. It isn't a war-town, it's a boom-town. There's occasional firing on the periphery, I read in the papers, and at night the flareships light up the river to see what Charlie is doing. Nobody thinks about the war. What people think about is what they're going to invest in here. Because what American business is doing here (with Japanese, Korean, Republic of China, Filipino, Australian, Indian and French business) is to use the armies as a holding operation until a firm economic hold on Southeast Asia is obtained for Western money.

By "Western" money I mean Japanese, Indian, Chinese, Filipino, and Australian money, too. In short, I don't mean "Western," I mean "Free Enterprise" money. The "Free Enterprise" Grocery Store has it made here: there won't be any Dienbienphu. The hold that the French once had has now been extended, so that everybody has a piece.

The only ones who won't get any are the Vietnamese.

The *S. S. Moon of the Orient,* which I boarded in San Francisco on Nov. 14, turned out to be a water-borne nursing-home. I was the youngest passenger. The crew was of my own generation. Which partly explains why it took us seventy-two days to make the crossing. The crew wasn't altogether to blame. East of the West Hebrides we ran into a sixty-mile-an-hour headwind, which would have backed us up clear to South Senility, Utah, had it not been for a tailwind of equal velocity. The captain maneuvered his craft sidewise but we were still in peril of being smashed in two until I advised him to try being becalmed. To show him what I meant, I went down to my cabin and lay becalmed. When I got up the sun was out, the seas were running smooth, and the captain was still running the vessel from an astrology handbook bought in Walgreen's.

"Guess weatha cwear up, guess choppy weatha, guess wain cwear the weatha," was all I could get out of *that* one. The only thing the captain didn't seem to be guessing about were the birds that kept following us. He kept going around the deck telling tax-paying Americans, "That bird are arbatross." Who ever heard of an albatross with a thirty-foot wingspread and *webbed* wings? Fortunately, most of the passengers died en route.

South of the Lower Northerlies we ran out of sailcloth. By good luck I'd brought along an extra roll of waxed paper just in case we ran out of paper napkins. When six more died the waxed paper gave out. We let the arbatrosses have *them*.

Well, I *told* you they weren't albatrosses.

It wasn't the storm that did most of the passengers in. The majority of them died simply because they were that old when they came aboard.

Tokyo isn't a city—it's an explosion. It's the most alive city I've ever seen. New York is poky by comparison. Twelve million people living elbow to elbow; yet maintaining individuality. They move faster than anybody—yet there seems no undue haste. *Control*—the traffic is controlled, the economic explosion is controlled; and the lives of individuals *look* controlled—I haven't been hit by a single panhandler; nobody has yet offered to act as a guide or a tout or to introduce me to his virgin sister. The only beggar I saw was a tall man draped in the black of a Buddhist priest and tinkling a bell for alms. I peeked under his hood—it was an American!

No tipping, no kissing, no handshaking, no hauling, mauling, yanking or back-slapping. It's part of a very big thing about personal dignity here—sustained even in milling throngs.

An incidental benefit of the incredible crush on the Tokyo subway is that it immobilizes pickpockets. If he has his hands up when he gets in, he can't get them down to your wallet. If he has them down, he can't get them up. Passengers' pockets are thus automatically protected—but unnecessarily so: the Japanese don't steal. I mean that. They don't think in those terms. A Japanese bartender may shake you down outrageously for a drink; but he won't go after your poke directly.

At the racetrack they leave their binoculars beside their racing forms. That's part of the big thing about personal honor, I suspect. Also everyone is working. Twelve million people—and there's a labor *shortage!*

Personal cleanliness is also striking. If you buy so much as a two-bit cellophane-wrapped sandwich out of a machine, there is a small, moist napkin for your hands enclosed. Immaculate people. And as courteous as they are tidy. By seven in the morning streets of even the poor sections are spick-and-span. I took a tour of what a Japanese friend here terms "a slum." *He* don't know what a slum is.

The friend in the photo is Suji Terayama, a novelist and dramatist who, as far as I can figure it out, is a kind of Japanese Andy Warhol. This I gather, is because he has an underground theater. By "underground" I don't mean out of sight. It's a theater under physical construction now. Terayama must be big around here, because newspapermen take his picture when he shows up at fights and at the races. He hasn't been translated into English but probably will be. He's only thirty-three; the son of a farmer of Northern Japan who was killed in World War II.

The intensity of Japanese interest in writing, painting and the arts gives me the idea that Tokyo is going to be, in a time not too far away, what Paris was in the 1880s—the center of the arts for every country. It has all the feel of Paris now. It is so *new*, so *fast* and so *joyous*—an enjoyers' city.

The wonderful knack the Japanese have is for forever experimenting, trying to do things new ways—originating—and yet keeping their ancient forms. For example, the office building opposite my window here looks more like a gigantic tree than a business building. It has a central beam, like an eleven-storey oak with a dark-green cast; and the offices cling to its trunk like foliage.

Trees, water and rocks—these are the ancient forms in which the Japanese enclose new feeling. I saw *Antony and Cleopatra,* in Japanese, in a theater that made me feel I was watching the play in between great sea-walls. The play itself was good for the first three hours. But by the time Antony had died and been resurrected three times, I felt it was time to go. It may *still* be going on. It was too slow and obvious for my own taste.

The impression the Japanese often give, of being cold, is misleading. They are a passionate people but with a controlled passion. On the stage they get wildly demonstrative; but not on the street. Except, of course, when it's political, as in Shinjuku recently when the Shinjuku students —as well as workers—battled police for five hours trying to stop trains carrying American fuel through the area.

I've always thought I could make it as a standup comic, and that suspicion is now confirmed. I don't even have to stand up here. All I have to do is sit down in a snack bar with a sign in English outside—COFFEE & HOT DOG—and ask for coffee and a hot dog. The place breaks up. Apparently the "coffee" part isn't hilarious. It's the "hot dog" business. I've mentioned hot dogs to countermen and vendors in Chicago, but they don't have the sense of humor of the Japanese. Curiously, if I say "Hawta dog," all I get is a hot dog; and no laughs at all. Sometimes I don't say *anything* and they break up. Marvelous sense of humor.

A pretty twenty-two-year-old Japanese girl asked me, "You like to play *patinko* wid me?" I'd like to play *anything* wid her. *Particularly patinko*.

135

"*Pachinko* is a monologue of the lonely," Suji Terayama assured me. "The life here is outwardly joyous and full of amusements. But people are not amused. How sad their private lives are can be seen when young men stand for hours feeding small steel balls into a machine."

Yet it seems to take very little to get Japanese people laughing. They break up at a touch. For example, my telephone rings and a male voice informs me: "I spreak no Engrish. I spreak only Japanese"—laughter.

"I speak only English," I assured the voice, "I can't speak Japanese." This, it seems, is funny, too.

Voice: "Hord line one morment prease."

I hord line.

Second male voice: "This man spreak no Engrish. He speak onry Japanese."

"I can't speak Japanese. Only English."

This time they *both* break up.

Finally: "Srank you very much. Good-bye."

This happens several times a day. I'd like to get in on the joke, too.

Prostitution is illegal here. It was outlawed in 1957. Then what are those miniskirted lovelies doing smiling to me under a red lantern? If they're secretaries, they're working awfully late.

What the Japanese do with neon is to make a fairyland of this city at night: the signs don't pitch, like American ads, by hard-selling: *Buy!* They seduce your eyes in purple, chartreuse, violet, orange, chinese red, pale pale blue, silver and green—signs that move in squares, in circles, up, down and sidewise in an alphabet consisting of pictures rather than letters. English is the second language; but it's running a poor second. French is third, and not too far behind to catch up. The French seem to be better liked here than Americans. Well, they never blasted a Japanese city as a demonstration of military might, for one reason.

It would be one of the great ironies of history if, in return for the most deathly strike any people ever inflicted upon another, the East should return that explosion with a life-giving one: if the arts of the West should be drawn away from Paris, London and New York to the great cities of the Orient. After witnessing the condition of the arts in Chicago, one can only hope something like that is happening.

These people are nothing if not logical—especially if you're caught jay-walking in the middle of Tokyo traffic. These little cars keep at sixty, and they don't stop when there's no red light. It's *Jump, mother*—and mother jumps. So you see, that stuff about "Day of Infamy" is all wrong —they were just going that way, that's all.

I'll modify my observation about no kissing—mothers kiss their babies. I can't help wondering if in the privacy of their homes husbands kiss their wives—or do they keep bowing?

This bowing isn't just politeness. It's part of conversation: discussion is punctuated by bowing. The woman's deep bow to the man as she is introduced, and his short bow in return, indicate, I take it, that his station is higher than her own. Which is still how it is in Japan.

My two Japanese friends—Terayama and the twenty-two-year-old girl, Keiko—are modern young people whose ways and dress and interests are Western. Yet, after we had spent a day together Keiko told me, "Mr. Terayama aparigize because he cannot do Lady-First."

After a minute, I got it: I'd been opening doors for her to go first, helping her on with her coat, all the customary American deferences of the man to the woman. But a young Japanese man, like Terayama, doesn't even *think* of such deference—and the Japanese girl doesn't expect it. "Mr. Terayama must not aparigize because he is Japanese man."

It's perfectly natural for a man to hit his wife or daughter, Keiko believes, "if she deserve." But it is *never* all right for a woman to strike a man. Which accounts, in part, for the relative contentment of Japanese women, compared to the dissatisfied, irritable, unresponsive and boring American female. They have better taste, too.

"What is it that men find so rare and desirable in Japanese women?" Jacqueline Paul inquires in her illustrated opinion of modern Japanese life, *Japan Quest,* and answers herself: "I see it as the acceptance (real or apparent) of male dominance. Self-effacement in the interests of the man, a charming facade maintained by mannerisms which hide the true feelings, and proper behavior as prescribed by custom; these are the repertoire. If a woman is to earn approval, she must act in conformity with the preconceived role in which a man has placed her. In order to appear feminine to men (and to women as well) she must appear to accept things-as-they-are with a soft humility.

"The men love it, of course. And of course they get bored."

WHAT COUNTRY DO YOU
THINK YOU'RE IN?

IN the season of the elephant-mango, when motorbike riders wear rain-coats backwards, I lived in a hotel on an avenue once named *Rue Catinat*. That is now Tu-Do-Street. The year was 1969.

It was also that season when cricket-hunters come down Cong-Ly with bamboo-poles and glue-pots. And all cricket fighters hope for the rains that come on the summer monsoons. For crickets fight harder then.

I communicated with only three people in that hotel: a black GI living with a Vietnamese girl, who called himself Duke; Pham-Quynn, an eleven-year-old cricket-fancier; and a woman in a white *aodai* called Giang; for whom Pham served as a procurer. Giang was his mother.

Duke's girl complained of the prices of American whiskey and cigarettes on the black markets. So I changed his green money into piastres, through an Indian bookseller; changed the piastres into Military Payment Certificates with a Chinese leather-goods merchant; then bought whiskey and cigarettes, as well as soap and comic-books, for Duke at the PX. Where he got green money I didn't inquire. And how long he'd been awol I didn't conjecture.

Pham spoke to Duke and myself in GI English; to Duke's girl in Vietnamese; and used sign-language with his mother.

To eight a.m. motorbike riders down Tu-Do, Pasteur and Cong-Ly, red warning lights meant only to slow down to 40; yellow meant *GO!* And the green signaled the right of way to all riders to wheel up on the walks. Then an air of mischief, touched by desperation, began dividing Honda from Harley and trishaw from taxi. As if the mischievous headlines were inspiring them to out-gun, out-ride, out-risk and out-dare one another both ways down the Tran Hung-Dao:

REDS DECIMATED
REDS REPULSED

LT. JUMPS ON GRENADE
NVA WALKS INTO TRAP
NVA RALLIES TO CHIEU HOI
HOI CHANH LEADS GIS TO CACHE
PRESIDENT RAPS WHISKEY-DRINKING INTELLECTUALS
SEE ACCEPTANCE BY VANQUISHED VC

The same lieutenant leaped upon the same grenade every morning. Day after day the NVA walked into the same trap. The President rapped the same intellectuals drinking the same whiskey. Reds who weren't immediately decimated were instantly repulsed. The few who strangely survived rallied to the Open Arms-*Chieu Hoi* program—"rallying" here meaning that an NVA defector had led Americans to a cache of Russian-made arms, slaughtered eighteen of his former comrades to establish his loyalty to the Saigon Government; and then had jumped on a grenade to save democracy. While vanquished VC wandered aimlessly about looking for somebody to put them to work. Preferably in the Cholon PX.

Yet the mortars still came in and yet bike-riders flung *plastiques*. Gunship and fireship searched the skies and docks; while MP patrols cruised the darkened alleys.

Whenever I saw a motorbike upturned, its wheels spinning slowly and more slowly, above a rider whose face was now part of the pavement, and a policeman looking languidly down at the rider's splattered head, I realized that traffic accidents were part of the struggle to win the hearts and minds of men.

Giang wasn't trying to win hearts or minds. It was all she could do to hold onto her own. Though her features were Vietnamese, her expression was French. For her eyes, commonly languid among Vietnamese, were energetic. The openness of her glance, not unusual in women of Paris, was unique on Tu-Do. She was deaf and mute.

Once she was standing in the hotel entrance, toward evening, and made way for me as I entered. She flashed her wide white smile, then folded her hands against her cheek and closed her eyes, feigning sleep. I thought it was a good idea.

Later I had dinner, alone, on the riverboat restaurant *Phat Diem*. On a river with a view of a shore that looked, in the evening air, like the beginning of a contented country, I decided to invite Giang and Pham to have dinner with me here the following Sunday.

When I asked Pham, he ran, exhilarated, to inform his mother. She came to the door, in her white *aodai,* and nodded confirmation to me. She seemed pleased.

I told Duke that I had invited Giang and Pham to the *Phat Diem.*

"Numba Ten," Duke's girl put in.

"What's the matter with *her*?" I asked Duke.

"She says that, in this country, it's smart not to get involved."

"What kind of country does she think she's in anyhow?" I asked Duke.

When I rapped Giang's door the following Sunday, Pham opened it—dressed less for an afternoon on a riverboat than for an alley. He was barefoot, uncombed, was holding a peanut butter jar, and had a GI toothbrush hanging around his neck. I'd expected Giang to have him ready and to be ready herself. I didn't want to be on the Saigon River after dark.

Pham indicated that his mother was home; but she didn't appear. And instead of getting ready, Pham insisted on showing me the stupid cricket, that he called Skippy, in the peanut butter jar. A few grains of rice and the remains of a spider lay on the jar's bottom. Feeling both disappointed and annoyed with Giang, I got up to go; but Pham took my hand.

"Tau Chit Choot," he told me, and led me down to the street: we were going to a cricket fight.

Every trade had its own tune in Saigon, and each tune its own pitch. The fellow wheeling along the curb, rattling a chain as he cycled, was asking for knives to grind or scissors to sharpen. The little man, afoot with a big shears as if preparing to cut his way through the throng, had nougats ready for cutting if only you'd buy. The ten-year-old boy blowing piercingly on a tin whistle was whistling for bike or motorbike tires on which to put patches for whatever you'd pay. The woman getting a chirping cry out of coca-cola tops strung on a wire, was offering to massage me, on the street, for fifty piastres.

The boy beating a pair of strung balls with a pair of drumsticks, in a three-step beat, was an advance-man, announcing the coming of steamed rice; in a Chinese soup-wagon hauled by his mother. If the beat was slower it wasn't steamed rice. It was the woman who'd dye your trousers while you waited.

While whistles kept shrilling, sirens kept warning, horns kept squawking, ducks kept quacking, and toy-tanks kept zapping chopchop eaters at their chopstick bowls, a girl with a basket on her head came crying, among charcoal fires and children squatting to pee, *"Ay vit lon! Ay vit lon!"* like a querulous bird.

Down an areaway so narrow only one could pass, we came into a shadowed and gutted shack where a couple dozen men and boys, safe from the National Police, were crowding around a battered and rusted washtub.

The washtub was the ring. A stout Vietnamese was the matchmaker. He held all bets and took a percentage off the winner. He was the Maurice Stans of the cricket-fighting world.

How long ago Charcoal Crickets and Fire Crickets plunged Southeast Asia into a holy *cicada,* or war of mutual cricket-extermination—literally biting off one another's antennae to spite their stupid faces, is lost in the mists of cricket-history.

All we know for certain is that the Charcoal bug, being black, cannot bear the presence of the Fire Cricket; who is just as much of a bug because he can't *endure* the sight of the darker insect.

Since neither one has eyes, how does either distinguish between friend and foe? We are trapped here in an ecological mystery to which no satisfactory solution has been offered either by science or Wm. F. Buckley, Jr. (whose own blind charges have afforded so much diversion to TV viewers).

Certain arthropodists contend that colors have odors: that the smell of black infuriates the Fire Cricket while the Charcoal Cricket sees red when he smells yellow. But this is mere circumvention. For, if so, wouldn't the Charcoal Cricket keep beating out his brains against chartreuse houses? And what would keep Fire Crickets from attacking Cadillacs? The fact is that both species are noseless as well as eyeless. Back to the old drawingboard, Professor.

Because it's territorial instinct—let me make this perfectly clear—which arouses both species to fight to the death at the touch of antennae. This touch being provided—I'm sure you've already guessed—by a human being whose territorial instinct is aroused by the hand of another human on his wallet.

But if the stupid bugs didn't go about dressed in contrasting trunks, like opponents on the Friday Night Fights, there wouldn't be any fights-to-the-death. For the simple reason that nobody would be able to tell whose boy won and whose lost.

Pham brushed the antennae of his fighter carefully, with his GI toothbrush, until it stood up on its hind legs, tense for battle. When his antennae touched that of the Fire Cricket opposing him, the battle was joined.

Skippy looked pretty good in there at first. He got a strong hold of the Fire Cricket and spun him onto his back with all six firelegs kicking helplessly. Pham cheered. But instead of finishing his opponent off, Skippy just stood waving at the crowd. That bug purely *loved* applause.

The Fire Cricket's owner called time out. He tied a thread to the yellow cricket's leg and spun the bug around his head. Whether this was to restore the insect's sense or drive him even crazier I still have no idea.

Yet it worked. As soon as the yellow cricket was back on his legs, he jumped across the ring, the thread still dangling, and bit off Skippy's head. Skippy stood one moment, still acknowledging applause. Then his body followed his severed head. The Fire Cricket was lifted up, the black thread still dangling, put back in the winner's jar and fed a fresh spider.

Pham had put a lot of work into feeding and brushing and training that stupid bug, and he looked solemn as we passed among copper-gong beaters, shaven-head bonzes bearing umbrellas; and old women whose mouths were bloody with betel, spitting as they came.

Children came hauling between donkey-cart shafts; children being many and donkeys few.

Then a chopper, flying much too low, beat down all sound and rumor of sound: for a moment after it passed silence held all the choking air.

Then the cry "*Ay vit lon!*" broke through again and all the market's voices hurried back as if invited by that cry. What *was* that girl selling?

Half a dozen of Giang's deaf-mute colleagues were waiting for her in front of the hotel.

One, who looked no older than fifteen, handed Pham a folded note and nodded toward me. Pham handed it to me and I put it in my pocket; still folded.

Duke was waiting for me at my door, which surprised me. He didn't speak until I'd offered him a drink.

"Did you hear the blast?" he asked me at last.

"Which one?"

"On the river. They blew up the *Phat Diem.*"

I reached for the note as if feeling, suddenly, that whatever it was, I needed it. It was written with painstaking effort:

> I sorry. I afraid go by Phat Diem
> Be not mad please.
>
> > Giang

I handed it to Duke, who grinned when he read it; inspected the blank side then handed it back. Yet he said nothing.

"Some coincident," was all I could think to say.

"What coincident?" Duke wanted to know. "The woman was trying to tell you something but you were too dumb to get it, that's all. What did you want her to do? Hand you a plan of the operation? Put you on her grapevine?''

"She's not politically involved," I protested.

"For God's *sake*," Duke became impatient, "she's *Vietnamese*, isn't she? How can she *not* be involved?" Then added after a minute, "It was just lucky for you she didn't have something against you, that was all."

"What if she had?"

"Why, she would have kept the date, then ducked with the boy, that's all. What country do you think *you're* in, buddy?"

POLICE AND MAMA-SANS GET IT ALL

THE street called Huong-Dieu slants through a slum pervaded by the yellowish scents of raw fish, urine, and charcoal fires. You push your way through throngs of yam-and-mango vendors, Vietnamese veterans still wearing their field uniforms the better to beg, women between the shafts of donkey-carts, and small girls who tug your sleeve but speak not a word; from one sunstriped alley to the next until you reach 22 Huong-Dieu.

Up a stairwell so worn its wood looked gnawed, I passed into a narrow passage, made narrower by heavy red draperies, and into a room where women sat or lay upon a dozen beds. Some wore slacks, some miniskirts and some were in their slips. Above, several candles burned in Buddhist altars. Only one had a Christ impaled above her. I favored Jesus as being the lesser fire hazard. I was in a camp of refugee whores.

An upended container, marked US ARMY in rusting white paint, held water for both washing and drinking. Yet the room was so spacious that 22 Huong-Dieu, I surmised, must once have been a luxurious French hotel; there were still gas fixtures from that long-gone time. Now the water was off and lights were out and all the carefree times were done.

"Where Xuong?" I asked one of the women.

"What numba?"

I'd first spoken to Xuong in the Central Market. I'd been shopping for oranges. Not the little green-skinned lumps that pass for oranges in Saigon—I wanted those big yellow California Sunkist dandies imported from the nearest American commissary.

A foreigner pays half a dollar each for them; a Vietnamese gets them for a quarter. Moreover, when a foreigner buys six, he winds up with five. These market women are really deft.

I asked Xuong to buy a dozen for me and gave her the piastres. When she returned with oranges *and* the change, I was impressed; it was the first time I'd seen a Vietnamese return change to a foreigner. I gave three oranges to her eight-year-old boy to show my appreciation.

"O, me wuv *you* too *much*," she thanked me, and added, indicating the boy as we walked out of the market, "him Hiep." I would have walked her further but she seemed embarrassed.

"Me Xuong," she told me, "2 Huong-Dieu," and walked away.

When I ran out of oranges I went to find her. Had she told me her number instead of her name she could have saved me a troubled search. In a troubled season.

"What numba?"

Then Hiep jumped out of some cranny, put his arms about me and his head against my chest, and bummed me for a cigarette. He wouldn't lead me to his mother until I'd given him a light. Then he pocketed the matches.

Xuong was sitting cross-legged on Bed 16 with neither a Christ nor a Buddha above her. Her nose had no bridge and her right cheek bore a long slant scar that must once have been livid but had long since turned ash-grey.

"Numba-One Mama-san co*dock*," she explained instead of saying hello; touching a safety-razor blade to her temple with a slanting motion to show me how Numba-One Mama had co*docked* her. "O, me wuv *you* too *much*," she remembered; and put the thin blade down. Two middle-teeth of her uppers were gold. Her skin was unblemished nonetheless.

The girl on the next bed put on shades, though the light was dim, and turned up the volume of her transistor as though to raise a sound-curtain between the beds. Some of the beds had drawstring curtains. One woman took her laundry off the curtains and drew the strings. The Mama-san, a woman in her seventies, no bigger than a child, was led in by Hiep.

"Short-tam?" the old woman wanted to know. "Long-tam? Numba One gel."

The girl on the next bed took off her shades, turned down the volume and came out flat against Short Time: "Short tam didi fast. Long tam Numba One." A girl lying on her back in a far corner agreed and added, indifferently, "Me wuv you too much too." Then Mama came out, independent of the opinions of anyone else, for Long Tam.

The only dissenter was Hiep, who kept pulling the bed's drawstrings and trying to push his mother onto the bed. He was plainly afraid that unless it was Short Time, it might be no time at all. A bird in the hand was Hiep's thinking.

A quorum having finally been attained, the girl on the next bed put her shades back on and turned up the volume while Xuong began to get dressed for the street. She had a slight limp, yet she never went out on the street without looking neat.

Mama-san took me aside to tell me her sorrows. She had been, when young, she assured me in a mixture of French and GI English, a dancer in Paris. I gave her the benefit of the doubt. Perhaps she *had* danced a step or two down the Boulevard Sebastapol *circa* 1917. Up from some Cambodian hamlet to the lights of Montmartre, then down to the alleys of Saigon. Where now she raced curfew, corner to corner, night after night, upstairs and down on her seventy-year-old legs.

Xuong came out of the curtains wearing a white blouse and a dark pleated skirt. But Hiep clung to her and wouldn't let her leave him.

"Give cigarette," Xuong explained.

"Eight years old and pimping your mother," I congratulated the child, "here, son, take the whole pack."

On the street I gave Xuong cab fare to my hotel. I walked in the opposite direction to be certain I wasn't being checked by one of the White Mice. Then took another cab to the hotel.

What a lovely city this once must have been, I reflected, driving north on the Rue Pasteur, when it was still flowered and wooded. Now its gardens are sandbags and barbed wire. If you want a flower you can buy an artifical one in any market.

Xuong left her ID card at the hotel desk under the eyes of four bell-boys. Before the night-chameleons had fled the walls, one of them would be rapping my door for 500 piastres for entertaining a guest. But there wouldn't be a tip in it for him. I always knew they'd like me in Saigon.

"*Beaucoup* piastres," was Xuong's first reaction to my second-class yet air-conditioned nest. "How much for *all*?"

"36,000 P. a month."

Xuong rolled her eyes at a sum so fantastic. "Hundred P. a day for me and Hiep," she filled me in on what it cost her and her son to survive. Her rent comes out of her own half of her fees. The other half, she assured me, is divided between the Mama-san from the Rue Sebastopol and the First District Police.

Police—the White Mice—and mama-sans alike are terribly hard on these village women. Country girls sometimes have a tough and sinewy pride; so co*docking* them becomes more or less routine. If a mama-san's razor doesn't subdue one, the First District will be happy to take her in hand. After living in darkness a month, on rice cooked in muddy water, never knowing at what moment she's going to be slapped silly again, then being turned back to mama with her head shaven, the girl may wish she'd settled with mama out of court.

Mama doesn't feel she's asking too much of the girl—just to hold up five fingers or 10, meaning 500 piastres for short time or 1000 for long.

Each holds up her fingers in the end: police and mama-sans get it all.

Around the Hotel Caravelle and the Continental Palace, women are available who are never co*docked*. Who never hold up five fingers or 10, and are never shaven by police. These are city women from Vung Tau, Dalat, Danang, Saigon and Hué. Generally, they're better looking than the refugee women, and always better dressed. Most are Catholic and have had some French schooling. The village women are commonly Buddhists and speak no French at all.

These restaurant courtesans, more mistresses than whores, don't sleep with a man because he pays for a dinner. They pick and choose and take no chances on the common soldier. Most dress in the traditional *aodai*, and are, essentially, conservative women. They are for men with bank accounts in New Delhi, Cincinnati, Athens, Stockholm, Hamburg, Buenos Aires, Paris, and Manila.

Some of them must marry a bank account in Cincinnati: anything to get out of Saigon.

Xuong came out of the bathroom holding a bar of soap.

"How much?"

"Fifty P."

"Fifty for you, fifteen for me," she informed me smugly, and returned to experimenting with hot and cold running water. Then gave a yelp of surprise and came out drying her neck, looking both pleased and rueful. She'd gotten an unexpected sprinkling from the shower. Xuong was a fast learner; even if she was a little heavy around the hips.

The refrigerator was a lesser mystery; some of its contents curiosities. "What name?" she'd want to know, holding up a can or jar. I had to open instant coffee, soluble chocolate, powdered orange juice, and let her taste them all before she could be satisfied. Now she had a tea-bag in her hand. "What name?" When I brought a cup of hot water, she tore open the bag and poured the leaves into the water. She had the right combination anyhow.

Then she discovered a manicure scissors. She pushed me back on the bed, pulled off my socks, and I had to submit to a toenail paring. She enjoyed the work so I let her go on, meanwhile watching a bug on the wall above her head. He'd been living in the room before I'd moved in, and my thinking had been that if he didn't bite me, I wouldn't bite him. Live and let live was how I'd looked at it. Because if he were the kind of bug I suspected he was, he was The King. Now watching Xuong working on my big toe, he began applauding with his feelers. The rascal was growing bold.

Xuong transferred her scissors to her other hand, smacked the brute with her palm, and went back to paring. Five gets you ten that the stain The King left on that wall remains there to this day.

Xuong was older than most of Saigon's refugee whores. For her own refugee time had begun when her father had been killed fighting against the French, or fighting for the French; or for refusing to fight anybody; it all depended on who Xuong was talking to.

Some of these women have been made homeless by B-52s and some by bulldozers. Some by search-and-destroy, and others by search-and-cordon. Some fled the NLF. Some the Americans. Some because a father said a plague on both your houses; or because he rowed down a river nobody had told him was no longer his own. Some are lost because a pilot had to lighten a bombload; others for revealing a cache of rice. Some because a brother informed to the NLF; others because someone informed to the Americans. And some by the defoliant called Blue Bamboo.

Some by knives and some by mines; some by fire and some by water. One says her husband would not have been killed had he not been bareheaded in the paddy. The war has been going on so long, the woman has sold her grief to so many, it is no matter now whether she herself did the informing or was informed upon. Nor upon whose side her father died while being pacified. All she knows is that her name was once Xuong-thi-Nhan; and that it is now Number 16. It all comes under the general heading of winning hearts and minds.

Xuong was a big girl and a resolute one. My fingernails had to be manicured, too. I tried to get free while she was shining my bedroom slippers and almost made it. But she put the slippers down and began to massage me.

Later she showed me needle-marks, on her arms, with pride. She wanted me to know that she took anti-VD shots every week. She was reassuring me. Then she splashed about in the tub like a great baby. I fell asleep hoping she wouldn't drown.

In the middle of the night, I wakened to find the lights still on, the radio going, and something still transpiring in the bathtub. I rolled out of bed.

Xuong, naked in the tub, was stomping the hell out of every shirt, pair of socks, shorts, and tops I owned, regardless of fabric, fast colors, or condition of cleanliness. She'd found it unthinkable to let all that lovely bathwater down the drain without putting it to some use first. Her hips may have been a bit heavy; but she made up for that in frugality.

Personally, I felt it was a little early in the day to be getting out a laundry. Yet, by the way her big breasts bounced as she stomped, it was plain she was having a ball. So I turned off the radio and went back to bed. When I woke in the morning, Xuong was gone and so were most of my clothes. She'd left me one shirt, one pair of pants, and my shoes.

I didn't want company that evening. I got a knock all the same. Xuong, with laundry ironed and my pants pressed. I went for my wallet.

She looked hurt. "No money," she reproved me. And kicked off her shoes. I would have preferred paying her. I didn't think I could stand another toenail paring this soon.

A lot of good it did me. So what do you know; instead of a Numba One Gel, what I had on my hands was a pedicurist, laundress, masseuse, bodyguard, nurse, cook, seamstress, market-woman, vermin-exterminator, economist, pants-presser, shoe-shiner, and bed-warmer. At the least a mistress; at the most a wife. I didn't have a shirt-button missing. And clean underwear has its own appeal. I just wasn't prepared to set up housekeeping.

"I find Numba One hou' for you," she seemed to read my mind, "you come see."

Now she was in real estate.

So we went down a walk so narrow that no light had ever fallen across its walls, into a passage littered with droppings of children and dogs, down a hall, then up a ladder to a floor that sagged beneath my feet. Into a room about 8 x 10 containing an iron cot bearing a mattress stained with rust or blood. We were home.

Xuong switched on a floor fan and looked at me as much as to say, "Didn't I tell you it would be great?" Well, we had electric power at least.

I just sat on that beat-up bedspring and boggled; this was how people actually lived in the world, born into rooms like this: eat, sleep, pray, make love, and die in such kennels. Whole lifetimes. The floor fan creaked and skreaked. It didn't like the place any more than I did.

"Numba One!" Xuong assured me.

"Numba Ten!" I assured her.

"Numba Ten for you, Numba One for me," she reminded me.

When she knocked the following evening, I didn't answer the door. She knew I was there all the same.

"*You* Numba Ten!" she denounced me from the other side of the door.

A chameleon on the wall fled for cover.

The night before I moved, Xuong caught me in. My bags were packed and my escape-route plain. I let her stay. She bathed but didn't splash about. And wouldn't turn out the lights until I'd turned off the ceiling fan.

"Make bad wind," she explained her superstition: death comes on a night-wind.

ILL WIND STRIKES SOLDIER

*A soldier slept soundly in his home at Trinh Minh The Street,
but alarmed his wife when she heard him uttering indistinct
cries. She sped him to a hospital but he died upon arrival.
There was speculation that the soldier had died of an ill wind.*
—Vietnam Guardian

We had breakfast in a Chinese noodle cafe. When she rose, I glanced up. Then let her go. She didn't turn and look back at the door. She didn't look back from the street. She didn't look back at all.

Those shots she took ought to help one of us, I reflected glumly.

I'll say this much for Xuong: she fought with all she had to get out of a whore's bed and back into a wife's.

POOR GIRLS OF KOWLOON

THOUGH the Macao Palace, the big gambling casino afloat in the harbor, shines blazing-bright all night, the streets of the hot little enclave behind it are dimly lit. If history hasn't quite brought Macao to a dead-still halt, it has certainly made it hard to find one's way around after dark.

The gambling isn't for Americans unless one is a slot-machine bug. At both the Macao Palace and the Estoril, the big game is *dai-sui*: The Big and the Small. There is also chemin-de-fer, roulette, pakapoo, boule and black-jack.

I don't play other people's games and I wouldn't be caught dead yanking the lever of a slot machine. But there was no poker. And the crap table was out of action. So, through streets so humid the banyan trees kept sweating, I wandered into a carnival grounds. There wasn't any carnival but some fools were standing around betting on fighting crickets. I lost twenty-five patacas. I *told* you not to play other people's games.

The first Christians to gain a foothold for Jesus in Asia were Portuguese Jesuits, and theirs was a Portuguese Christ. Though Lisbon had to kneel to the Spanish throne, the missionaries of Macao refused to recognize the domination of Spain and sustained their defiance for sixty years. When Portugal then regained her independence, Lisbon rewarded the bishopric of Macao by endowing the city with the title: City of the Name of God, There is None More Loyal.

The Portuguese had a good thing in the name of God. Trade between China and Japan having been forbidden by the Ming emperors, Portuguese sea-captains carried Chinese silk to Japan and Japanese silver, in payment, back to China. The carrying charge covered more than expenses.

And while the captains cut themselves a bit of silk for purses to hold their silver, Portuguese bishops covered the action by bearing Jesus, without favoritism, to mandarin and Samurai alike. Macao's Church of St. Paul, whose magnificence can be seen even in its ruins, was built by Japanese Christians and dedicated to The Mother of God.

151

For four hundred years, in this Mediterranean nest of the South China Sea, Chinese and Portuguese handled one another so well that both races subsisted comfortably, without racial friction, on tourism, fishing, gambling, manufacturing incense, firecrackers, and the underground traffic in gold. So skillful were the Portuguese in the uses of neutralism that the enclave wasn't occupied by the Japanese during World War II.

Graveyard memorials testify to a curious emigration. In the mid-nineteenth century, when the overwhelming tide of western emigration was *to* the West, Westerners came to Macao against that tide. George Chinnery, a minor master and the best British painter ever to live in China, came to Macao because it was the farthest port, away from his wife, of which he'd ever heard. But after he'd settled in she showed up, bag and baggage, all the same. He finally rid himself of her by hiding out in Canton.

The smell of Macao is that of saltfish. The streets of Macao are Portugal. But when a street runs down to the sea, it becomes Chinese. The sea is Chinese. The rain is Chinese rain. The sea-haze that makes rain and mountains one is a Chinese haze. The Chinese here never became a Mediterranean folk. But the Mediterraneans, and Westerners too, British, Irish, Americans, Middle-Europeans, all, eventually, went bamboo.

The success of the Jews in maintaining their unity, as a people, in Russia and Poland and France, didn't succeed in China. There are the remains of synagogues in China; and ancestral memories of Judaism, too. There are even Chinese who claim Jewish descent. But in the end the Jews, too, went bamboo.

Macao offered sanctuary to Westerners who not only felt that the world was moving too fast, but in the wrong direction. Now here it's come almost to a stop; but is no longer a sanctuary. When Big Brother Mao's loudspeakers began thundering Newspeak and Nothink in 1966, the enclave had to capitulate to its dehumanization. Looters and arsonists received rewards; those who tried to preserve order were punished. Political prisoners, bound hand and foot, were handed over to their deaths. The Portuguese flag is still permitted to fly over the enclave. But Big Brother owns all the poles.

Maoist movie houses make most of their money off American westerns. After the good guys beat the bad guys, the Chairman harangues the audience from the screen and the soundtrack bursts into *Anchors Aweigh*. The audience has the impression that the Chairman wrote the song.

POOR GIRLS of Kowloon sometimes prefer to earn their livings in ballrooms rather than in sweatbaths or bars. If such choice seems narrow, it can be even a tighter squeeze than that. Because working in a sweatbath requires an apprenticeship as a masseuse; and working in a ballroom requires some command of English. But in a bar all she has to be able to do is say yes.

On a night when mist made the lamps of Nathan Road burn amber, a cab-driver wheeled me to The Oriental Ballroom. I'd missed the 5 till 9 tea dance; but was in time for the 9-1 a.m. night dance. The inside of the program listed, in both Chinese and English, the names of my hostesses:

PLEASE INDICATE IN FRONT
OF THE LADY'S NAME
WHOM YOU WANTED TO INVITE
IN THE NAME LIST.

PLEASE NOTE:
Hostess leaving the ballroom for private party bookings. Will be charge double price as per our regulations.
Dance-ticket charges: $5.50 including tax (time limit for each ticket 5-15 minutes).
Cover charge for visiting lady partners $5.00.

The latter charge discourages patrons trying to beat the house by bringing a girlfriend of their own.

Over a hundred young Chinese women make their livings at The Oriental. Some of their names are adoptive, some use their own: Tammy Ho, Cherry, Pek Yuck, See see, Poi poi, Veiginia Lee, Dominique, Susarna Wong, Wong Man, Wong Way, Sar sar and, simply, Daisy. Tea and Coca-Cola are the only drinks served. Didn't I tell you The Oriental is a high-class hall?

A portly young Chinese man escorted me to a table and inquired, politely, whether I preferred an English-speaking friend. I thought that might work out better than one who'd have to depend upon my Mandarin. Then I had a bad moment in which I was sure I'd let myself in for an evening with some kukefied ruin whose best days were long gone. When I looked up and saw her my bad moment was done. I lost no time getting to my feet.

Her name was Maria Chan. A slender girl, of perhaps twenty-four, with a heart-shaped face and quiet air. We ordered tea. I wanted to make a good impression so I asked if she would have dinner with me.

"You buy me out, we go where you want," she assured me, "but I have dinner already."

It cost a hundred and fifty Hongkong dollars to buy Miss Chan out —about twenty-five dollars American. Which wasn't too high considering where I had it in mind to go.

"Hundred-fifty is just for time," she dispensed with *that* fantasy. So we took a cab to Victoria Peak and drank orange juice in an English garden. A wind kept blowing a mist off the harbor. Miss Chan was as reserved as she was beautiful.

She was Cantonese—"*Pure* Cantonese," as she put it—and her right name was Mong-tse. My thinking was to find some way to take her out without buying her out.

"I am not free," she explained simply, "Mr. Ding makes my arrangements."

"Who is Mr. Ding?"

"My Leader."

"The man who introduced us?"

She nodded: "Every Leader has twelve girls. When a girl wants a day off she must ask her Leader. I have two days a month free, but I don't go out. I sleep, I rest. The work is hard to do every night. Appearance takes much time. I begin to make my appearance three hours before I go to the ballroom. I stay until one A.M. In a week I will receive half of the money you pay Mr. Ding. Leaders are very smart. If you say you are sick and go out somewhere, he find out. Leader have spies."

Maria had had a couple years of high school, but had had to drop out because she is the oldest of nine children. She has four younger brothers. Brothers count more than sisters in Kowloon. The boy has to be given the opportunity of education even though the older sister has to go on the streets.

When the hour grew late we took a cab down the peak.

"Where do you live" Miss Chan asked me.

I told her the address of the guest-house in which I was staying and added, to give her a lead, "It's a *very* small room. Two people could just about fit in it."

She smiled. My fears of being overcrowded were groundless. When the cab pulled up to my door she patted my shoulder. "You're a nice fellow," Miss Chan assured me; and gave me her cheek to kiss.

I kissed it.

Goodnight, Maria Chan.

"Hongkong," according to *Pravda,* is "an evil-smelling malignant growth on the body of China where millions of Chinese are exploited and oppressed by brutal colonial masters.''

On the contrary, it is the most tolerant of territories and the least marked by colonialism. Low taxes, no controls, fast profits and free enterprise offer more opportunities here to refugees than any other sanctuary on earth. The place is like some gigantic grocery where anyone who can get his hands on a shelf of goods—noodles, leather, jade, jewels, silk, coconuts, hardware, watches, furs, carpets, silver or gold —is in business for himself. I don't know how this dumping-ground for twentieth-century techniques makes it by nineteenth-century economics; yet it flourishes. And nobody worries just because it would take no more than a telephone call from Peking to cut it off from the Western world.

Nine-tenths of the colony must, at any rate, be handed back to China in 1997, when the British lease on the New Territories expires. Meanwhile printers circulate a reversible double-faced rotogravure job with Chairman Mao's face on one side and that of General Chiang on the other. This can be put in a store window on the Communist Liberation Day, October 1; then reversed, nine days later, on the Nationalists' Day. Some of these photographs bear the legend: *Made in Japan.*

So you can buy *Playboy* or *China Reconstructs* at the same newsstand and *Kung Hai Fat Choy! (Happy New Year and May You Make a Fortune!)* is the cry.

The *Oriental Rio* is a gigantic Motor-vessel, a sister-ship of the *Oriental Jade,* and has been in the service of the Republic of China nineteen years. She is bearing some hundred elderly Americans—in addition to her cargo—back to The Big PX.

Most of the Americans are from Southern California and have been riding this monster for three months. Mr. K.C. Tung, the ship's single owner, sold world-tours to these Californians for a bargain price of three thousand dollars each.

It turned out to be no bargain. But then it's been no bargain for Mr. Tung either. The air conditioning went out somewhere on the equator, the plumbing is unreliable and the Americans are bored to exhaustion.

For their boredom, however, Mr. Tung can hardly be blamed. If they hadn't been bored to exhaustion by Southern California, they wouldn't have boarded the *Rio.* It's their own lives that have left them so empty. The peak of dinner conversation is hit when one woman observes that the butterballs have a prettier design than the butterballs served in Mombasa; and everyone inspects the butterballs to verify this observation.

When the purser informed me that we'd be putting into Kaohsiung for two weeks, for refitting, it occurred to me two weeks was hardly long enough, considering the shape most of the passengers were in. As it turns out, however, it's the ship which is to be refitted.

If you happen not to have heard of Kaohsiung, consider that nobody in Kaohsiung has heard of Gary, Indiana. Which, incidentally, Kaohsiung resembles: a country kind of town under a pall of industrial smoke; set down between the sea and ancestral hills. Where the traffic moves mostly on bicycles, and taxies keep up an all-day honking—the point of which is not so much to warn off bicycles, but to call attention to the drivers.

The lobbies of air-conditioned hotels break up rows of low, wooden, hundred-year-old tenements. Beggar-women beseige tourists. Department stores are thronging with customers and are loaded with goods. The cost of a haircut, a basket of fruit or a loaf of bread is almost too small to believe. But private cars and telephones are out of the reach of all but a few.

Mr. K.C. Tung is one of the very few. He was a shipyard worker here when General Chiang retreated from the mainland. Now he owns the *Oriental Rio* and eighty-nine other cargo-liners. He came aboard in Kowloon and spoke to the passengers; but didn't identify himself. I'm sorry I didn't know to whom I was talking. I would have asked him for one of his smaller ships. He would have had to give me one or lose face.

People, like cats, assume their owners' sense of values. When you hit a port where the bellboy hurries ahead to open a door for you, then stands aside to let you pass; where the desk clerk inquires, in the same tone as when he asks if you want air conditioning, whether you also want a girl; and where your lady-barber cleans your ears, you're in an Accommodation Nation. Taiwan is an Accommodation Nation and there can be such a thing as just too *much* accommodation. I don't mind having a lady clean my ears but I'd rather open doors for myself. The procurers of Kaohsiung surpass those of Saigon in persistency.

Taiwanese are proud of being able to decline U.S. aid. The country is making it on its own. Buildings, protected by bamboo scaffoldings, are going up everywhere. But wages are low and prospects unpromising for young people. Everybody wants to go to Hongkong.

Like the intellectuals of Hongkong, those of Taiwan are Chinese nationalists. Yet few are Nationalists. Severed from their cultural heritage by Big Brother, they find their protector to be Big Brother's brother. Imperilled by the dehumanization of the mainland, they understand now how, when the pendulum of revolution swings back, it is the artists and intellectuals who are the first to be cut down.

An American poet can have it both ways: he can be resolutely against the establishment, earn its awards and remain unafraid of travelling abroad. The artist of Taiwan can't have it either way. Because he has fled from the mainland doesn't mean he has found freedom. Both regimes are tyrannies. In neither can he survive if he expresses himself individualistically.

"All we have is Chiang," a thirty-two-year-old editor assured me ruefully, meaning that Chiang allows him to survive where Mao would not. He came to Taipei "as a little soldier"—as he puts it—fifteen years ago. His family, on the mainland, now believes him to be dead and he intends to let them think so. If he corresponded with them he'd endanger them. And it would be harder on his mother to know he was alive, and to be unable to see him, then to let her resign herself to his death.

No wonder he sounds rueful.

The weather alone sufficed to make one rueful. The morning I boarded the Kaohsiung-Keelung bus it began to rain. It rained the whole ten-hour ride, and was still raining when, the next morning, I looked out of my window of the Hotel Mandarin in Taipei.

The hotel lobby was crowded with passengers waiting for their water-borne nursing-home to take them to Yokohama. There was nothing to do but hit the streets of Taipei; rain or no rain.

What do you do on a rainy morning in a big city that has no burlesque houses and all the movies are in an alien tongue? You find a sweatbath-massage parlor and investigate the city's subculture, of course. Any itinerant journalist can tell you *that*.

The most interesting distinction between the Asian and the American sweatbath, I had perceived in Saigon, is that the masseurs of the Orient are masseuses. And that there is a world of difference, not only between sweatbaths, but between masseuses.

If the price is cheap and the bath-floor is dirty and there is no steam, it's run by Vietnamese. If the bath is immaculate, the steam is steaming and the price is higher, the owner is Japanese. If the masseuse comes in barebreasted, she's not Japanese. If she gives you a few languid caresses, asks "You like *spesal*?" it's a Vietnamese brother, not a bath. But if she stretches you out *prone*, wraps a towel around your middle, and goes to *work*, she's either Japanese or has a Japanese boss. The Japanese don't confuse their enterprises. If you're looking for a whore, go to a whorehouse; if you're looking for a sweatbath and massage, that's what you pay for and that's *all* you get.

Oriental sweatbaths don't advertise "Chinese attendants" or "Vietnamese hostesses." The billing always claims that the masseuses are Japanese or French. Yet I never met a French masseuse. Speaking literally, of course.

"Taipei's reputation among bachelors rests primarily on Peitou," the guidebook informed me, "a hot-springs resort just twenty minutes by cab from the city. A legacy of the Japanese, who ruled Taiwan until 1945, Peitou provides what are perhaps the most complete bathing facilities in the East. The difference between Peitou and similar places in Japan is that at Peitou the girl gets into the sulphur bath with you."

"*Peitou!*" I instructed the cab-driver in front of the Hotel Mandarin.

Attention Please—a polite warning, in English, was hung above the sauna room, at the entrance to the pool—*We cannot accept those who tattooed to take a sauna bath. We propose the man tattooed to take the private room of Turkish bath.*

That's one way of avoiding trouble with American seamen, I surmised.

The sauna was Japanese: all bamboo panelling, tile and dry heat. Two middle-aged Chinese men, sitting crosslegged, were reading newspapers. I returned to my locker and brought back *Portnoy's Complaint*. (Any Portnoy in a storm!) It struck me as a sort of pornographied rehash of Bruce Jay Friedman's *Stern*. When I'd gotten up a sweat I jumped into the hot pool, then the cold. Then wandered around, in a kimono, until I found a massage table.

The masseuse, wearing a pair of white briefs and a bra, was a gentle, even shy-appearing woman in her early thirties. I lay on my stomach while she massaged my torso. When she got up on the table, straddling me the better to work on my rib cage, I didn't mind. After squirrel-eyeing her right thigh awhile I let my right arm swing back and took a gentle hold of it; just to see what her reaction would be.

"No," she told me quietly. I let go.

With my face pressed into a small pillow, I had time to think things over. My thinking was that I'd taken hold of the wrong thigh. I tried the left one.

The pillow came out from under my face in a gentle movement, my face went softly down into a cushioned declevity in the table, a powerful hand rested on the nape of my neck. I removed my hand from the thigh.

I suffered no discomfort. But the point had been made plain. When she'd finished massaging my legs she stood up, planted her feet on my calves and began walking up and down my spine. The curious part of this little jaunt was that, although it took away my breath, it was wonderfully relaxing. She didn't do it as though she were mad at me. Nor, I must add sadly, as though she were in love, either.

Next was the big soap-up soap-down scene where, seated on a stool in front of a mirror, she fussed about first with warm water then with cold. Fanned me dry and, sitting beside me, produced what appeared to be a pair of chopsticks tipped by cotton batting. Before I realized what she was about, she was probing my pointy ears. The result was embarrassing: I've been moderately diligent, through the years, in splashing a palmful of water at these curious appendages every morning. But my ears had never been *cleaned*. Is this something other Americans do and only I don't? Isn't American advertising missing a billion-dollar opportunity in concentrating upon nicotine-stained teeth and overlooking the imminent peril of deafness caused by unclean ears?

I was ready for the *tête-à-tête* in the sulphur bath. So was she. She pointed to the door that led to the pool and I flopped in. A moment later she came out nude. She had small breasts and a graceful walk.

Too graceful. When she reached the edge of the pool she stood a moment with one hand extended; then found the ladder. At the top of the ladder she turned her head as if wondering where I was at. I made a splashing sound and she smiled; yet her eyes weren't directly on me. She came down the ladder, swam slowly in my direction, then stood up, smiling, with one hand held out tentatively.

It didn't come to me until then that she was blind.

Who Sent for You?

Dear Joel Wells,

Kindly cancel my complaint about Accommodation Nations being *too* accommodating.

Everybody loved me in Cholon: bartenders and bargirls, landlords and cab drivers, pedicab-pushers, trishaw-wheelers, black-market money-changers, head-waiters and market-women; beggars, cripples, leaping pimps and weeping lepers.

Where have all those procuring clerks and eager bellboys gone? Why don't taxies wheel up to where I'm waiting whether I want a cab or no? Where are all those smiling faces of Saigon and Kaohsiung? Where have the miniskirted lovelies standing in bar-doors gone?

Nobody loved me in Kobe. Nobody pulled my sleeve in Nagoya. Here are fifty thousand humans milling down the Ginza and not *one* needs me! I tell you, men, it's plain hell when you get into a country that has self-respect.

Another complaint about Japan: they'll tell you that English is the second language; but I think it must be the twenty-ninth. If you want a restaurant, a barber shop, a movie, or a sweatbath, learn Japanese. And don't mess around with American green, because not even the cabbies will accept it here. You deal in *yen*. There are places where a traveller's check can be cashed—but try your hand at an American Express Order and you're in for a hard time.

Not that the Japanese set out, deliberately, to give you a hard time. The attitude is simply that nobody sent for you, did they? Everybody has his own gig, everybody's in a hurry; nobody knows what you're talking about; and if you don't know how to ask for what you want, why did you come *here*?

The realization dawns at last, upon the confused tourist, that, despite American conquest, despite Hiroshima, despite American know-how and American investment and American movies, the conviction of Caucasian superiority hasn't had the faintest impact upon Japanese pride.

Another assumption, which can be cleared up by a stroll down the Ginza, is that it's a close thing when comparison is made between the American and the Oriental woman. If it was *ever* a close thing, it must have been before the American woman began looking more like Duke Wayne than like Eve.

Argue, if you will, about Chuck Davy's chances against Kid Gavilan, Silky Sullivan's chance against Tim-Tam or how many successive games Luke Appling will be able to play—the debate about Oriental *vs*. American women is over, too. And it was a mismatch as bad as Joe Louis *vs*. Johnny Paycheck.

Nor is this simply because the Oriental woman has more grace, a finer complexion, dresses unpretentiously and possesses poise. It's because she has the inner composure derived from knowing she *is* a woman. The reason the American woman overdresses, flops when she sits, strides when she walks, booms when she speaks and gets stoned on half a martini, is because she doesn't feel sure she *is* a woman. And that is also the reason for her perpetual complaint—"What happened to the *men*? There aren't any *men* any more. *Virile* men."

Perhaps one reason is that, when she is confronted by male virility, she goes to such great lengths to destroy it. Which also throws some light on the reason for American men still going bamboo.

All of which may be to imply that the Japanese woman is enabled to be a simpler person because her life has been arranged for her by an ancestral society. An implication which would be untrue. The young woman here who has come up in the generation since 1945 is often in deep conflict with her society. She is divided between the traditional role of subservience to the male, and her awakening to the possibility of having a life as fulfilling as that of her boyfriend or husband.

From childhood she is trained to efface herself in the presence of the male, whether father, husband, brother or son. In order to be accepted by men—as well as by other women—she must assume humility.

And if this gentle femininity is so attractive to the woman-dominated Western man, it bores the Japanese husband silly. It is his prerogative to occupy himself as he chooses in the outside world, so long as he provides groceries for his family. If he buys her a TV and takes his family on an outing once a year, the other days are all his own. In fact, the businessman who goes home to his family immediately from work is regarded as lacking manliness. And while it is unthinkable that she should be unfaithful, it is assumed that he has the right to sleep around as his desires may take him. This leads one to suspect that the air of quiet contentment one finds so common among Japanese women—and so rarely among American ones—may camouflage resignation. Or even despair.

Cabin B-52 is way *way* down in Mr. Tung's ship. It has no porthole and the only sound is that of engines beating against the deep Pacific's floor. It's no larger than the room in which Miss Chan declined to overcrowd me. And there are a couple of unattached American women aboard eager to do some overcrowding. But no thank you—not that they're middle-aged but that their eyes are *round*.

The only passenger with whom I can conduct a sane and humorous conversation is an Italian whom I call *Commandante*. The *Commandante* is a strongly built, vigorous fellow of fifty-six, who commanded an Italian battleship in World War II. He accompanied the Italian naval brass to Japan to cement relationships with the Japanese naval brass. The Italian officers were given fantastically hospitable reception: the reception went on all night in the spirit of highest good-fellowship. Then word came that Italy had surrendered; and the Italian guests were pitched, directly from the banquet table, into a prison camp. *Commandante* was there two years but he has lived in Tokyo ever since.

In my first letter to *The Critic,* written from San Francisco, I wrote: "Japan belongs to *us.*" Sorry about that. Japan doesn't belong to us

161

any more than she belonged to the Italian naval brass. And the *Commandante,* as Italianate a man as one could find, confesses that he, too, has gone bamboo.

His transistor had kept us in touch with the moon-flight. The towers of San Francisco came into view, through a fog, on the morning of the day that the astronauts landed on the moon.

I was leaning on the rail of the *Oriental Rio* when the sun dispersed the fog and I saw that wondrous city once again. Yet, the sight caught me feeling less elated than reminiscent.

My father's father was one Nels Ahlgren, born to a shopkeeper of Stockholm. When his (Ahlgren's) father died, the son found a much-marked Old Testament. He'd never read it. When he did, it drove him bonkers. He memorized The Book word for word, changed his name to Isaac Ben Abraham and adopted Orthodox Judiasm as his faith. That's how it happened that my own father was born, in 1868, in San Francisco.

A hundred and one years to make the mind boggle: news of Lincoln's assassination had not yet had full impact on this city then. Now I was sailing into it on a day when men were going to walk on the moon!

San Francisco was my father's birthplace because Isaac Ben Abraham (now ready for a funny farm for pseudo-intellectuals) was waiting for a ship to take him to The Holy Land. He, his wife and son caught the ship and he preached Zionism to Zionists, in Jerusalem, until his wife lost her job. She had to go to the American Embassy to get passage back to America.

Isaac Ben Abraham came along. The family was so broke, coming back, that the passengers took up a collection for them. The mistake the passengers made was in giving the alms to the husband instead of to the wife. He brooded over the American bills for a while—then threw the money overboard because it had George Washington's picture on the bills.

George Washington was a man, was Isaac's thinking; man is made in the image of God; and the Holy Book commands: Thou Shalt Make No Graven Image.

Yet who am *I* to put that old man down? Haven't I done the same thing with American bills, throwing them into mutuel windows instead of into the sea—and without so idealistic a justification? In fact, I'm not coming to an American shore any more affluent then he did in that long-ago year.

And as for embracing Judaism so uncritically, wasn't he doing the same thing the *Commandante* had done; and myself? Weren't all three of us looking for hope to the East?

Wasn't it simply old Isaac's way of going bamboo?

To sum up, in one aphorism, all the wisdom I acquired in nine months in the Orient:

Never eat in a place with sliding doors unless you're crazy about raw fish.

AFTER THE BUFFALO

I. How Do I Look Boys Dead or Alive

The North was one country and the South another. But the men of the wooded seaboard valleys said A Plague On Both Your Houses.

These were slaveless yeomen who never saw the sense, with a continent of game stretching before them, in breaking their backs in other men's fields. They were rifle-and-fishing-rod folk whom other whites called "white trash" and Negroes called "po' buckra." Seeking neither to bind the labor of other men to themselves nor permitting their own labor to be so bound, they came to town only now and then.

Yet came often enough to perceive that the proscriptive rights of master over man had been transferred whole from plantation to mill. And when, between the landed gentry of the South and the proprietary interests of the North, war at last broke out, they didn't come to town anymore at all.

But went deeper and deeper into the forests until hiding became a way of life with them.

Yet among red roses their women had planted about their cabins, a shadowed bloom sometimes gleamed whitely.

They did not take it for a sign. They took it for a forest flower and paid it little mind. Not knowing that the soil upon which their cabins rested had been waiting, volcanic aeons gone, for a certain seed.

The ultimate price the huntsman paid, for mistaking a field fiber to be a forest flower, was having to take what the cotton planter offered him for his trees and streams. Caught between the reaching greed of Northern industry and the equal greed of the planters, the slaveless yeoman was pressed from his woods into a wobbly old wagon piled high with the junk of a dying frontier.

As the wagon began to roll, through woods once his, already ringing with axes in the hands of bound men, the sense of loss the huntsman endured must surely have been hard.

164

The loss his descendants were to sustain would be yet harder. Unwanted by Southern agriculture and unneeded by Northern industry, he was taking his hunters' skills to a frontier already lacking use for them. By the time his wagon ferried the wide Missouri, he was already a drifter of no trade: master of no man to be mastered by none. A landless illiterate; already a kind of outlaw.

"I'll bet you didn't know the world was so wide," he might have told his son when the wagon reached the Great Plains.

"No," the son might have replied, "but I always knew what I'd have for breakfast."

For though he might belong to a woman or a faith or just to his hounds; to a passion, an aspiration or a hope, after the buffalo the hunter would never again find his own true country.

For what The West was all about was not whether Man should be free, but who should be Man's master. The issues which were joined in The Making of the West were whether gold or silver should be the standard of money; whether timber or mining should own this or that range; whether oil or railroads should govern this or that state.

After the buffalo, when the hands that had gotten the gold had gotten the silver and copper as well, when timber and railroads became single empires and governors found that there were enough mines and wells and rails to go around, the frontiersman was left with a couple hounds and a string-tailed mare in a shanty on a claim.

The banks were now the hunters; the hunter was their prey. For the flower that was not a flower had severed him at his roots.

Small wonder that the huntsman's sons said a plague on all your houses.

If the Border War didn't, precisely speaking, breed bad men, it certainly turned them loose. "Jayhawkers," "nigger-stealers" and "bushwackers" were commonly men whose skills in hunting game had been transferred, by the slave-*vs.*-free controversy, to hunting men:

> *They rode in one morning at breaking of day,*
> *They came to burn Lawrence they came not to stay;*
> *With guns all a-waving and horses all foam,*
> *And Quantrell riding his famous big roan.*
> *The boys they were drunken with powder and wine;*
> *They came to burn Lawrence just over the line.*

After the buffalo, the frontier hunter might move from ranch to ranch; follow the oil booms or the wheat; drive spikes or mules. But he wouldn't be banking the silver and he wouldn't be riding in Pullmans. His name would be on no government contract for meat or wool. And all his songs celebrating the great outlaws of the Southwest would be variations of a sense of having been deeply wronged:

> *Now as through the world I wander,*
> *I see lots of funny men;*
> *Some rob you with a six-gun,*
> *Some with a fountain pen.*

The trickle of wagons and walkers moving west became a dispersion.

Came now the Sleep-by-day-fly-by-nighties, Get-rich-quickies with W's on their foreheads, hiders, escapers and St. Louis whoremongers with many a lightfoot whore.

The fugitive slave had headed north. The Bad Nigger fled west.

John Henry was a Good Nigger because he died with his hammer in his hand; having nicely killed himself for a white section boss. John Hardy was a black gambling man but this didn't make him a Bad Nigger. He didn't make that till he shot a white man down on the West Virginia Line.

Another black wonder was Po' Laz'rus, who'd always been a Good Nigger. He was a Louisiana levee-camp big-timberman who endured being worked from dawn to dark. It was worms in the grits that cut it with Po' Laz'rus.

He came down the middle of the mess-hall table wielding a brace of blue-steel revolvers and taking care to put his big muddy boots in every man's plate. Then, by way of saying good-bye to the white boss, he stuck up the commissary and got away with the payroll. When dem cotton bolls turns rotten you cain't pick very much cotton in dem old cotton fields down south.

When his face was posted in every post office—WANTED DEAD OR ALIVE—Laz'rus, pleased at his widening fame, sent one of the posters back to his levee-camp comrades inscribed: *How do I look boys dead or alive?*

> *How do I look boys, dead or alive?*
> *How do I look boys, dead or alive?*
> *Dead or alive boys, dead or alive?*
> *It's a hard road, dead or alive.*

*   *   *

New sheriff sent me my pitcher,
"Come up and see me, dead or alive."
"Come up and see me, dead or alive."

New sheriff sent me a letter,
Said he'd clothe and feed me,
Dead or alive, dead or alive.
It's a hard road, dead or alive.

I'm sorry I cain't come sir,
Dead or alive, dead or alive.
Got to go see my sweet little thing,
Dead or alive, dead or alive.

How do I look boys, dead or alive?

Nobody knows who Po' Laz'rus was any more than anyone knows who Jesus Christ was. All we know is that both were poor men who defied armed authority; were betrayed, taken; and died wounded in the side:

O then they taken Po' Laz'rus
An lay him in the commissary gallery.
He said, "my wounded side, Lord,
Lord, my wounded side."

From Jesus Christ to Jesse James, an innocent insistence that the outlaw is a kind of saviour pervades the celebration of all their names. As in the song Woody Guthrie used to sing to the tune of *Jesse James*:

When Jesus came to town,
Poor workin' people,
They followed him around.
He sent to the preacher;
He sent to the sheriff;
And told them all the same:
"Take all your money
And give it to the poor."
So they laid Jesus Christ in his grave.
The people held their breath
When they heard of Jesus' death,

> *And wondered how he ever came to die.*
> *Twas the landlords and the soldiers*
> *Who nailed him in the sky,*
> *And laid poor Jesus in his grave.*

Shades of great outlaws crossed the Atlantic to haunt the Appalachians and the Ozarks:

> *A brace of loaded pistols,*
> *He carried night and day.*
> *He robbed not from the poor,*
> *But on the King's Highway.*
> *Bold, gay and undaunted*
> *Stood young Brennan on the moor—*

Like John Henry, John Hardy, and Po' Laz'rus, Young Brennan remained a shade. But the opening of the American Southwest brought the photographer to make shades tangible. Outlaws became living realities. The chronicle of the just man who, by stamina, guile and courage outwits authority armed in its hundreds, becomes tangible history with the flight and pursuit of Gregorio Cortez.

II. So Many Mountain Rangers to Take One Mexican?

On a summer morning of 1901, Sheriff Brack Morris, of Karnes County, Texas, rode up to the tenant farm of the brothers Romuldo and Gregorio Cortez, accompanied by two deputies. The brothers understood little English. What little they understood now sufficed: they were being charged with horse-theft. And Karnes County justice was served, when a Mexican was charged with horse-stealing, by hanging the nearest Mexican.

And as the only crime the brothers had committed was that of being Mexicans, Gregorio said he would not permit himself to be taken.

A deputy translated this as "I refuse to let a white man arrest me." Brack Morris then shot down Romuldo and fired at Gregorio. Gregorio shot and killed Morris. The deputies fled.

By the time they returned with a hanging posse, Gregorio had gotten his family and his dying brother off the farm and into the hands of friends.

Thereupon began a chronicle of flight and pursuit sufficiently heroic to set a pattern for all subsequent manhunts in the Southwest. In all the annals of Texas there had never been a Mexican fugitive who hadn't ridden hellbent for the Rio Grande. Gregorio Cortez headed straight north—*walking!* While Texas mounties were covering every three yards of the Rio Grande, Cortez was taking a leisurely breakfast in the dead sheriff's home town.

What methods Sheriff Bob Glover, of Gonzales County, may have employed in interrogating the women and children of Cortez' family is not known; yet he learned that Cortez was hiding out at the home of one Robledo.

Glover's posse attacked the Robledo home from all sides, with the Napoleonic Glover leading the assault on horseback. Cortez shot him off his horse, cold-stone-dead, with a single shot. Then ran, barefooted, for the brush.

Convinced that they were now engaged by a gang of *banditi,* Glover's troops kept answering their own fire until one constable was dead and several wounded; as well as Robledo's wife and one of his children. They then hanged Encarnación, Robledo's thirteen-year-old son, and left the field triumphantly. Cortez came back for his shoes.

He had walked a hundred miles in the two days since he'd killed Brack Morris. Now he borrowed a mare that he rode to her death; and carrying the saddle, continued walking north. Not until then did Cortez commit the crime of which he'd been accused. He stole a horse; and turned at last for the border. The law picked up his trail. Both bloodhounds and press began baying for blood.

"Since Glover was killed," The *San Antonio Express* complained, "Southwest Texas has swarmed with men in pursuit of him. Some of the best trailers in the country have been following him and he has thrown them all off. His methods are peculiar. He travels a great deal at night and never follows the trails. He stays in the brush as much as possible. His trail runs along straight and smooth for several miles, convincing the trailers he is following a certain general direction, when the trail starts at right angles. Then it doubles back. Another trick of Cortez is to stop, walk around in a circle, then reverse, then cross his circle and stop in a grassy place. This trick gives the trailers the most trouble as they lose hours picking up the trail once more."

Special trains, bearing men, horses and bloodhounds, were now moving east and west across Texas, keeping in touch with one another by telegraph and telephone. Whenever Cortez was sighted, a posse with fresh horses would be transported by rail to the scene. The trail would be lost once more; the pursuers would board another train and resume the search. An anonymous *guitarrero* began singing—

They let loose the bloodhound dogs;
They followed him from afar.
But trying to take Cortez
Was like following a star.

The Major sheriff said
As if he were going to cry,
"Cortez, hand over your weapons
As we want to take you alive."

Then asked Gregorio Cortez,
His pistol in his hand,
"So many mountain Rangers
To take one Mexican?"

Como decimos asi es,
En mil novecientos uno
El dia ventidos de junio
Fue capturado Cortez.

(As we say, so it is;
In nineteen hundred and one,
On the 22nd day of June
Cortez was captured.)

Otro dia por la manana
El solo se presento:
"Por la buena si me llevan
Lo que es de otro modo no."

(He surrendered on the next day, in the morning
He surrendered of his own accord;
"You can take me if I am willing,
But by no other way.")

With his pistols concealed in a bag slung across his shoulder, Cortez
had walked into a sheep camp near the town of Dolores on the north
bank of the Rio Grande. Mistaking one Gonzales for a friend, he gave
him his pistols to be reloaded. With a thousand-dollar reward on his head,
one Gonzales took the pistols to a captain of the Texas Rangers. But

as the reward depended upon Cortez' conviction for murder, Gonzales' betrayal earned him only two-hundred dollars.

The pursuit had only begun. Cortez was taken to Gonzales, Texas, where, strangely, he was tried for the killing of the constable during the fight at the Robledo ranch; though it was already known that the constable had been killed by one of the posse. Yet feeling against Cortez was running so high, he barely missed being hanged for the shooting. One juror, A.L. Sanders, held out against the death penalty. Cortez was, instead, sentenced to fifty years.

Ten days later an attempt was made to take him from his cell and lynch him; but Sheriff F.M. Fly stood off the mob. Meanwhile his brother, Romuldo, died of the wound inflicted by Morris.

In 1902 the Texas Court of Criminal Appeals reversed the verdict of guilty found against Cortez in the shooting of the constable. By then Cortez had been sentenced, in Karnes County, to be hanged for the murder of Morris.

Eight months later the Court of Criminal Appeals threw this verdict out on grounds of prejudice.

He was then tried in Pleasanton for the horse-theft, sentenced to two years, and the verdict again reversed.

He was tried at Goliad, again for the murder of Morris. The jury disagreed. At Corpus Christi a jury finally found that Cortez had shot Morris in self-defense while the sheriff was making an unauthorized arrest.

Cortez was then tried at Columbus for the murder of Glover, found guilty and sentenced to life imprisonment. He entered the Texas State Penitentiary at Huntsville on January 1, 1905.

After serving twelve years and nine months he was offered a full pardon. But because of his recalcitrance before the court, the pardon was made conditional.

"Deep regret I have always felt for the sad occurrence," he explained to the board, "but repentance I have never felt. For I could never bring myself to the hypocritical state as to so plead to gain an end that was my just due."

Three years after his pardon, at the age of forty-one, Gregorio Cortez died during his own wedding ceremony. His place among American outlaws is memorable because, of them all, he was the most innocent. No other sustained the right of a man to his own life with such uncompromising dignity.

III.   The Pursuit of the Pixie-Eared Elephant

A female elephant named Raji escaped from a circus near Lansing, Michigan, several years ago. She attacked nobody. Raji simply walked off the circus grounds and began wandering the outskirts of town. Four thousand men, women and children turned out with squirrel guns, World War II bayonets, rakes, barrel-staves, bows and arrows, BB guns, baseball bats and housebricks for The Great Elephant Hunt.

They pelted, hacked, slashed, stoned and tore the defenseless brute all around Lansing, until someone had the simple decency to shoot her through the head.

The lynching of Raji was scarcely more degrading to the people of Lansing than the defamation the people of Dallas worked on the bodies of Bonnie Parker and Clyde Barrow on their own killing-ground.

Before officers had arrived to control the crowd, Bonnie's hair had been clipped off, her bloody dress had been torn to shreds and her purse rifled. Somebody was prying off her rings and someone else was trying to cut off one of Clyde's ears when a doctor got there. Bonnie's last request, made to her mother, that she be brought home after she'd been killed, could not be fulfilled because of the multitude thronging the streets around the funeral home. They would have hacked the wooden casket to splinters for the sake of having souvenirs. Hot-dog and soft-drink vendors turned a pretty penny.

Denied dignity in their lives, the press denied it to them in death as well. Thus the manner of their lives was more nearly that of two terrified foxes than that of a man and a woman. And the manner of their deaths evoked a roar of approval from the Texas press.

Clyde Barrow apparently took to his heels long before he had gained a pursuer. For the immediate use to which he put his first car—a stripped-down speedster—was to get himself chased purely for the sake of pursuit.

"It's so much fun to go fast," he told his sister, "it's easier to run away." A policeman had given him a whistle, so he'd stepped on the gas and a lifelong flight had begun.

He fled on foot, he fled by car; he hid behind barns and slept in woods; one escape he attempted on muleback.

When he wanted to see his kinfolk he drove past their home and threw a pop bottle, with a note concealed inside, advising them of a safe meeting-place. If the depth of a man's fear may be measured by the violence with which he reacts when cornered, then the dread Clyde Barrow contained literally *propelled* him.

He was born on the run. His chief preoccupation thereafter was in arranging chases. Poor Bonnie.

That Barrow's deep dread was of women is one of those Freudian simplifications convenient to writers of introductions to books about people they never knew. This is nicely verified by another writer of introductions, Mr. John Toland, in a volume of conjectures, surmises and easy assumptions called *The Dillinger Days*.

"He [Clyde Barrow]," Mr. Toland writes, "was a small twenty-three-year-old man of medium build with wavy, dark brown hair slicked down in the middle. He had pixie ears, a weak chin, soft hazel eyes . . . and homosexual tendencies."

Since this sounds as if Barrow was born twenty-three-years of age with his hair parted in the middle, we wonder whether he may have parted it differently after he grew up. It's credible that he did; as small men of medium build customarily parted their hair in the middle in this era. As well as large men of medium build.

I can accept his having "pixie ears"—whatever *they* are—upon the assumption that if you have one pixie ear you're likely to have a pair. But as tendencies are infinitely more difficult to discern than pixie ears —even by people who know the suspect intimately—one can only marvel at this hack's presumption. Clyde Barrow might have been a latent heterosexual without even his mother knowing.

Mr. Toland also assures us that Barrow's drivers, Wm. Daniel Jones and Henry Methvyn, were hired "not only to assist in the robberies but to help satisfy Bonnie's sexual aberrations." Again one wants to ask, "Vas you dere, Sharlie?"

Or is making love in an automobile aberrative? Nothing was commoner in the thirties; it is only the congestion of traffic on the throughways and accessibility of motels that make it less common today.

What if Bonnie *did* take off into the woods with one of the kids? That still doesn't verify Mr. Toland's implication that Clyde was peeking from behind a bush. That Clyde was catching up on his sleep in the back seat is more likely. And when, on waking, found the front seat, a blanket and the kids missing, may have not minded greatly. Exhausted as he must have been, he was, possibly, relieved.

"All in all," Clyde's sister avers, "Bonnie Parker was the answer to a sister's prayer for a wife for a best-loved brother." Assuming that Sis might be unperceptive about the relationship, my own inclination is still to give Bonnie and Clyde the benefit of the doubt.

For the myth of monstrousness, so assiduously circulated by the press when the pair were being pursued, is the source of Mr. Toland's assumption that Bonnie and Clyde were both perverted.

This myth was assisted by fantasies contained in a twenty-eight-page confession made by W.D. Jones. W.D. asserted that he was chained to trees by Barrow in order to prevent his escape; that he feared for his life every moment with them.

The confession was made when he *was* truly in fear of his life; he made it in exchange for a life sentence when charged with the murder of Doyle Johnson at Belton, Texas. Given a chance to lie himself out of the electric chair, one can hardly blame a teenager. But that it was himself, and not Barrow, who murdered Johnson, as Clyde's sister claims, is highly likely. After all, Clyde Barrow didn't do *all* the gunning-down. W.D. did his share.

And so did another "quiet country boy with clear blue eyes"—to employ Mr. Toland's description of both W.D. and Henry Methvyn. Methvyn, too, escaped the chair by a repetition of W.D.'s fantasies. It is too hard to believe that Barrow was able to keep a revolver pointed, day and night, at a driver's head, while being pursued by federal, state and municipal police all over the Southwest.

We can assume that neither of those blue-eyed youths was any too bright. Nor was Barrow. And surely Bonnie must have been dealing with only half the deck.

Was her unfaltering devotion to Clyde or to herself? Was it herself or Barrow with whom she was sufficiently fascinated to expiate her life proving such devotion? Her earliest aspirations to be a tightrope walker, an actress or an operatic star, are not unusual in a little girl. Yet one wonders whether these hopeless ambitions might not have been later sustained by becoming the cynosure of multitudes. Might she not have been acting out a *True Confessions* epic that could end no other way than in death beside her dying lover?

Nonetheless, devotion there was; and awesome devotion at that. What comes through is an old-fashioned loyalty you don't get any more: the loyalty of Buck Barrow, blinded, delirious and dying, calling for someone to take Blanche to safety. The loyalty of Clyde Barrow, creeping through a battalion of possemen to find Bonnie, wounded in the brush; or W.D., himself wounded, fording a river with Bonnie on his back. Nor did either Bonnie's family or Clyde's ever fail to accept the pair, at any hour of the night, regardless of risk to themselves.

Lynching a defenseless person's name is even easier than stoning a befuddled elephant. The newspapers indulged themselves freely in making monsters out of Bonnie and Clyde. I have never seen a newspaper, magazine or book about these two that took into account their beginnings and the climate of their times.

Neither Barrow's forebears nor Bonnie's had performed gallant deeds for ladies in farthingales against a background of trellised honeysuckle and the scent of magnolia. Their homes had not been pillared mansions bearing Greek entablature. Their homes had been cabins and shanties and wagons. Yet it had not been the gentlemen of the Old South, but these wilderness castaways, among whom the myth of the cavalier persisted most strongly.

Driven out of England by Cromwell, the myth found sanctuary in the American South. And flowered its finest amid cotton-mill waste. And in those small grubby towns where Main Street was rutted by wagon-wheels; and the last gas-lamp on the outskirts looked tired all night long.

A myth sustained, during the Civil War, not by Southern commanders and politicians, but by the Southern farmer, hillman and tradesman of the rank and file. These were the ones whose savagery in battle kept alive a myth as unreal as a dream: a dream that they were fighting and dying in defense of white-columned mansions; although their own fences were sagging and unpainted. A Quixotic belief, though their own lives were brutal and mean, that they fought to save their honor. And it was this fantasy, when the war was lost, which informed their refusal to accept defeat:

> *I'm a good old rebel soldier*
> *And that's just what I am;*
> *And for this Yankee nation*
> *I do not give a damn.*

> *I hate the starry banner*
> *That's stained with Southern blood;*
> *I hate the pizen Yankees*
> *'N fit 'em all I could.*

> *Followed old Marse Robert*
> *For four years nearabout;*
> *Got wounded at Manassas*
> *And starved at Point Lookout.*
> *I cotched the rheumatism*
> *From fightin' in the snow;*
> *But I kilt a chance of Yankees*
> *'N wish I'd of kilt some mo'.*

Three hundred thousand Yankees
Are stiff in Southern dust;
We got three hundred thousand
Befo' they conquered us.
They died of Southern fever
And Southern steel and shot;
I wish we'd of got three million
Instead of what we got.

I hate the Yankee nation
And the uniform of blue;
I hate the constitution
Of this great republic too.
I hate the Freedmen's Bureau
With all its mess and fuss;
O the thievin' lyin' Yankees
I hate 'em wus 'n wus.

I cain't take up my musket
To fight 'em any mo';
But I ain't gonna love 'em
'N that is sartin sure.
I don't want no pardon
For what I've done around;
'N I won't be reconstructed
'N I do not give a damn. *

It was such Fight-Till-The-Last-Dog-Dies boys, some of whom had never mounted a horse before the war, who became the nuclei of the guerrilla warfare; which was to afford the tradition in which the James boys, Quantrell and Cole Younger continued to ride after the war was done.

To what this preposterous tradition had degenerated by the nineteen-thirties may be gathered by the spectacle of Clyde Barrow bumping about a cornfield in a Ford V-8; and abandoning it to attempt an escape on a mule.

Who *were* Bonnie and Clyde? They were outcasts of the cotton frontier. They were children of the wilderness whose wilderness had been razed; who came to maturity in the hardest of times. Clyde might have

*As sung by Frank Warner, *The Unreconstructed Rebel*, Elektra Recording jh504b.

survived to a sad old age by chopping cotton. Bonnie might have knocked about as a sharecropper's wife or a prostitute until worn out by hard use. The two chose, instead, to give everyone a run for their lives. And, having once committed themselves, made a run which verged upon the uncanny.

As a true desperado, Barrow never had the class of John Dillinger. Yet, when Dillinger was killed nobody doubted that he was dead. But Bonnie and Clyde created a myth of invincibility which survived their deaths. They are the only American outlaws, other than Jesse James, who achieved an aura of the supernatural.

Kings' Daughters Hospital in Perry, Texas, looked more like an armory than a hospital when Buck Barrow lay dying there within a locked and guarded room. The hospital corridor was lined with police, and police surrounded the hospital grounds.

Bonnie and Clyde, crazed with pain and bleeding from their wounds, were miles away hiding in a ditch.

Yet nurses, policemen, doctors and citizens all over town were *certain* that Bonnie and Clyde would come racing up the hospital drive, machine-gunning everyone in their way, fight their way up to Buck's room, take him off his deathbed and make a getaway.

Bonnie herself had known better than that for many months. She concluded one of her simple poems:

> *Some day they'll go down together*
> *They'll bury them side by side;*
> *To a few it'll be grief*
> *To the law a relief—*
> *But it's death to Bonnie and Clyde.*

Bonnie Parker and Clyde Barrow were not gunned down simply because they were outlaws. They were killed because their outlawry was so profitless. There are no payoffs, no kickbacks, no graft and no fees involved in rawjaw robbery. Had they had the enterprise—as others had—to arrange fake bank robberies for a percentage of the take, they might have become respectable and prosperous members of a business community.

But their methods belonged to a time that had passed. They were bow-and-arrow people in an age of the fountain pen. One way or another they had to be disposed of.

Ultimately they weren't disposed of simply because they had disposed of others: they were killed because they kept getting in the way.

THE CORTEZ GANG

THE brothers Cortez—Romuldo and Gregorio—were farmers, in the year 1901, in the Texas County called "Karnes" by the Anglo-Americans; and "El Carmen" by the Mexicans.

Romuldo Cortez owned two fine sorrel horses of nearly identical size and markings. But one was lame. An American neighbor, envious of Romuldo's horses, offered to trade a mare he owned for one of Romuldo's sorrels. Romuldo declined, but the American was persistent. He pressured Romuldo to trade; yet Romuldo would not. In a part of Texas, and in a time when Mexicans were not considered to be white men, Romuldo's refusal amounted to arrogance.

So Romuldo decided to trick the American. Knowing that the man drove a buggy, on certain mornings, down a certain road to town, he arranged to be astride his lame sorrel, under a big mesquite bordering a fence with the horse's spavined leg concealed by the mesquite. When the American drove up and saw the Mexican idly eating mesquite, he stopped to resume his bargaining.

"I would consider trading," Romuldo conceded at last, "but I'm afraid you might renege on the deal later."

"I'm an American, not a Mexican," the American boasted. "I keep my word."

The agreement was then reached that Romuldo, still astride the sorrel, would take it to the American's home, leave it there and take the American's mare in return. The American then drove on in his buggy, well content that he'd made a sharp deal.

When Romuldo told Gregorio of the trick he had played, Gregorio heard with only half an ear. He was troubled because his wife had sighed in her sleep all night. Once he'd wakened her to ask her what the matter was. She did not know. All she could say that "my heart is trying to tell me something sad—what, I do not know."

The American who'd been out-horse-traded complained to Sheriff W.T. "Brack" Morris. Morris, forty-one, had put in twenty years as an officer of the law in Texas. He'd become sheriff of Karnes County in 1896 and, in 1901, was serving his third term. His reputation was that of a man who was fast and accurate with a revolver. It does not appear that he was vicious.

He disregarded the complaint of the out-traded American. Horse-trading was a matter of *caveat emptor*: the man should have either watched out for himself or kept his mouth shut later.

He did, however, act upon an inquiry of Sheriff Avant, of neighboring Atascos County, who was in search of a horse-thief described as a medium-sized Mexican wearing a red, broad-brimmed Mexican hat. Morris began checking on Mexicans, around Kenedy, Texas, who'd acquired horses in recent weeks.

When he set out to question the Cortezes, he took two deputies with him—Boone Choate, as interpreter, and one John Trimmell. Morris and Trimmell were armed. Choate was not. The three rode out to the Cortez place in the sheriff's surrey.

Half a mile from the house Trimmell got out to espy the area while Morris and Choate went to the house.

Gregorio was lying on the porch with his head in his wife's lap, with a revolver stuck in his belt in front. When the surrey stopped, he slid the gun around until it was even with his hip pocket and out of sight. He said to Romuldo "See what they want."

Romuldo talked to Morris and Choate, then walked back to Gregorio and said, *"Te quieren."*

What Romuldo meant by this was only, "Somebody wants to speak to you." But Choate understood it to mean, "You are wanted." And assumed from this that Gregorio was already a man wanted by the law.

Gregorio came up and stood near Romuldo at the fence, with Romuldo standing nearer to Choate. Gregorio kept a bit of distance between himself and the Americans. Romuldo was unarmed and Gregorio's gun was not visible.

Choate then asked Gregorio if he or his brother had recently acquired a horse. Gregorio said he had not. Because, to Gregorio, a horse and a mare are two different animals. Had Choate asked if he'd acquired a mare, he would no doubt have said yes. Choate had said *caballo* instead of *yegua*.

Morris then dismounted from the surrey and approached the Cortezes, telling Choate to inform them that he was going to arrest them. Morris was to the right of the two men and about twelve feet away when Choate translated.

Choate later testified, at Cortez's trial, that Cortez had then said, "A *mi no me arreste nada,"* and had translated this as "No white man can arrest me." Later Choate changed this wording to, *"A mi no me arreste nadie."*

What Cortez had actually said was, "You can't arrest me for nothing."

Morris then drew his weapon; Romuldo rushed at him in a crouch, as though to grapple with him, and Morris shot him through the mouth. He then shot at Gregorio and missed, and Gregorio then shot Morris. The impact of his forty-four almost knocked Morris down. Morris fired two or three more times, but missed. Gregorio shot him again. Morris began to reel and stagger, going along the wire fence toward the gate. He fell before he reached the gate; and Gregorio shot him again as he lay on the ground.

Choate ran into the chaparral and headed toward the gate where they'd left Trimmell, half a mile away. By the time Choate reached Trimmell, he fancied that he had been fleeing from a gang of armed Mexicans. This idea of Choate's, that Cortez constituted a gang, became the premise upon which the pursuit of Cortez was conducted.

Meanwhile, back at the ranch, Morris was still alive. He'd been shot three times—in the right arm, the right shoulder, and the lower intestine. The arm wound was the most serious because the shot had severed an artery. Cortez took Morris' pistol and left the sheriff lying. He took Romuldo into the house, washed his face, loaded him into the sheriff's surrey and drove off to Romuldo's house. His son, Valeriano, brought the rest of the family to Romuldo's, where Cortez loaded the family into a wagon and got them headed for the home of a friend in Kenedy. He saddled a sorrel mare for himself and a horse for Romuldo—his plan being to get Romuldo into Kenedy for medical treatment after dark.

Morris got to his feet, staggered out of the gate, and bled to death in the brush some two hundred yards from where he'd been shot.

It was ten miles in a straight line from the Cortez place to Kenedy. But the route that Gregorio was taking with Romuldo, through the bush, was longer and infinitely more difficult. Romuldo could no longer seat his horse. Gregorio had finally to lay him down under a tree. With Romuldo growing feverish, they lay in the brush, five miles from the Cortez place, from early afternoon until dark. By this time a posse of fifty men were searching for them.

The posse, though it searched all that day and all that night, not only failed to discover the Cortezes five miles away, but failed to find the body of the sheriff, two hundred yards away. They assumed by now that they were fighting a bandit gang, who had spirited the sheriff away. Morris' body was not discovered until the following morning.

Gregorio was heading to Kenedy with Romuldo, swaying in the saddle before him. Romuldo was so much heavier than Gregorio that Gregorio could not hold him when he began to slip out of the saddle. He finally had to abandon his horse and carry his brother five miles into Kenedy. He got Romuldo into the house with his family.

The pursuit of Gregorio Cortez had begun.

No Mexican in flight had ever gone in any direction except toward the Mexican border. All the several posses struck south.

"The trail of the Mexican leads toward the Rio Grande," the newspapers reported. And posses waited at every possible crossing of the river. No Mexican in flight had ever fled in any other direction save that of the Mexican border before.

Gregorio Cortez was heading due north. And he wasn't riding. He was trying to get out of the Anglo lynching belt into territory where he could get a fair trial. If he could get north of the Colorado, he'd be out of the lynching belt.

From Kenedy in Karnes County it is sixty-five miles in a straight line. He averaged two miles an hour for forty straight hours, through brush and the roughest kind of country, wearing a pair of shoes with narrow, pointed heels.

He made the eight miles from Kenedy to Runge by eight the following morning and entered the town for breakfast at a Mexican restaurant on the outskirts of town. He was not aware that Runge was the hometown of the sheriff he had killed. Morris' funeral was being held that day, to be followed by an indignation meeting. Cortez didn't hang around town.

Thirty-four hours after he had left Kenedy he was at Belmont, fifty-five miles away by direct route. There he ate at a friend's and in the afternoon began walking again: toward Ottine and the house of Martin Robledo. He arrived there about sundown, ate, and then told Robledo of the killing of Morris. Robledo agreed that he should hide there a few days, as the Robledo place was so isolated and wooded.

There were seven others at the Robledos: Martin, his wife, and their three sons—Bonifacio (18), Tomas (16), and Encarnación (13)—Ramon Rodriguez (a half-grown boy living with the Robledos), and a visitor, Martin Sandoval.

Gonzalez County Sheriff Robert Glover had been a close friend of the Sheriff whom Cortez had shot down. He arrested Cortez's women and pressured them—by what means is only to be surmised—until one of them informed him that Cortez was heading for the home of Martin Robledo.

Robledo lived in a wooded and isolated house on the Schnabel Ranch in Gonzalez County, near Ottine, Texas. Schnabel was himself a constable.

Glover's posse, organized around Kenedy, consisted of fifty men, who were entrained for Ottine. It was established at Cortez's trial, that the posse began drinking en route. By the time that Cortez had eaten at the Robledos and came out on the house's gallery, barefooted, Glover had eight men concealed in the brush surrounding Robledo's house.

Glover's plan of action was to have Deputy Swift approach from the rear. Glover and Crispin Alcantar—the only Mexican in the posse—were to approach from the east side, and the other five deputies from the west. All were dismounted except Glover.

When the eight men rushed the house, the two Robledos and Sandoval escaped into the brush. Cortez was on the southeast side when Glover charged on his mount, firing as he came. Cortez shot him dead off the horse. Then ran, barefooted, into the brush and stepped into a patch of burrs. He removed his vest and bound his feet, now bleeding, with it. From the house he heard persistent gunfire.

Refugia Robledo, Robledo's wife, had been left in the house with the Rodriguez boy and her own two sons. Swift saw the Rodriguez boy running inside the house and shot him. He also shot Refugia Robledo; but, as she was standing in front of her sons, he did not shoot them.

Hearing the firing inside the house, posse men outside assumed they were being attacked and began firing upon one another. Schnabel was shot dead by a blast so close that it left powdermarks on his skin.

With two of its men dead, the posse men avenged themselves by hanging the thirteen-year-old Encarnación from a tree until his tongue protruded and he was close to death. Their purpose, they later explained, was to obtain information about the whereabouts of the mythical "Cortez Gang."

The posse took Martin and Mrs. Robledo, her two sons, and Sandoval prisoners, and Refugia was charged with the murder of Schnabel. Deputy Tom Harper testified that he saw the Robledo woman fire at Schnabel from the window and that he fired twice at her when he had seen Schnabel fall. Other members of the posse charged Harper with having killed Schnabel himself. Neither Mrs. Robledo nor Harper were ever brought to trial for the killing of Schnabel.

The posse also informed the newspapers that they had found ten Winchester rifles and a lard bucket full of cartridges on the Robledo premises. Later they reduced the number to eight. Even later, at Cortez's trial, this number was reduced to one Winchester and a single-barreled shotgun. Deputy Swift then testified that neither weapon had been fired the night of the shootings.

After the posse men had left the Robledo place with their prisoners, Cortez returned to the house, got his shoes, and began walking again.

This time he walked south, ten miles, to the house of Ceferino Flores on the banks of the Guadalupe River. Flores took Morris' pistol and hid it, giving Cortez his own revolver. He saddled his own horse, another sorrel mare, for Cortez. Cortez left, pursued by bloodhounds, across the Guadalupe River. The posse paused to hang Flores in the manner they had hung Encarnación Robledo—until his tongue protruded. Flores later got two years in the penitentiary for aiding Cortez's escape.

It is fifty miles from the Guadalupe to the San Antonio River. Cortez rode many times that many miles in the next two days and one night. He often doubled back, stopped to shoot at his pursuers, then rode on, circling about, leaving false leads.

On Sunday noon, as he crossed the Cibolo Creek near Stockdale, his trail was picked up by a fresh posse and his mare began giving out. Yet he galloped her for six more hours, running in circles and zigzags between Stockdale and Floresville, sometimes with the posse less than five hundred yards behind him. At six in the afternoon the sorrel mare fell dead.

Cortez slipped off her saddle and bridle and hid in the brush until dark. Then he made his way out of the net and found, in a pasture, a Spanish mare about thirteen hands high. He rode this mare from Floresville to Cotulla, three hundred miles through brush and rough country, through rivers and over barbed-wire fences, in three days. The pursuing posse lost six horses trying to catch the Spanish mare.

By this time special trains were moving on the Corpus Christi-Laredo Railroad, bearing horses, dogs, and men in their hundreds, keeping in touch by telegraph. Wherever Cortez was sighted, fresh posses would be placed in pursuit.

"The only hope," *The San Antonio Express* reported in a page-one story, "is to fill up the whole country with men and search every avenue of escape. Business has been practically suspended as all the men are out searching the country. New men are joining the hunt every day. The woods are full of searching parties."

From Floresville Cortez rode twenty-five miles along the San Antonio looking for a fording place. When he heard the dogs coming, he cut off his shirt-tails and blindfolded the mare, forcing her into the river. When stopped by a barbed-wire fence, he filed off the top so that the mare could jump the lower strand. Several times he rounded up cattle and used them to cover his trail. Once, desperate with thirst, he drove a bunch of cattle to a waterhole guarded by armed men, deceiving them into thinking he was a *vaquero*.

When the Spanish mare went lame, after cutting herself on leaping a wire, he rode her into thicket near Cotulla, took off her saddle, which he hung to a Coma tree, and went into a thicket with a posse right behind him.

By ten o'clock on Thursday, June twentieth, the mare had been found and the thicket surrounded.

Gregorio Cortez was trapped.

While the posse men sat around the thicket waiting for him to come out, he slipped out and, in full daylight, got into Cotulla, the town from which the posse had come. He figured, again rightly, that most of the men were in the brush and he'd be safer in town.

Cortez, again on foot, walked into Cotulla at noon, with his pistols in a *morral*—a feed-bag of woven ixtle that border rancheros use as a catchall—over his shoulder. He stopped at the home of a Mexican woman, who gave him food and water; then he walked right through the heart of town.

Below Cotulla the Nueces River cuts the Cotulla-Laredo Road. The bridge across the Nueces was guarded by posse men. Cortez went under the bridge, bathed in the river, crossed to the other side and rested. He then followed railroad tracks to the town of Twohig. He arrived there just as a posse had left, going east. He went to the outskirts of the town, lay down by a watertank and slept all night the night of the twentieth: all day of the twenty-first; and all the next night while the posses were still waiting for him to come out of the thicket at Cotulla. It was 2:30 P.M. of the twenty-first before the posse men figured out there was nobody in the thicket. And had not been for some time.

Again the tracking began. This time somewhat facilitated because Cortez's broken shoes left easily recognizable prints. Despite this advantage, Cortez made so many circuitous routes to wipe out his tracks that the posse began to lose heart. They convinced themselves that he had been furnished with another horse by "The Cortez Gang" and had crossed the Rio Grande. The posse men began returning to their homes.

Cortez woke from his three-day sleep on his twenty-sixth birthday, June 21, 1901. He walked into the little ranch village of El Suaz, bought a new pair of trousers and a shirt and converted the dollar and a half of American money he had left into Mexican currency. He threw away his old shirt, wrapped his pistols in his old trousers, put them in his *morral* and began walking toward the Rio Grande, thirty miles distant.

He had to avoid not only American guards, but Mexican as well; because of an extradition agreement between the U.S. and Mexico.

He left the railroad tracks and turned south toward the old Spanish settlement of Dolores, just above Laredo. At noon he arrived at the sheep camp of a man named Abran de la Garza. He was now, at least, out of the lynching belt. Local detachments, made up largely of Mexican-Americans, now constituted the posses.

While this protected him against lynching without trial, which any of the East Texas posses would have conducted, it also made his capture more likely; because his movements were known to the Mexican community. His movements among the Mexicans were now not so likely to be closely kept secrets.

Also, a thousand American dollars had now been offered in reward. Which reward appears to have been what one Jesus Gonzalez, also known as "El Teco," had in mind when he recognized Cortez at the sheep camp.

El Teco had been a friend of Cortez. Cortez trusted him sufficiently to give him his guns to clean. El Teco did not have to go far to earn the reward. There was a posse only two hundred yards away. El Teco brought back two rangers: Rogers and Merrem. Rogers opened the door of the hut where Cortez was sleeping and unarmed, drew down on him and took him prisoner.

The casualties inflicted by the Texas Rangers, and by various posses throughout Texas, before this simple capture, included:

In the Guadalupe Bottoms: One Mexican killed, one wounded, four arrested as members of "The Cortez Gang."

At Ottine: Two Mexicans killed and one arrested as members of "The Cortez Gang."

At Belmont: One Mexican hanged to death, another shot dead, one wounded by rifle fire; a fourth suffered a skull fracture when hit by a rifle barrel: all for denying membership in "The Cortez Gang." The hanged man was hanged many times. With three hundred Texans watching, he was repeatedly, when on the verge of death, brought back to consciousness and hanged again for refusing to give information about "The Cortez Gang."

At Benavides: One Mexican killed as a member of "The Cortez Gang."

At Willow Springs: One Mexican killed as a suspected member of "The Cortez Gang."

At San Diego: One Mexican killed, one seriously wounded, a third captured as members of "The Cortez Gang." When it became established that the Mexicans killed at San Diego by Texas Rangers had nothing to do with Cortez, the press comment was simply: "They were probably all horse-thieves anyhow."

At Kenedy: Posse man Robert Benton was seriously wounded while moving around in the dark, by friends mistaking him for a member of "The Cortez Gang." Cortez was thirty miles away when this shooting occurred.

Sheriff Jackman of Hays County dispatched the "cheering news" that he was hot on the trail of Gregorio Cortez. Cortez was riding a roan horse, the sheriff reported, and was armed with three six-shooters; that he was heading toward Austin and cutting all telephone and telegraph wires on the way. Posses from Austin and San Antonio and other points converged on the rider of the roan; who wasn't armed and wasn't Cortez.

The posses from Runge, Sheriff Morris' home town, gave up the chase of Cortez because "the fugitive had all the advantage, being supplied with fresh horses all the time." In short, a posse could not be expected to apprehend a man unless his horse died under him.

Actually, this was the posse which Cortez evaded simply by walking past them.

Eight hundred "thoroughly armed" posse men were assembled in Gonzalez County to combat "The Cortez Gang"; reported to be numerous and armed with the "latest 30 x 30 Marlin Winchester rifles."

Sheriff Moss of Refugio County assured reporters that he shot a horse from under Cortez in a desperate encounter several years before. This statement is refuted by evidence that Cortez had never been in any trouble with the law before the death of Brack Morris.

The state of Texas now held prisoner almost every known member of the Cortez family; including Cortez's mother and his three-year-old son, Crispin. Romuldo, the wives of Gregorio and Romuldo, and Gregorio's children had been thrown into the Karnes City Jail the morning after authorities had discovered Romuldo at the house in Kenedy; to which Gregorio had carried him in his arms.

The adults were kept in separate cells, while Valeriano, his six-year-old brother and his ten-year-old sister were held in a single cell. The three-year-old was allowed to be with his mother. After the capture of Gregorio the three eldest children were released. But the other adults and the infant were kept in custody four months. Gregorio was sentenced to death *in absentia*, at Karnes City.

An older brother of Cortez, Tomas, was arrested during the pursuit of Gregorio and sentenced to five years in the penitentiary on a charge of horse-theft.

The first Mexican-American organization to appeal for funds for the defense of Gregorio Cortez was the Miguel Hidalgo Workers Society of San Antonio. Money was collected through workers' societies, individual donations, rancheros, professional men and benefit performances. His defense of himself held a powerful appeal to a minority long intimidated. And it was in this climate that some unknown guitarist composed "The Ballad of Gregorio Cortez."

In Mexico City Cortez was made to speak directly through a balladeer, directly to an audience in an appeal for funds. At street corners blind singers took up the ballad, while children collected the coins.

T.E. Mitchell of Laredo, Texas, advertised in *The San Antonio Express*:

> FOR SALE: Gregorio Cortez, Sheriff Killer,
> photographed as captured, send 24¢

Other Anglo-Texans came to Cortez's defense. R.B. Abernathy of Gonzales, the county in which the Battle of Belmont had been fought, and where prejudice against Cortez was strongest, worked four years in defense of Cortez without financial reward and without hope of financial gain. Nor can he be considered to have been courting the Mexican vote: Mexicans were then barred from the primaries in Gonzalez as well as in neighboring counties.

The widespread passion to lynch Cortez without trial was cooled off after Cortez was taken to San Antonio instead of back to Karnes. Karnes City people were waiting for Cortez at the train which, they supposed, would deliver him to them. Instead, only three posse men got out: Cortez was being held in San Antonio. The Karnes people, who had hoped to lynch him, gradually compromised; with the hope and belief that he would be hanged anyhow.

Had he been tried for the killings of Morris and Glover, he may have been. Curiously enough, he was tried for the killing of Schnabel; whose death, it was already common knowledge, was caused by one of his fellow-deputies.

The Americans reneged on the promised reward of a thousand dollars. Gonzalez got two hundred and the rest of the grand was divided up among deputies; including one who'd taken no part in the capture of Cortez. Rogers, who'd made the capture, refused to take reward money.

The charge that Mrs. Robledo had fired at the deputies, in the Battle of Belmont, was refutable by the fact that none of the weapons in the Robledo house had been fired. Yet, the charge was not dropped until she agreed to state that she had seen Cortez kill Glover on one side of the house, then run around the other side and kill Schnabel. One Manuel

Tom also perjured himself by testifying that Cortez had confessed to him that he'd been on the side of the house by the barn where Schnabel had been shot. Upon being asked the Spanish word that Cortez had used for "barn" in the purported confession, Tom said *Casa*: house.

The trial of Cortez for the shooting of Schnabel was a mere formality. Judge, sheriffs and jurors had reached the decision that Cortez was to be hanged—except one. One A.L. Sanders, believing Cortez innocent, hung the jury. He hung the jury until he received word that there was a serious illness in his family and that he was needed at home. He then compromised with the eleven who'd decided Cortez must die for a sentence of fifty years on a charge of second-degree murder.

The verdict outraged everybody. Cortez cursed court, judge and jury all the way from the courthouse to the jail.

A.L. Sanders wasn't satisfied either. He went to the defense lawyers, informed them of why he had compromised on the verdict. The defense lawyers promptly filed for a new trial. The judge, as promptly, denied it; and fined Sanders a hundred dollars.

A week later Romuldo Cortez died in the Karnes City jail. The official report was that he had died of his wound.

Morris' shot had gone into his open mouth and through his left cheek, knocking out some teeth, and had lodged in his shoulder. Valeriano Cortez recalls that when he visited his uncle in the jail, Romuldo was well enough to walk around his cell, only a few days after he'd been arrested, and to joke with the jailer. He was then a two-hundred-pound man in the prime of life. Two months later he was dead.

An attempt to lynch Cortez in the Gonzalez County Jail was frustrated by Sheriff F.M. Fly. The attempt, the sheriff claimed, was by three hundred to three hundred fifty men from Karnes County.

A week after the lynching attempt, a deputy sheriff, A.A.Lyons, killed one Mexican and wounded another in Runge, Morris' home town. He claimed that the Mexicans had "surrounded him"; but not that they were armed. One had struck at him with his coat. He therefore, he asserted, did not anticipate "any trouble whatsoever in clearing himself of any charge that might be made"; and he was right.

On January 15, 1902, the Texas Court of Criminal Appeals reversed the Gonzalez verdict on Cortez on the basis of witness Tom's unique translation of *casa* as "barn". Cortez was not tried again for the murder of Schnabel.

Cortez was next taken to Karnes City to stand trial for the murder of Brack Morris. The families of Morris and Glover sat in the front row where they could be pointed out to the jurors. The jury took two ballots, one for the degree of murder and one for the penalty. First-degree murder was the verdict; and hanging the penalty. Eight months later the Court of Criminal Appeals reversed the verdict on the grounds of prejudice.

Cortez was next taken to Pleasanton, where he was sentenced to two years for the theft of the mare he had stolen while in flight. Although the conviction was reversed, the verdict was later used, when he was moved for retrial, at Goliad, for the shooting of Morris, to identify him as a convicted horse-thief; who had killed Morris when the latter had attempted to arrest him for that crime.

At the Goliad retrial seven jurors decided for first-degree murder and four for second-degree; and one for acquittal. The case went to Wharton County, where it was dismissed by the district judge for want of jurisdiction.

The case then went to Corpus Christi, where Cortez was again tried, April 25-30, 1904. There a jury of Anglo-American farmers found Cortez not guilty of the murder of Morris, claiming that Morris had attempted an unauthorized arrest; and that Cortez had shot him in self-defense.

Cortez, at the reading of this verdict, turned to the jury and, obviously deeply touched, bowed to the jury and said, *"Gracias."*

Meanwhile, back in Columbus, Cortez had been found guilty of the murder of Glover and sentenced to life imprisonment. Cortez's lawyers expected this verdict to be reversed because it had been based upon the assumption that Cortez had been a fugitive from justice rather than as a fugitive from lynch law. The defense had made the mistake of building its case on the contention that Cortez had not fired the shots that had killed Glover, which he had. The Court of Criminal Appeals therefore upheld the conviction and Cortez entered the Huntsville Penitentiary on January 1, 1905, to serve a life sentence.

Cortez had now been in eleven Texas jails, in eleven counties, over three and a half years. The fight for pardon began immediately.

A new light was now cast upon Cortez's personality.

Leonor Cortez had been the chief witness at the Karnes trial in her husband's defense. At the Corpus Christi trial she did not appear and the defense felt it necessary to explain that she was no longer married to Cortez and was "prejudiced against her former husband." Since so many defense witnesses had either fled or changed their stories, under pressure from the Karnes County leaders who wanted Cortez hanged, it might be assumed that Leonor Cortez had been pressured to abandon Gregorio.

Yet, Cortez, when he married again, was to refer to his new bride as the only woman who'd remained faithful to him in his ordeal. And at least once again Cortez was to refer to yet another woman as the only person who'd been faithful to him. Both women (and there may have been at least a third) made public statements that they had loved Gregorio for many years and that both had been engaged to marry him before the shooting of Morris. Although Cortez was only twenty-six when he was captured, he had had ten or eleven years of roaming the country unaccompanied by his family. It can then be reasonably surmised that Cortez's wife did not divorce him because of local pressure; but because his trial revived the attention of women to whom he'd made love.

Gregorio Cortez married Estefana Garza in the Columbus, Texas, jail on December 23, 1904.

Sheriff Bridge not only made all arrangements for the marriage, but the pair were given the whole upper story of the jail as a bridal suite for the week between the ceremonies and the incarceration, for life, of Cortez in the penitentiary at Huntsville.

His prison certificate reads: Occupation—barber. Habits—temperate. Education—limited.

Largely through the persistent intercession of Colonel F.A. Chapa, publisher of *El Imparcial* of San Antonio, Cortez received a conditional pardon after he had served twelve years' imprisonment; nine at Huntsville.

The Board of Pardons recommended a full pardon. Governor Colquitta, also inclined toward a full pardon, may have been modified by a letter he'd received from Cortez two weeks before signing the pardon:

"Deep regret I have always felt for the sad occurrence; but no repentance I have felt, for I could never bring myself to the hypocritical state as to plead to gain an end that was my just due."

This tone indicates the area in which Cortez's heroism lies: not in the speed and accuracy of his gunplay; nor his courage nor stamina in flight. But in the dignity he preserved, through more than a dozen trials, in rejecting all efforts to make him beg for his life. It was probably this attitude which so affected the men who held him in custody. The prison chaplain, the warden and the chief clerk at Huntsville were among those who petitioned the governor for full pardon for Cortez.

Three letters petitioning pardon appear to have been dictated in Spanish and typed by the same person. Two are signed by Cortez and one by "Senorita E. Martinez" with the explanation: "Represented by: Esther Martinez, his sweetheart." The letter defining his lack of repentance is also signed by Miss Martinez, "to whom I was engaged to be married at the time this trouble arose. She alone has remained true, devoted and faithful to me during my long and terrible fourteen years of misfortune."

No mention is made of the fact that, "at the time this trouble arose" he was married to Leonor Diaz Cortez. Nor to the fact that he had married Estefana Garza at Columbus, Texas.

Miss Martinez's letter reveals a curious conviction, among Spanish-American women, that a governor may release a prisoner if a woman claims him for marriage. Her letter repeats the request, "if you will give him to me," several times.

Cortez did not marry Miss Martinez when he was pardoned. He went instead to Nuevo Laredo to establish residence in Mexico at a moment when that country was in the throes of revolution. Northern Mexico was up in arms against Huerta, who had succeeded Madero upon the latter's assassination. Nuevo Laredo was still held by Huerta troops. Cortez's son, Valeriano, says that Cortez went to Nuevo Laredo to join the Huerta forces at the request of Colonel Chapa. And joined the Huerta forces to satisfy his obligation to Colonel Chapa.

The Huertista mistook Cortez for a spy. He was in immediate danger of being shot; but papers, provided for him in San Antonio, prevented that. The Huertista then shaved his head and put him in the infantry as a private soldier.

Later Cortez was mounted and given a squad of *rurales* to command. He was wounded. One rumor has it that he was captured and escaped before being executed. He returned to Jones County, Texas, and remarried. Whom he married is not known as he died on the evening of the wedding. Valeriano Cortez believes his father was poisoned at the wedding.

He was buried, at the age of forty-one, in a little cemetery eight miles outside of Anson, Texas. A niece of Cortez says that as late as 1925 there was a headstone with the name of Gregorio Cortez marking his grave.

Thus lies Gregorio Cortez, five hundred miles from the border on which he was born. And which he had once come within a few miles of crossing on a little sorrel mare.

THE HOUSE OF THE
HUNDRED GRASSFIRES

IT was during that rumorous dappled hour when evening spreads like the latest scandal, before the night's true traffic starts. When such whore's foliage as vermilion bras and chartreuse panties still hang, in the airless heat of backyard lines, between G-strings that once were silver. A joint-tog jungle festooned by garments of such bright shame as stay washable. Above a vegetation of contraceptives lying in puddles of gray decay.

This is the early-buyers' hour when women dust their navels for afternoon bugs who can't wait till evening to fly: all those hurrying from loneliness in order to preserve their solitude later. The city was full of lonesome monsters who couldn't get drunk any more.

At The Hundred Grassfires the night's first girl stood in the night's first door; feeling sweat molding her pink pajama to her thighs.

The whole street felt molded, thigh to thigh. Perdido Street was a basement valet shop with both irons working. In the round of her armpits the girl felt sweat creeping in the down.

She did not solicit; it was too hot for that. She had lived fifteen years in Chicago without once feeling warm; now she had lived almost ten in New Orleans without once feeling cool.

It was so hot that at the sight of a man she could feel both of their watery navels stick. So she merely crooked her small finger now and then and let it go at that.

The courts were against these cork-heeled puppets, the police were against them as well. Politicians used them; editors mocked them. Doctors disdained them. Judges and ministers were sustained by them. Daughters, sisters and wives were perpetually outraged by them. So mothers organized against them. Their own pimps conspired regularly against them.

Now a man wearing a shadow for a cap marched up and down, across the street, below a curious sign—

BEWARE THE WRATH TO COME

The missions were dispatching mercenaries announcing that Christ Himself had decided against them.

The man under the sign cut slantwise across the street to give the girl full benefit of his warning. She turned her hip to give him a bit of her backside; simply to show how little she needed him. Like all the women who kept the doors, Chicago Kitty knew that, like the police, the columnists, the courts, the doctors, the preachers and the pimps, he wanted to save her only to have her. For all the indignation these women provoked, no one ever wanted them to be anything but whores.

The prostitute never sent for anyone's husband. Husbands came to her. She never sent for a brother or son; sons and brothers came to her.

In the parlor behind Kitty sat other outlaws, eight nine ten, who had died of uselessness one by one. Yet now they lived on, behind veritable prairie-fires of wishes, while prying salt-water taffy from between their teeth. Envy and ennui divided each.

"A light drizzle wound be good for trade," Kitty heard a man's voice say behind her, "but a heavy fall would ruin it."

That would be that appleknocker, an apprentice pimp calling himself Big Stingaree, recently arrived from nowhere in a red shirt and high-heeled Spanish boots; who'd be gone once more before the heels ran down.

The juke began complaining about everybody—

It isn't fair for you to taunt me
You only want me for today

A small man wearing a clerical collar, under a face favoring a raccoon's, skipped up—he was built like a bag of sand and somewhat favored a badger, too. As Kitty stepped aside to let him pass, she caught a whiff of violet talc. The juke went on complaining—

It isn't fair for you to want me
You only want me for today.

A moment later she followed him inside just to see what he really wanted.

He was pulling off his collar—then flinging it across the room, then challenging the house:

"Bring on your beasts of the wild!"

"Are you sure you're in the right place, mister?" the appleknocker pimp, standing a full head higher, inquired.

"Oh, I know what you people do here," Bag-of-Sand lowered his voice confidentially—"*I* know what you do."

"What we do best," a girl holding a poodle dyed pink remarked, "is pitch people out on their skulls."

Bag-of-Sand laughed into the palm of his hand.

"*Exactly* what do you think you're geared to, mister?" the apprentice pimp wanted to know, stepping closer.

"Exactly what am I *geared* to?" Bag-of-Sand glanced up. "My dear young man, I'm exactly geared to the girlies; *exactly*. Otherwise why would I be here *exactly?* Or is this a hardware store?" And turning his back on the slow-witted macker, he began an explanation of the Immaculate Conception that not even Mama, the mulatto madam of The Hundred Grassfires, had ever heard before.

"Parthenogenesis is scientifically possible," he explained as though the question had been troubling him for some time, "but it can only occur in the haploid chromosomes. As these are only half the size of the somatic chromosomes, they result in dwarfism. *That* was what happened to Mary."

"The hell with all that," the apprentice pimp decided. "How about some action?"

"Let him speak," Mama overruled the apprentice, "I know I'll never die sanctified. But I *do* hope at least to die blessed."

Bag-of-Sand began pacing up and down, in a sweat from more than the climate; one hand on his belly and one on his head—"and furthermore I'll tell you how the Church covered up the scientific truth that Jesus Christ *was* a dwarf. Every time the Church fathers came to a biblical reference to Jesus as 'tiny,' 'little,' 'undersized,' or 'small,' they changed it to 'humble,' 'meek,' 'gentle,' 'modest,' or 'sweet.' I've done research all over the world on this and I can tell you: The Church has perpetuated a hoax!"

"Are you for action or *aren't* you, buddy?" Big Stingaree wanted to know.

"Well, in May, 1929, I wrote C-U-N-T on a convent wall in red chalk—how's *that* for action?"

Big Stingaree clapped his hand to his forehead and staggered backward to show that the mind boggled at the very thought.

"Not only *that*"—Bag-of-Sand seemed anxious to paint as black a picture of himself as possible—"*I was wearing the cloth at the time!*"

"No matter how you look at it," Mama deliberated solemnly, "it's a bad situation. I hope you've confessed, young man."

"Not formally," Bag-of-Sand explained, "but later in the same year, while passing the same convent, I wrote *Jesus Saves* where I'd written that other."

"What were you wearing," Mama wanted to know, "when you wrote *Jesus Saves* where you'd written *that other*?"

"A sports jacket and huarachos."

"I see," Mama said sorrowfully. "You write something like *that* while wearing the cloth and then come back six months later dressed like Bing Crosby, scribble *Jesus Saves,* and think you've missed purgatory. It isn't as easy as all that, young man."

"The Pope himself couldn't get you off now," Big Stingaree decided. "How about a bit of action as long as you're sunk anyhow?"

Bag-of-Sand agreed. For he was geared to the girlies just as he'd said.

In fact, this ghee could scarcely remember one day to the next where he'd lain the night before. And as often as not, he wound up in the very same sack as he had at noon disheveled.

Twitchet-struck and pussy-simple, snatch-mad and skirt-sick, he was a side-street solitary who had nothing but a petticoat with seven ruffles on it in his mind. One who dreamed by night of nothing but what he'd do to the girls tomorrow. This was a sinner whose family had once had him committed because he had decided he didn't want to be a priest after all. Any man who didn't want to be a priest was obviously out of his mind. There had been simply nothing left to do but to commit him.

What had thereafter emerged, obsessed by myths, was no longer of either the church or the world, but the ghost of a ghost who roamed a curious twilit land between the world and the church.

A land where the thousand images of sex stood transfixed like stone ruins in a desert place. Lost in a world where sex had gone blind, deaf, mute, cold: and alone as a seaward stone.

"So long as I'm sunk I might as well have some fun out of sinking," he reasoned Jesuitically. Then, turning to the girl holding the poodle dyed pink, he inquired, "What may your little friend's name be, miss?"

"Heavensent," the girl assured him.

"Why, then Heaven must have sent him," Bag-of-Sand deduced. And offering the girl his arm, all three, girl, poodle and defrocked priest, proceeded up the unsanctified stair.

Now the blinds, drawn fast, held the room in a dappled gloom where dimly fell the shadows, one by one, of bars. And in this dusk like a jailhouse dusk the juke sang on and on.

> *In our little penthouse*
> *We'll always contrive*
> *To keep love and romance always alive*
> *Just over the Hudson*
> *Just over the drive—*

The moment the song stopped, the creaking of the overhead fans began, regular and slow. The women shifted restlessly from doorway to divan, lighting fresh cigarettes or opening fresh Dr. Peppers at each new post; yet never finishing either a drink or a cigarette.

"You never know when a trick is a cop or somebody missing one bubble," the Chicago girl complained.

"When he starts in to strangle you, chances are he ain't a cop," Kitty explained, "it's why I keep saying it would be best if every trick took two girls. Then when he got your neck in his hands, your buddy could holler for help."

They never finished anything. Restlessness was their common affliction. Reba was sure the fan was giving her a chill, Floralee wanted to sing; and Kitty had to know why she wasn't permitted to spike a Coke with gin. While Mama worried lest she should die unblessed.

The girls crowded forward in their watery gloom, shading their eyes against the street: No one had seen the cab drive up.

It came out of nowhere. Like a cab that wheels all night through a misting dream.

All saw step forth in the greenish light a naval lieutenant in full regalia; a seagoing executive in rimless glasses: A hero of sea fights yet unfought. Bearing like a rainbow across his sky-blue breast all the honors a peacetime navy could pin.

Bag-of-Sand, wherever he'd gone, was immediately forgotten when this sight stepped out on Perdido Street.

Mama simply *scuttled* to the curb. Mama had never captured a prospect so glorious to behold.

Yet he seemed reluctant of capture. For he held Mama there in some earnest discussion; speaking low so as to keep his driver from hearing.

"Mammy-freak," Mama *thought* she heard him saying, "stick out so fah behind she hahdly got time to make a child behave."

Mama took one step closer. "I don't quite catch what you're saying, Officer."

196

He cupped his lips, leaning toward her—"*Made a lemon pie. Made me a lemon pie, little lemon pie all mah own.*"

Mama took a step back. "Lemon?" she asked. "All your own?"

"The very day I broke the churn."

"Then I have just the girl for you," Mama decided. For whatever this rascal had in mind, she couldn't afford to lose a customer so prosperous. "Every man likes a little change now and then. I know exactly how you feel."

He drew himself up. "*Nobody* knows how a mammy-freak feels," he informed her point-blank. "How could anyone but another mammy-freak know how a mammy-freak feels?"

If it was an organization, he was the president. Mama simply turned to go, but he held her back with a wheedling touch. "You know yourself," he cajoled her, "how they stick out in back."

"*Who* stick out in back?"

"Why, *all* of them; especially when they get in a hurry. Now, *admit* it."

Mama shook off his hand. "*Who* stick out? *Who* get in a hurry? Admit *what*?" Mama was getting angry but she didn't know at what.

"Why, old black mammies, of course," he told her as though everyone knew old black mammies were the coming thing.

"Maybe you ought to come inside before it rains," Mama invited him, suddenly feeling she'd be safer in the parlor.

"It isn't going to rain." Navy sounded certain as God and began unfolding a little apron from under his coat. He bent to tie it about her waist. It was striped green and white like peppermint; as he tied it Mama plucked without strength at the apron's price-tag. He picked the tag off himself and the cab dusted off in disgust.

"A good many black-mammy-freaks visit you, I presume?" the officer assumed.

"It's been several days since one called," Mama told him. Standing in her Aunt Jemima apron, she now felt *she* had become the prospect.

"My men call me 'Commander,' " he announced.

"That," Mama decided inwardly, "isn't what my chicks are going to call you."

And led him inside The Hundred Grassfires like leading a child home.

Inside the parlor the six-year-old black boy with the mind of a forty-year-old pimp, the one his grandmother called Warren Gameliel but whom the women called the King of the Indoor Thieves, stood on a divan wearing shoes that belonged to a grown man and nothing else but a shirt.

A shirt that barely reached his navel, revealing a hide not exactly high yellow. The King was in fact closer to high brown. He was even closer to dark brown.

Warren Gameliel was black as a kettle in hell.

Truth to tell, the King looked to be a cross between a Black Angus calf and something fished out of the Mississippi on a moonless night. One shade darker and this kid would have disappeared.

"Meet my grandson," Mama introduced him to the Commander. "Ain't he just *fine?*"

Turning his head proudly upon his iron-colored throat, the King fluttered his lashes modestly at the woman's flattery.

"Age six years, waist thirty-two and a half, weight one hundred and two, and she asks is he fine," the woman called Hallie Dear mocked Mama fondly. The big overdressed man saluted the small naked one.

"Pledge allegiance, Boy-Baby," Mama encouraged the King to perform his single accomplishment. But the King simply planted his black toes wider, as though saying he'd have to know more about this gold-braid wheeler-dealer before he'd pledge his teething ring.

Then Reba honked with hollow glee: under the shirt the boy was reacting to the scent of the half-naked woman like a baby bull.

"I do it *back*," the King made his intention known.

"Ain't you *shamed*," Mama reproved him in a voice that simply *donged* with pride, "gettin' a *upper* right in front of ladies?"

"He'll be a pimp like everyone else," Kitty prophesied.

"I worked for loryers," Reba entered the stakes, "we specialized in tort'n'seizure."

These women regarded Hallie Dear with an intermixture of admiration and pity. They felt she held herself aloof because she'd once taught school. At the same time they perceived that she was defenseless. Floralee alone loved and trusted the older woman.

But was there anyone Floralee *didn't* trust? If this pale lost blonde wasn't down the stairs by the time street-lamps came on, somebody went up and fetched her down. For should lamps come on or lamps stay dark, all was one to this pale lost blonde.

Nobody had counted (since nobody cared) how many lamps had gone down since the night she had stood where marquee lights flickered in an uncertain rain; and a cabbie had held a door wide for her. She had gotten in and offered him a pressed flower for her fare.

"I sing just *ever* so purty, mister," she assured the officer now. "Only modesty songs, of course; for I don't know vulgary words. May I recite a modesty poem?"

"Wait till you hear *this* loony holler," Kitty warned him. "I think all they did in them hills was bury their dead."

"Don't begrudge the child," Mama put her arm about Floralee's shoulder to indicate *she* wasn't one to begrudge *any* child, "she got the innocence God protects."

"He's got a strange notion of protection then, that's *my* opinion," Kitty told how she felt about everything.

And turned her back on the parlor.

What must I do to win a diadem

Floralee burst into song strung on a silver string—

When I reach that shining strand?

"*Shh,* honey," Mama tried to quiet the demented girl, and turning apologetically to the naval prospect, explained, "this one is a regular angel."

"She's a whore like everyone else," Kitty announced with her back still turned. Floralee cupped her face in her hands to hide her blush of shame.

"Anybody can be a whore," added Kitty.

"Is that true?" the commander asked Mama seriously. "Can any one woman become a whore? Any woman at all?"

"Anyone at all," Mama seemed optimistic. "Aren't we all created free and equal?"

"Where do you keep your submarines?" Kitty turned abruptly on the officer.

"Why ask me a thing like that?"

"It would help me in my work—I'm a spy on the side." Nobody laughed when Kitty turned to the juke.

"I feel rotten about everybody but myself," she said aloud.

"I got half my choppers out 'n no ovalries," Reba remembered, "the doctor said he never seen nothin' like it. So what? I can still be a practical nurse without ovalries, can't I? Hey! How'd you like all the cigarettes you can smoke, General? Just go down to American Tobacco 'n give my name; they'll give you all you can haul in one trip."

"Baby," the girl called Big Five marveled, "I don't know what you're on, but *I* never heard nothing like it, either."

"I do it back," the King insisted, but Mama yanked the gold-braid cap, which he had taken off the commander's head, far down over his eyes. As if by shutting off his vision she might improve his manners.

"I *do* it," the infant insisted, warning everyone of what would happen the second he got this damned hat out of his eyes.

Somebody got the juke going. Somebody said, "Make mine a double." And somebody else called for gin—

Mama don't 'low no gee-tar playin' here

the juke cried in dread—

Mama don't 'low no banjo-playin' here—

"Oh, I can sing purtier *far* than that," Floralee boasted amid pleas, claims, threats, and tiny squeals. For now the women vied openly for the commander's attention. While the King worked his thighs in a rage of blinded love but still couldn't get that cap out of his eyes.

"I want you girls to respect our guest!" Mama began shouting, though nobody had yet gotten around to insulting him. "Look *up* to this man. Hear this! Hear this! Warren Gameliel, you little black fool, get the commander's hat off your head this *instant!*"

"Mama!" Hallie began scolding Mama, "stop giving orders! We're not in a battle!"

"This man represents the entire Atlantic fleet combined!" Mama cried out. "Warren Gameliel! Pledge allegiance!"

"She's just being carried away," Hallie explained to the officer. Brushing the other girls aside, she framed his face in her hands until he returned the look she gave.

"If you don't behave, I'll send you to the nigger school," Mama threatened the King.

Outside the drunks were coming out of the country's last speakeasies and the street-lamps began to move like the breasts of a young girl under the hands of a man who has bought too many. Warren Gameliel reached out blindly and secured a black stranglehold on the officer's neck.

And in an odd little silence a girl's voice said, "I was drunk, the jukebox was playing; I began to cry." And all the air felt troubled by some cheap cologne.

"Our guest wants to say hello," Hallie guessed; and pulled Navy's head right against her breast. He nodded strengthless assent.

She helped him to rise and he rose; more like a sick man than one drunk.

200

"Send two double-gins to my room," Hallie ordered Mama. "The rest of you drink whatever you want."

A kerosene lamp lit Hallie's room—one that might have served a whore of old Babylon: a narrow bed in hope of bread; a basin in hope of purity. A beaded portiere to keep mosquitoes out yet let a little music in. A scent of punk from an incense stick to burn off odors of whiskey or tobacco. A calendar from the year before and an image above it of something or other in hope of forgiveness for this or that. A whole world to millions since the first girl sold; and a world to millions yet.

The lamp's brown glow on her amber gown made of Hallie a golden woman. For her eyes burned with a gray-green fire; and about her throat she wore a yellow band. Her gown fell off one shoulder but was kept from falling farther by the rise of her breast.

"No matter how often I trick," she murmured aloud, "as soon as I'm with a man, I get shaky."

"No need of even taking off your clothes," he told her. "Nothing is going to happen."

Hallie, always defensive about her darkness, was ready to be hurt: "Some men like dark girls best."

"Nothing to do with it," he explained, "I was brought up in a special way. Yet I'll pay you for your time. I don't mean charity."

"I never turn down charity," Hallie told him candidly, "I have too much pride for that. What kind of whore would I be *then*?" She held herself proudly upon her dishonored bed.

"I'm from Virginia," he now thought she should know, "we go back to the Old Dominion."

"It's nice to have two homes, I'm sure," she congratulated him.

He smiled gently; then cupped her ear to confide something—"*It's where Old Black Mammy come by with a broom 'n 'most knock you down—'Stay outa mah way when ah'm cleanin', boy!'—but when you stay out of the way here she come with bucket 'n mop 'n 'most knock you down again—'Boy, when you gonna learn to behave?'—'n when you start behavin', she come right at you—'Boy! You got nuthin' to do all day but stand in mah way?'*" His voice took on a secret excitement. "*Wham! She give it to you good, Old Black Mammy got a heavy hand —'Boy, you fixin' to git yourself soaked?'*"

He composed himself.

"Mister," Hallie asked at last, "how long you been in this condition?"

The big flushed man, boylike yet strangely aged, ran his hand across his hair to be sure its part was in place. He was one of those men whose teeth are so well kept and whose hair is so well groomed that both appear to be false.

"Black Mammy's been dead nineteen years," he told Hallie, returning to his white pronunciation. "Hand and foot that woman waited on us; and when the day came that found her crippled, who was there left to wait on her? 'Mammy,' I told her, 'you waited on me, now it's my turn to wait on you.' " A mischievous light came into his eyes: "That wasn't *all* I told her."

"All *right*—what else?"

"I told her, 'You made *me* behave, now it's my turn to make *you* behave.' "

"Mister," Hallie told him, "I really don't take your meaning—couldn't you get to the point?"

He crossed his large hands and looked at her evenly.

"I was working the churn when the handle snapped. The water from it was flooding the porch. When Black Mammy saw what I'd done, she aimed her hand at me. I slipped and fell trying to get away, so she paddled me face down. I started hollering, pretending she was half killing me, when it really hardly hurt at all. That was the first time she made me *behave.*"

Hallie saw light however faintly.

"What happened *exactly?*"

"*Exactly?* Exactly what happens when a man is having a girl, exactly. And I've never been able to make it any other way since." He laughed in the watery light. "Exactly."

Hallie waited.

"That was when I was ten. She died when I was twenty-one. And the day she died, the last motion she made was to give me a backhanded slap on my bottom. To let me know she had understood all along." He put his hand to his forehead. "I'm terribly tired, I don't know why."

"She must have been grateful for your care," was all Hallie could think to say. For it came to her that this wasn't a monster of the nastier sort: but only a boy playing commander with his nose still running.

"She was. As I'm grateful today for her. Who else but Mammy ever felt I was worth human care?"

"Mister," Hallie told him quietly, "you don't need a girl. You need a doctor."

"There aren't any doctors for black-mammy freaks," he explained dryly; as though he'd tried looking one up in the city directory.

"Then just try to rest," Hallie told him. "I'll do what I can."

"There's money in my wallet. It's in my coat," he instructed her.

She took the coat off the chair and found the wallet. "I won't take it all," she assured him.

He didn't look interested in her count.

He looked stricken.

Fast as she could pin, Hallie began preparing Mama for a great impersonation.

"You don't think he stole his ship's money, do you?" Mama had to know. "He isn't going to get us all in trouble, is he?"

"You never made an easier dollar your whole enduring life," Hallie reassured her. "He's just a green boy kept on black titty too long. All you got to remember is he keeps getting in your way. Don't hit him too hard—just hard enough. Make it look good. Getting whupped by his old black mammy is what he come here for—turn around so I can pin you." She began stuffing a small pillow into Mama's bosom. "The more you stick out in front the more you stick out behind. I'll have you sticking out so far you'll look like Madam Queen."

"Girl, I was *born* in this country. You won't catch *me* hitting no member of our armed forces."

It was plain Mama hadn't caught the play.

"*Mama*," Hallie pleaded, "*forget* the man's uniform. I'm trying to tell you he isn't like other men."

Mama stiffened like a retriever. "Honey, he ain't one of them *O*-verts? I won't cater to *them*. Not for *no* amount."

"If he were, he'd be better off," Hallie reassured her, "now turn around." And pinned skirt over skirt till Mama, weighted down, sank heavily into a chair.

"Honey, I'm starting to sweat," she complained.

"Sweat till you shine," Hallie encouraged her, "but don't show your face till I give you the sign." And stepped through the portiere.

Beneath the ruin of the commander's gold-braid hat, the King of the Indoor Thieves had collapsed at last; his undershirt tangled about his throat as if someone had tried to improve his manners by finishing him off altogether. He snored till his toes were spread; he stretched till he creaked in dreams. Dreams of some final assault for an earth about to be his for keeps.

"All of you stop talking out of the corners of your mouth like you were Edward G. Robinson and everybody was in the can," Hallie quieted the women. "You've got a guest tonight that means gold from way back. Try to show manners."

For down the stair with an admiral's tread came the hero of sea fights as good as won. Looking like the dogs had had him under the house. With a gin glass latched to his hand.

Hallie crooked one finger toward the portiere and Mama came forth with forehead shining, bandana and broom; all sweat and Aunt Jemima in a peppermint apron that hung like candy.

The second he saw her, Commander dropped his glass. "I didn't *mean* to do that," he apologized immediately, and began trying to clean the floor with his sleeve, glass, splinters, and all, immediately making a worse mess than before.

Mama seated herself across from him in her preposterous gear. The girls exchanged looks; part fear and part wonder.

"I'm a Protestant by birth but a Catholic by descent." Mama felt it was time to explain the curious no-man's land of her faith. "I've shod the horse all around." Meaning she had had four husbands. "So I'm not acceptable to the Church. But if I can't die sanctified I *do* hope to die blessed."

His elbow touched Floralee's glass. It tottered; he reached as if to keep it from tipping and knocked it over instead. The girl pushed back her chair and he began mopping it up with a silk handkerchief; although all he was doing actually was swishing the handkerchief around in it. "Go on with your story," he told Mama, "I'm *sorry* to be so clumsy."

Mama had lost the thread. All she could remember was that she'd shod the horse all around.

"Three of them were thieves and one was a legit man—I'd never marry another legit man. Do you know that you're safer living with a man who kills for hire than with a man who has never killed? That's because one knows what killing is; the other don't."

"Why," Commander remarked, "in that case, ill-fame women ought to make better wives than legitimate girls."

Nobody knew what to say to that.

"Navy, I think that's the nicest thing I've heard anyone say since I've been in the trade," Hallie said at last.

His elbow tipped Mama's glass into her lap.

"Now don't tell me *that* 'just happen,' " Mama scolded him in earnest now. "Mister, my frank opinion is you done that a-purpose."

"Honest I didn't, Mammy," he lied patently.

"*Don't* whup him, Mama," Floralee pleaded for him.

"I'm *sure* he won't do it again," Hallie defended him, too.

"Give me *one* more chance, Mama," he whimpered.

"Only out of respect for your uniform," Mama issued final warning, "and one more is *all* you gets." She turned to shake out her skirts, somebody tittered and somebody honked and she whirled just in time to catch the Commander with two fingers to his nose. Mama scarcely knew what to feel.

"Why, that isn't the least *bit* nice, a man of your background to have such manners—"

"He didn't *mean* anything, Mama," Hallie was sure.

"*Don't* whup him," Floralee begged.

"*Cross my heart* I didn't mean anything," Commander swore in that same unbearable small-boy whine that in itself entitled him to a thrashing.

"Oh, he *meant* it all right," Kitty informed, "I seen him with my naked eye. And I have a *very* naked eye."

"I *will* try to do better, Mammy," he promised too humbly. "Oh, I *will* try to behave. Oh, I *will* be a good boy, cross my heart 'n hope—" Standing up to cross himself, his hand caught the tablecloth and brought cloth, bottles, decanters, ashtrays, Cokes and a centerpiece of artificial pansies crashing to the floor.

In the silence everyone heard a small clock saying "sick-sick-sick."

Then Mammy went even blacker with rage as he went whiter with fright. Now she went at him with no pretending, and he flung his two hundred and fourteen pounds under the table in true fear.

"*Don't* whup me, Mammy," they heard him pleading. "*Please* don't whup me just this *one* time."

Hallie tried to hold her and Floralee helped, because Mama *could* do murder when out of control. Reba fastened onto Mama's waist to hold her back. Kitty stood to one side not caring particularly who got killed so long as blood was spilled.

"Beat him blue!" Big Five joined Mama's forces. "If you can't do it, I will!" and dove right for him.

"He's *Mama's* date, not yours," Hallie hauled Big Five back and held her until she calmed down—holding a strip of gold-braided blue serge in her hand ripped from the officer's sleeve.

"I'm just a little boy," they heard somebody under the table whine, "*please* don't hurt me."

"Now he's *really* asking for it," Kitty commented.

Just as the apprentice pimp showed up at last, complete in sombrero and boots newly shined. He was the only one capable of holding Mama in a true rage and Mama herself knew this. When he got both arms around her, she ceased to struggle and began to cry. He and Hallie got

Mama into a chair; where she daubed at her eyes with his big bandana.

Big Five got hold of one of the commander's silken ankles and Floralee the other. Between them they succeeded in pulling him forth.

He lay on his stomach, rump elevated to invite kicks, eyes closed with rapture. Big Five pushed him onto his side. Then, by inserting one toe underneath him, rolled him over like lifting a great drugged cat onto the flat of his back.

He lay face up, his eyes still shut.

"He got no right to lay around so loose, without being drunk or sick, either one," Big Five expressed her disgust, "somebody get some water."

"I don't have any *water*," Floralee reported in her light sweet voice and a white pitcher in her hand—"Wouldn't beer do as well?"—and emptied it full in the officer's face.

Then, looking down into her pitcher, the girl saddened: "Now it's empty." And she looked ready to cry.

"You could use Cokes," Hallie told her.

Now who but Hallie Dear would have thought of *that*? Floralee gathered the half-finished bottles standing on ledge and divan, and in no time at all had her pitcher refilled. But this time she poured it down the front of the Commander's shirt.

"That *was* fun," she reported hopefully to Hallie, and lifting his legs and holding them, began to sing—

> Don't throw bouquets at me
> Don't laugh at my jokes too much—

while all the while the commander lay licking his big ox-tongue like a Coke-dripping Lazarus too languid to rise.

"I've been everywhere God got land," Hallie told him, "but you are the *most* disgusting sight yet seen—you can drop his legs any time," she told Floralee. Who promptly let both legs fall at once.

"I had a very strong hankering to go to sea at one time myself," the apprentice pimp recalled, kicking the big man lightly: "Get up, officer."

But nobody really knew what to do with this hero of sea fights yet unfought.

Except the King of the Indoor Thieves. *He* always knew what to do.

"I do it *back*," he repeated. And with no further ado, straddled the fallen leader and began urinating upon him with solemn delight. "I'm

206

a sonofabitch," he explained, "I *do* do it back!" And fluttered his lashes above the torrent.

"Why!" Mama came suddenly to herself in a burst of sunrisen pride, "Why! Listen to *that*! A child of six using the language of a child of ten! Hear this! Hear this! Salute the Atlantic fleet!"

"Mama," Hallie sought to calm the older woman, "I respect the Atlantic fleet as much as the next person, but I do feel this child is going too far."

Mama came to attention, eyes straight forward, put her palm to her forehead in the hand-salute and began the Pledge of Allegiance. The King brought his own hand up to his forehead and stood at attention as well as he could while continuing to urinate.

The big man on the floor looked up. He opened his eyes so blue, so commanding. "That was the nicest party I've had in eleven years," he announced, rising at last.

Someone handed him his crushed hat and his soiled coat.

At the door he smiled; but no one smiled back.

Mama lowered herself, inch by inch in all her finery, onto a divan. She felt like the real thing in black mammies. But all she did was sigh. Just sigh.

Outside, she heard the night's last drunk pause as if listening for a friendly voice; then cry out: "God forgive me for my sins! Empty saddles in the old corral!"

And passed on toward the breaking day.

Half in wake and half in sleeping, Mama heard the jukebox weeping—

> *From all of society we'll stay aloof*
> *And live in propriety here on the roof*

When the juke began to bark, she wakened. Down the stairs the poodle dyed pink came bounding and barking all the way. Behind him came the girl who owned him, crying to Heaven: "Heavensent! Heavensent!"

And behind her, holding the banister with one hand, Bag-of-Sand came feeling his way down.

If he'd been out of shape when he went upstairs, he was really disheveled now. He came down like a man fearing to break his neck at every step. And when he made it all the way down, he found himself facing the apprentice pimp; who seemed to have grown in size somehow.

"*Are* you for action or *aren't* you, buddy?" the would-be pimp wanted to know.

Bag-of-Sand got past him and stood in the middle of the parlor boggling blindly about.

"I can sing like a damned bird," Floralee told him, "only how did I fly in *here*?"

Bag-of-Sand turned slowly away. But at the door he turned.

"Good-night, girls," he told them. "Someday I'll tell you about the time I reviled the Virgin for fifteen minutes."

And he passed, like the commander had passed; through a dark doorway into a darker dream.

"Go out and get the morning papers," Mama instructed Floralee, "I want to see what the white folks are up to."

PREVIOUS DAYS

FURLONGS away from those bright-red arrows directing horse-players to the daily-double windows, every racetrack has one shadowy cage identifying itself begrudgingly as:

PREVIOUS DAYS

After the $20-on-the-nose sure-thing that broke stride; after the $15-across-the-board shot that went wide; after all the tips that came straight from the barn have run out, Previous Days is where Yesterday's Bettor goes to cash a $3.80 place ticket: thus redeeming the follies of all his yesterdays.

And Remembrance being but a sequence of bright changes that broke stride (Recollection itself having run a bit wide), I recently found myself shuffling through a handful of memories like so many dead tickets that once had been certain winners: discovering several still redeemable. Within the shadows of previous days.

I remember taking a shortcut through an alley, when I was about ten, and seeing three women leaning, as though fascinated, across an alley gate; they were held fascinated by something in that backyard. I looked, too.

Somebody had trapped a huge rat, in a circular trap of frying-pan size. The trap had fastened the rat by its nose. It was bleeding and trying to pull free. The women didn't know what to do.

A Sunday-morning iceman, tongs resting across his shoulder, straw hat on his head and toothpick in teeth, looking ready for anything, came up and took command.

"A bucket of water!" he issued the orders of the day.

One of the women raced into the house and came out with a mop bucket so full that it spilled a bit when she put it down beside the rat. Mr. Ready-for-Anything flung trap, rat and all into the bucket. We crowded around to watch the brute drown.

It didn't even sink. The trap was of wood and supported it like a buoy. Around and around it went, bleeding as it swam; while we stood waiting for it to bleed to death. Now not even the iceman knew what to do.

A small girl, wearing a white communion veil, skipped up, banged the rat behind one ear with a housebrick, waited just long enough to see it sink, then went skipping off down the alley with the brick still in her hand.

Some iceman.

Any kid looking for battle could get it just by tapping you on your shoulder and saying, "There's your carty." If you didn't accept the challenge, all he had to do was say, "Well, I gave you your carty," and walk away. And though you later succeeded greatly and he failed miserably, he remained, all your life, because of your cowardice that day, your superior.

A variation of this challenge was once offered me by a kid named Walter Dinnerbell. (That was his real name and he was smaller than I was.) He came up to me in the schoolyard of the Park Manor School and warned me, "I can change you into a cat."

I scoffed.

"Do you *dare* me?"

I thought it over carefully. I was *almost* certain he couldn't. But then you could never be *absolutely* certain.

"No," I decided not to take the chance, "I *don't* dare you."

Many times since then I've wished that I had that chance over again. "Yes," I'd say firmly, "I *do* dare you."

On the other hand, why take unnecessary risks?

A kid called Vinnie was perfect hell on substitute teachers. One day a young girl introduced herself as Miss Leibowitz, our substitute music teacher. What move would Vinnie make *this* time? We wondered.

For starters he did nothing but make funny noises.

"*Who* is making that *animal* noise?" Miss Leibowitz asked gently. She was a gentle girl and a rather pretty one. "Have we a little *animal* in our class?"

Nobody snitched on Vinnie. The girl turned to the piano and sang as she played:

> *Soft o'er the fountain*
> *Gently falls the Southern moon*

*   *   *

She had a nice voice. When she nodded at us we all joined in:

> 'nita, wah-ah-ah-'nita
> Comes the day too soon—

Vinnie was ready. I sensed it.

"That was awright, Teach," he assured her in his high nasal voice. "Now how about a couple bars of *Jew-roos-alum de Golden*?"

At thirteen my sister was a film buff. She'd seen every Saturday-afternoon film that had shown at the Park Manor Theater since she'd been eleven. Had theaters already begun giving away dishes in 1915? I don't know. All I know is that every soup and cereal dish—yes, and some dessert dishes also—that we owned, had the face and autograph of a film star stamped upon them. I've eaten oatmeal off the lovely lips of Viola Dana and spooned gravy from the doomed brow of Wallace Reid.

If I got the Wallace Reid plate and Sis had the Viola Dana, we'd trade no matter *what* covered the faces. The trouble was that my mother forbade dipping plates to see who was under the noodles and she made an awful lot of soup. By the time you'd knocked off the gravy on the mashed potatoes it would be too late to trade. We didn't eat *up*, we ate *toward*. And while I was drying the dishes, and Sis was washing them, she'd sing:

> *Charlie Chaplin with his feet*
> *Stepped all over poor Blanche Sweet.*

That one broke me up. My father thought Sis should be on the stage.

I was five and in love with a girl of six. Her name was Ethel, she lived upstairs, she was Catholic; and she liked me too. She could read and write, and as soon as I could read and write, too, we'd be married at St. Columbanus.

The wide stone steps and the high stone cross of St. Columbanus rose directly across from our windows at 7139 South Park. I could even see the rabbit warren, where one of the fathers bred Belgian hares, in a patch of greenery.

Every morning I watched Ethel climb those steps and disappear into the shadowed, still, and holy mystery where one learned to write and read. Love and marriage, priests and hares, the cross that hung pendant from her throat and the cross that guarded her high overhead, merged into a hope of salvation: I would be saved when I learned to read and write. I prayed for the day, a year away, when Ethel would lead me by the hand up those holy stairs.

For reasons I didn't understand I wasn't permitted to go inside St. Columbanus. But Ethel took me to look at the hares.

"They're Jesus' bunnies," she explained.

When a ragged white cloud drifted across a summer morning's sky, Ethel made me look up to see: "That's the beard of Jesus in the sky."

Once, toward evening, we looked up from our play to see the church was raising its cross, like a command, against a sky pouring an orange-red light across the last of day.

Ethel genuflected, pulled me down beside her and whispered terrifyingly: *"Gawd's blood is burning! Pray!"*

"Why?" I whispered back.

"So you'll see the face of Gawd!"

"Is that the same as 'God'?"

"Don't say 'God.' Say *'Gawd.' Or you'll never see sweet Jesus' face!"*

That girl was purely *gone* on Jesus.

Anything either of us owned belonged to the other, and one day we found a nickel together. Ethel led me to the school store at 71st and Rhodes, opposite the Park Manor School, and I thought we were going for candy. We weren't. She exchanged the nickel for five pennies, made me put my eye to a stereopticon while she turned the crank; that flipped a series of bright postcards depicting the stations of the cross. I saw Christ make Calvary four times; then asked her if she'd like to look.

"I've already seen it," she assured me; and played our last penny so I could see it a fifth time.

My report on the recent crucifixion to my family received a mixed reaction.

"That girl is a Holy Wonder, isn't she?" my father inquired mildly.

"That was better than candy," my mother decided, "at least you *learned* something."

"*I* would have bought candy," Sis boasted smugly; "*I'm* an atheist." She was going to be a schoolteacher.

On the first day of school—September, 1915—she took me down 71st Street to Rhodes Avenue. I tried to pull away, protesting that we were going the wrong direction. She marched me into the kindergarten of the Park Manor School and turned me over to a Miss Burke.

I took one look around: No fathers, no rabbits, no Jesus, no Ethel.

And set up a howl that wouldn't quit until Miss Burke shoved me into her portable clothes closet and locked the door.

I stood in the dark, among coats and umbrellas, until the door opened and another howler was shoved inside. We stood silently confronting one another in the dark. I couldn't see his face and he couldn't see mine.

"What do you want to do?" he asked me at last.

"Fight!" I decided at the same moment he did, and we went for one another.

The closet trembled and tilted, umbrellas fell, a box of hats fell and covered the floor but we fought on. Miss Burke flung open the door and made us stand, each in opposite corners of the room, while she read *Little Black Sambo* to the well-behaved kids encircling her around the floor. She reported my action to my sister and my sister reported home.

"I don't want to go to that school," I explained, "I want to go to Ethel's school."

"You can't go to Ethel's school," my mother explained firmly, "you're not Catholic."

I raced upstairs to give Ethel the bad news. She took it well yet seemed bemused.

"If you're not Catholic *what* are you?" she wondered.

"I'll go downstairs and find out," I offered, wondering what was left. But Ethel kept me. She took my hand and led me to her dressing table. There were so many rosaries, crucifixes, bleeding hearts, and chromos of John the Baptist adoring the infant Jesus, I wasn't taken at all by surprise when she splashed me with holy water and issued a Papal Bull:

"*Now* you're Catholic."

I raced downstairs to find my mother, father, and sister already at the supper table.

"Ethel just baptized me! I'm a Catholic!" I announced breathlessly.

"That's a real smart girl," my father commented, "one of these days she'll have her own convent."

"You're *not* going to St. Columbanus," my mother spoke with finality, "you're going to Park Manor. Now eat your soup."

"*I'm* an atheist," my sister reminded us.

"Be whatever you want," my mother gave her full rein, "just finish your carrots before you start on the tapioca."

When my tapioca was half-finished, I tilted the dish—and the lovely face of Blanche Sweet, with a braid like a halo above it, smiled at me with understanding.

"*I want to see the face of Gawd!*" I demanded, and poured the rest of the tapioca onto the floor. My mother cracked me a solid slap and

I wept into the empty plate, pressing my face against Blanche Sweet's waiting lips.

I used to pal around with an old-time *Form* player, Jesse Blue, who didn't like sharing hard-won information with total strangers.

We were in the clubhouse at Hialeah, where the tables were close together, and J.B. began talking louder and bigger than ordinarily. The reason was a woman who kept leaning an ear toward us, under her parasol, to see if she could pick up a hot one. I caught the play and began talking in terms of a hundred on the nose and hundred to place. She leaned closer to hear what the Big Shots' plans were.

"Get me five hundred on the nose on Number 7," Jesse whispered hoarsely, but loudly enough for that parasoled ear to hear. She got up and hurried to the window. After she'd gone J.B. and I put up three dollars each for a combination ticket on the Number 2.

Our horse placed. Number 7 ran dead last.

J.B. came back from the cashier's window with the fifteen dollars we'd won and said to me, "Here's *your* seven-fifty."

Then he sat down and grinned right *at* the woman.

She cracked him flat across the head with the handle of the parasol; then went back to her chair and never looked our way again.

If I haven't learned much, I've learned this much: faced with a seemingly impossible task but with no alternative but to do it, you'll do it.

Shortly after I got out of the Army, in 1945, I fell in love with a West Madison Street hooker. She was twenty-two, a country girl who'd become street-wise, cynical, comical, and vulnerable. I didn't know she was on heroin. I'd never met a user. All I knew about drug addiction was what I'd read in the Sunday supplements.

And I was too square, when I did find out, to grasp what that meant. No habit on earth but could not be broken by simple willpower: I really *believed* that! And became absolutely determined to break hers.

I was living in a two-room $10-a-month rear-lot flat on Wabansia and Bosworth. I cut off her connection and put her to bed there. "I don't want you to see what I look like when I'm kicking," was her only protest. But she was already too sick to protest further.

Did I say *sick?* For what began hitting that child toward evening, "sick" is no word. And that was only the beginning. By midnight she'd gone blind. I was really into something now: the girl was either going to die or go mad, that was plain. I had to leave her to find help.

I had never seen her connection. All I had to go on was that his name was Max. Try locating a heroin pusher named Max on West Madison between midnight and 4 A.M. some rainy morning. Can you imagine a square, still in his Army jacket and fatigue cap, stopping every doorway hooker with the curious approach, "I'm a friend of Margo's and she needs help." They fled into the shadows, they fled into halls; they vanished in silence or just turned away.

Finally I went into a White Tower hamburger stand, on the northwest corner of Aberdeen and Madison, that had a full view of the street. And sat there watching the night-people pass in hope of spotting someone who looked like a pusher. Even though I had no idea what a pusher looked like.

A little lame man, wearing double-lensed glasses and a cap shadowing his eyes, came in and sat at the counter. He looked so wrong he had to be *somebody*. I sat beside him looking into the mirror trying to catch his eye. He wasn't trying to catch mine. I didn't speak until he had a cup of coffee almost to his lips.

"I'm a friend of Margo's," I told him softly, "she needs help."

The cup clattered against his teeth. He had to put it down to keep from spilling it. It took him a minute to get up his nerve to look at me in the mirror. Then he looked relieved.

"She ought to know better than to send a square down here," he told me irritably.

He was Max.

We heard her calling feebly for help before we opened my door. She had thrown herself out of the bed and, having no strength to get back in, was lying blindly, face down, in a pool of her own perspiration.

"What do you think you're doing?" Max began scolding her before he touched her—and a kind of miracle happened. A faint pink flush touched her cheeks at the sound of his voice, a faint smile came to her mouth; and, by the time we had her back on the bed, she'd begun getting well before the needle had touched her.

"Did you see that?" the lame pusher asked me.

I saw it all right. And I still bless that small begoggled outcast. And when I read one of those scapegoat pieces about the "viciousness" of drug pushers, and extolling the basic humanitarianism of the nark-squad hero, I'm saddened. Because it isn't Margo and it isn't Max who keeps the traffic moving: it's that same nark-squad hero with a small, brown paper bag that hustlers and pushers alike have to keep filled if they want to stay on the street.

I remember a kid called Specs who was punchy about guns. He had a habit of sticking a finger in your face and saying "Stick 'em up!" Nobody paid him any heed. Not even when he started doing it with a toy gun. I was walking with an ex-fighter one night when Specs stepped out of a doorway, said "Stick 'em up!" and pointed the toy gun.

"Let him go, Vince," I told my friend, "I know him."

Another time Specs went into a bar where he was known and pointed the gun at the bartender: "Stick 'em up!" The bartender put his hands up. Then Specs saw a cop at the end of the bar and changed his mind: "Put 'em down!" The bartender put his hands down on a bottle, reached over the bar and knocked Specs cold. He woke up in the Stockyards Station.

After that Specs never touched anything that looked like a gun, and never said "Stick 'em up!" to anyone. But he began drinking. Hard. He drank so hard that his hands began to tremble whenever he lifted a shot-glass. Finally his mother took him to a psychoanalyst. "Tell the doctor *everything,*" she instructed Specs.

"What did the doctor ask you?" she asked Specs later.

"He asked me if I drank."

"What did you tell him?"

"Very little."

Specs' mother could hardly believe it.

"Why did you tell a lie like *that?*"

"It isn't a lie, mother," Specs defended his answer—"Most of it *spills.*"

I once knew an interesting clothes-store thief. He was arrested at the wheel of a car in which a couple thousand dollars worth of men's suits had been piled and he didn't have a bill of sale for one of them. The clothes-store owner, to exploit the publicity attending the robbery, ran a large ad in a St. Louis paper: PEOPLE WILL DO ANYTHING TO GET OUR CLOTHES—and signed it with the thief's name. The thief beat the rap and sued the store owner for invasion of privacy.

This was the same thief with whom I once went to a dance in East St. Louis. He asked a young woman to dance with him but she declined. So he took one step back and said—so loudly that everyone on the floor could hear—"WHY SHOULD I GIVE *YOU* 25 CENTS?"

When I asked him, later, why he'd deliberately embarrassed the poor girl that way, he answered, "They can't take a knockout back, can they?" And that was all the explanation he'd give me.

I heard a fellow, accused in court of passing counterfeit hundred-dollar bills, make the simplest justification possible: "I got them for fifteen dollars, so I thought it was a pretty good deal."

"I can tell a feeler the moment he comes in," the cop who guards the monkey house at Lincoln Park once assured me. "He gets right into the crowd, starts working his way up to the cage but he ain't interested in monkeys. I can tell a feeler by the way he walks."

"I can usually spot a jumper," the desk clerk at a North LaSalle Street hotel informed me. "It's usually a woman asking for a room with a view. If it's a man, he'll want to know what the checking-out hour is, whether he can have a room near the bar, will he be able to get telephone messages without coming down to the desk—he'll have you filling him in on every possible detail; yet he'll forget to ask you the rate.

"When times are good we get as many as two a month. When times are hard we get them oftener. But very, *very* few jumpers actually jump. All I mean by a 'jumper' is someone who has it in mind. Carrying through is altogether another matter. The man will wait until a bellboy is in the room with him to stop him. The woman will phone the desk to tell you what she has in mind and give you time to get to her.

"In the five years I've been here only two made it. One a young girl and one a middle-aged woman who really made it. The girl just broke her back. But we all have a bit of the jumper in us. If not in the back of the head then in the heart."

There was a St. Louis businessman who was so intense about the Cardinals that he bet $10,000 on his mortgaged home and the Cardinals lost in the tenth inning, 3-2.

"Our house just took a bad hop over Red Schoendienst's head," his wife was heard to tell someone over the phone.

The businessman died a few months later. His wife found him in bed, the sheet over his head and his ear still pressed to a transistor set that was still humming the final score: Mets 6. Cardinals 4.

"It wasn't the Mets that killed him," his wife decided, "it was the Cardinals."

I once got into a poker game in the rear of a North Broadway barber shop which was this kind of poker game: If the cops didn't pinch it somebody would heist it.

This night a player—call him Ziggy—went broke and went away mad. Half an hour later there was a knock, "It's me, Ziggy."

"Ziggy got some fresh bread," somebody said. "Let him in." The barber opened the door and two strangers came in. All they said was, "Leave the money on the board, boys."

I folded the twenty I had in my hand and dropped it discreetly behind a refrigerator.

One of the strangers showed the barber a paper. "Federal warrant," he explained.

"How do I know it's a federal warrant?" the barber tried to argue.

"Because he *says* it is," the other stranger assured everybody, "and we need this for evidence," he added; and started picking up the hundred-odd dollars in the pot.

I went over to the refrigerator and recovered my twenty.

"What are you doing behind the icebox?" one of the strangers wanted to know.

"I threw a twenty there when you came in because I thought it was a heist," I explained.

"Okay," he said, "put ten on the table and keep the change."

After they left the barber congratulated me on my presence of mind in throwing the twenty behind the refrigerator. But the others derided me for being in too much of a hurry to get my twenty back.

"How did *I* know they were cops?" I asked them.

"What makes you think they *were*?" they asked me.

Whether I saved $10 or lost $10 by making that behind-the-icebox move I don't know to this day.

Any more than I know whether that game was heisted or pinched.

But we never let Ziggy take a chair again.

I was drinking with a couple miners, in the kitchen of a whorehouse on Wyoming Street in Butte, Montana, when one of the women, a good-looking, dark-haired girl no more than nineteen, walked in, smiled sweetly and sat down at the table. The madame handed her a menu, spotted by many *soups de jour,* from the Hotel Finlen.

"Jo-Ann likes to pick out," the madame explained.

"Where are you from, honey?" I asked the girl.

"Ten dollars," she replied.

I decided to think that over. Then one of the miners decided to have a try.

"How much to say hello, sweetheart?" he asked her.

"Columbus, Ohio," Jo-Ann answered.

I looked at the miner. The miner looked at me.

"Jo-Ann don't have her hearing," the madame finally explained, "she reads lips."

"She sure don't read them very damn good," the miner complained.

"Go fuck yourself," Jo-Ann assured him quickly.

And went back to picking out.

I once tended bar for an old bachelor who lived above his bar. That was on Wabansia a few doors east of the CB & Q tracks. It was a two-story frame building, long unpainted, and every time a train roared past the whole building shook.

The old man had drilled a hole in the floor above the cash register so he could see if I pocketed any change; but I knew the hole was there. I could also sense when he was watching.

One night a lone customer bought a 25-cent schooner of beer, laid down a new half-dollar, and said, "Keep the change." I figured, at first, to keep the whole half. Then my conscience twinged and I told the customer, "Heads it's mine, tails it's the old man's," and tossed it on the bar. It came up tails but I decided to keep it anyhow and put it in my pocket.

"Put that in the register, son," the old man told me through the hole. "I won it fair and square."

When old-timers say that someone has gone on the arfy-darfy they don't mean he's simply taken it on the lam. They mean he has disappeared himself with a bunch of money; or jewels that once belonged to somebody else.

Some say "gone on the uffy-duffy."

The greatest American underground comedian, other than Lenny Bruce, was Lord Richard Buckley. He had a bar, called Chez Buckley, on Western Avenue just opposite Riverview Park in the early 1940s.

He would call three people from the audience—male or female—and instruct them merely to move their lips whenever he tapped them on the shoulder. Then we heard the voices of Amos, Andy, and Brother Crawford emanating from the three stooges. It was highly confusing.

He also had a kid he called Junior who resembled Jackie Vernon. Junior would stand, with a spotlight on him, looking through a toilet seat at the audience with the blankest grin conceivable. Buckley would say, "Register despair, Junior." Junior's grin would freeze right there. "Now register happiness, Junior. Now register hate." Buckley would go through the gamut of human emotions from love to terror. The emptier of all emotion Junior appeared, the funnier the act became.

Well, *I* thought it was funny anyhow.

*   *   *

Bankers who'd been losing heavily on the market, in the twenties, sometimes arranged with a professional bank robber to stage a prearranged holdup. They'd tell him where the $25,000 was and set a time.

When the robber would read, in the papers, that the bank had been robbed of a hundred thousand, he'd know the banker was home free.

A teller, who wasn't in on the fix, once watched this thief taking ten thousand dollars. And, for some reason, assumed the man was *supposed* to be taking it. He didn't report it. With the result that he was sentenced to five years in Atlanta.

He'd finished over two years when he was told he was to have a new cellmate: and in walks the man he'd watched stealing the ten thousand.

There was once a house of prostitution near Willow Springs that had a steel door. Two guards, armed with MG's, guarded it. There was also a man-killing police dog; kept half-starved and held on a wire.

It was run by an ex-Rams football player, a big, *very* big boy. He wore a white football sweater and a referee's whistle around his neck. No matter how late the women worked, he roused them at 10 A.M. with blasts of his whistle—"time for workout, girls!" Although none of them had had more than three hours sleep, they had to double-time around the house in their pajamas.

At 5 P.M. he roused them out with the whistle again and they'd have to go into a huddle around him. "Let's all pitch in and make this evening one that'll make the boss proud of us all," he'd try to inspire them. Then he'd review half a dozen ways of accosting a customer, all of which the women had known since they'd been children. He called this "school."

"He made us practice everything but passing," a woman who worked there recalled to me recently.

Past-posters broke many bookies in the decade of the forties. The past-poster was the party who put down a heavy bet on a horse that had already won.

There were many ways of getting information before the bookie had it; with time enough left to place the bet.

One way was to send a radio flash, right from the track, to a partner parked within sight of the bookie. The third partner took a signal from the man in the parked car and made the bet.

Or the second man could phone the bookie and ask for Mr. Harris. The bookie would holler, "Is there a Mr. Harris here?" Nobody named Harris. But the past-poster standing by had the message: "Harris" was the code name of the winner. Since he'd been hanging around the joint all day, the bookie had no reason to suspect him when he put a couple of hundred dollars on an off-horse.

Once we outsmarted ourselves. The horse that the flash had given us had been given too soon: the horse had been disqualified for rough riding.

"I *almost* did it today, Dave," I told the bookie, whom I'd very nearly had on the hook for $2,000, that same evening in a restaurant.

"I don't know what you did," he admitted, "but I know you *almost* did it."

There is also a window named IMMEDIATE REFUND.

At Cahokia Downs a horse named *Popcorn Butch* threw his rider in the gate, then raced the entire length of the track before he could be reined. Bettors were instructed that those holding tickets on the horse would receive an immediate refund.

Then here comes a clown, his two-dollar refund in his hand, his face split into the biggest grin of self-satisfaction I've ever witnessed.

"I figured it that way!" he kept telling everyone, waving the two dollars, "I *figured* it that way!"

I knew a fellow who had an argument one morning in East St. Louis with a friend, and the friend stabbed him in the stomach. The friend then took him to a hospital where he was sewed up after giving the explanation that he'd fallen on a piece of glass.

In the afternoon the fool goes bowling! He ripped one of the stitches open and sealed the fresh wound with Mystic Tape. He must have been feeling pretty good because in the evening he visited a whore and bled to death in her bed.

The girl rolled him into her kitchen and went back to work. Then, about five hours later, she finally reported the incident to the police.

The police found him in full rigor with the Mystic Tape stuck in his hair. The cops traced him back to the friend who'd stabbed him in the morning. They found the friend in a hospital, sitting at the bedside of his wife; whom he'd shot in the afternoon. "Everything would have been perfect," he explained to the arresting officers, "if only the Mystic Tape had held."

No one has ever seen a cashier's window, at any racecourse on earth, named PERSONAL INJURY.

Yet there is such a cashier. And you can collect enough there to keep you in daily-doubles all season; without sustaining so much as a black-and-blue mark. If you have a good lawyer.

Because every track maintains a fund to meet suits brought by people who fall off stools in the clubhouse bar onto their skulls; who get hot coffee spilled on new dresses in the clubhouse restaurant; who dislocate a knee trying to get to a mutuel window when the flag is up; or are nipped by an embittered mare from whom they are trying to get hot information.

I used to know a big-bellied blowhard, mockingly nicknamed "The Judge," who'd sustained numerous black-and-blue marks. He'd carried cards in boilermakers', ironworkers', steamfitters' and carpenters' locals in his day. But his working day had seldom lasted longer than twenty-four hours.

Cables had tripped him, rivets had burned him, lighting fixtures had shocked him, falling planks had stunned him; ladders had collapsed themselves beneath him and moving trucks had let him fall out of their cabs into traffic. When he learned that Cahokia Downs had been quietly putting aside a percentage of the profits, against claims of personal injury, The Judge went back to work.

I was sitting with him in the Cahokia clubhouse, studying the breeding of a seven-year-old mare named *Jealous Widow,* and had just decided to put two dollars across the board on her, when the chair collapsed.

Not The Judge's. Mine.

The Judge hadn't tampered with it. Neither had I. It was just a rotten chair, that was all.

When The Judge looked up from his own studies to tout me onto something, he observed that I wasn't there. This was because I was on my back on the clubhouse floor clutching the *Racing Form.* Unhurt, I foolishly began to get up.

"*Stay down, fool!*" The Judge commanded me hoarsely. "*You've broke your back!*"

I grasped his concept. As long as I was lying down I had something going for me. Once I got up it would be too late to lie down again. I stayed down.

Two ushers lifted me into a fireman's carry and began toting me away.

Ordinarily, people would have followed. Especially the morbidly curious. But the only thing horse players are morbidly curious about is the next race: they're so preoccupied they'd step over the dying.

"What have you got in this one?" one of the ushers asked the other as they carried me.

"*Moon River,*" the other youth answered.

"I'm going on *Duke's Girl,*" the other revealed.

In the infirmary they laid me out on a hospital bed beside a screen.

"Get me a combination ticket on *Jealous Widow*," I asked the only honest-looking one of the two. He took my six dollars as though everyone who fell off a clubhouse chair bought combination tickets.

A buxom, middle-aged nurse came from behind the screen to give me a buxom middle-aged smile.

"Lie still till the doctor comes," she instructed me. She picked up the phone and told the message center to page the doctor.

"Dr. Karsky, report to the infirmary," I heard the loudspeaker system pleading.

I wouldn't have to go through all *that* to get him, I reasoned: I'd just go down to the rail and *fetch* him. But I didn't think it appropriate, when the doctor came in, to ask him what *he* had going. What was on my mind was whether that usher was going to get me down on *Jealous Widow* or book the bet himself.

"What happened?" Dr. Karsky asked me.

"I fell."

"Down a stair?"

"No. Off a chair."

"Your own chair?"

I saw what he was getting at. "No. A clubhouse chair."

"Lie still and take it easy," he advised me; and hurried out.

It wasn't hard to figure out why he hurried. A plaintiff putting in a claim on the basis of a rotten chair would need the chair as evidence.

But, unless I underestimated The Judge, that chair was already out of sight. The Judge would salvage it in order to put in a fifty percent claim on whatever I might collect. He would also need it in event the management's lawyer made him an offer. The Judge would testify for either side.

"Flag is up!" I heard the loudspeakers announce.

"They're off!"

All I could catch was that *Jealous Widow* was up there somewhere. So was *Moon River*. I could tell that *Jealous Widow* was still contending when they came into the stretch for home. Then the clamor drowned out all other sound. Then silence. A *long* silence.

Photo finish. I closed my eyes and composed myself.

Until a shout came up from both clubhouse and grandstand and then I *had* to see. I got off the table cautiously, tiptoed to the door and got a glimpse of the tote-board. Number 6. *Jealous Widow*! I couldn't make out the prices yet I was content.

I was climbing back onto the bed when the nurse walked out from behind the screen.

"Did you win?" she asked sweetly.

"Yes," I had to confess.

"Then you'd better look up that usher," she advised me with finality. There was no reason for climbing back on the bed. I'd blown my personal injury suit.

I found the usher and he was a good kid after all. He'd made the bet and handed me thirty-four dollars and fifty cents. I kept thirty and thanked him.

The Judge didn't look pleased to see me.

"I thought you'd be on your way to the hospital by now," he told me, sounding terribly disappointed.

"I decided it wasn't worth a lawsuit," I apologized.

The Judge dragged the broken chair out from under the table, where he'd covered it with my *Form*. I carried it to a corner so he wouldn't get the idea of tripping over it.

When I got back he was gathering his tip-sheets, charts, and program.

"I can't stand a man who don't pay his own way," he advised me sternly.

And walked away.

When somebody says to me "I'm a fan of yours, Mr. Algren," I get on my guard. Because the moment that declaration is made, your unsolicited admirer expects something in return. It still happens that someone rings my doorbell and calls up the stairs, "I'm a fan of yours!"

"I'm not running for office," is my standard reply before shutting the door.

Holy wonders and carty-givers, leaping grievers and past-posters, jumpers, feelers, and Mystic Tape-hopers, we all keep a bit of the jumper in our hearts.

Now if I just follow the red neon arrows and go down one flight, I'll get something back on yesterday's place ticket.

EPITAPH

It's all in the wrist, with a deck or a cue,
And Frankie Machine had the touch.
He had the touch, and a golden arm—
"Hold up, Arm," he would plead,
Kissing his rosary once for help
With the faders sweating it out and—
Zing!—there it was—Little Joe or Eighter from Decatur
Double-trey the hard way, Dice be Nice,
When you get a hunch bet a bunch
It don't mean a thing if it don't cross that string
Make me five to keep me alive
Tell 'em where you got it 'n how easy it was—
We remember Frankie Machine
And the arm that always held up.

We remember in the morning light
When the cards are boxed and the long cues racked
Straight up and down like all-night hours
With the hot rush-hours past.

For it's all in the wrist with a deck or a cue
And if he crapped out when we thought he was due
It must have been that the dice were rolled,
For he had the touch and his arm was gold.
Rack up his cue, leave the steerer his hat:
The arm that held up has failed at last.

Yet why does the light down the dealer's slot
Sift soft as light in a troubled dream?
(A dream, they say, of a golden arm
That belonged to the dealer we called Machine.)

THE PASSION OF UPSIDE-DOWN-EMIL
a story from life's other side

THE summer that we lived next door to Upside-Down-Emil was a long time ago. Emil was a lithe, wan youth who'd been a tightrope walker in the old country. And was determined to perfect his profession in the new.

He practiced, every morning of the week, on a cable strung from his back porch to his one-car garage: a free circus, every morning, for every kid on the block.

Wearing a red turtleneck sweater, long faded to rose, Emil traversed the air from his porch to his garage, glided to earth, then trotted lightly back to walk the air once more. We cheered. Nothing like it had ever happened on Moorman Street before.

Then, on Friday twilights, he materialized in a belted trenchcoat, cranked his Model-T: and off he went wheeling with his taillight winking mysteriously.

When Emil left it felt to me like good-bye to summer. When I heard the Monday morning cry—"Emil on wire up!" summer had returned.

Emil was back. He rode the air and we rode the fence and all the air seemed daring.

From scenes like these yet greater scenes would come, I sensed.

They did.

Emil fitted a pulley to a cable, soldered it onto an ironworker's helmet, clapped the helmet onto his head, turned himself upside-down and rolled upsy-downsy to his garage.

A burst of applause—then the youth hit the ground on his face. Bashing his forehead and bending the hell out of the pulley.

"Emil's balance is so good upside-down, he can't stand straight up anymore," my mother pointed out—and rapped me one that spun me half across our kitchen—"Let *that* be a warning to *you*."

Neither straight up nor upside-down, nobody walked that wonderful wire that week. Emil was inside, thinking.

What he thought of was a double-cable, one drawn from porch to garage and a lower hooked from garage to porch. I saw the problem: How would he make it onto the lower strand?

He accomplished this by somersaulting, feet first, onto the lower cable; then turned himself upside-down again and glided triumphantly home.

I stood on my head. My father rapped me. "Why can't you be a good boy like I was when I was a boy?" he wanted to know.

Hard times returned to the backyards of home. Emil had to travel farther for less money. His fees, it was said, were going into his gas tank instead of the bank.

"Emil will think of something," I promised my mother.

"May it be to walk on his feet," she hoped.

"When I was your age I had a job," my father remembered.

Emil jacked up the Model-T and crawled beneath. He was converting it into an oil-burner. My father took alarm.

"The Stanley Steamer has already been invented!" he called the news to Emil down through the Ford's open hood. "It didn't work out!"

Emil crawled out.

"For me," he informed the world, "works *out*."

And he crawled back under. His will was forged of the same stuff as his cables. Yet it wasn't so flexible. He lay on the freezing November earth with only his canvas sneakers visible. His toes twitched with cold. All our good times were past.

"Work in your garage," my father instructed him, "it's going to snow."

"Too dark," Emil explained from somewhere among the spark plugs.

"Now he's saving electricity," my father reported.

"If that young man had a mind," my mother decided, "he'd be dangerous."

Her washing was whipping white—when a long, oleaginous, dark and dripageous, gelatinous pall of coal-oil smog, too heavy to clear a clothesline yet light enough to clear every fence, emerged by the yard from the hood of the Model-T. It enwrapped the sheets till they dragged to the ground, blackened slips, shirts, brassieres, pillow cases, panties and pants, and raised perfect hell with Mrs. Kowalczyk's front-room curtains. Someone phoned the precinct captain. Someone else called the alderman. Someone else reported the disaster to the Red Cross. Finally two cops drove up. They hauled Emil out from under the Model-T.

He tottered on the step of the wagon, and would have fallen, had not one of the cops caught him.

Thirty days in the psyche ward did for *that* pale youth. He went to work for a factory that made endless belting; and some magic that had been in the world was gone.

The house he had lived in went empty. The wind broke the windows that nobody had boarded. A storm blew down the cable he'd walked on. It dangled loosely, rattling against the porch or the fence as the winds took it; until my father cut it down so we could get some sleep.

Emil worked on an endless belt, endlessly making endless belting, until a machine was devised for his job. So Emil went to the bars. He never tried anything again except whiskey. He became a kind of crippled fly of the tavern corners. If you'd promise him a drink he'd stand on his head for you and drink the shot in that position; letting the whiskey run down into his eyes.

Once a bartender, in an idle hour, made Emil get down on all fours and rode him around the bar, shouting, "One more lap! One more lap! Get all the money! One more lap!"

Emil begged for drinks. When a customer wouldn't buy him a whiskey he'd beg for a beer. If he were refused again, he would stand beside the customer until a cockroach ran across the bar. He never had to wait long. Emil would scoop up the roach, throw it into his mouth and pretend to be choking.

"Give this man something to drink!" the customer would shout to the bartender, and the bartender would bring a beer and a shot. Then Emil would spit the roach out, and drink the shot and the beer while the customer watched.

"How can you *do* anything so disgusting?" one customer asked Emil after paying for the drinks.

"That's show biz," Emil replied.

People don't have fun like they used to have, do they?

MERRY CHRISTMAS MR. MARK

OUT around 71st and Cottage Grove around this time of year, just before Mr. Volstead took over, we used to sell something called the *Saturday Evening Blade*. In front of the saloon on the southwest corner of that intersection that was, right across the street from the north gate of Woodland cemetery. We'd worked up any number of swindles there.

When a customer handed over a nickel for a copy and would wait for his change, with one palm extended while his eyes were preoccupied with the Blade's screaming headlines, the swindle would be to lay a penny in the palm, click a second penny on top of that—and then to click the third without letting it loose at all. The mark would shove his pennies in his pocket and never even know he'd been hyped.

Sometimes, if the chump didn't have anything smaller than a two-bit piece we'd duck into the saloon for change—and duck out the Ladies' Entrance. Merry Christmas, Mr. Mark.

We called the old red-and-yellow wooden four-wheeler that came to the end of the line there the Toonerville Trolley. There was almost always some fool on the rear platform waiting for the Blade to see who'd gotten killed today. We'd time it so as to hand him those blood-red headlines just as the trolley began its creaking jaunt west toward Halsted—the hustle then was to stumble alongside the car trying to reach the fool's change hand but never quite reaching it. That was no small stunt, the shape that trolley was in, even for a 10-year-old. Sometimes you'd have to have a coughing spell to slow you up.

Once one kid pulled that coughing routine and the mark got off the car and came back for his change, cough or no cough. He didn't care if the kid had TB. Some mark.

Around Christmastime the big paper guys had cards printed and sold them to us little paper guys for a nickel apiece. They read something like this:

229

Christmas comes but once a year
When it comes it brings good cheer
So open your heart without a tear
And remember the newsie standing here.

That got them, every time. Especially if there was a light fall of snow. And the swindle in the card routine was this: After he'd paid for the verse and would be thinking he owned it, you'd have to tell him no, it was your only card, you just wanted him to see the sentiment on it, it had cost you a nickel, so please mister could you have it back?

That was thirty Chicago Christmases and Lord-Knows-How-Many-Swindles ago. That saloon is long gone, whole populations have been buried in that cemetery, and the Toonerville Trolley is now a street-car bus. But that big mark of a Santa still keeps coming around, year after year.

It begins to look to me like he must be in on some fast hustle himself. Maybe it's a kickback on those toys he pushes. Maybe he got something on somebody.

Maybe he knows something we don't know.

I GUESS YOU FELLOWS
JUST DON'T WANT ME

I once knew a here-and-there sort of fellow who was so here-then-there that the police would always pick him up before he could get somewhere.

The officers would never admit—no, not in a hundred years—that they kept picking this fellow up just for being *around*. "We're *forced* to pick him up," one told me, "because he's so *suspicious*."

"It's not so simple a matter as mere suspicion," the desk sergeant tried to explain, "it's because he's suspicious of *himself*. If a man is suspicious of himself, why shouldn't we be?"

If the police had just said straight out that they picked him up because his neck was on crooked they would have been on solid ground. You could hardly fault the law for a man's neck being on one side. The law didn't put it on that way.

But, as though crookedneckedness wasn't enough to get him picked up, this fellow would stand around with his cap pulled down far enough over his eyes as to constitute intent to commit a misdemeanor if not a felony, on street corners where buses never stopped. If he'd just pulled that cap off his eyes and gone up to the bus-stop, crooked neck or no crooked neck, it wouldn't have made the least difference. He would have been picked up all the same. Because by that hour the buses are all back in the barns and *every* corner is a wrong corner. This fellow seemed bright enough in other ways. His trouble was he had an IQ beyond psychology.

Another affliction this fellow had was having a record over five inches long. The way he'd gotten it was by getting himself picked up only a block away from a bar where a pearl-handled .22 caliber pistol and ninety-eight dollars and sixty cents had just been stolen. Sure enough, this fellow was found to be carrying a pearl-handled .22 caliber pistol. The officers accused him of having *robbed* it.

"Why should I rob another man's weapon," he demanded to know, "when I've got ninety-eight dollars in my wallet?"

"How much you got in your pocket?" one of the shrewder officers asked immediately.

"Sixty cents," this fellow answered proudly. But when they took an account it was found he had a total of a hundred and four dollars in the wallet and twenty-six cents in his pockets. He was sentenced to six months for failing to account for the $5.66 discrepancy. He had to give the pistol back, too.

As soon as he got out he began doing everything he knew how to do to keep from getting a record a full half-foot long. And what he knew how to do better than anything was moving electric typewriters, computing machines, lamps, swivel chairs, and cherrywood desks out of the back doors of Milwaukee Avenue office-furniture stores while a couple of cops were guarding the front to see that no one walked down the alley. The fellow called this "helping out" because he did it unarmed.

When the cops handed him five or ten dollars he would accept it. But he would never take an adding machine, or a carton of fountain pens or a shipment of typewriter ribbons off the law. Which goes to show that even though his neck was on crooked his thinking was pretty straight.

Whether this fellow's affliction was hereditary or had been acquired by looking back over his shoulder I never did find out. And if I gave you another hundred years to guess what we nicknamed this fellow, you'd never hit it. Right off you'd say "Crooked-neck" or "Dizzy" or "Dodger" or "Rabbit" or something like that. But it wasn't *anything* like that. What we called this fellow was Ipso. Which was short for Ipso Facto.

Because you'd be talking to him here and, when you looked around, he was over there. So you'd ask him where he was going and he'd say, "I'm on my way—*ipso facto*." Or, when the cops thought he was starting to look suspicious of himself again, they'd stop him and ask, "Who are you going to rob tonight, Ipso? Who are you waiting around here to kill? How much did you make picking pockets at Wrigley Field yesterday?"

"I wasn't at Cubs Park yesterday," Ipso would answer.

"*Where* were you?"

"Sox Park," Ipso would say; because he was ashamed to tell them he'd spent the whole day riding the roller-coaster at Riverview.

"The Sox are out of town," the cops would say, "get in, *Ipso Facto*."

Now what Ipso Facto meant by *Ipso Facto* was "I'll see you around."

But what the cops thought "Ipso Facto" meant was "Be damned quick about it." Ipso would accept the cops' interpretation.

Then, of course, in the query room it would come down to a matter of being booked on suspicion or of helping the boys out.

The first time Ipso was picked up he asked the officers, "What for?"

"You look suspicious," one explained; and held the car-mirror so Ipso would see himself in it.

"You're right," Ipso had to agree, "I really *do* look suspicious."

But when they wanted to take his prints that time, Ipso asked them, "What for? I haven't robbed nobody."

"But if you should change your mind we'd *need* them." the fingerprint man explained in a kindly manner.

"I see your point of view," Ipso had agreed; and put his hands on the pad.

He felt relieved after they's gotten his prints.

"When they told me I could go home it was better than confession," Ipso admitted to me, "that was why I didn't go straight home."

"Where'd you go?"

"Nowheres. I just sat down in the cops' waiting room and read a copy of *St. Jude's Magazine.* When they asked me what I was hanging around for I told them I thought maybe they wanted me for a Lie Detector Test."

Ipso's draftboard was a bit startled when he materialized at the induction center. Being three inches over six feet, weighing only 129 pounds, and the manner in which his head was set on his shoulders wouldn't have attracted special attention had it not been for the tiny American flag waving from the left lens of Ipso's tortoise-shell specs. The pin holding the frame had been lost; so Ipso had inserted the stem of the tiny flag to keep the glasses from falling off. Removing the flag from its stem would not only have been unpatriotic, Ipso explained, but would also constitute a felony.

All the inducting officer could think to ask was, "Are you going to be on *our* side?"

"I'd like to die for my country," Ipso announced, "but I have bad teeth."

"That's all right," the officer decided, having recovered from his first surprise, "we don't want you to bite the enemy."

It was only his neck which deprived Ipso of becoming a force for law and order in Chicago. Had they ever let *him* ask the questions in the query room, he would have asked all the right questions:

"If you weren't planning to mug some drunk, when you were hanging around that bar, why don't you let us have your prints in event you should change your mind?"

"If you're not guilty of something, why are you trying to make fools of us by having us stand around asking you questions?"

"If you're so innocent what are you bleeding about?"

"If you're not *guilty* of something, you must be innocent of something—and that's even more serious."

Ipso hated work. He hated work so much that he not only hated people who went to work but he hated unemployed people who had friends who were working. All he did, himself, besides moving office furniture, was to drive a cab a couple nights a week.

He drove sitting in the middle of the seat. Had he sat under the wheel his flag, projecting out of the window, would have caused the driver behind to think he was about to make a U-turn.

When a passenger would ask why he drove in this position, Ipso would answer, "I was a pursuit pilot, sir." Why a stupid answer like that worked I never understood. Wouldn't you think *somebody* would have said, "Get the hell under that wheel where you belong?" Yet nobody ever did.

We were playing the Kosciusko Arrows, for five dollars a man, on a hot, dry, dusty Sunday morning, on the lot bounded by Ashland Avenue and Bosworth Street. We were two runs behind with one out in the ninth when Ipso came to bat with a man on second. The manager flashed the bunt sign to the third-base coach; who flashed it to Ipso.

Ipso stepped back out of the box, because he didn't get the signal. The coach flashed it again but it was no use. Ipso had forgotten it.

"Bunt you meathead!" the manager shouted at the top of his lungs from the bench. "B-U-N-T—BUNT!"

The pitcher gave Ipso a fast ball and he laid down a perfect sacrifice bunt—and *slid* into first base.

He waited there, while the right fielder and the first baseman hunted for the ball, long enough to adjust his flag. Then he took off and slid into second base. The pitcher went over to help the right fielder help the first baseman and right fielder find the ball. Ipso dusted himself off again. Then he adjusted his flag.

"I guess you fellows just don't want me," he finally told the second baseman; and took off for third. This time he used a hook slide.

The Kosciusko second basemen went over to help the pitcher help the right fielder help the first baseman to find the ball. Ipso dusted himself off again. His flag was still in place.

"I guess you don't want me neither," he told the third baseman. And took off for home.

Ten feet from the plate he took the ball out of his pocket and tossed it to the catcher; who tagged him out so hard he knocked Ipso down.

Ipso didn't get up right away. He just lay there, turning his lopsided head one way and another and saying to himself, "I had it coming! I had it coming!" Miraculously, the flag was still waving.

All Ipso would answer for some days after that, when asked for an explanation, was *"ipso facto."* But, about a month after, sitting in a bar, I asked him why he'd given up that ball.

"If I'd scored a tying run on a stolen ball I wouldn't be a *good* guy," he told me. "I *deserved* to be tagged out."

"That is highly honorable of you, Ipso," I had to admit, "but how come your conscience didn't bother you, the night before, when you were hauling two thousand dollars' worth of somebody else's furniture down the alley? How could you get conscience-stricken about a sixty-nine-cent baseball the next morning?"

"What does *costs* have to do with it?" Ipso asked me. "Sports is one thing and robbin' is another. Everybody stands a pinch now and then—but *nobody* steals first base."

"Then it was stealing first base, and not stealing the ball, that made you get yourself tagged out?"

"Of *course*. Lots of good guys go robbin'. But *no* good guy slides into first."

"Frank Frisch did it at the Polo Grounds," I had to remind Ipso, "and started a riot."

"I wish you would've told me that before the game," Ipso reflected wistfully, "we'd all be five bucks richer today."

And adjusted his little flag.

EVERYTHING INSIDE IS A PENNY

A winter of a single wind has driven snow against the ads that once offered baby talcum and Log Cabin Syrup. But no el stops here anymore. Rains have ripped the ad that promised dancing lessons at the Merry Gardens; its tatters are less merry now. Waltz king and waltzers alike are gone. The 12th Street beau with cap tipped for love in Garfield Park, the Monday-morning salesgirl with lashes still Maybellined by Sunday night, the Mogen David wino with Happy New Year snow on his shoulders, none get off here anymore. Only a rail of rounded iron guards a peanut machine whose glass is cracked and its peanuts long vended. Snow-shadows race like children in the blood-red glow cast by two railroad lamps; up the drift of snow against the rail and then tobogganing down. They stop to rock the platform, lamps and all, when the midnight B train passes; and the lamps dip and tip like flares left burning on a raft abandoned at sea. The B train's echo trails the B train. Then a fog shot with neon closes down; the coldest that ever fell. Yet riders of late winter locals sometimes hear a piano playing faintly somewhere below the ties, like a piano out of times long gone: on a night when tavern doors were opened to the street for the first night of the year.

> *Oh! Gee! say gee, you ought to see my Gee Gee*
> *From the Fiji Isle*
> *Gosh Gee, say Gee, you ought to be with Gee Gee*
> *She does a twister much better than her sister—*

The long car leans to the land where old els wait for winter to pass. The walker on the midnight platform, adrift above the town, is left like a walker adrift in a dream. A dream dreamt by any old el rider.

For the blue-and-white legend that once named this station, its ads that once bragged and its pigeons that made summer strut, all have passed in the wash of this sea of blue snows.

Leaving two railroad lamps arock in the echo and ebb of the B train's final passing.

* * *

My father was a fixer of tools, a fixer of machinery; a fixer of tables
gone wobbly and windows that had stuck; doors that had warped and
furnaces that had clogged. His labor was fixing, eternally fixing: the plaster that had cracked, the wallpaper that had splintered and the lathe that
had broken. Other men wished secretly to be forever drunken. He wished
secretly to be forever fixing:

The step that had rotted, the rain pipe that had rusted, the hinge that
had loosened, the fence wind had bent. He moved among pistons and
vises and cylinders, he healed boilers and ministered to valves: hoses
had to be coiled with care lest they crack; clocks had to be wound against
losing time; wiring had to be insulated against fire. He used electrical
tape like a doctor applying a tourniquet: he was a geneticist of lathes
and prolonged the lives of brushes stiff with sclerosis of paint. His ear
was not so well attuned to human speech as it was to the delicate play
of gears: his dreams moved on ball bearings; and within them he sensed
that one dream-bearing was more worn than the others.

Puttying or soldering, welding or binding, my father was a fixer of
machinery in basements and garages.

He could get a piece of machinery to work for him that would work
for no one else; but he could not get other men to pay him any mind
at all.

"If you're so damned smart, why ain't you a foreman?" I would hear
my mother going for him when the bulb that lit the kitchen and the lamp
that lit the door were the only lights foretelling the beginning of a winter
day—and was still going at him in the bedroom after dark when supper
dishes had been put away and the gas lamp burned before the door once
more.

Yet in the hours between she paid her lot no mind, sometimes singing
to herself—

> *Take me out for a joy-ride*
> *A girl-ride, a boy-ride*
> *I'm as reckless as I can be*
> *I don't care what becomes of me.*

There were no heroes nor heroines on my father's side of the family;
although he had many brothers and sisters. My mother's family, on the
other hand, consisted of nothing but heroes and heroines—of whom the
most heroic was Uncle-Theodore-the Great-Lakes-Sailor.

Uncle Theodore had had a fistfight with the cook on the deck of the steamer *Chicora* that the ship's captain had stopped: which of the brawlers had begun it he didn't care to hear; but one would have to pack his gear and get off the *Chicora*. Some captain.

Uncle Theodore packed his gear and walked ashore at Benton Harbor after shaking hands with everybody but the captain.

He should have said good-bye to the captain, too. For the *Chicora* went down with all hands on her next trip.

Down with all hands to leave not a trace on the unshaken waters. Not an overturned lifeboat nor a sailor boy's cap. Not a beer cork nor a clay pipe nor a smudge of oil. Cutters scoured the waves for days but found no sign. Then the waves froze over; the wind blew the memory of their names into winter. Spring began as though the *Chicora* had never been.

But a son of the *Chicora's* fireman built a glass-bottomed boat in his Chicago backyard, determined to find the wreck on the lake's shifting floor or go down himself. Five days after he had put out, the glass-bottomed craft capsized.

Down went the brave son of the brave fireman to join the brave crew of the brave ship *Chicora* below the cowardly waves. Down to the uselessly shifting sands; yet determined all the way down. And left no more sign than his father had.

My mother spoke of these upsets as though the glass-bottomed disaster were the greater. But my father insisted that the youth who had followed his father had been simply one more glass-bottomed damned fool.

"Not all the damned fools are at the bottom of the lake," my mother observed.

How having a relative, who didn't happen to go down with the *Chicora*, made anyone an authority on shipping disasters, my father claimed he failed to see.

How a man could work six years for the Yellow Cab Company and not get to be foreman was what my mother failed to see.

How a man could get to be a foreman when he had a woman who never let him rest was another thing my father failed to see.

If a man didn't have a woman to inspire him he could *never* be a millionaire was how things looked to my mother.

If a man has to be nagged into being a millionaire he's better off to stay poor was my father's decision.

Some men couldn't even be *nagged* into being a millionaire my mother implied.

Then she might as well save her breath, my father concluded; and threw the cat off the davenport.

"That's right, blame everything on the poor cat." My mother encouraged us all to penalize the cat for our poverty.

"What good is a cat that won't hunt mice?" my father wanted to know; with the *Saturday Evening Blade* across his face.

"He can't hunt mice because he's handicapped," my mother explained.

"Then let him hunt a handicapped mouse," my father suggested.

"He can't hunt because he can't smell," my mother insisted, "when you cut off a kitten's whiskers he'll never smell anything."

"Has he tried using his nose?" my father inquired softly.

I'd snipped the brute's whiskers off with my sister's nail scissors; but to this very day I cannot help but feel that the real reason that cat never caught mice was, purely and simply, that it didn't want to take unnecessary chances. It was accident-prone and knew it. Especially when I was near.

When it limped home trying to lick red paint off its fur, however, that was none of my doing. I simply hadn't thought of it. The stuff stuck pretty good; especially onto the softer fur around its paws. Both my mother and father agreed that nobody could have done anything as idiotic as ducking a cat into a can of red paint except Johnny Sheeley; but they were both wrong.

The kid who had done it, the kid to watch out for, the real neighborhood nut wasn't really Johnny Sheeley. It was Baldy Costello.

Baldy raised hell with us littler kids. He was *really* mean and *really* bald, too. And *really* accident-prone. The 71st Street trolley, that had never run anyone down in its life, chomped off two of Baldy's toes. The shock, it was said, was what had caused his hair to fall out; but I think that was only a handy excuse. That kid never really *wanted* to have hair.

The backs of both his hands were tattooed with decalcomania papers we called "cockomanies"; and sometimes his forearms, too. He shoved me off my handmade pushmobile, raced it down to 71st Street and left it lying in the middle of the tracks. My sister recovered it before it got smashed; but I never cared for that pushmobile anymore.

Baldy was a thief who always got caught. Whether anyone had actually seen him take the money out of a purse or not was not important; because he always spent it immediately on cockomanies. When money was missing in the neighborhood, Baldy was sure to show up half an hour later covered from forehead to forearms with red, green and purple designs.

A few years later he became one of the first men to sit in Cook County's electric chair upon conviction of murder and rape.

Didn't I *tell* you he was accident-prone?

*   *   *

There was no way of prying my mother off an idea nor an idea off my mother. One afternoon as our winter life was running toward spring, I was busy addressing valentines to put into a box on the teacher's desk the following day. She would then call out the names of everybody's valentine in what was a kind of runoff election to determine who was the most popular girl and boy in the class.

There were 48 kids in the class and I had 46 greetings.

"Are you sending one to Mildred Ford?" my mother asked.

Mildred Ford was the only Negro kid in the Park Manor school at that time. How she got there never was told. It was just my luck that she should show up for Valentine's Day.

I had no answer; so I made none.

Mildred Ford, by tacit agreement, had been ruled off the turf.

No answer didn't work. When I'd finished the 46th heart-shaped greeting, my mother scooped up the bundle.

"You can't send valentines to anybody unless you send one to everybody," she told me.

"*Nobody* sends a valentine to a *nigger,* Ma."

"You heard what I said."

The situation was bewildering. Here but a moment ago the world had consisted of 47 of us to one of *them;* and now I was being told to switch sides. For *what*? Just to make it 46 to 2?

The situation, as Governor Faubus expressed it on a later occasion, was untenable.

"Nobody sent her any last year, Ma." I fell back on tradition.

"Then this is the year to begin," she decided.

It wasn't, you understand, that I had anything against that child personally. It was just that I felt it would be better for *her* if we proceeded more gradually; in another school on a different holiday. I was afraid that a promotion to second-class citizenship, if it came too suddenly, might leave the girl unbalanced the rest of her life. My friends still tell me I ought to stop putting the interests of others above my own; but I can't help myself.

The valentine that Miss Ford received from me possessed as much wit as could be bought for a penny at that time: It showed a tearful puppy pleading, "Don't Treat Me Like a Dog, Be My Valentine"—about as far as you could go and still stay segregated in 1918.

All I could see of her, from where I sat, was a pair of nappy pigtails, each tied with a blue ribbon-bow; bent above the one card she had received.

I never spoke to Mildred Ford, she never spoke to me. She didn't thank me for the valentine. But, as she passed me when class let out, she gave me a glance that plainly spoke—"You're on the *other* side."

I had not known until that moment that there was another side.

* * *

Out of odd lore and remnants of old rains, memory ties rainbows of forgetfulness about old lost years.

Out of old rains new rainbows.

An image of Jesus hung above the piano in Ethel's home; but above our piano nobody but Uncle Harry looked down. Yet there was a resemblance: both had died young of a wound in the heart. But Uncle Harry's was hidden under the buttons of his Spanish-American uniform.

That uniform still hung in our closet with a threat about it, because my mother planned to cut it down to fit me, to wear to school on the anniversary of the sinking of the battleship Maine. That would be just about what might be expected of a kid who had asked a black girl to be his sweetheart.

Ethel's faith in Gawd encouraged me to wait at the window every evening to see His colors rage the sunset sky. Yet I did not feel I had as much to do with Him, nor He with me, as with the lamplighter who came later.

Came riding a dark bike softly: softly as the snow came riding. God's colors would begin to die on tree and walk and street, when the lamplighter propped his ladder against the night to defend us. Touched a torch to a filament that came up green. Then turned to blue against the drifted snow.

I followed him with my eyes to see a line of light come on like tethered fireflies. God's colors passed but the night flares burned steadily on.

> *For we are very lucky*
> *With a lamp before the door—*
> *And Leerie stops to light it—*
> * * *

I read in a book my sister had gotten for me at a library—

As he lights so many more.

My memory of that Chicago winter is made of blue-green gas flares across a shining sheet of ice so black and snow so white it was a marvel to me to recall that under that ice-sheet tomatoes had lately flowered.

St. Columbanus kids stood around the ice pond's rim with skates under their arms; for an inch of water was already spreading to the pond's edges. When they tested the ice it squeaked the first squeak of spring.

In March came the true thaw, running waters in running weather, when we raced the sky to school and raced it home once more. The St. Columbanus kids began lingering on the steps of their church—then the light, that had closed each night like a door behind their cross, began to linger, too. As if to see what they would be up to next.

Then the fly-a-kite spring came on and I fled through the ruins of Victory Gardens pulling a great orange grin of a kite higher than the cross of St. Columbanus; with Ethel screaming behind me.

When it soared so high it no longer grinned, I anchored it and Ethel sent a message up: I LOVE MY SAVIOR. I don't know what had frightened that kid so.

Ethel's father had died without last rites and her mother had paid a priest $100 to keep her late husband from spending eternity in Purgatory. The priest, Ethel now told us between sobs, had returned to tell the family that all the $100 had done was to get the old man to his knees. It would take another $100 to get him out. But Ethel's mother had answered, "If the old man is on his knees, let him jump the rest of the way;" and had sent the priest on his way. The blasphemy had provoked Ethel's decision to run away from home.

Ethel's mother opened the kitchen door, tossed in an armful of the girl's clothing onto the floor—"And don't come home!" she announced; and slammed the door on her pious daughter.

The cast-out girl stood silently. Then her features began working.

"He'll never see the face of *Gawd*!" she howled her grief and love. "He'll never see *His* face!"

"Then let him look at His ass," my father made a swift decision.

*   *   *

On weekdays I got a penny to spend and blew my nose into a rag. But on Sundays I got 10 cents and a clean handkerchief. Weekdays gave only the meanest kind of choice: that between two yellow jaw-breakers or licorice whips or a piece of chewing wax shaped like a wine bottle with a few drops of sugar water inside. But Sundays offered a choice between a chocolate or vanilla or strawberry sundae.

Sundays were for sundaes; the very same day that Ethel was my girl and I was the one with the dime. Ethel owned weekdays because she was closer to Gawd. But Sundays belonged to me because I was the one who knew the way to the country where maraschino cherries lived atop vanilla ice-cream cones. Where strawberries loved whipped cream and pineapple syrup ran down both sides of banana splits. It was all butter-cream frosting there; where caramels lived in candy pans and Green River fizzed beside root beer. It was always root-beer and ginger-ale time; it was always time for lemonade there. Where walnuts lived in butter-cream fudge and pecans lived in chocolate. It was the one place where vanilla, chocolate and strawberry embraced. Ethel's church was St. Columbanus but mine was John the Greek's: The Store Where Ice Cream Came True.

Yet even there Ethel couldn't forget Gawd. She was really dotty on Jesus. The minute John the Greek brought us two glasses of water, that kid would start sprinkling me. I didn't mind the wetting as the day was warm. But as she had already used holy water on me without any result, I didn't see how a couple glasses of soda-fountain water would do any good.

And as though that weren't enough superstition for one Sunday, she would dare me to step on a crack in the walk all the way home. If I did, Gawd would strike me dead, she decided.

I didn't believe a word of it. I put both feet down flat, deliberately, on each crack of the walk, all the way home.

Nothing happened.

"You wait and see," she warned me.

Another Sunday, though the weather was still cool, Ethel and her mother and my mother and myself took a basket lunch and swimming suits and went to the Jackson Park beach.

A replica of Columbus' flagship, the *Santa Maria*, had been standing around the Jackson Park lagoon since the World's Fair of 1893. We took our lunch on the grass in view of its rotting hulk. Ethel and her mother went to the women's bathhouse and I went to the men's to change into swimming suits.

My mother wasn't going swimming herself and she felt the weather was too cool for swimming. If I wanted to go in the water, I would have to put the suit on over my winter underwear.

When I came out of the bathhouse Ethel's mother took one look and started to laugh. Then my mother laughed. It must have been a pitiful sight. When Ethel began to laugh, however, I felt really brought down.

In pauses in our play, after that Sunday, Ethel would survey me gravely—then give me a smile of thinnest mockery as she saw me once more in a swimming suit drawn on over a suit of long underwear. Ground lost by such experience is not easily regained.

As the roll-a-hoop spring came on blue as peace. By the light that now lingered, the light that now held, I stood bowed against the gas lamp crying warning—"eight-nine-ten-*redlight*!" As the roll-a-hoop spring raced to a summer of redlight pursuit.

A terrier got hit in the street by a car that kept going. We heard its yelp and watched it drag itself to the curb. Ethel gave it last rites.

The next morning she got me out of bed to give it a Catholic burial. I hadn't even known the brute was a Christian.

We took turns digging with a toy shovel. When it was deep enough Ethel began crossing herself and I stepped back until she should tell me to throw in the deceased.

Johnny Sheeley came up, put his six quarts of milk down, and took the shovel from me. The grave wasn't deep enough, it seemed.

At his first stroke, the shovel bent and Johnny looked humiliated.

"Wait for me," he asked us. We stood around until he came back bearing a man-sized shovel.

Johnny dug until we grew tired of watching him and wandered off to hunt four-leaf clovers. When we came back he had dug himself to his waist.

The dead terrier lay beside the milk. Ethel threw in an extra prayer for the dog and I practiced crossing myself until it was time for lunch.

From our front window, I watched Johnny on the warm noon, digging for his life. He had, it was plain, forgotten both dog and milk, dirty home and dirty mother. In the early afternoon Ethel came down to fetch me and we went out to watch Johnny for lack of anything else to do.

"You're going to catch it if you don't get home," Ethel shouted down into the hole from which we could still see Johnny's sweat-tousled head. Her answer was a shovelful of dirt from which we both jumped back.

Johnny dug until we saw his mother coming—somebody had snitched! She was a formidable harridan who supported half a dozen sons and daughters with her backyard dairy; doing more herself than her whole retarded brood combined. Johnny tried to scramble out, but couldn't get a hold. His mother had to get two of his retarded brothers out of bed to pull him up.

When they got him up, without a word they both began punching him, while his mother slapped him with the broad of her hand. Johnny ducked into a running crouch and all three followed, punching and slapping; the old woman carrying the soured milk in her left hand while she slapped at his ears with her right.

The battle went across South Park Avenue, with Ethel and me following, drawn by horror and joy, through a narrow way between the building and up the alley between South Park and Vernon Avenue, when Ethel's mother and mine both hollered us back into our own yards. I don't remember whether the terrier ever got buried.

I know the great hole remained there until my father filled it with the shovel Johnny had left, and Ethel and I had to return the shovel as some sort of punishment. Nobody knew what we had to be punished for, but my punishment was always the same: I was excommunicated from the Catholic Church. I don't see how my father was qualified to excommunicate anybody; but he did it all the same.

This time it was my mother who thought the action was comical and my father who went around growling that somebody ought to have that milk-delivery kid locked up before he started thinking about girls.

So far as I know, Johnny never got any ideas about girls that were any funnier than anyone else's.

In the late sunflowered summer of 1918 I took my fiancée to John the Greek's confectionery on the corner of Vernon Avenue and 71st Street. She ordered a strawberry sundae and I ordered chocolate and John put his favorite record on his mechanical piano and sang along with the song for us—

> *If you don't like your Uncle Sammy*
> *If you don't like the red, white and blue*
> *Go back from whence you came*
> *Whatever land its name*
> *Don't bite the hand that's feeding you—*

In the corn-stalked autumn of 1918 I built a new pushmobile out of an orange crate and fitted it with a candle holder. When my father got off the 71st Street trolley he could see me flickering toward him in the dark. And held my hand all the way home.

That was the last autumn my mother took me to see my grandmother and grandfather.

We walked together below the Lake Street el, and a grandfatherly light came down through the Lake Street ties.

All the way to the West Side House.

The West Side House was where my grandfather sat sealing cigars of his own making with a lick of his tongue. The band he wrapped each cigar in said it was a Father & Son Cigar.

And he had promised to tell me a secret he had not told any of his other grandchildren.

And the secret that I was never to tell was that he, himself, personally, *my own grandfather*, had thought up the name of the Father & Son Cigar! That he was therefore the *inventor* of the Father & Son Cigar! And that he had applied for a patent on the name: FATHER & SON CIGAR.

And that it was a *good* cigar.

I was proud to have the man who had invented the Father & Son Cigar for a grandfather.

Then he made the wooden half-figure of a clown on his worktable blow real smoke at me and we went upstairs to dinner.

Behind my grandfather's West Side House stood the *Sommerhaus*, a little old-world cottage with blinds.

It was always summer in the *Sommerhaus*.

The old man sat at dinner with his wife at his right hand and all his married daughters, and all his married sons, and his grandchildren running in and out of the *Sommerhaus*. He was proud that all of his grandchildren had been born in the States.

But I was the only one in the whole tribe for whom he made a wooden clown that blew real smoke.

I was the only one the old man ever told *who* thought up the name of the Father & Son Cigar.

And that it was a *good* cigar.

After dinner Uncle Bill sat at the player piano and played *The Faded Coat of Blue* and Aunt Toby sang the words. Aunt Toby didn't look exactly faint and hungry the way it said in the song—

> *He sank faint and hungry*
> *Among the vanquished brave*
> *And they laid him sad and lonely*
> *In a grave unknown*
> *O no more the bugle*
> *Calls the lonely one*
> *Rest, noble spirit*
> *In thy grave unknown—*

but I figured it must be because she had just had dinner.

Then in no time at all it was time to go home and I walked back with my mother below the Lake Street el.

A grandfatherly light drifted like yellow cigar smoke between the ties and my mother hummed cheerfully—

> *Take me for a joy-ride*
> *A girl-ride, a boy-ride*
> *I'm as reckless as I can be*
> *I don't care what becomes of me—*

all the way home.

Halloween night Ethel and I put on false faces and went up and down 71st Street chalking windows of laundry, undertaker, delicatessen and butcher shop. Dotty as ever, Ethel chalked a cross on John the Greek's and I wrote below the cross—EVERYTHING INSIDE IS A PENNY! and we both ran off screaming. On my way home from the Park Manor School the next noon, all the store windows had been washed clean except John the Greek's.

John's window stayed chalked. On Sunday morning police broke the lock and found John hanging by his belt above the candy tins. I don't know how it had happened but I now knew there *was* something terrible padding the world; and began to skip the sidewalk cracks just to make sure *it* wouldn't get *me*.

I skipped the cracks with particular care when passing the Hanged Man's Place. Frost froze the cracks over and the Hanged Man's windows went white.

I rubbed off the frost with my mitten and peered in: dust and cold had laid a gray hand across the bottles of Green River and Coca-Cola. The great jar of fresh strawberry syrup had fermented, then split the bowl, bubbled over the counter. It hung in a long frozen drip like a string of raw meat.

The magic of strawberry was gone. The magic of its smells and the magic of its color all hung in a freezing dust.

That night I said the German prayer my mother had taught me out of her own childhood:

> *Ich bin klein*
> *Mein Herz ist rein*
> *Darf niemand' drin wohnen*
> *Bloss Gott und die Engel allein.*
>
>   **   *   **

Yet somewhere between that St. Valentine's Day and the Store Where Ice Cream Came True I had realized that where God's colors raged behind a lifted cross was no business of mine: that these were for people who lived upstairs and not for people who lived down.

*   *   *

My father was a working man in a day when the working hour was from 6 A.M. to 6 P.M. He left the house before daylight six days a week and returned home after dark six days a week, year in and year out.

He worked for McCormick Reaper and Otis Elevator and Packard and the Yellow Cab Company in a time when there was no sick leave, no vacations, no seniority and no social security. There was nothing for him to do but to get a hold as a machinist and to hold as hard as he could as long as he could.

He was a good holder but he was unable to keep any one job for more than four or five years because he couldn't handle other men. He could handle any piece of machinery; if left alone. But he was as unable to give orders as he was to take them. He was a tenacious holder; but after four or five years he would hit a foreman. This would happen so blindly that he would be as stunned by it as the man he had hit.

When he walked into the kitchen at noon with his tool chest under his arm my mother knew it had happened again. The first time this happened I was frightened, because I had never seen him, during the week, in the middle of the day. I had the feeling my mother was going to go for him like never before.

That was one time she didn't go at him at all.

Then for days we lived under an oppression of which only the tool chest in the corner of the kitchen spoke. On the morning I rose to find the tool chest and the old man gone to work together, the sense of ominousness lifted; and life began once more.

He was a fixer of machinery in basements and garages who had seen the Electrified Fountain in Lincoln Park.

My father was a farm youth who had come to the city to see Little Egypt dance, and had stayed on to work for many great plants: for they offered him twice the wages that others were getting for doing the same work.

He liked earning twice as much as anybody else and would stay on the job loyally until some picket would take him aside and ask him how he would like to have his head blown off his shoulders.

My father would say that he would like to wait until after lunch if that wasn't asking too much.

He had witnessed the fight between police and anarchists on the Black Road near the McCormick works. He had heard Samuel Fielden speak on the Lake Front; yet his most vivid memory was of Honey-Throat Regan singing *If He Can Fight Like He Can Love/Goodby/Germany.*

My father avoided being killed in situations simmering with violence simply because he didn't hear anything simmering.

*   *   *

The day falls with a colder light today, between the Lake Street ties, than once fell between the blinds of the *Sommerhaus.*

It was always summer in the *Sommerhaus,* the old-world house lit by a grandfatherly light; where grandchildren ran in and out before dinner.

When I was the only one, of all those children, to whom the old man told the name of the inventor of the Father & Son Cigar.

And the farm boy from Black Oak who worked for McCormick Reaper and Otis Elevator and Packard and Yellow Cab became an old man on a West Side bed. An old man who lay without knowing that his wife and son stood looking down at him.

They saw his right hand take the fingers of his left as though something had gone wrong with the fingers; and saw he was trying to fix the machinery of his left hand with the machinery of his right.

They saw him pass from life into death still trying to fix machinery.

His old woman saw him go; yet she did not weep.

So the son knew that, for all his fixing, the old man hadn't fixed anything that mattered.

Now a winter of a single wind drives snow against the blue-and-white legend that once said LAKE STREET. But the ads that once bragged and pigeons that made summer strut, drunkard and lover both alike, have passed into neon mists adrift above the town.

Captain and crewman, all alike, are down with all hands on the proud ship *Chicora*; lost without trace in the ice of South Haven.

Sunken without sign on the unshaken waters.

THE RYEBREAD TREES OF SPRING

OTHER springs have come on strong before. That one where David walked, I've heard, was something quite new in the field. It turned the fields a greener green and flecked the figs of old Gilboa with gold. Yet here in Chicago in the big green middle of a brand-new all-American beginning to everything, I think no spring before was geared this high.

At the Sunday morning newsstand the papers hadn't been tossed in yet by the news truck. The newsy hadn't showed up yet. My mind was filled with that Russian dog that had two heads.

That was the reason I was up so early. I knew the *Tribune* could explain everything. I walked on.

Into a spring strutting like Marilyn Monroe defying traffic lights. That seemed to stand for a moment to one side as if listening to someone like June Christy singing about how it's really spring that hangs her up the most, and you think: that must be as fine as any girl can sound. Till spring herself comes on with lyrics of her own, making the lyrics up as she goes along. A spring that tops the very best, then tops herself and, breaking off, announces to all young men from everywhere, that there is a garden where smorgasbord grows from ryebread trees, the Garden Where All Things Are Possible. And all young men are invited to help themselves and all is free: *Allt är möjlig i gården hänger smör-gåsbord från ri bröd träden.*

A spring, that is to say, telling all young men all things are possible. That if you are a young man from Stockholm with a right hand too fast to follow, and the reason you do not use it against sparring partners is that it has such awful power it will take a man's head off five inches below his shoulders and snap it like a twig and all of that, then somewhere in the room is a reporter who, for one fleeting moment thinks—*allt är möjlig*—all is possible—and you've sown a seed in the climate of belief. All that then remains to be done is to write a round-robin letter to sports editors and sign yourself: The Unacknowledged Champion of Everything. Leave the rest to spring.

"All right, but what about the dog?" I thought I heard someone call, but when I looked around there was nothing but a used-car lot with this year's models already awake and last year's still drowsing about. A cherry-colored pennon above them waved me a cherry-colored good morning.

A morning to bring poets running to see which one can sound the most like Mr. Thomas used to sound.

Between the sidewalk and the street a narrow streak of city grass grew so green one breath would breathe it into fire. Would Joseph Rostenkowski, Ward Committeeman, approve a spring that left things growing in the street? I wondered. Yet it really wasn't so much a Ward Committeeman's spring as it was a State's Attorney's, an Ed Hanrahan spring, and that's the dandiest kind because it knows where spring is legally entitled to grow and where it is not.

"It is my proud privilege and special pleasure to announce that the State's Attorney's Office has arranged for spring to arrive four days early to both sides of West Division Street. Eastbound traffic will be rerouted past students crossing at St. John's High School. So will westbound traffic as students must not be run down from either direction. Courtesy fees in payment of violation of traffic regulations are not payable on the street; but officers will carry even change just in case. It's the proud privilege and special pleasure of this office to announce that tickets to Riverview Park are now available on a bipartisan basis to well-behaved children under twelve at Wieboldt's well-behaved department store."

Sometimes I think a streak of common grass burning between sidewalk and street is as hard a thing to understand as a dog with another dog's head growing out of its neck.

Once a candidate for local office offered a hundred dollars as first prize for a poem about Chicago. A hundred dollars was a lot of money then as now, so I sent in a poem about Chicago being freight-handler and hog-butcher to the world and how freight-cars roll in here on little cat feet. And signed it "Edward St. Vincent Millay" in order to make a strong impression.

I should have signed it "Edward St. Vincent Hanrahan" because I didn't win. The poem that took the hundred began

Chicago is a stallion wild
Windstretched and untame

I know that doesn't seem real great on paper, but just you try saying it out loud in a whiskey-tavern. You'll find, as we of the Poetry Trade like to put it, that it "gains momentum."

We of the Poetry Trade know how to say a thing to keep the layman in his place. You have to keep the layman in place in any line. "Give a layman a hand," we say, "and he'll take a whole knuckle."

"It's true as Proust" is still another—but this one has to be sort of dropped with an indifferent air. I dropped it like that in front of a bartender once--"this Schlitz is true as Proust"—just like that—and before I knew it he had drawn me two Pabsts.

I tried the bit about Chicago being a stallion wild on him; but he didn't even draw a Pabst. He just stood there. So I pressed him about did he think Chicago *really* was a stallion wild? But all he did was keep standing. So I said, "It's big as Whitman." Then he started that just *standing there* again. He was *all* layman.

Another time someone asked Allen Ginsberg what *he* thought about Chicago and the way Mr. Ginsberg put it was: "Death is a message that was never sent." A friend of Mr. Ginsberg's stepped up and said what *he* thought about Chicago. And that was, simply, "MEOW!" He said this "MEOW!" in such a wonderful lifelike way that everyone understood what he had in mind: He thought he was a cat.

"Do you know what you'd have if you put Mr. Ginsberg's brains in a cat?" I asked him and he didn't know. So I told him—"a crazy cat."

But another friend of Mr. Ginsberg's knew that *he* had the *real* solution:

"Chicago is a *rose*," he said before anyone could stop him. The fellow had thrown the whole game away on one bad pitch.

For myself I simply couldn't stop thinking about that Russian dog. Had the Russians beaten us to it again? How could anyone be absolutely sure that Morris Fishbein might not have relatives in Russia? How, in fact, could anyone be sure of anything? What was there to stop the Russians from teaching the dog to sing, "I Ain't Got No Body" and thus turn a purely scientific experiment into a grisly prank? To come down to it, I realized I myself didn't even know which head I was thinking about. I needed a *Tribune* badly.

The Augusta Bakery was still closed, but it was giving away free smells. You have to go around the alley where they load the morning delivery trucks to get one; but you can have all you want so long as you don't get in the way of the man carrying bread trays. I picked old-country-rye with seeds to smell first, even though I hadn't yet had orange juice. This is a very heavy whiff to hit a person's stomach with no warning, but I was hungry. Next I tried egg-bread plain, but they hadn't used enough eggs. After that I had a French do-nut, the light kind without frosting. I didn't hang around for pineapple cheese rolls because something began to get me in my middle like that June Christy coming on about it being spring that hangs her up the most again, and that is exactly what was doing it: spring was coming on again. Like spring. I walked on.

Into a spring of old-time church-chimes, old clocks ticking remembrances of things people used to say and sing they don't say or sing any more. I remembered a fellow used to come on between strip acts at the old Rialto. He weighed in around ninety pounds and wore a bright orange tie that hung past his knees and his face was so little and so pale behind it that it made the business of being a man something very comical in itself. The song he sang best was *Oh Why Did I Pick a Lemon in the Garden of Love Where Only Peaches Grow?* His name was Kenny Brenna and if it wasn't for me both his name and the song would be lost to posterity.

A big green trolley-bus whose windshield said CHARTERED came racing its empty seats down the middle of the street. Yet in the very last seat a woman's face, pale as heroin, looked out; the only one who rode. *"Zaza Zazaza,"* she told me. So I knew I was the only one, beside herself, who knew she rode.

I thought of a spring whose bright returning would bring, in the semi-windup featuring eighty rounds of boxing at the Marigold Gardens, a welterweight from Gary, Indiana, named Zale in the semi-windup. With EXTRA-ADDED ATTRACTION: Ruffy Silverstein wrestling Hans Schmidt, the Prussian Giant. Some spring that smells of egg-bread, plain; but short two eggs per loaf.

Turning off Ashland onto Cortez I saw one Puerto Rican sitting on top of a Keep-Our-City-Clean box far from Puerto Rico. He wore a red shirt open at the throat, cream-colored trousers fresh from the cleaners, and was combing his hair as if he had just killed somebody on North Clark. When he saw me coming he replaced the comb and began to riffle a deck of cards.

"Come to me here you," he ordered as I passed, "couple fast hands black-jack, just me and you." The riffle sounded heavy like a deck with one extra card. My guess was that it was a queen. The Polish boys who used to deal seconds around here never used a queen. The card you had to watch out for with them was the jack. Don't ask me why. If I knew why Porkies prefer a queen and Polskies a jack, I'd know about two-headed dogs, too. The whole thing was explained in the *Trib*; but I missed the issue. I simply have no luck no luck at all.

"Let me just talk to you, you," the dealer asked, but I kept passing for I knew now who he was. Just plain old Bill Saroyan still trying to get up his taxes; nobody else.

I once knew a spring that came on fiercely tootling, red-white-and-blue-whirlabell, a small girl on a Fourth-of-July tricycle with flags tied to the wheels, who left laughter trailing like a confetti-colored pennon down the long block behind her.

I knew another spring that walked in handsewn jeans, and rain-gray shirt and cap pulled low, below the wrack of a prison noon: whose lips inquired without moving, "Will you hold this for me?" and walked on never glancing back to where, the taped blade plunged five inches in, the paid informer lay.

I knew a spring that once dealt stud poker all night long, the first card and the last card closed, fifteen dollars on the last card or an open pair, dealing on and on past midnight and toward noon; in a room that smelled of burning punk and dead cigars and booze. And when the last bluff had been called and the last closed card was opened and the burning punk was fading, someone rapped the door: we all looked up.

And in came Summer in a yellow dress saying "the joint is raided, boys." And everybody laughed.

And once I saw a spring of lonesome jacks played by a girl in a pool of light at the end of a third-floor hall where no one comes all day. Crosslegged, ball and jacks, she made up a third-floor spring as she went along, just for girls who live behind numbered doors in halls where no one comes. As if she felt that the bright noontime city behind her might stay at noon, and never slowly darken, if she could find a magic saying to say with ball and jacks. Yet the city behind her was already darkening.

Near the corner of Chicago Avenue and Wolcott two walls squeezed out an old blown bum, one who had been squeezed between many old walls—barracks, flophouse, barroom, and cell—that are made to squeeze men in. This one had been squeezed between walls where old bricks sweat and slowly drip in a cold, uncaring sweat. He came toward me now with one sleeve slowly squeezing the other and both elbows squeezing his middle. He had to hold his head bent a bit forward because something unseen kept squeezing his neck. His cheekbones were ground in a heavy vise that only a shot of Old Stillborn could loosen. This was the vised man Time and The Goat had caught between them. When Time and The Goat begin to press there is nothing on earth can help a man but Old Stillborn. He held out a card old brown beggary had begotten. I put it to my eyes and let them squeeze themselves to me:

254

DONT WORRY

DONT HURRY

BETTER TO

BE LATE TO

THE GOLDEN

GATE THAN

ARRIVE IN

HELL ON TIME

He wanted a nickel for his philosophy, although both the philosophy and the card he offered it on were secondhand. I handed him a coin—then realized too late that it was a *quarter*! My mistake must have been reflected on my face, because he snapped his card back out of my hand, looked me up and down with real derision and asked impatiently—"What are you waiting for—change?" Then turned, laughing lightly, on his heel. And left me standing without a quarter. And no philosophy whatsoever.

Well, what do you know, he hadn't been a mere wino after all. I'd been touched by a true Mortimer Adler of the alleys; one who knew how to collect on the philosophy of others, and bank the money for himself. If that fellow had a PhD, I realized, he'd be dangerous.

Passing the used-car lot again, the new year's models looked brighter than ever, but last year's were still drowsing. The cherry-colored pennon that had waved to me had itself gone back on the nod, folded over upon itself above a 1956 Chevy. A *Tribune* truck sped past and I broke into a run, still clutching my card, because I wanted to be the very first to read what they had thought up in the Tribune Tower the night before.

I had begun to doubt whether Chicago was really a stallion wild after all. I was sure it's no damned rose. I doubt it's even a rose that says "MEOW!" although that seems to be nearer than thinking of it as a cat that smells like a rose.

What it's really closer to being is just an endless stretch of crisscrossing streets where men from everywhere have come to see how close they can come to killing one another without losing a customer and still stay out of jail.

A small girl was sitting on the stand in a new print frock with a green balloon tethered to her hand.

"Has someone forgotten you, honey?" I asked her. She studied me thoughtfully.

"Where *you* been all night?" She wanted to know.

The way she put that made me think for a moment I might be up against a midget—but what would a midget be doing holding a green balloon?

"You *might* pick up the morning papers," she suggested in that tone so near to scorn. "Or *am* I asking too much?"

Chicago isn't the best town in the world to be seen conversing with an unaccompanied child, and there have been so many laws passed against crime in general lately that I might not even have a defense in pleading that my accuser was a fifty-six-year-old midget. There might be something about talking to unaccompanied midgets. I am all for law and order on Sunday morning, so I put the papers beside her without unbinding them, thinking that might be interpreted later as a ruse to gain time.

Am I asking too much? Of any Sunday-morning balloon-man's spring in Chicago, that it lift the wishes of all young men in landlocked bars a little, waiting for their lifelong lives to start?

Or raise the hopes of Sunday-morning sidestreet solitaries all over town, to let them drift slowly and low above St. John Cantius and high, then higher, over St. Bonifacius and St. Columbkille, toward that wonderful garden where all things are possible? To all those now merely waiting for rain or bread or love or peace with a pinch of the salt of magic in it that will last till the big dark falls.

Allt är möjlig i gården hänger smörgåsbord från ri bröd träden.

The garden where all things are possible. And all is free.

All is free to young men in landlocked bars on landlocked streets.

In a spring inviting every young man with a right hand too fast to follow to be the Unacknowledged Champion of Everything.

If anyone has been killed on North Clark Street recently, it wasn't me.

DIFFERENT CLOWNS FOR
DIFFERENT TOWNS

IT was a bright summer's morning, in 1931, when I walked into the City News Bureau to receive my first start in Chicago journalism.

The late Isaac Gershman, then directing the bureau, gave it to me.

He began by assuring me that his list of applicants was already so long that there was no point in his even asking my name. Then he asked it anyhow! His newshawk's intuition had gone to work. And, like the man of action Isaac Gershman was, he acted on that intuition.

"Add this man's name to our list of applicants!" he instructed his secretary.

His secretary happened to be out of the room at the moment. But, like the woman of action she was, she returned.

Gershman looked up the moment she entered the room.

"What can I do for *you*?" he asked me.

"You were going to put my name on some list."

The man reacted swiftly. "Put this man's name on some list!" he told the young woman.

I told her what my name was.

She put it on some list.

"*I'll* phone you as soon as we have an opening," she promised. To other applicants, I sensed, she merely said "*We'll* phone you."

When she came back from lunch she told me to go home.

But what if the opening should materialize while I was on my way home? By the time I got back to the bureau it might have closed again! I decided to play it safe by staying in the area. I went to the Little Paris Burlesk on South State. That was right *in* the area.

My relationship to the City News Bureau has remained intensely personal ever since. Much of the credit for this goes to the Little Paris Burlesk.

Now transpired one of those mystical coincidences which, looking back through the mists of four decades, will baffle science: *The Little*

Paris did not close its doors until 1959, the same year that the White Sox won their first American League pennant in four decades!

No sooner had the White Sox won the pennant than Emmett Dedmon of the *Sun-Times* sent for me and Fire Superintendent Quinn set off air-raid warnings at midnight. I was to write human interest stuff from the grandstand.

"Mr. Dedmon," I responded courteously, "thank you for giving me my second start in Early Chicago Journalism," saluted briskly and left. I cabbed out to my parents' home on the Northwest Side to give them the good news. A stranger came to the door. I'd forgotten that my folks had moved in 1936.

I ought to have remembered as they'd moved the day after I'd run away from home. That's something *else* I've never been able to figure out.

The moment each game was finished, I cabbed north to Dedmon's office, composing my story on the way. Dedmon, wearing a green eye-shade, would be striding up and down shouting things like, "Hit that story! The presses are rolling! Get on the streets before the *Trib*! *Scoop* 'em!" To which nobody paid the least attention. It wasn't until some years later, when I chanced to see a revival of "The Front Page," that I realized he'd been doing Hildy Johnson.

Whether Hildy would have sent me to Los Angeles, had the Sox extended the series, is one of those great Ifs of history which scholars will debate into infinity; like whether the Weathermen did, or did not, spring Dr. Leary; or whether he got himself out by failing to realize he was in. In which case I fail to see what difference it makes.

Considering that my second start in Early Chicago Journalism had lasted three days longer than my first start, I was gathering momentum. How often now I look back, nostagically, wishing that the Little Paris was still open so I could get away from the hurly-burly of the press room. Or did I miss my big chance by not applying at the *Northwest Side News*?

I owe my next beginning to the *Sun-Times*. For it chose a moment, when the world seemed strangely quiet, to express a feeling it had had for some time but hadn't been able to place before:

"We have had a feeling which has persisted for some time that squalor is going out of fashion in Chicago. Perhaps this is largely due to the postwar war on slums, our mayor's efforts in tidying up the streets, the popularity of cheering colors and the wide interest in art and music shown by the public.

"All these, and more, have added up to a feeling that the good old-fashioned, smelly squalor immortalized by men of literary genius is definitely on the way out.''

What overpaid idiot wrote *that* editorial I never troubled to inquire. All I'm sure of is that, if Roman Pucinski can get elected to public office, *anybody* can be a managing editor.

As Goldie Hawn once put it: different strokes for different folks.

Back in the *Chicago American* press room Dirty Maggie had been thinking, for some time, that I needed a fresh start. When two old-time thieves were curbed, on North Broadway, by a squadrol, and I happened, by some strange chance, to be sitting between them in the front seat, Maggie sprang into action.

When a stick of marijuana was discovered under the dashboard she became really *eager*. And when Otto Preminger's *Man with the Golden Arm* materialized, in the same week, for a rerun on Otto Preminger's TV sets, she grew hysterical.

The proof of my innocence was incontestable: had I been aware that there was a stick of tea under the dashboard, it wouldn't have been there when we were busted because I would have had it smoked to the final ash by then.

''The man who wrote a novel about a narcotics addict himself appeared today in narcotics court,'' Maggie put it on the wires coast to coast. Then she phoned the arresting officers to determine whether the car we'd been curbed in hadn't been stolen.

What a beauty of a scoop! I can see it now: ''Writer trapped in hot-car ring! Claims dope in car was not for sales purposes. Divorced author, once found guilty of typewriter theft in Texas, out on bond pending trial.''

Unhappily for Dirty Mag, there was a bill of sale for the car. And, as Papa Hemingway might have put it, it was a good bill. Judge Wendt, apparently unimpressed by Mag's screeching, looked sympathetically at the state's attorney, asked him ''What has the loser got to say?'' and dismissed the case in less than five minutes. The driver of the car, however, was fined for going through a yellow light.

But the Prosecution for the *American* wasn't ready to accept dismissal of the case that readily.

''Congratulations to Nelson Algren on beating the narcotics rap!'' she topped her column the following morning.

Different strokes for different folks.

''The more we put into welfare the worse the immorality becomes,'' was the theme of a column of Jack Mabley's, which gave me my third or fourth local start—I'm losing count.

"We are making it profitable to have babies out of wedlock." The columnist advanced the concept that the higher incidence of immorality on the South Side, as compared to the suburbs, is directly proportional to the incidence of public welfare.

Not pausing to consider that adulterers who aren't on welfare aren't tailed by caseworkers.

"The soaring rate of illegitimacies," he warned all homeowners between Chatham Fields and Lake Forest about overdoing generosity, "shows that the more help you give, the more indolent the recipient becomes! Where will the vicious cycle of bastardy end?"

Somewhere between Winnetka and Glenview would by *my* guess.

Yet the ploy worked well enough to lend him momentum toward a managing-editorship.

So it isn't surprising that the same columnist pulled one of the weirdest U-turns, transforming himself from a wild bull into a bunny-man, in the history of Early Chicago Journalism.

In the same crusading tone as he'd warned the suburbs about the vicious cycle of bastardy going on in the ghetto at their expense, he anticipated the purposes of the antiwar demonstrators during Convention Week of 1968. According, I assume, to orders from above.

But there it was: hippie chicks were going to work as hookers in order to put LSD into delegates' drinks, beat-up cars were to be abandoned on the thruways in order to jam traffic. LSD would be dissolved in our drinking water—the whole gamut of fantasies that makes frightened men buy newspapers.

"The defense is massive manpower," Mabley warned.

And saw the consequences of his own irresponsibility.

Horrifying View of the Police State he reported, having witnessed police beating up a cripple in the course of their rioting. He was so outraged at such useless cruelty that he put down his head and charged the whole police department. He charged so hard that he charged offstage.

When he next materialized he was wearing a bunny-suit and was organizing a defense fund for policemen indicted on charges of brutality.

His organization of the fund was so successful that now Chicago police need have no further fear of clubbing anyone, crippled or able-bodied; so long as they take off their badges first.

"I was involved in the fund," he explained later, "because after the convention disorders, when there was public speculation on federal indictments of policemen as political balance for the indictments of eight radicals, I thought the idea was so outrageous I said I would start a fund to defend the policemen the day any indictments were returned. I didn't think the federal government would have the nerve to indict. But . . . the awesome federal government went into action to try to put these policemen into prison . . . the cost of proving their innocence, in money and the emotional impact on the men and their families, was terrible.''

The cost of putting people into prison for protesting the most cowardly military assault in American history, and the emotional impact upon *them* and *their* families, however, is just another touch of brightness to lighten the gloom of our subway decor.

A fighter who'd just been knocked out by Archie Moore, came around to Moore's dressing room to ask for Moore's autograph. But he was moved by awe. Mabley just feels that a bunny-suit is more becoming to his personality.

"I don't think a newspaper should be like a mean dog," Mike Royko once commented, "that trots down the street, slashes your leg and keeps on trotting."

What Royko didn't figure was on the mean dog doing a U-turn, coming back to take another slash and *then* keep trotting.

A few years ago I was introduced to a fortyish-looking fellow who told me his name was Gershman. As he was a newspaper man, I recalled I'd once met a man of the same name, several decades ago, at the City News Bureau.

"That was my father, Isaac Gershman," the younger Gershman assured me.

"Then I have a message for him," I thought quickly, "tell him if I don't hear from him in the next six months I'll be forced to seek employment elsewhere."

Well, how would *you* feel if *you'd* been Rod Serling when Ron Ziegler came along?

Different strokes for different folks.

Different clowns for different towns.

GO! GO! GO! FORTY YEARS AGO

THERE was an October forty Octobers gone, when a lamplighter on a Pathfinder bike, carrying a torch across its handlebars, came down South Park Avenue, between 71st and 72nd, every evening; and the White Sox were going to whip Cincinnati.

The cross of St. Columbanus, from its Prairie Avenue height, looked down on the prairie our windows faced. It was by the light behind that cross, as the autumn day died and the first gas-lamps came on, that I realized that the time to stop playing Run Sheepie Run had come.

The time for me to start being a major leaguer had arrived. The Sox were certain to beat Cincinnati.

Their names were Jackson and Risberg and Felsch and Cicotte. Their names were Collins and Faber and Schalk. Their names were Williams and Weaver and Gandil.

Their names were also Chick and Buck and Happy. Their names were Red and Swede. Their names were Lefty and Shoeless Joe. Joe alone could whip Cincinnati.

I was cutting close to eleven years of age and yet had no name like Lefty or Buck. Or Red or Chick or Happy. I couldn't be Lefty because I was righty; I couldn't be Red because I was tow-haired. I couldn't be Shoeless because that my mother wouldn't allow. It looked like I was never going to be anybody.

That I was already dangerously near to being nobody came to me the day I approached some kids with a dime-store rocket in my hand.

"Who wants to play throw?" I asked, flipping my ball from hand to hand.

"Girls play throw. *We* play catch," they let me know, and walked away.

That setback started me out, one Sunday morning from 71st Street, walking to White Sox Park at 35th and Shields. With the dime-store rocket in my pocket. Outside Comiskey Park, mounted police were trying to keep a mob of locked-out fans from crashing the centerfield fence;

which was then wooden. Inside the park, with the White Sox and the New York Yankees fighting for first place in the 1920 pennant race, Cicotte was pitching to Ruth.

The crush of the mob swept police, horses and myself onto the field and I scampered into the centerfield bleachers. The papers described the crashing of the great fence as RIOT AT WHITE SOX PARK! Overnight I became the kid who had not only survived a riot—with its connotations of the race-rioting of a couple years before—but had seen Eddie Cicotte strike out Babe Ruth.

I was made. My existence was recognized by the world of men. I had survived in the world where men play catch. The kids who'd walked away from me not only now accepted me, but permitted me to have a favorite player. I picked Swede Risberg. My name, for the next decade, was "Swede."

Player-cards were a penny for a strip of ten. We cut them into individual cards, dipped them in wax to stiffen them; and snapped them at the cracks dividing the walks. The cry was "five up!" "ten up!" or, when the gambling fever rose, "*twenty* up!" This was sheer madness; but eliminated small bettors. Baseball having become a national gambling fever, as well as a national sport, we'd joined in the corruption that was turning everything into a business.

I traded my cards off for an agate and six steelies. Someone brought out dice. From the halls of state to the sidewalks, the whole country was out after the easy buck. And their names were Rothstein and Attell; Sinclair and Doheny; Insull and Ponzi. And when Comiskey hired Alfred Austrian, and Rothstein retained Wm. G. Fallon, to save Comiskey's image as well as Rothstein's skin, the big E sign went up on the center-field scoreboard in White Sox Park.

Shadows of helicopters fled across the outfield last Thursday. Someone flew Tony Martin from Hollywood to sing the national anthem. Before he'd finished the Sox had scored twice.

When Early Wynn doubled in the third, someone ran out to give him his jacket and a woman behind me asked someone, "Aren't they going to play it out?" She thought that, because Wynn was dressing, he was going home.

Although I'd come to the park fearing that there might be a roped-off area for Black Sox fans paroled for the series, I finally began to enjoy the feeling of being right there in the middle of first-class citizens.

In that strenuous third inning there was a moment, after Al Smith's first hit, that there appeared to be only·one member of the Dodger infield upright. It looked like Antietam Creek. It was this spectacle, of prostrate athletes, that made me suspect Lopez may be more than just a good manager. He may also be the world's foremost expert on making opposition look silly.

The woman who'd been afraid that Wynn was going to go home asked her husband what the score was. "11-0 in the 4th, dear," he told her. "Does that mean it's going to be 22-0 in the 8th?" she wanted to know.

Chuck Churn looked pretty fast. He looked almost as fast as Lou Kretlow. There was one pitch in there as fast as Van Lingle Mungo and nobody has ever thrown harder than *that*. Now if Churn can keep his stuff out of the grandstand he may begin getting people out.

All in all it was a good-natured crowd. I kept my Sox hat throughout, prepared, at any moment, to invoke Algren's Invincible Evil Eye whammy; which, once turned on, cannot be turned off. Sitting only nineteen furlongs to the right of Al Smith, I had a dead aim for the plate.

But I let it go. After all, I was forty years late. Had I had it developed when I was eleven, and Buck Weaver was playing third, I would have put it on Kenesaw Mountain Landis. And Weaver would still be out there, with a big grin under his cap, inching up on the Dodger batters one by one. And every one of them as unnerved as Cobb used to be when Weaver began inching up *him*.

There was no need of intimidating the Dodgers. Every one of them, from the moment he looked at Early Wynn with that chaw of tobacco in his jaw, getting ready to throw at him, looked ready to faint.

When I got inside Comiskey Park, for the second game, the field was deserted; apparently confirming the prediction, made in this column yesterday, that the Dodgers might return to Brooklyn—or whoever it was that sent them—without playing it out.

However, four members of the Fifth Army Color Guard, by marching across the field with three of them in step, inspired Brooklyn—or is it Los Angeles now?—to change their minds. They were going to try again!

The flag-raising went much better than yesterday: they got it higher than half-mast. Nat (King) Cole offered *his* version of the national anthem. Considering his many other obligations I thought this was considerate of him; that song has been in need of rewriting since 1812.

Watching thousands of Americans eating hot dogs, it struck me that, although I saw not one who looked like he'd lay down his life for Democracy, there were certainly multitudes who would fight to the death to see Luis Aparicio lead off with a double; which is precisely what Luis did.

A woman in blue corduroy, showing signs of early mileage in both her face and the corduroy, sat beside me with a cardboard horn, almost as big as herself, in her lap. Yet it lay there disconsolately; as if it had simply been left there by somebody else. She didn't come to life until Junior Gilliam came up and connected so solidly that I stood up to see the end of the ball's flight in the lower left-field grandstand—just as Ted Kluszewski, on first, began coming down from his leap for it, rolled like a wheel and came up holding the ball! Gilliam, leaning on his bat, looked like he thought his own hit had landed in the grandstand that Kluszewski must have brought a ball of his own to the park all the way from Argo, for just such an emergency.

It was the right moment for Blue Corduroy to blow her damned horn; but she missed it. She hadn't seen anything to blow a horn about, it looked like. Or just didn't give a damn one way or another.

It wasn't until after Charley Neal's second homer dropped in by inches, and Kluszewski missed by the same margin, that I felt the fickle finger of fate swinging toward the Dodgers.

Yet I felt the Dodgers were flying in the face of the Furies, when they pulled Podres for a pinch-hitter, as he was getting stronger by the inning. Another reason I felt the Dodger management was making a big mistake was because the pinch-hitter was somebody named Aram Puntformacion or something: an Armenian football player who may or may not be a cousin of William Saroyan's. He'd batted against Early Wynn, in the first game as though he must be *somehow* related.

Puntformacion appeared bemused, as if wrapped in reflection about those seventy thousand Assyrians that once bemused Saroyan. He lurched absent-mindedly in the direction of the first pitch; then stood as though waiting for the second pitch until somebody suggested he start running as he'd just hit a home run.

One of Bill Veeck's rose-bearing ushers handed Blue Corduroy a rose in celebration of the occasion. She took it and put it into her lap with a gentle gesture. Then, as if suddenly stricken by the full impact of the occasion, stood up and blew the stupid horn a blast as though Veeck had just awarded her the grandstand. Then sat down as suddenly as she'd stood up; looking abashed. What got into *her*? I wondered. By this time Puntformacion was rounding second.

"Two days here, it's about time somebody give me *something*," she apologized.

Then the big Chicago afternoon light came down like the light of no other city.

Puntformacion crossed the home plate at last. And I knew that the White Sox were going where Shoeless Joe had gone.

Floating Down The Old Green River On The Good Ship Rock And Rye was the song we liked best on our crank-handled Vic. *Cohen On The Telephone* was another favorite. *America I Love You* was also popular; but had a crack in it that caused the refrain to repeat, when it got to "from ocean to ocean a nation's devotion—devotion—devotion—devotion"—

Days of the Kissell car, the Japanese bun and the daring one-inch heel; when there were people who yet remembered The Bismarck Gardens. That stood where the Marigold stands today. Who remembers when people went to Lincoln Park to see the fountain that operated electrically?

My father smoked Father & Son cigars and had once gone to Sam T. Jack's Burlesk. I myself had seen the *Eastland* lying on its side in the river: my mother had taken me downtown just to see it. And all the way home she spoke the sorrowful name of the proud steamer *Chicora*; down with all hands in the ice off South Haven.

Yet that was my mother's past, my father's past, and had nothing really to do with *me*.

Yesterday The Dodgers put over six runs in the fourth inning. Early Wynn still looked like a twenty-game winner to me; between line drives. When Barker got on on a squibbling single I told myself, "There's a man who knows in his heart that he just stole first base." And the woman beside me began calling on God: "Let it rain," she prayed, "let it rain."

God paid no heed. So she went over his head directly to Al Lopez: "Put in that .625 hitter, Lopez! Put in that .625 hitter you been keeping on the bench!"

I asked the lady, courteously, who she might have in mind, on the White Sox roster, that was hitting over .600.

"Honey Romano," she assured me; looking surprised that I hadn't heard all about it.

I was still for Wynn, I was still for Fox; I was still for Big Klu. Because Los Angeles has always impressed me as being a city wired only loosely to reality. Furthermore, I've never been able to take football seriously and Armenians have always seemed implausible to me.

Which was why, when Chuck Essegian, the Armenian football player from Stanford, hit his second homerun of the series as a pinch-hitter, and the band struck up *California, Here I Come,* it wasn't rain I was praying for; but a 4-11 alarm that would bring the Loyalists of the Chicago Fire Department out just in time to hose Comiskey Park down South State Street.

As the music faded, a dull apprehension moved across the stands. The

266

music, going farther and farther away, sounded to me like it was playing *Lili Marlene* in another country; and the year was 1943.

I remembered the way Wee Bonnie Baker had sounded, singing *O Johnny O Johnny O* in 1939; and the way the scrub pine and red sands of North Caroline looked when a PX juke box played *Milkman Keep Those Bottles Quiet* in 1942.

Long after the .625 hitter had popped out I sat looking at the rain behind the lights.

The little people of the rain were having infield practice of their own. Mistaking—as hep-ghosts often do—the arc-lights around the park for so many moons.

I've seen hep-ghosts playing throw before. And once, in another rain, I watched the ghosts of blue-moon hookers, old-time cruisers out of times long gone, chase each other, leaping drunk, across an all-night billboard advertising Mogen David wine.

Yesterday, after the rain had let up to no more than a light drizzle, and the infield hep-ghosts had gone back to the dugouts, I saw a tall man, his hands on his knees, in a muddied uniform, waiting in left field. As I watched. he began walking toward the dugout; his head slightly bent.

I noticed that he'd left his glove on the field: as though he knew he wouldn't be needing it anymore.

The vendor outside the park was still shouting *"Go! Go! Go! Forty years ago!"*

BALLET FOR OPENING DAY

The Swede Was a Hard Guy

He had grown up believing it was talent made a man big. If you were good enough, and dedicated yourself, you could get to the top. Wasn't that enough of a reward? But when he got there he'd found out otherwise. They all fed off him, the men who ran the show and pulled the strings that kept it working. They used him and used him, and when they'd used him up they would dump him. In the years he'd been up they'd always made him feel like a hero to the people of America. But all the time they paid him peanuts. The Newspaper men who came to watch him pitch and wrote stories about him made more money than he did. Comiskey made half a million dollars a year off his right arm.

> Eliot Asinof on Eddie Cicotte
> in *Eight Men Out: The Black Sox*
> *and the 1919 World Series.*

Charles A. Comiskey liked being called "The Grand Old Man of Baseball." He liked it so much that he hired a little man to see that messages unbefitting his grandeur never reached him.

This required vigilance on the little man's part. There were people around town—some of them working on newspapers—who wanted to tell the old man that he wasn't even grand enough to be The Grand Old Man of Horseshoe-Pitching. They thought he was too cheap to be grand.

Eastern fans, indeed, began jeering Mr. Comiskey's players as "Black Sox" before that appellation signified anything more scandalous than neglecting to launder their uniforms. The old man was so begrudging about laundry bills that his players looked as if they'd put on their

268

uniforms opening day in the coalyard behind Mr. Comiskey's park; and hadn't changed them since.

Three dollars per man *per diem* was the White Sox dining-room budget on the road. This inspired merriment among players who could crop a sirloin without paying for a potato out of their own pockets.

Yet the old man didn't stint sports-writers. He loaded press-tables with liquor and food. And he had affection for children, too. So much that he would often present an autographed baseball, without charge, to the son of a public official; providing that a photographer were on hand. There is no record of the old man ever taking a baseball back from the son of any affluent official.

His little man was also handy at getting Joe Jackson to sign on the dotted line. Hap Felsch proved no problem either. Since Jackson was illiterate, and Felsch didn't give a damn, the little man wasn't demonstrating a highly specialized skill.

Where he ran into trouble was with Eddie Collins. Collins was a college graduate and could read fine print. He'd had sufficient foresight, when signing with Connie Mack at Philadelphia, to have his contract stipulate that, in event of his being traded, his $14,500 salary would be sustained.

Comiskey's other stars were drawing between $2,500 and $5,000. The little man sweated to break Collins' contract; yet it held.

Had the old man's parsimoniousness not been dangerous it would have been comical. For no other factor contributed to the corruption of Comiskey's players so directly as the old man's venality. He now had a shortstop making the same plays, for $3,000, for which his second baseman was earning $14,500. There wasn't a club in either league that wouldn't have doubled Swede Risberg's salary.

Nor that of any of the other White Sox regulars. Gandil was playing first base for $4,500; while Cincinnati was paying double that to an infielder whom Gandil outclassed in every department. Cincinnati's heaviest hitter was making $11,000; Jackson, outhitting him by fifty points, was getting $5,000.

Eddie Cicotte had brought Comiskey a pennant, in 1917, by winning 29 games; yet Comiskey had refused him a raise. Instead, he'd offered the pitcher a ten-thousand-dollar bonus if he won 30 games in 1919. (1918 having been a foreshortened season.) When Cicotte had won 28 the old man benched him; upon the pious pretension that he was saving his star's arm for the World Series.

Baseball had always been a betting game. The great American sports explosion, that followed the end of World War I, heightened stakes.

When players' salaries failed to follow the massive profits being made by the owners, gamblers began paying off certain players. The players wanted in, too.

Whenever one of these scandals broke—and they broke in both major leagues—the owners conducted "investigations" to sustain the public image of baseball as an honest game; yet were careful not to touch the thousand-dollar bettors sitting behind home plate. Their detectives collared the boys betting nickels in the bleachers instead.

Like the Pullman Company, baseball recognized no labor organization, fixed its own wage rates and working conditions. Any player attempting to negotiate a contract, other than with the one that had purchased him, was automatically expelled from organized baseball. He couldn't even play minor league ball under his own name. If an owner's terms left a player dissatisfied, he had one alternative: he could throw in his glove.

Chick Gandil had been batting around .300 for nine seasons. He had the strongest hands of any first baseman in either league. "The only first baseman who doesn't need a glove," one writer said of him.

When, in the face of fast-rising attendance, Comiskey cut players' salaries, Gandil was ready to throw in that glove.

Gandil
Riding the Western rails since boyhood
Between copper camp and lumber camp
Fighting weight one hundred and ninety-seven pounds
Copper-mine boilermaker, border boxer,
Semi-pro ballplayer
A big-handed boy taking his ease in Western bars
Who'd once fought with a broken jaw
In a hundred-and-fifty-dollar winner-take-all bordertown brawl
Yet had fought on and taken the hundred-fifty:
He could still feel the welded break
Like a copper thread running his jaw.
"He has the best first-baseman's hands in the business"
Ring Lardner wrote of him.
He didn't mention the blackleg gambler's fingers.
Nor the Westerner's pure gall:
Everyone knew that Chick Gandil
Had the nerve of a government mule.
Yet strangely lost that nerve among the tinhorn sporty-O's
Of the Eastern hotel lobbies.
J.J. Sport Sullivan looked like the biggest man in Boston to Chick.

J.J. paid for the whiskey and the women
J.J. paid for the good cigars
J.J. said "Chick, I want you to meet George M. Cohan:
"Mr. Cohan, meet Mr. Gandil. Mr. Gandil, meet Mr. Cohan."
J.J. said, "Chick, I want you to meet Harry Sinclair.
"Mr. Sinclair, meet Mr. Gandil. Mr. Gandil, Meet Mr. Sinclair."
And when all J.J. required
To get Mr. Sinclair down for a ten thousand-dollar wager,
Was Mr. Sinclair's word
Gandil rubbed the welded break in his jaw
Recalling the chintzy forty-five dollars per man
"Token of appreciation"
The White Sox had assessed themselves—
For four Detroit pitchers who'd whipped Boston
Three successive end-of-the-season games.
Thus bringing the 1917 pennant to Mr. Comiskey's park.
It came to Chick Gandil then
That the word of some men was good.
Like Mr. Sinclair's.
And the word of other men was no good at all.
Like Mr. Comiskey's.
The old man had promised the team individual bonuses
If they brought him a pennant that year.
Yet he hadn't himself shown up at the clubhouse celebration
When they'd won it for him.
Instead he'd sent the little man—whose name was Grabiner—
With a case of champagne.
"*Here's* your bonus," the little man had explained.
Cheating was wrong only if you didn't own a baseball park.
That much was plain.
And it hadn't even been good champagne.
And every man in the clubhouse knew, while drinking it
That the "token of appreciation"
Hadn't been for the Tiger pitchers beating Boston.
It had been payment for four games they'd thrown to Chicago.
Collins—simon-pure Eddie—hadn't liked it.
He hadn't liked it at all.
But when Gandil told Risberg to collect forty-five dollars per man
And to collect from Collins first
Collins had paid up; so the others had followed.
Until Risberg confronted Weaver.

"Count me out," Weaver told Risberg.
Gandil had to count Weaver out:
The only man who didn't go along with the 1917 fix.
The Swede was a hard guy:
He wasn't that hard to Buck Weaver.

Weaver
The sportswriters had named him "Error-A-Day-Weaver"
When he'd first come west from softcoal country
And his hitting had been even softer.
Kid Gleason developed him into a .300 hitter
By switching him at the plate
And into the finest fielding third-baseman in either league.
His habit of grinning, while inching up on a batter
So unnerved Ty Cobb that he refused to bunt against Weaver:
The only third-baseman whose throw Cobb couldn't out-run.
Buck could wear a pitcher down, foul after foul after foul
Till the man blew sky-high.
A joyous boy, all heart and hard-trying
A territorial animal
Who guarded the spiked sand around third like his life.
And wound up coaching a girl's softball team
With no heart left in him at all.

Risberg
He was a rangy San Franciscan who took to fighting as easily as to baseball; and occasionally confused these crafts. At Oakland he'd protested a third strike simply by stepping up to an umpire and knocking him cold with a short chop to the jaw. "Call *that* a third strike," he'd commented while other umpires were trying to bring the umpire around. And walked back to his dugout.

He had prescience. He'd begin moving to his left with the pitch, knock down a drive through the middle and cut the runner down with a peg only hands of iron could handle.

Gandil had the iron hands.

Swede Risberg would have looked dazzling anywhere; except playing beside Eddie Collins. Everything Risberg did, Collins did with more flash. When Risberg singled, Collins doubled. When Risberg doubled, Collins doubled and stole third.

Himself a grammar-school dropout and strictly a boy for the girls and the booze, it hurt to be outplayed by a college graduate who didn't drink, smoke or chew. What hurt even more was getting less than $3,000 for making the same plays the graduate was being paid $14,500 to make.

The team was divided. The wild boys weren't talking to the stay-in-shape boys; the stay-in-shapers weren't speaking to *them*. The wild boys were Risberg, Gandil, Felsch and McMullin. The stay-in-shapers were Collins, Faber, Schalk and Kerr. Cicotte, Williams and Weaver drank with the wild boys yet stayed in shape; and still talked to the Collins faction. Joe Jackson talked to anybody who'd talk to him.

Yet there wasn't a hole in that infield. That infield came together as if it had been seamed. On the diamond they were brothers.

Felsch

Oscar Felsch must have known, in the womb, that being alive was going to be fun. For he came forth looking for it. And it was even more fun than he'd been expecting: *everything* was fun!

At school he made the teachers happy the day he dropped out. It made Hap happy to leave school. And it made the girls and fellows at the factory happy to have Hap. Factories, Hap saw right off, were fun.

What was most fun of all was baseball. Getting paid to play it made it even more fun than *that*. When a White Sox scout spotted him shagging flies on a Milwaikee sandlot, and asked Felsch if he'd like to come to Chicago, Hap decided that *that* might be fun, too.

There was no use, Kid Gleason found, trying to teach Hap anything. What he was taught he'd forget the next day. On the other hand, there was nothing he had to learn. He was a natural hitter, a natural fielder, a natural runner and could throw with any man in the league. The only thing that kept him from being among such classically great outfielders as Cobb, Speaker and Hooper, was that they played for the season. Hap played for the day.

The fans came out early just to watch Happy Felsch shag pregame flies. He got so much fun out of playing so hard that Comiskey deducted the fun from his salary.

After the scandal he shagged flies on Milwaukee sandlots, opened a bar and raised six kids.

Shagging flies was fun. Having kids was fun. Running a bar was fun. When barflies heckled him about the series, he understood the boys were just having a little fun.

Yet, if they kept at him too long, he'd stop them.

"I was jobbed," he'd tell them at last. They'd shut up then.

For they knew then that, for Hap Felsch, all the fun was finally done.

* * *

273

Cicotte

Eddie Cicotte, the French-Canadian family-man, was a worrier. He worried about the debt still owed on his Michigan farm. He worried about sending his daughters to a reputable college. But mostly he worried because he'd been pitching winning baseball for fourteen years and yet had nothing to fall back on should his knuckle-ball fail him for a single season. He worried because one bad season would drop him back into the bushes, pitching for whoever would have him. He was thirty-five years old and all he could do was throw a knuckle-ball better than anyone else in the world.

Williams

Claude Williams was a Missourian who kept his grievance to himself. He also kept a book in his head on every batter in the league. He could figure a batter's weakness, or his strength, by pitching to him only once: after that he went to the book in his head whenever the man came up again.

He never hurried a pitch. Off the diamond he was quiet and introspective. On the mound he became unaware of anybody else in the world but the batter, the catcher behind him, and himself. He worked so deliberately, and so methodically, that it was not unusual for him to pitch a full nine innings without giving a single walk.

What Williams had was a curve that might break as slowly and hesitatingly as a child's balloon—or might come in like a streak of light with a vicious twist to its tail. If you tried waiting him out you'd be called out on strikes.

He'd won 23 games in 1917 and was now getting $3,000.

Yet, as a man who kept his grievance to himself, he kept his fears to himself as well.

Jackson

Joseph Jefferson Jackson was an illiterate son of an illiterate share-cropper, earning thirty-five dollars a month in a South Carolina cotton mill. When its management discovered, when Joe was thirteen, that nobody could get him out on a baseball diamond, he was raised to seventy-five dollars; and didn't have to do anything but play baseball.

A small girl handed him a hairpin "for good luck" before a game and he had a good day. Since then he'd never gone out on a diamond without a hairpin in his hip pocket. If he saw a hairpin and failed to pick it up he'd go hitless: Jackson believed that.

He'd light a candle in a dark room and stare at the flame, one eye shut, until the eye went blind. Then he'd stare with the other eye. This improved his batting eye: Jackson believed that, too.

Why he felt he had to sharpen his vision nobody knew. They still couldn't get him out. He'd hit .408 in his first full season, in 1911, and had been hitting near that ever since.

When Connie Mack paid $350.00 for his contract, to see what he looked like in Philadelphia, he slipped off the train at Richmond and went back to Greenville. He was afraid of leaving his family.

Mack instructed a coach to go down there and bring back the whole tribe. This time Jackson got all the way to the ball park and got to bat twice. He got two hits. Then it began to rain.

It rained for two days. When it stopped raining Joe was gone again; family and all. His teammates had been heckling him because he could neither read nor write. Jackson had no defenses.

Mack farmed him out to Savannah, where he met his wife. She got him back to Philadelphia.

One day, in Detroit, he lined out a terrific drive and came into third standing up.

"Hey! Jackson!" a fan challenged him loudly, "Can you spell 'cat'?"

"Hey! Mister!" Jackson shouted back just as loudly, "Can you spell 'shit'?" Joe Jackson was getting sophisticated.

Yet never so sophisticated that he could play baseball badly for a price. When he fielded a ball he couldn't shortleg it. When he went to bat he *had* to hit. His peg came in with express-train speed dead-center across the plate. He was death on runners who thought they could score from second on a grass-cutting single.

His flaw was fear. He saw himself as an ignorant rube among erudite, city-wise Northerners. If he wasn't a dummy, how was it that he was the only one on the team who couldn't read or write?

He got along with Lefty Williams because Williams, too, was a Southerner.

Had it not been for baseball, Joseph Jefferson Jackson would never have gotten more out of life than Brandon Mill, South Carolina, could offer a cotton-mill hand. He would never have left town.

And came to wish to God he never had.

Gleason

He'd been a major-leaguer, first as a pitcher, then as a second-baseman, for twenty years: a well-balanced man and a well-balanced manager, who sympathized with his players' dissatisfaction. He had himself stayed out of organized baseball for a year because of a salary dispute with Comiskey.

Yet, when the players threatened to strike in the summer of 1919, he got them onto the field. He'd talk to Comiskey himself about getting them bonuses, he assured them. But when Comiskey had anyone by the short hairs, he held till the hairs bled. He refused even to discuss salaries with his manager.

Gleason smelled the fix—yet had no way of knowing it wasn't a fixed fix. Boston gamblers had suckered New York bettors, in 1912, by leaking word that Tammany Hall had rigged the series for the Giants to beat the Red Sox. The ploy worked so well that the odds tilted to the Giants. New York bettors didn't even catch on, when they were paying off, that the men they were paying were the very ones who'd spread the phoney rumors on which they'd wagered.

Burns and Maharg

Sleepy Bill Burns had two unique gifts: he could drop off to sleep at will and he could wake up finding he'd been traded. He'd dozed through four major league seasons on benches at Cincinnati, Chicago, Philadelphia, Washington and Detroit. Every time he woke up he found he'd been traded again. And always congratulated his new manager at having gotten his team a bargain.

After losing 55 games while winning 27, managers didn't want him even in exchange for players of which they wanted badly to be rid. Sleepy Bill went off to tell everyone in Texas how he'd won 27 games in the big leagues.

He made a fast killing in oil at Ranger, Texas. And returned to Cincinnati, his pockets stuffed with leases, to tell his old teammates how he'd hit oil. They let him pitch batting practice. Then he left to tell everyone in New York how good he'd looked in pitching practice.

Burns was the kind of clown who'd have trouble finding his own way out of an outhouse unless somebody opened the door. But when somebody did, Burns would be standing there with an armful of fresh roses.

The man who opened the outhouse door for him was no prize package himself. He may have been the "Peaches" Graham who'd caught major-league ball in the National League for ten years, and had been Grover Cleveland Alexander's roommate. Or he may have been the Bill Graham whose major-league career consisted of scabbing, for a single game, during the Detroit Tigers' strike of 1912. The Tiger management had had to put a full team on the field, to sustain its franchise. Somebody named Graham was available.

Following this distinguished service to organized baseball, Graham felt he'd gone about as far as a man could in baseball, and turned to boxing. Somebody explained to him that, if he spelled "Graham" backwards, the name would become "Maharg." It was as "Billy Maharg" that he'd fought, as a middleweight around Philadelphia. Buffs paid to watch him taking punishment.

When Bill Burns phoned him from New York, he was happy to run up there to see an old friend now in the bucks.

He found Burns with Gandil and Cicotte at the Ansonia, and gathered that the series was for sale for a hundred grand.

Burns asked Maharg if he had a Philadelphia connection big enough to swing it.

The boys in Philly advised Maharg to proposition The Big Bankroll.

McMullin

McMullin? How did a utility infielder get in *here?* Who was going to bribe a player who wasn't going to play?

Because he was behind a set of lockers when Cicotte and The Swede, assuming they were alone, were sounding one another out on Gandil's notion of blowing a couple games for a payoff. McMullin materialized and said he'd like to help blow a game or two, too. How he'd manage that from the bench he didn't have to explain; because The Swede counted him in.

McMullin was the Swede's bar-buddy. The Swede never counted a bar-buddy out.

McMullin not only counted himself in, but became as active in the operation as though he'd conceived the fix himself.

The Big Bankroll

Abraham Rothstein was a just man. He adjudicated a garment industry dispute so justly that, at a dinner honoring him, the Governor of the state, Alfred E. Smith, described him as Abe the Just.

Abe the Just had one son who was also just. He prayed for another. Be careful of what you pray for lest it be granted. What Abe got was Arnold.

Arnold contained a *dybbuk* with dollar signs for eyes. *American* dollars. What Arnold wanted Arnold got. What Arnold wanted was *cash*: *All* of it.

When Abe the Just emptied his pockets on *shabbas*, in order to stand purified in the presence of his God, twelve-year-old Arnold borrowed the cash, organized a crap game, loaned the losers his profits at usurious rates—and had the original cash back on Papa's table before the old man got back from the temple. Arnold was something else.

By the time he was sixteen he was booking bets out of John McGraw's poolroom. McGraw knew that nobody could beat Arnold. Not the way Arnold booked.

A Brooklyn bookie once phoned to ask Arnold if he could handle a thousand-dollar bet. Arnold didn't turn the bet down. He didn't take it either. He strung it. He told the bookie he'd get back to him but he didn't get back. And made sure the bookie didn't get back to him.

If the horse ran out he hadn't covered it. If the horse won, he had.

The horse won: the bookie owed him a grand. The bookie argued that the bet hadn't been confirmed. Arnold sent Monk Eastman to settle the argument.

The bookie didn't argue with Monk. Nobody argued with Monk. Monk didn't even exist on an arguable level. Whether he existed on any human level at all was doubtful. All Monk knew was that when Arnold sent him for money, he brought money back to Arnold.

Monk knew how to get to Brooklyn and how to get the money—but how to get back? He'd forgotten how he'd gotten there. Monk had somebody telephone Arnold and Arnold sent somebody to bring Monk back.

That's how it is when you string bets from Brooklyn.

Arnold strung his days as he strung his bets. He never said No to a proposition; and never committed himself to any.

Operating two gambling houses, under police protection, he amassed a fortune. He converted a hundred-thousand-dollar mansion, in Saratoga, into a gambling house, cabaret and restaurant; where the cuisine was of such excellence that prices were unlisted. That would have been *vulgar*.

He made Saratoga a place where flash wealth could promenade as high style; and vulgarity could purchase the illusion of good taste. By the hot summer of 1919 the ghetto Gatsby had enough money to sustain himself in luxury if he lived another century. Yet he could no more have stopped gambling than he could have stopped the circulation of his blood. It was a surprisingly long interval before somebody stopped it for him.

The first whispers of a series fix probably came to him through the fox who served him as a pair of ears with a nose between: Albert Knoehr.

* * *

Albert Knoehr

"The newspapers made the decisions those days," the fox explained long after he'd fought professionally 365 times and had never been knocked out, "the trick was to let the yokel hold you even. I always felt bad when the papers gave me a shade. The line I liked to read was: 'The champion was entitled to no more than a draw.' "

He'd fought eleven years and had been in real trouble only once. Against Harlem Tommy Murphy both men had been half-blinded by blood by the end of the first round. In what must have been the bloodiest fight ever held in a ring, they'd fought on for nineteen more. At the end of twenty nobody but the referee could tell them apart.

The referee picked Murphy. Well, you can't win 'em all.

He was Abe Attell—born Albert Knoehr—dubbed "The Little Champ" by the press; and he hadn't grown humpbacked carrying bums into newspaper decisions without making friends among sure-thing gamblers. And such fly-by-night veterans of the double double-cross as occasionally met themselves coming back from short-changing their mothers. He was Rothstein's kind of kid.

The pair of country clowns who worked their way into A.R.'s box, after the third race at Jamaica on September 23, 1919, were not Rothstein's kind of kid. He got out of their way before they could put a story on him. And yet, after the fourth race, he dispatched Attell to find out what the clowns had had in mind.

Attell returned to report that one was an ex-pitcher; the other an ex-fighter. Their story was that eight White Sox players were ready to throw the World Series to Cincinnati for a hundred thousand dollars.

There was no way the Cincinnati Reds could beat the Chicago White Sox five games out of nine. No way. The Sox had the hitters, the pitchers, the fielders and the runners. All the Reds would be able to do would be to put on their uniforms and take turns at bat. They would have to play over their heads just to keep from being shut out.

Cicotte would beat them three games off by himself.

Lefty Williams would beat them twice.

Unless Cicotte were fixed.

If Cicotte were fixed, Williams could be fixed.

If Williams could be fixed, so could Risberg, Felsch and Jackson.

Cicotte was the key.

For sure-thing gamblers it was the sure-thing of a lifetime. For, if the players went along only a single game, they'd be hooked, under threat of exposure, for the series.

And if they threw the series (Rothstein must surely have foreseen), they'd be hooked for the season of 1920, too. They'd throw the games they were told to throw then. And be paid what the Sure-Thingers thought they were worth. They wouldn't get off the hook until the whole thing began stinking to the roof of the grandstand.

How long that would take was a matter of conjecture. But there'd be fat paydays as long as it lasted. By that time there'd be so many mobs involved, with so many prepaid perjurors, that no investigative commission would be able to finger anybody.

Except, of course, the clowns in uniforms.

Rothstein wasn't the kind of a man to pass up a good fix.

Rothstein to Attell: "It won't work."

Attell to Burns and Maharg: "It won't work."

Rothstein to Attell: "Forget it."

Attell to Burns and Maharg: "Forget it."

Rothstein to Burns and Maharg, in the lobby of the Astor: "Count me out."

Rothstein thus protected himself of a future charge of conspiracy. This left him free, should Burns and Maharg find another backer, to place his own bets. He had a faceless man, whose name was either "Evans" or "Brown," to make faceless bets. All The Big Bankroll had to do now was to watch The Little Champ.

All The Little Champ had to do was to watch Evans. Or was it Brown?

Rothstein didn't have to watch Attell long. Flat in the face of his unqualified refusal to back the conspiracy, Attell assured Burns and Maharg that Rothstein had changed his mind: A.R. would bank the deal up to a hundred thousand dollars.

Not doubting Attell for a moment, Burns wired Maharg:

ARNOLD R HAS GONE THROUGH WITH EVERYTHING. GOT EIGHT
IN. LEAVING FOR CINCINNATI AT 4:30. BILL BURNS.

A man signing his own name to a telegram revealing a national conspiracy was one whom Rothstein had hardly underestimated in avoiding.

Three days later Rothstein had a note from Sport Sullivan, asking to see him. Rothstein had never met him; but knew he was a big frog in the back-country. He received him.

For ten thousand dollars each—Sullivan came right to the point—eight White Sox players were prepared to blow the series to the Reds.

"On whose word?"

"Chick Gandil's."

"That's weak collateral."

Yet he instructed "Brown"—Nate Evans—to hand the visitor forty thousand dollars. The balance, payable upon delivery of the series, would be held in a safety vault in Chicago, Rothstein assured Sullivan.

Fair enough, Sullivan agreed, pocketing forty thousand.

One condition: Cicotte would have to give the sign, that the fix was on, by hitting the first batter with a pitched ball.

Understood.

That Burns and Maharg were working the same street as Gandil and Sullivan didn't trouble Rothstein. "When nine guys sleep with the same girl, it's pretty hard to prove that the tenth is the father," was his thinking.

He sent Nate Evans to Cincinnati with a bankroll to hook suckers. He himself got on the phone to Harry F. Sinclair, with whom he shared an interest in horse-racing. He guided the conversation to the series until he'd hooked Sinclair for $90,000.

Later, in his hotel lobby, he ran into the greatest single-roll crapshooter in the Western World: Nick The Greek Dandolis. When you met the Greek he either had fifty thousand in cash in hand or he couldn't buy a newspaper.

Rothstein, the lay-back-and-wait gambler, had broken this plunger oftener than either man could remember—the last time for a quarter of a million dollars. Now The Greek was flat again: he'd been waiting for Rothstein in hope A.R. would stake him. Rothstein peeled twenty-five thousand off the top of his roll and told The Greek to bet the bundle on Cincinnati.

If Arnold Rothstein couldn't be content until he owned all the thousand-dollar American bills in the world, Sport Sullivan couldn't rest till he had all the hundreds.

When he put down $29,000 on Cincinnati, at the Chicago Board of Trade, expecting 3-1 odds and finding the best he could get was even money, he was infuriated: somebody had beaten him to the broker's with a big bundle.

That he was betting other men's money didn't modify his sense of betrayal. By the time he found Gandil, Sport was tight up.

So was Gandil. He'd had a phone call from a brash fellow named Jake Lingle, a newspaper reporter. "The word is out," the brash fellow had assured Gandil brashly, "the series is in the bag." Gandil hung up on Lingle. He didn't even have Cicotte in the bag and reporters were already beginning to hold their noses.

Gandil had lost his awe of Sullivan. Being a bookmaker in Boston wasn't big enough for a national conspiracy, Gandil was becoming aware. They'd started something that was growing bigger as it gathered speed—and that couldn't be stopped. He had The Swede leaning on him, too.

When you had The Swede leaning on you, you couldn't afford awe of anybody.

"Where's the money?" he demanded of Sullivan.

"How many payoffs you trying to make, Gandil?" Sullivan accused him immediately—"How many other people you working with?"

It would have come to blows—had each not needed the other. After they'd cooled it, Sullivan handed Gandil ten grand for Cicotte. And explained that heavy money was being dropped on the Reds.

Small wonder. The Little Champ was atop a table, in a hotel lobby in Cincinnati, taking all Chicago bets. Suckers were struggling to give him their money. He hooked them one by one.

Later, looking for prey in the lobby, he spotted George M. Cohan. Not only was Attell miffed at Rothstein, for preferring to work with Sullivan instead of with himself and Burns and Maharg, but he now saw a chance to do a big shot a favor: that might one day be returned with interest. He cut into Cohan.

Cohan had just put thirty thousand, with a man named Brown, on the White Sox.

"Take a tip from The Little Champ," Attell wised Cohan up, "you just bet thirty thousand dollars with Arnold Rothstein. And the series is fixed."

Cohan phoned Sam Harris, his partner in New York, to put thirty thousand on Cincinnati. He'd covered himself.

Attell tailed "Brown"—Nate Evans—until Evans got another mark into conversation. Attell caught the mark's eye and signaled him, from behind Evans' back—"Lay off. Lay off." When the mark walked away, Attell disappeared himself until Evans cornered another, and repeated his performance. He loved the feeling that he was cutting into The Big Bankroll's bankroll. So much so that he wasn't aware that *he* was being tailed.

Burns and Maharg had business with The Little Champ. Where was the hundred thousand, they wanted to know when they'd finally cornered him.

Attell didn't even blink. All you had to do to get out of a lie was to compound a bigger one. Get the players together, he instructed Burns and Maharg. He would handle them himself.

The evening before the opening game, seven players showed up in Attell's room. Weaver was counting himself out.

His instructions from Rothstein, Attell confided in the athletes, was to stagger payments at twenty thousand dollars per game. The man had to protect himself, didn't he? They all knew that Rothstein's word was his bond—didn't they? And as soon as A.R. gave the word, he, Attell, would pay them off. Then he waved a telegram addressed to himself:

AM WIRING YOU TWENTY GRAND AND WAIVING IDENTIFICATION—AR

That nobody in the room, including Attell, had the foggiest notion of what "waiving identification" meant, mattered not at all. What mattered was that it *was* a telegram; and that it was signed with Rothstein's initials.

Even Risberg was mollified. Cicotte had already been mollified. He had sewn ten thousand dollars into the lining of his coat.

Attell saw them waver and got in the clincher: Cicotte would blow the first game and Williams the second.

The players almost pulled themselves together then: if they didn't win behind Cicotte and Williams they surely weren't going to win behind The Busher, Dick Kerr, Collins' friend.

Attell must have made a mental note right there. Kerr had won 13 games and lost 8, with great support. Without that support, Cincinnati would beat Kerr, too.

The fourth game, it was then agreed, they would win behind Cicotte.

Then Attell, who never knew when to stop when he had a good thing made, nearly wrecked his own ploy. He told Gandil he'd hand him twenty thousand dollars on the sidelines, just before the game.

The prospect of handing out thousand-dollar bills along the White Sox bench must have momentarily boggled Gandil's mind. It must have boggled all their minds; because Attell got them out of the room before they'd recovered their senses.

Maharg was the first to come to. How did they know, he asked Burns, that that telegram had been genuine? Western Union, they found, had no record of anyone sending a telegram to the Hotel Sinton signed "A.R."

If Attell had been lying about the telegram, the light began to dawn at last, he may have been lying from the beginning about Rothstein's backing. They must have felt like men, tiptoeing through shallows, who find themselves plunging into bottomless depths.

Curiously enough, a telegram signed "A.R." *had* arrived at the Sinton. But Rothstein hadn't sent it. Attell had had a friend in New York send it.

Joe Jackson returned to the bench, following pregame practice the day the series opened in Cincinnati. He sat off by himself, looking sullen. Joe was hurting. Gleason went over and looked at him.

"What's the matter, Jackson?"

"I don't wanna play!" Jackson blurted out.

"You *what*?"

Jackson began shouting, "I don't wanna play! I don't wanna play!" Then, at the top of his voice: "You can tell that to the boss, too!"

Gleason leaned over him and whispered hoarsely:

"You'll play, Jackson. You'll play."

To Lefty Williams, Gleason paid no heed. The left-hander was scheduled to pitch the second game. All he had to do today was to watch Eddie Cicotte.

Now he sat, between the bat boy and the water cooler, watching Cicotte's practice pitches to Schalk.

When the first Cincinnati batter, Max Rath, came up, Williams canted his hand across his eyes. Cicotte's first pitch cut the heart of the plate for a called strike. The second hit Rath between the shoulder blades.

At one minute before 3 P.M. on October 1, 1919, Rothstein walked into the Green Room of the Hotel Ansonia. Most of the several hundred chairs were already occupied. The chairs faced a diamond-shaped chart representing the playing field in Cincinnati. The game would be reported, pitch by pitch, by telegraph; with red and white markers, representing the players, being moved according to the report. Rothstein stood against the wall.

When Cicotte's second pitch hit Rath, Rothstein left. He hailed a cab and was sped to his broker. He placed another hundred thousand there on Cincinnati: on the series. Rothstein never bet individual games.

Cicotte blew the game single-handedly in the fourth. He not only crossed Schalk's signals, but fielded so badly that the Reds scored five runs. Final score: Cincinnati 9/Chicago 1.

Eddie Cicotte was earning that farm.

Jackson's condition was pitiful. Williams had handed him a dirty envelope containing $5,000 and he'd been afraid not to take it. His pocket was fixed and his heart was sick.

He was afraid of Gandil and even more afraid of Risberg. He was also afraid of Gleason, Comiskey, Grabiner, Collins and Schalk. He couldn't swing at a bad pitch and he couldn't throw badly. One fly ball dropped between himself and Felsch: that was as close as he came to making a series error; while outhitting everyone on both clubs. Yet he felt he wasn't playing to win.

Buck Weaver was. He was not only playing flawlessly: he was playing ferociously. His thinking was to take Sullivan's money, take Attell's money, take Burns' or Maharg's or anybody's money—then go out and whip Cincinnati four straight and take the winners' end of the purse as well.

Buck Weaver was the only one, apparently, who was in his right mind.

When Lefty Williams walked two men, in one game, he'd had a wild day. In the fourth inning of the second game he walked three men in a row; none of them dangerous.

Then, with men on second and third, he delivered a pitch so high that Schalk had to go off the ground to prevent a wild pitch. Schalk called time out. He walked out to the mound holding the ball, to talk to Williams. Williams wasn't talking: he demanded the ball. The next batter lined out a single, scoring two men. Final score: Cincinnati 4/Chicago 2.

Yet the game wasn't over for Schalk. He waited for Williams, on the ramp under the stands. When Williams came out of the clubhouse, Schalk hauled him to the wall and clobbered him, both hands, until other players pulled him off. Williams hadn't even fought back.

"He crossed me three times in the fourth inning," Schalk explained to Gleason, "he wouldn't throw a curve."

Gleason went looking for Williams. He found Chick Gandil, fully dressed, sitting in the locker room.

"Did you have a good day, Gandil?" he asked.

"Did you?" Gandil inquired in turn.

Gleason got his hands around Gandil's throat so firmly that, when Gandil stood up, Gleason was lifted off the ground and yet held on. When he finally shook Gleason off, Gandil turned and walked away. He hadn't fought back either.

Gleason went to Comiskey. Comiskey reached Heydler, the President of the National League, on a midnight train bound for Chicago. Heydler waked Ban Johnson, the American League President at 3 A.M. in another compartment of the same train.

"That's the yelp of a beaten cur!" Johnson decided about Comiskey; and went back to sleep. Comiskey and Johnson weren't passionately fond of each other.

Abe Attell was stashing money. He had so much to stash that he'd called in helpers: the brothers Ben and Lou Levi and one "Bennett."

Abe, Lou, and "Bennett" were stacking it on tables, tying it into pillow-cases, folding it into wallets, hiding it under rugs, planting it in sugar bowls and stuffing it into shoes in event of a raid. They were even putting some in their pants against a rainy day.

Burns and Maharg, come to collect the players' payoff, had to stand around awhile before they could get anyone's attention. It was plainly to be seen that either these fellows had been wonderfully lucky or the first two games hadn't been honest.

Burns reminded Attell that the players had forty thousand dollars coming to them.

"It's all out on bets," Attell dismissed the question, "besides, who needs *them*?"

Attell's stupidity and greed, Burns realized, was not only endangering the whole fix: it was likely to get somebody killed. Burns went after him.

"Bennett"—real name Zelser—stepped between the men. Burns restrained himself; but reminded Attell that Williams, in losing a game while still managing to look good, had been masterful. He also reminded Attell that the players had kept their part of the bargain. The brothers took Attell aside for a conference. Finally Attell pulled ten thousand dollars out from under a mattress and placed it in Burns' hand.

"That's the whole bit," he announced, "*all* of it."

Burns stared at the bills. What made Attell think the players, promised a hundred thousand, would settle for ten?

"*You* give it to them," he told Maharg helplessly.

Maharg was a bum—but he wasn't *that* big a bum. He recoiled. Burns was crooked. He wasn't *that* crooked. The advantage Attell held over both was his touch of pure reptile.

Burns, still bemused, went for the door with the ten grand still in his hand. Attell stopped him before he reached it.

"Tell them bums to win the third game," he instructed Burns and Maharg.

The pair left quietly.

Beyond the problem of how to tell the players they'd been double-crossed, was another: how were they going to bet the third game *now*? The one pitcher the players didn't want to win behind was Kerr. But how could they go on blowing games without a payoff?

The players themselves, except for Weaver, hadn't figured it out. Weaver had no problem because he wasn't playing for a payoff. Indeed, he was playing as if to *prove* he wasn't bought. Weaver couldn't *bear* to lose.

Nor could Schalk. It was Schalk who decided the third game. For gamblers and players alike.

Unable to figure it, wanting to be sure, Burns phoned Gandil the morning of the game. How was it going to go?

"The boys have talked it over," Gandil reassured him. "They've decided to go along. The game will go the same way as the first two."

Although Dick Kerr had neither the power, the experience nor the control of Cicotte and Williams, Schalk had made a winning pitcher of him in his first year in the majors. Kerr never crossed Schalk on a pitch.

Schalk, sharply aware that the first two games had been thrown, never called for a pitch that would give Risberg a chance to blow the game. For all the chances Risberg got that day, he might as well have been sitting on the bench beside his bar-buddy, McMullin. Cincinnati got three scratch singles and not a man got past second. Final score: Chicago 3/Cincinnati 0. Gandil, who'd singled in two runs, was a hero.

Burns walked into Gandil's room that evening, inwardly fuming but trying to look friendly. Cicotte, Risberg, McMullin and Williams were there. Attell had twenty thousand dollars more to pay off, he assured the little group.

The group expressed no interest.

Burns then gave his game away: he'd bet on the Reds. He'd crashed. So had Maharg. So had Attell.

Now he needed his thousand.

Thousand what?

Thousand dollars.

What thousand dollars?

His ten percent of the ten thousand he'd gotten from Attell and delivered.

Gandil studied him a moment.

"It's all out on bets," he assured Burns.

"Gimme a grand or I'll tell everything!"

Gandil turned away. Burns looked around. Nobody in the room was interested in him anymore.

That was the end of the 1919 World Series for Sleepy Bill Burns.

Until he got on the witness stand a year later.

In the fifth inning of the fourth game, with the score 0-0, Cicotte fielded an easy grounder, then threw it over Gandil's head into the grandstand. The next batter lined a clean single to left. Jackson fielded the ball cleanly and threw on a dead line to the plate to catch the runner rounding third. Cicotte deflected Jackson's throw with his glove. The runner scored. Cicotte was *still* trying to earn his ten thousand. Final score: Cincinnati 2/Chicago 0.

In the fifth game, still in Chicago, Williams didn't give Cincinnati a hit for five innings. In the sixth he gave up three hits and a walk. Combined with Felsch's wild throw, four runs scored.

The Reds needed only one more game.

In the tenth inning of the sixth game, with the score tied, the fix unfixed itself. Without talking it over, the players, as one, felt themselves free to win. Weaver doubled, Jackson singled and Gandil singled in the winning run. Final score: Chicago 5/Cincinnati 4.

It took less than a hundred minutes to win the seventh game. Jackson drove in two runs with a long double, and Cicotte dominated the batters. Final score: Chicago 4/Cincinnati 1.

Whose side were these guys on? Rothstein wondered. If Williams won the eighth game the series would be tied. And Kerr, who'd already beaten the Reds twice without support, would be hot to put them down once again.

Arnold Rothstein abhorred violence, personally. What he abhorred even more was losing half a million dollars. If somebody had to be killed somebody had to be killed. He sent for Sullivan.

Rothstein gave him the full treatment: cold yet courteous.

There wasn't going to be a ninth game.

Not only was Williams going to lose it: he was going to lose it in the first inning.

Those were Rothstein's instructions.

Then Rothstein smiled.

Back in Boston, the meaning of that smile came upon Sullivan.

He'd thought all he was investing was money. Now he knew he'd invested his life. He phoned The Man in the Bowler Hat.

The Man in the Bowler was known to be scrupulous in fulfilling his own obligations; and presumed others to be equally scrupulous.

He worked by contract. His business was simply to advise a designated party of a course of action he was to follow. He always specified the course; he did not have to specify the consequences of failing to follow it.

Are there children, he inquired of Sullivan.

No children.

Unfortunate. With children it was simpler. A wife?

Yes, there was a wife.

The price was cheap. $500.00. Sullivan wired the money immediately.

Watching Rothstein, Sullivan, Burns, Maharg and Attell and Gandil making their moves now, half a century after, is like watching a civilization of beetles in a dusty Mason jar.

The three in the center who keep circling blindly for a way out, are Burns, Maharg and Gandil. The sluggish one, trying to keep up but always one move behind, is Sullivan. The one in the middle, who doesn't move at all yet seems most aware of the movements of the others, is Rothstein. The one moving fastest, and most evasively, around the periphery, is Attell.

Somehow, other than sustaining a solid punch in his mouth, Attell survives best of all.

When Williams and his wife returned to their hotel, following dinner the evening before the eighth game, a man in a bowler blocked the hotel entrance. He dismissed Williams' wife.

Williams was to lose the next day, the man advised the pitcher. Williams turned away. The man got him by the wrist and held him.

They weren't talking about money, he explained: all the money had been paid. The question, rather, was whether or not Mrs. Williams was to go on living.

Williams was going to lose the next day. Not only was he going to lose, but he was going to be knocked out. Not only was he going to be knocked out, but he was going to be knocked out in the first inning.

No other way.

Williams' last practice-pitch, the following day, broke so sharply that Schalk almost dropped it. Going back to the mound, Williams glanced at the box, behind third base, where his wife was sitting.

The second Cincinnati batter dropped a soft liner to short center for a single. The next batter singled sharply to right. Williams, the most unhurried pitcher in baseball, began pitching hurriedly. Roush doubled to left, scoring a man in front of him.

After fifteen pitches, Williams had given four hits and three runs, and still had only one man out. Gleason took him out. Final score: Cincinnati 11/Chicago 4.

On the witness stand, a year after, he said nothing of the man in the bowler. He kept his grievance to himself.

Time has diminished Kenesaw Mountain Landis. Those laurels, gained by an aristocratic bearing and imperiousness, have long withered. The verdict we once applauded as one of Olympian sagacity was nothing more, it has become plain, than a legal mugging by an enraptured Puritan.

"Birds of a feather flock together!" he justified the expulsion of eight players from organized baseball—"association with gamblers and crooks can expect no leniency!"

The judgement did not, however, apply to birds who owned baseball parks: theirs was plumage of another feather. It meant that Buck Weaver's failure—to inform the front office of a conspiracy—had to be punished ruthlessly. But that the silence of Comiskey, with equal knowledge of corruption, deserved only praise.

What good would it have done Weaver to inform? Gleason had ranted about Comiskey's office, after the 1919 series, that the team had sold out: Comiskey had sat silent. Jackson, frightened and bewildered, had tried to talk to him; but had been turned out. And a year later Collins had come in to tell the old man that the team had sold the last games, in the last series of the 1920 season, the Sox had lost to Boston. The old man had refused to listen.

Could other owners have punished Comiskey's stars without suffering loss themselves, they would have been content to put all eight behind bars. Had they been able merely to destroy Comiskey and pick up his players, they would have been delighted. Had they been able to indict Rothstein without involving Comiskey, they would have sent him up the river for as long as law would allow. But there was no way of exposing corruption on the diamond, or in the boxes behind the backstop, without destroying the overall image of baseball as an honest game and its owners as incorruptible.

When the Cleveland Indians, the New York Yankees and the Chicago White Sox tied into a three-way contention for the 1920 pennant, and American multitudes were thronging into the parks, the question of whether gamblers were controlling players could hardly have been more inopportune.

The baseball establishment conspired desperately to keep the scandal from blowing the roof off the grandstand. Journals like *Baseball Magazine* and *Sporting News,* that fed at the owners' troughs, denounced every reporter who expressed suspicion.

Yet, when the scandal blew the roof at last, there was the righteous and churchly pontiff of Comiskey Park in bed with the coldest confidence man on the Eastern seaboard. There was The Grand Old Man and The

Big Bankroll, under the maypole hand in hand, the one trying to save his franchise and his name; the other ready to pay off all down the line to keep from being subpoenaed.

Comiskey retained Alfred Austrian, a corporation lawyer. Rothstein retained William J. Fallon—The Great Mouthpiece. The first thing on which Austrian and Fallon agreed was that evidence already in had to disappear itself.

The evidence was the three signed confessions, obtained by an overly eager state's attorney, in Chicago. Rothstein paid eighty thousand dollars for them, through Fallon. How Austrian got them remains unknown. Curiously, Rothstein never destroyed them. Years later, when the scandal had subsided and the documents were no longer explosive, they reappeared in a Chicago courtroom.

What could Rothstein do, to save his own skin, other than cooperate with Comiskey to keep the rumors hushed? What, indeed, could the old man do? A serious investigation would force him to fire his stars—and what then? A precedent for snatching suspended athletes had already been set, by the New York Giants, in giving a contract to Hal Chase after Cincinnati had given the first-baseman the heave-ho for accepting bribes.

The prospect, facing Comiskey, of having his pitchers facing Jackson and Felsch, was no less nightmarish than the possibility of his hitters having to face Cicotte and Williams. Moreover, if charges failed to hold, how about eight libel suits; each the size of his park?

The old man's strategy was to hide behind press releases and offers of rewards, that he never intended to pay, for evidence against any of his players.

More ominous, to other owners, than the threat to Comiskey's franchise, was a District of Columbia Decision of April, 1919, defining the baseball establishment to be in restraint of trade and violation of the Sherman Anti-Trust Act.

The Baltimore Club, of the disbanded Federal League, had been dissolved in accordance with this decision. Exposure of corruption, the owners perceived, would not only mean severance of relations between major and minor leagues, but—worse—would make the Reserve Clause illegal.

Imposed by the owners in every contract, this clause enabled owners to hire and hold players as chattels. It left physical risk to be entirely the player's affair. A revision of the Reserve Clause would force owners to share responsibility for injuries sustained by the player that might terminate his career.

The National and American League owners met to confront this frightening prospect squarely. They doubled the price of bleacher seats and went home congratulating one another on being members of such an honest group.

But while the owners, *Baseball Magazine* and *Sporting News,* Alfred Austrian and William J. Fallon were blowing clouds of smoke across the diamonds, individual reporters were catching out the clowns.

Ring Lardner had caught on early. And, to show the stars that he was on, devised a parody for singing in the cocktail lounges of trains bearing the players to New York:

> *I'm forever blowing ball games*
> *Pretty ball games in the air. . . .*
> *Fortune's coming my way*
> *That's why I don't care—*
> *I'm forever blowing ball games*
> *And the gamblers treat us fair.*

Lardner wasn't merely commenting on the series of the previous fall. He was aware that, though in contention for the 1920 pennant, the boys were still blowing crucial games.

In New York he received a night-call from Kid Gleason: "Come up to Dinty Moore's. I'm at the bar with Attell. He's talking and I want you to hear it."

Lardner leaned on a corner of Dinty Moore's bar.

Rothstein had fixed the series, Attell was claiming. He himself had made bets, on the strength of rumors floating around: but everything he'd won on the first two games he'd lost by betting against Kerr in the third.

"There's your man, Kid," Attell assured Gleason—"Rothstein."

It seemed to Lardner that The Little Champ was panicking.

Harry Reutlinger of the *Chicago American* wasn't a baseball buff. But he became bored by newspaper accounts of the scandal that were no more than hearsay. "Who's the dumbest one of the bunch?" he inquired of several colleagues. "Felsch," each assured him.

Reutlinger came in on Felsch bearing a bottle of scotch.

Hap, nursing a broken toe, was in a bathrobe. Hap wasn't mad at anybody.

"I didn't like to be a squealer," he confessed to Reutlinger after a couple drinks, "and I knew that if I stayed out of the deal they'd go ahead without me and I'd be that much money out without accomplishing anything. Had I stood my ground I might have stopped the whole deal.

292

Don't make it appear I'm putting up an alibi. I got my five thousand. We all share the blame equally.''

Attell was roused out of bed early, in a morning shortly after, by a message from Maclay Hoyne, a Chicago D.A., inviting him to drop over to the Waldorf for a bit of a chat.

Frightened, Attell fled to Lindy's in hope of finding The Great Mouthpiece. As he was entering the restaurant a large-sized friend approached and Attell extended his hand. The large-sized friend smashed Attell full in the mouth with a large-sized fist: Attell hadn't been hit that hard since he'd fought Harlem Tommy Murphy.

Although his mouth was still bleeding when reporters gathered around him, that didn't stop the mouth from talking. When he found Fallon, Attell demanded that Fallon afford him protection from District Attorneys, The Press, Old Friends who busted him in the mouth and Arnold Rothstein.

Fallon was protective. He assured Attell that Rothstein was leaving for Europe and that he—Attell—would be wise to wait out the storm in Montreal. And provided Attell with funds to keep him there. He then advised Sport Sullivan that, since Attell was fleeing to Canada and Rothstein to Europe, Sullivan's best move would be to Mexico.

When the White Sox came to Boston, at the end of August, 1920, they had a half-game lead over Cleveland and New York. After both Cicotte and Williams had blown games they should have won, they returned to Chicago in third place. It was then that Collins reported to Comiskey that the games in Boston had been sold.

The Grand Old Man had a telegram on his desk:

I ACCEPT YOUR OFFER TO TELL WHAT I KNOW OF THE CROOKED WORLD SERIES OF 1919 AND WILL GO TO CHICAGO TO TESTIFY PROVIDED YOU HAVE A CERTIFIED CHECK FOR $10,000 WITH HARVEY WOODRUFF, SPORTS EDITOR OF THE CHICAGO TRIBUNE, TO BE TURNED OVER TO ME AFTER I TESTIFY.   (Signed)
                                                Billy Maharg

The old man didn't need to pay anyone $10,000 for evidence that his team was controlled by gamblers. Collins was offering it *gratis*. The old man gave Collins no answer. He simply turned away. Then he tore up the telegram.

The reporter who perceived that the players were still being controlled, by the same gamblers who'd enriched themselves on the 1919 series, and who put it all together, was Hugh Fullerton of the *Chicago Tribune*.

His own paper, roaring daily, like the Great Bull of Bashen, about corruption in public life, fled like a hare for cover when confronted by the need for an act of simple honesty. (A rabbitlike reaction which the paper still attempts to dignify as "The Tribune Tradition.") Fullerton had to look elsewhere for support.

The *New York Evening World* published the story and the cat was out of the bag. Its challenge was that, inasmuch as the owners had been in possession of knowledge of corruption, but had concealed it from the public, they too were conspiring with gamblers. A Grand Jury was convened in Chicago and subpoenas issued.

Having deployed those dangerous loudmouths, Sullivan and Attell, out of range of subpoenas, Fallon hurried Rothstein to Chicago to establish his client's innocence.

Rothstein was manhandled by the press; as Fallon had hoped he would be. By the time Rothstein rose to testify, his status was that of a visiting dignitary who'd been maltreated.

Having become aware of certain rumors, the visiting dignitary explained to the court—rumors as false as they had been persistent—he had decided that he owed American jurisprudence a clean and unequivocal statement of the facts behind the rumors.

"I've come here to vindicate myself," he assured the court, "the whole thing started when Attell and some other cheap gamblers decided to frame the series and I turned it down flat. Attell used my name to put it over. But I wasn't in on it, and didn't bet a cent on the series after I found out what was under way. I'm here to clear myself and I expect to get out of here with a clean bill of health."

And he did. Rothstein left the stand adjudged, by both the public and the court, to be guiltless. Hardly had he gotten back to New York when Attell materialized, bursting with threats.

He was going to Chicago to attest that Rothstein had dispatched Nate Brown to Chicago as his broker. That he (Rothstein) had hooked George M. Cohan and Harry F. Sinclair; among others. And that he (Rothstein) had perjured himself before the Chicago Grand Jury. Rothstein bought him off for fifty grand.

Nobody bought off Sleepy Bill Burns. And his testimony was sufficiently deft to switch the guilt to the players. The fix, he lied as he testified, had been conceived and planned by the players; that it had been the players who'd sought out the gamblers; not the gamblers the players. By the time he was through he'd not only cleared himself, Rothstein,

Attell, and Sullivan, but an entire bestiary of bush vipers, buzzards, jackals, and nocturnal predators from the jungles of St. Louis.

The gamblers had made the money. The players were left holding an empty bag.

A bag that looked emptier than ever by the time Cicotte, Jackson and Williams got through coming in on themselves.

Jackson finally phoned one Judge MacDonald. "I'm an honest man," he told the judge.

"I know you are not," MacDonald assured him, and hung up.

"I'll be right over," Jackson phoned back; and explained himself in chambers:

"Faber and Collins and Kerr and Schalk weren't in. I got to be careful now."

"You've been fairly careless to date," the judge pointed out—"why the sudden caution?"

It took Jackson a minute of thought to answer that:

"The Swede is a hard guy."

So he'd said it at last and was already wishing that he hadn't.

"We did our best to kick the third game," he testified, "but Kerr won it off by himself just on pitching. Only the gamblers thought we'd double-crossed them so they double-crossed us. They promised us twenty thousand but all I got was five in a dirty envelope.

"Now Risberg is threatening to bump me off if I talk. That's why I had a bailiff with me when I left the Grand Jury room. The Swede is a hard guy."

He kept saying that. As if he thought nobody was believing him: "The Swede is a *hard* guy. Some guys are hard but they know when to stop. The Swede don't know when to stop. If I was a bear 'n the Swede got a grudge against me, I'd be careful not to walk around nights without a couple other bears with me."

Risberg didn't try to save himself. All he wanted to do was take the halo off the college graduate's head. Detroit had thrown three games, he testified, to give the White Sox the 1917 pennant. Gandil had gotten up a thousand dollars from the White Sox players to pay off four Detroit pitchers. Bill James, of Detroit, had accepted the bribe. Yes, Collins had contributed forty-five dollars along with the others. The others, that is, except Weaver. Weaver hadn't put up a nickel.

But the Grand Jury wasn't interested in the 1917 fix. It was the 1919 fix it was trying to solve.

An assistant bailiff, who'd lost a twenty-seven-year-old moustache on the series, called out to Cicotte, when they were smuggling the pitcher from the Grand Jury Room to the sixth floor—"Did you get a bath, Eddie?"

Meaning an immunity bath.

But he'd already signed a waiver of immunity without knowing what he was signing. He cried on the stand and couldn't say whether it had been Attell or Gandil who'd gotten the remaining seventy-five grand.

"I've lived a thousand years in the last twelve months," was all he had to say when asked who he thought had put ten thousand dollars under his pillow. Then he climbed off the stand and nobody saw him for six weeks.

He showed up at his home at last; and perhaps he was still a kind of hero to the wife and kids. He went to work for Ford's Bennett and never talked baseball again.

Five years behind bars and two thousand dollars, each, in fines was what the eight faced if found guilty. And by the time that Cicotte, Jackson and Williams got through testifying against themselves—having been duped into waiving immunity by the States Attorney—Comiskey's man Austrian had to conspire with Rothstein's man Fallon to keep the eight from doing time behind bars. That was when the confessions—of Cicotte, Jackson and Williams—disappeared themselves.

That cost Rothstein a pretty penny. As paying the defendants' legal expenses, without the defendants knowing about it, cost The Grand Old Man an equally pretty penny.

Court and press, prosecution and defense, cooperated. The Grand Jury acquitted all eight men of the charge of conspiracy.

"If any of my players are not honest I'll shut the gates of the park I've spent a lifetime to build," the old man boasted for the public's benefit. When he posted a twenty-thousand-dollar reward for evidence against any one of his players, his sincerity could hardly be doubted. When he reduced the reward, a month after, to ten thousand dollars, nobody wondered. When the reward disappeared altogether nobody remarked that the offer had been nothing more than a PR gimmick.

"Write to Commy, write to Commy," the press pleaded, "tell him you know *he's* okay."

Lardner was one Hoosier who wasn't cheering. "Why were all the bonuses except Jackson's held up in the spring that followed the series?" he kept asking.

The old man never answered. He was too busy playing hero for newspapermen and saving his purse.

The players assumed that acquittal meant reinstatement.

They went out to celebrate in the same Italian restaurant in which the jurors were celebrating. Before the evening was over they'd pushed the tables together and everybody loved everybody. The celebrants had hardly gotten to bed before the new High Commissioner of baseball issued the final word on their careers:

> Regardless of the verdict of the juries, no player who throws a ball game, no player who undertakes or promises to throw a game, no player who sits in conference with a bunch of crooked players and gamblers where the ways and means of throwing a ball game are discussed and does not promptly tell his club about it, will never play professional baseball again. Weaver was present during the testimony of a witness, [Landis went on to justify his inclusion of Weaver in the ban by recalling the testimony of Bill Burns] who most specifically stated that Weaver was present at the conference, and yet the case went to the jury without any denial from Weaver on the witness stand . . .

The fact that Weaver had been denied his right to take the stand was a fact the judge found inconvenient; so he dismissed it. That Weaver had been denied his right to a separate trial was equally unworthy, the judge decided, of his consideration.

A petition, reminding the judge that not only had Weaver accepted no money, but had played errorless ball and hit .327 in the series, was signed by 14,000 fans in a single day. The judge remained unimpressed.

Weaver fought for years to get back into baseball. When his playing days were done, he fought on just to clear his name.

He died indicted.

Say they made a great ball club
Say it was the greatest
Say The Swede was a hard guy
Say he was the hardest
Say it all again fifty seasons after—
Then let it go at that.

Let it go at that:
Say the gamblers double-crossed them
Say Jackson was too ignorant and Felsch too dumb
Weaver too careful and Risberg too careless

Gandil too slick and Williams too silent
Say the press needed a villain so it could have a hero
Say because he'd been the best the longest
It had to be Cicotte.
Say it must have been because he didn't understand
How a man could be a hero in America one day
And a bad guy the next
That he cried on the stand.
Then let it go at that.

Yet a left-hander's wind keeps blowing this way then that
Around an abandoned ball park
Always blowing away from home.
And if a single typewriter keeps clacking derisively
High in the press-box
It's only the ghost of a high-collared Hoosier:
There's nobody in the press-box tonight.

The man in deep left field in the uniform muddied at the knees
With the shadows of fifty seasons behind him
Isn't who you think it is.
For Shoeless Joe is gone long gone
With a long yellow grassblade between his teeth
And a lucky hairpin in his hip pocket.
And what a patch of spiked sand around third looks like
Fifty years after
Only a turning wind may remember.

Only a wind that keeps turning, turning
Around an abandoned ball park.
That blows and blows, forever blowing
Away: always away from home.

A TICKET ON SKORONSKI

I don't know what you have to do to have somebody buy you a drink in this neighborhood. In the old days, when the Logan Squares won, Owner poured a drink for everyone. When Hippo Vaughn pitched, he bought even if Hippo lost. Now it's all changed. Now the good times are gone. Now Owner stops when he gets to me.

One night we were getting ready for four-handed poker—Owner, Fielder, Haircut Man and myself. Lottie-Behind-Bar was behind bar. Fielder kept shuffling a red deck.

"Last night I dreamed—" Fielder began.

"No dreams," Owner ordered him, "deal."

"I was leaning on the rail, I got a *big* ticket in my hand," Fielder told, "only it don't say what race. Don't say what track. Don't say Win. Don't say Place. Don't saw Show."

"For how much?" I asked.

"Don't say for how much. Horses are in gate. Flag goes down."

"What distance?" I asked.

"Don't say what distance. My horse busts out in front. Cuts to rail. Two lengths out! Three! Pulling away!"

"How do you know it's *your* horse?" Haircut Man wanted to know.

"In a dream," Lottie called across the bar, "you don't have to have all written. When you want horse to pull away horse pulls away."

"Deal, deal," Owner said.

"Skoronski is riding. Coming into backstretch, Skoronski stands up in the irons." Fielder stood up and hollered. "Whip him in, boy! Whip him in!"

He slammed the red deck against the blue.

"Sit, Wenceslaus," Lottie told him gently.

Fielder sat. And just sat—head down, holding the cards without knowing he held them; red against blue.

"You're breaking decks," Haircut Man told him.

"Then *stops*," Fielder said like sorrowing, "Skoronski *stops*."

"*Stops*?" Haircut Man asked nervous like it had been *his* dream.

"He couldn't get away with that," Lottie decided. "Not even Skoronski."

"*All* stop, Mother," Fielder insisted, "stop like when on film somebody is cranking, then stops cranking. Film *stops*, horses *stop*. Skoronski *stops*, Mother."

"Next time you see somebody cranking, ask for a job before he stops," Lottie told him.

"Jocks climb off. Kneel like track stars!" Fielder was getting excited again.

"Two bits Skoronski wins on foot," I said, and put my two dimes and four pennies in front of Haircut Man.

"What's the distance?" Haircut Man asked before he took my bet.

"Hundred yards to finish line!" Fielder told us, "I climb rail! Fielder running for Skoronski!"

Two hundred eighty-five pounds. When he sits, chair screaks. When he walks, floor screaks. I took my twenty-four cents back.

"Bang!" Fielder shouted. "Bang!"

"*Bang*?" I asked, "How did a *Bang!* get into this?"

"He got to carry gun so nobody steals his paycheck," Owner guessed.

"How I *run!*" Fielder shouted, "away from *all!* Like *wind!* The wind! The wind! Right across finish line!"

"Where did Skoronski go?" I asked.

"No!" Fielder cried out. "*I* am Skoronski!"

"Play cards, Wenceslaus," Lottie told him.

Fielder sat down. How he looked. Pale, so pale.

The game began as it always began; cards fell as they always fell.

A wind came up like wind does. Rain began like always. Juke played what it always plays.

We said the things we always say. Barflies drank what they always drink.

The blue-and-red beer sign over the door flicked on, flicked off. Dead bulbs and bad wiring make it hard to see who comes in that door.

A kid called Lopez came in with the papers and left the door open behind him. Lopez is either a grade-school dropout or a fifty-four-year-old disbarred jockey. Nobody knows which.

"Shut the door behind you, Lopez," Owner said.

I watched Lopez reaching for the door handle, standing inside so as not to get wet. The light over the door flickered out. Somebody came in.

Came in without walking around Lopez and stood in the shadow of the juke.

Lopez closed the door. "Race results?" he asked.

"No horse players in here," I told him.

"Then buy a paper to put on your head," Lopez said, "it's raining outside."

Nobody else had seen the one who came in. Only me. The blue-and-red light flickered on again.

"What are you going to do with your money? Be the richest guy in the cemetery?" Lottie asked Haircut Man when he won a hand.

"Mind the bar and shut the mouth." Owner told her.

"Watch how you talk to my mother," Fielder told Owner.

"When you can pay for your own drinks," Owner said, "you tell me how to talk. Don't worry. I see all that goes on."

"So do I," Fielder said, like under his breath. "*All.*"

"*You* keep mouth shut," Lottie called across the bar to Fielder.

"When Haircut Man gives me a job," Fielder let Owner know, "I won't spend one dirty nickel here."

Haircut Man said nothing. But Fielder's chance with him had come and gone.

"Fielder," Haircut Man told him ten years ago, "come to shop at eight o'clock. I learn you haircut business."

Fielder made it to the old man's shop at two in the afternoon, so drunk he had to sleep it off in one of the chairs with the outfielder's glove across his face. All he's done since is sell gum at doubleheaders. Takes his mitt along in case of a foul.

Who remembers when Fielder played? Who remembers Fielder, a boy like a deer?

"Where you going, old man?" Owner asked when Haircut Man got up.

"To wash face," the old man told him.

"To put his money in his shoe, he means," Lottie said, after the old man had shut the washroom door. Haircut Man wears Ground Gripper shoes. If he would put shoe trees in them they wouldn't turn up at the toes.

I was dealing when he came back from the washroom. "You look *pee*-kid, old man," I told him when he sat down.

We all had our cards in hand before he picked his up. He picked them up and began squeezing one card at a time. When he got to the fourth, he let one card fall to the table. Then another, then another. The last two fell to the floor. His head went forward on his chest.

"Wake up, old man!" Fielder reached across the table and began to rub Haircut Man's wrists. "Old man! Wake up!"

Owner ran behind Haircut Man's chair to take him under the shoulders.

"Telephone doctor!" Fielder shouted, taking up the old man's feet. "Keep head down!" he told Owner.

"*Feet* down!" Owner shouted at Fielder; but they went up, so Owner grabbed the ankles and pushed. Fielder yanked Haircut Man out of Owner's grip.

He carried Haircut Man all the way to the pinball machine and stretched him out face down with his heels against the scoreboard. Then—fast like a fish—Haircut Man flip-flopped so his face turned up. He looked better that way.

The one beside the juke had his cap down over his eyes.

Owner tried to get a fresh hold of the old man, but Fielder pushed him back.

"He's suppose to go the other way, Wenceslaus," Lottie decided.

"Why do you always take *his* side, Mother?" Fielder asked. And began massaging Haircut Man's chest.

I didn't think the old man looked right myself, with his shoes against the GAME COMPLETED sign. But I don't like to take sides.

"Massage his feet, You," Fielder ordered me.

I began rubbing fast, with both hands, taking care not to pinch the toes. The old man never done *me* harm.

"Not the *shoes*, dummy! The *feet*, the *feet*," Fielder hollered right *at* me. I don't mind being hollered, but not right *at*.

I unlaced one of the Ground Grippers. When I got it off I looked inside.

Then I took off the sock and held it up. But everybody was so busy watching Fielder massaging, nobody would even look at *my* work. I took the sock over to Lottie.

"What do I do with *this?*" I asked her.

"Don't give me no dead stiff's sock," she told me.

"How do you know he's dead?" I asked her, and up jumped Owner from the bar stool.

"Call doctor!" he hollered. "Call doctor!"

"Sit down," Lottie told him, "I already called Croaker."

"The old man owed me a drink," I told her, hanging the sock on the bar rail in case somebody wanted to shine it some day. "You can give it to me out of his estate."

"He didn't have no estate," Lottie decided.

"Not in his right shoe," I said. "Should I look in the left?"

"Here's Croaker," Lottie answered, and sure enough, some wax-moustache sport carrying a doctor bag was tipping the rain off the brim of his little felt hat into a spittoon beside the juke.

"Are you watering our roses," I asked him, "or starting a reservoir?"

"Only being neat," he told me.

"Buy me a drink," I said, "and I'll be on your side."

"I can't afford having people on my side," he told me, "Where's the sick man?"

"Nobody sick in here I know of, Doc," I told him.

"Look in the corner," Lottie directed him.

"Corner of *where*?" He thought she'd said *on* the corner.

"I'll take you there," I told him, "I know this neighborhood like a book."

Then he saw Fielder giving somebody a rubdown on the pinball machine and walked over. He picked up the Ground Gripper I'd set on the GAME COMPLETED sign and studied it. The toe curved up like a ski.

"Have this bronzed," he said, and handed it to Fielder and came back to the bar. Fielder stopped massaging and came over, too.

"Give this man a drink," the Doc told Lottie.

"I got no glass," I let everyone know.

"You don't have anything to put in one neither," Doc told me.

Some Doc.

"Let me introduce myself"—I thought he ought to know me bet-ter—"I'm the guy makes the people laugh. Watch *this*." And I went into my song-and-tennis-shoe shuffle:

> Take me down to Haircut Shop
> But please don't shave the neck
> Call me up by Picturephone
> But please don't call collect.

He wasn't watching. Nobody was watching.

Except him beside juke.

"I make the words up myself," I told Doc. He didn't answer; so I went around to where he could hear me better.

"You got a stet'oscope, Doc?" I asked him.

"In the bag," he told me.

"I could help you test the deceased," I offered, "maybe there's a faint murmur."

"If there's one thing I can't stand, it's a stiff," the Doc told Fielder; and took some sort of paper out of his pocket.

I knew what it was. I went around the bar and whispered to Lottie,

"Don't put it down he died in here. Owner might want to sell someday."

Lottie whispered to Owner, and when the Doc handed over the certificate, Owner pushed a bottle at him.

"Don't put it down he died in here, Doc," Owner told him. "Put it down he dropped on the walk outside."

The Doc crossed out a line and added one.

Owner signed. "I might want to sell sometime," he explained.

"Do I get a drink *now?*" I asked Lottie.

Lottie brought a bottle up.

Owner took it down. "When we settle the estate," he said.

"When will *that* be?" I asked him.

"When the dead come back from the grave," Owner promised.

I dropped my jaw, made my eyes to stare, and pulled in my cheeks. What I call Making My Deadface. I pushed the whole thing into Lottie's face.

"What the hell is this for?" she asked me.

"It's how *you're* going to look one day," I told her.

"It's how we'll all look one day," she told me.

I went over to Owner and made The Deadface. I made it deader than a *real* dead face.

"What's the matter with *you?*" he asked me.

"It's how we'll *all* look one day," I told him, "give me a drink while you still got time."

"Who wastes whiskey on the dying?" he asked me.

I went over to Fielder. He had the bottle in front of him and a shot poured. When he raised his elbow I put The Deadface up at him from under his arm. Fielder looked down at my Deadface looking up.

"You're looking better," he told me. Then they all drank their shots down.

I went back to Owner. "How many?"

"How many *what?*" he asked me.

"You said you'd buy me a shot if I brought back the dead," I reminded him.

"One shot is the limit," he told me.

"What I mean is," I told him, "how many dead do I have to bring back to get one shot?"

Owner looked over at the pinball machine. "One will do," he decided.

I went over to Haircut Man and whispered in his ear. "You got a royal flush, old man!"

He didn't even twitch. The old man was dead for sure.

I heard the Pulmotor Patrol sirening down Western. A minute later two firemen came in, one carrying an inhalator strapped to his back. The other one unstrapped it and put the mask over Haircut Man's face.

"Stand back. *Back* everybody," he began giving orders. "If you're going to lean over, put out your cigarette," he told me, "we're trying to give the man air."

"Why should I give up smoking for you?" I asked him, "you don't even come from this neighborhood."

"Everybody *back*," Fielder said; and put everybody back with one hand.

"If I can't get up close to an accident," I told Fielder, "I won't look at all."

I hung around but not to look at the old man. Somebody had to watch those firemen because the old man had a gold ring on his right ring finger. Lottie came over to help me watch, and I decided to watch Lottie. I looked around and caught Owner watching me. There wasn't anybody else left to watch the firemen except Fielder; and he was having a hard time because they were *both* watching him. I never saw so many suspicious people in one group in my life. When everybody got tired of watching each other, we all went back to the bar.

I stood between the firemen. They must have liked what they were drinking because they didn't ask me to try it out for them. And every time they drank they'd touch glasses. It made me wonder what they would do about congratulating each other if they ever brought anybody to.

"That old man passed out in here seven times since Christmas," I let them know, "and he came around by himself every time. Why would he stop at eight? If you fellows had kept your hands off him he'd be standing up here having a drink with us now. He was the best friend I ever had. He was like a father to me. I used to follow him to see he got home all right."

"It's a good thing he didn't go down an alley," one fireman told the other.

"Cops! We didn't report this!" Owner hollered.

"You want me to go for them?" I asked him, "I know where to find them."

"Then what are you waiting for? *Get* them."

"It's raining," I told Owner, "I need something to warm me up so's I don't catch my death."

Owner made up his mind. "We got one stiff on our hands, we might as well have two."

A Holy Father came in. One with a beard.

"I phoned for him," Lottie said.

"You got the wrong kind," I told her.

The Holy Father made some signs over Haircut Man. I went over, but it was hard to make out what he was saying. I slipped a dime into the pinball machine, and just as the Father crossed himself, the machine lit up. I scored 850 before Owner came over and shut it off.

"You said you were going for the cops," he reminded me.

"What do I have to *do* to get a drink?" I asked.

"Put a sheet over him," the Holy Father told Owner.

"How can I find cops with a sheet over me, Father?" I asked him.

"He doesn't mean you," Fielder told me, "he's talking about our dead pal."

"Put a sheet over our pal," Owner told Lottie.

"You don't have to do *everything* the man tells you, Mother," Fielder told Lottie.

"She don't have to do *anything* she don't *want* to," Owner told Fielder.

Lottie touched Fielder with one finger to shut him up, and went into the back room. She came out with a wrinkled sheet.

"You forgot your pillow, Mother," Fielder told her.

"If you need a package of Juicy Fruit, Father," Lottie told the Holy Father, "look for my son in Cubs' Park."

"In the bleachers," Owner put in, "they don't let him sell in the grandstand."

"If you'll stop telling people I sell gum, Mother," Fielder told Lottie, "I'll stop telling them you're my mother."

"I don't hold that against her," Owner said, "we all make mistakes."

Fielder put up his fist, big as Owner's whole face, right under Owner's nose. Owner didn't even blink. He just put his hand on the bar towel and waited until Fielder's knuckles touched his nose. Then *swish*—smack across Fielder's face with the towel.

Fielder grabbed the towel. Owner let go of it. And there was Fielder wiping his face with the very towel that had just smacked him.

Lottie kept tucking the sheet around Haircut Man so she wouldn't have to take notice of the events across the bar. One corner of the sheet said HOTEL MARK TWAIN in green letters.

"Know who *that* is?" I asked the Holy Father, pointing at the signed photograph of Jim Vaughn above the bar, "that's Hippo Vaughn from the Chicago Cubs. Nobody had to say to Hippo, 'Buy me a drink, Hippo.' Hippo didn't wait for *that*. He poured it *for* you, and put a fiver

306

in your pocket whether you asked for it or not. Anything Hippo had you could have.''

Holy Father wasn't listening. Nobody was listening.

Only him beside juke.

Lottie put my cap on my head. "Take a run for the cops," she told me; and the way she said it I decided I would.

Look for the cops on a rainy night the same way you'd look for a cat—somewhere out of the wet and cold; next to a wall or under a shed. I went down the alley behind the Krakow Bakery, because that's where it's always warmest. They were parked with a cardboard box over the flash, listening to Pat Suzuki singing her heart belonged to an older man. Outside of that and being parked wrong, they were keeping crime at bay by smelling rye bread in the making. I rapped the window and one cop rolled it down. He looked like I was going to pinch him.

He was Firebox, a fellow I went to school with. He'd gotten his start by running for the truant officer to break up crap games after he'd lost his lunch money. On the force twenty-two years and never made a pinch. You never know where talent will show up next.

"Come and get a dead guy," I told Firebox.

"Who shot him?" he asked me.

"Nobody shot him."

"Then how do you know he's dead?"

"Because somebody put a sheet over him and he didn't pull it off."

The other cop woke up. "That ain't our jurisdiction," he told Firebox.

I knew this one too. We call him Transistor because if he catches you with a stolen one he don't turn you in. He just takes it off you and you can buy it back for what it cost in the store you stole it from. It's better than getting busted.

"What do you want *us* for?" Transistor wanted to know.

"Go get a dead guy out of a place," I told him.

"Try the fireman's carry," he told me. "We're crime-fighters; not litter-bearers."

"I think we ought to take a look," Firebox decided, and I knew what he was thinking. "Where is this stiff?"

"Carefree Corner. You know—Owner's joint."

"Where Fielder hangs?" Transistor asked.

"Fielder *sent* me."

"I caught Hippo Vaughn," he told me, "get in."

I got in the back seat and away we go.

"You don't look like Bill Killefer to me," I told Transistor.

"I didn't *say* I was on the Cubs," he told me. He meant he caught Hippo for the Logan Squares, after Hippo's big-league days were over.

"Fielder was fast, them days," he said.

"He isn't fast any more," I told him.

"I know," Transistor said.

There was a crowd in front of Owner's. Firebox went inside and right up to the pinball machine, and pulled back the sheet and began running his hand across the old man's skull.

"What's he doing?" Lottie asked me.

"Looking for bullet holes," I explained.

"He wasn't shot," Lottie told Firebox. "He had a coronary."

Firebox began running his hand up along the old man's spine.

"He's *still* looking for bullet holes," I told Lottie.

"The man had a *heart* attack," Lottie told Firebox.

"Why didn't you say so in the first place?" Firebox said. Transistor began stuffing the old man's shirt back down into his pants. You never can tell where a stiff is likely to wear a money belt.

"What is the deceased's name in full?" Firebox wanted to know.

"Put down any name you want," Owner told him, "just don't say he died in here."

"We might want to sell sometime," Lottie explained.

"Where do you get that *we*?" Owner asked her.

"Don't worry, Mother," Fielder told Lottie, "you still have your pillow."

"A forty-year-old son," Lottie told the Holy Father, "and he sells gum."

"What did you say the old man's name was?" Firebox repeated.

"He didn't have no name," I explained, "we just called him Haircut Man."

"What's *your* name?" Firebox asked me.

"I don't have one neither," I told him. "They just call me 'You.'"

"Then stay out of this, You."

"If you want the old man's name," Owner spoke up, "maybe it's in his wallet."

"See what the name in the wallet is," I told Fielder, "I'm not working for the Department myself."

"Mother was the old man's best friend," Fielder offered. "Maybe *she* knows his real name. Then nobody has to look in his wallet."

Cops are careful about reaching for a wallet on a drunk or a stiff. If the wallet is empty they get the blame.

The kid, Lopez, was still there, with one newspaper left. Firebox lifted him up level with the old man. All he had to do was reach.

"I can't," Lopez yelled, kicking with both feet, "if I reach, I'll drop my paper."

I took hold of his paper but Lopez locked it under his arm. "If you want the paper, *buy* it," he hollered.

Firebox put a dime in his little paw, and Lopez let go of the paper and reached and got the wallet. He hung on to it while Firebox carried him to the bar. The wallet didn't bulge, and when Lopez held it upside down, six plaid trading stamps fell out. He shook it. That was all.

"Look inside," Owner told him.

Lopez opened the wallet wide, stuck his nose into it, sniffed into the corners; then took his nose out.

"Gone on the arfy-darfy," he announced, and Firebox set him down. I started my soft shoe bit.

> *What do you want for the little you got*
> *For the little you got you don't got a lot*
> *You kept your money in your big dirty shoes*
> *From the graveyard who collects?*

Nobody was paying me any attention. Nobody ever does.

"Who would have thought the old man would die broke?" Lottie asked Owner, looking him right in the eye.

"My own opinion," Owner answered, "is that he didn't." And looked *me* right in the eye.

"Ambulance!" Lopez hollered before any of the rest of us heard a siren.

Firebox looked down at him. "Where's my change?"

"*What* change?" Lopez asked looking up.

"I give you a dime for your dirty yesterday's paper. I got three cents coming, Shorty."

Lopez don't like being called Shorty.

"I don't carry change," he told Firebox.

"People pay you in seven-cent pieces?" Firebox asked him.

"Why don't you search him, Firebox?" I suggested.

"He can frisk me but he can't search me," Lopez told the Department.

A dozen people followed the stretcher-bearers in. Owner put two bottles on the bar and got ready to pour. It looked like a good night for Owner. But no one came near the bar. They all wanted to help the stretcher guys carry the stiff to the dead-wagon. The stretcher guys wouldn't let them. All they could do was follow the stretcher out.

I stood by the bar next to Holy Father. I was trying to remember whether Haircut Man was still wearing a ring the last time I looked. If he was, one stretcher-bearer was in a good position to get married. All he needed was a blind whore.

"Were you a friend of the deceased?" Firebox asked Lottie.

"Hardly knew the old man," Lottie said fast.

"I thought you knew him *well*, Mother," Fielder put in, "I thought he said he always helped you out when you weren't working."

"Why should I take money from strangers when my son works steady?" Lottie asked him straight.

"All right," Fielder said, "all *right*, Mother. I *know* you worked for me all my life. Now why don't you go out and get a job for yourself?"

He turned away from her and walked up to the calendar that hangs on the washroom door. He just stood there looking at it with his back turned to us. Then he took the mitt out of his hip pocket, put it on and swung at the calendar. The door shook. The calendar bounced.

"*I* am Skoronski!" he hollered at it. Then he swung again. The calendar fell. Fielder looked down at it like trying to figure out what made it fall. But when he turned his face to us he was smiling. He came to the bar still wearing his glove.

"Drinks for everybody," he invited everyone. And put money down.

"My son sells gum," Lottie explained to the cops.

Then she put her arms on the bar and put her face down on her arms. She moved her shoulders a little. I don't think she was crying. I didn't hear crying-sounds.

Owner picked up the money, rang it up and brought down the bottle and filled the glasses. Fielder lifted his glass with his left hand.

"Say a prayer for the guy," he toasted Haircut Man.

Lottie looked up then. She'd been crying alright.

"Wenceslaus," she told Fielder, "how God is going to punish!"

The one beside the juke had gone.

ODE TO AN ABSCONDING BOOKIE

Where have you gone Sam the Jackal?
How can it be that through miles and miles
Of wires and wires
No message can reach us on a day this blue?

For the ducks that swim the infield quacked us no warning quack
Foretelling MODEST MAIDEN, in good form,
Well-bred and well thought of by her neighbors
Well-regarded by her muckers and respected by her groom,
Well-behaved while being shod and well-placed in the gate—
Distance suits—
And off at nine to five—
On a track announced as Fast yet that looked no more than Good
Would break with maiden-modesty
To find her stride too late.

Too late Sam the Jackal?
How could this be so when no skywritten prophecy gave us
The post-time tip
That GALLANT RALLY wearing one-eyed blinkers and racing evenly
Would rally gallantly at the top of the lane?
Yet lack the necessary speed?

Necessary speed? What can be the meaning of this Sam the Jackal?

We would like to understand how GAME COMMAND
Nine times out and never out of money
Responding to brisk pressure would battle gamely for command
To quit cold at the eight-pole.
Quit cold Sam the Jackal? After battling for command?
Is there something you weren't telling us you'd like to tell us now?

311

For all you said was RECKLESS LOVE was one sad dog
Held together by scotch tape and Absorbene
That no bookie had to fear.
I hate to take your money boys
You added when we put up ten apiece on RECKLESS at 44-1
And pocketing our fifty.

Now nobody is blaming *anybody* Sam the Jackal
We would only like to know
How it could happen that NEVER BETTER—
Only needs good ride—
Got the ride that he'd been needing while never feeling better
Easily outgaming horses who never had felt worse
Leaving GAME COMMAND and MODEST MAIDEN tied fast to the
        rail.
To just miss.

JUST MISS Sam the Jackal? What the hell is going on here?
Whom has been kidding whom?
We didn't need to see the rerun: we were standing at the scale
When RECKLESS LOVE came past the stands
Striped by a daily-double sun
And sheer astonishment.
Steadily improving
At forty-four to one.

Bulled way between rivals. Won driving.

We were waiting where we always wait
Beside the fifty-buck partition
Exchanging self-congratulations
While doing some addition
And disdaining well-backed entries who find their strides too late.
When it came to one and all of us
That you were a little late yourself.
Too late too late too late Sam the Jackal?

On a night when the moon has a disbarred rider's eyes
And tip-sheets are borne upon a wind
Blowing from *Just Missed* into nowhere
And cats freeze to death on fire-escapes

You shall come to us again
Returning forgotten hoofbeats to the backstretch of our dreams.

O skywrite something for us Sam the Jackal
Before post-time tomorrow
Leave us grasp your manly hand
Leave us see your sunlit smile
Give us a sign: some omen
For trustful hearts now desolate who once knew you best—
Like *Wither Thou Goest I Shall Go*
Will Pay Sixty Cents on the Dollar

Or at least a forwarding address.

BULLRING OF THE SUMMER NIGHT

LOCKED into the darkness of an endless starting gate, the rider saw field lamps burning in a mist; bordering a straightaway rains had left so shining that every lamp looked tethered.

Yet he heard no horses restive in their gates nor starters' warning cries. No gate had ever been this dark nor any crowd this still. The field lamps began casting moving shadows all down the straightaway. His horse came asweat as the flag went up, at the restless shadows the high lamps cast: he shared his horse's fear. *Scratch the whole field* he tried to cry out as every gate clanged open but his own.

Lamed riders afoot, all in black silks, broke in a jostling pack, whip and spur to be first to the rail. All limped and several fell. Some fell and could not rise. His horse hooked itself across the still-locked steel, its forelegs racing air.

He stood in the irons to double the reins and felt his right rein ripping. He reached for the mane but there was no mane—*rot in the reins* he thought, falling from a great height slowly—*rot in the reins* all along.

And wakened feeling disappointed in everything.

Somebody's big hand was lying lightly across his forehead. He pulled away from the hand.

Kate was standing above him. The tumult of her hair, uncombed and reddish-orange, looked to be aflame because of the yellow bug-repellent bulb burning behind her. She was offering him coffee in a tin cup.

Tin cups were for water not for coffee.

"For God's sake," he sat up to refuse the cup, "you have to shove a person across a room to wake him up?"

He looks so young yet so old, she thought, Floweree looks so grey in the dark before day.

"You were tossing, I thought you were fevery." She placed the cup with care in reach of his hand.

"*Fevery?*" he mocked her, "What in God's name is *fevery*?"

"I only have a country vocabulary," she explained; and let it go at

314

that. It was going to be another mean day for them both; that was plain. With nothing the way it had been before the Mexican had begun nipping him at the wire. He'll be pecking at me now for my Ozark talk, she knew with resignation; or for being a head taller and half again his size. Or for looking years younger while being years older. Or for being born in the mountains or raised on a river. Or for not minding when people call me Catfish. Or for wearing a GI cap. Or for wearing horse pins around the barn—What does he think I should use for bandaging?—Glue? Then he'll get on me for owning a horse that does a mile and seventy without coming asweat by morning yet starts washing in the paddock that same night. A pure wonder he hasn't yet faulted me for his falls at Waterford. Maybe he does in his jealous mind.

For all of his pecking (she'd taken note) took care to avoid its true salty cause; for it was *her* trailer, *her* table and *her* bed. Hollis Floweree was scarcely the man to take chances with a good thing. Unless he had money in his pocket.

"If you're going to blow out Red," she reminded him, "you better get moving."

"Blow him out yourself," he advised her.

Might not have things worked out better, had she not made it too easy for him at the beginning, Kate wondered now. All she'd done, of course, had been to take off his boots when he'd had too much whiskey in him; to let him sleep it off on her bed.

Yet they'd lifted a few together before, at other parks, when he'd been riding better; and nothing had even begun to happen between them before. That he'd still been using a cane and had had his saddle in hock when he'd come here from Waterford hadn't had anything to do with her taking off his boots. She hoped for her own sake now as well as for his.

Or had the falls—three in two months—*had* something to do with it? Yet the Mexican had not yet taken either a drink or a fall. And *his* boots had come off just as easily.

How can he hold *that* against me, she asked herself. Don't he know that was *before*?

There was the salty cause Floweree wouldn't risk pecking.

Unrequited love wasn't what was souring him so, she felt sure. It had to be because the rider who outraced him so often was the same who'd nipped him at the wire in bed. A touchy group, these riders; whose need of proving themselves could be felt in their mounting of women as well as of horses.

Excepting, of course, that Mexican thief. Whose mastery of all mounts came to him so naturally that he felt no need of proving himself to any. Horses sensed it as quickly as women.

"What time is it?" Floweree asked.

"Nigh to day."

"*Night to day*—What kind of time is *that*, for God's sake, *night to day*? Didn't they even learn you to tell *time* in them hills?"

"Them weren't hills," Kate corrected him, "them were mountains. Though I do have to admit we lived pretty far back."

Stripped to his waist, Floweree stood with his disproportionately big hands clasping his cup the way a child holds a gift he fears may be snatched away.

"So far back the owls screwed the chickens," he decided; "that's *my* opinion."

"The farther back you live," she returned the usual answer to the usual taunt, "the tougher you get. And we lived in the last house in town."

She handed him his boots with one hand and the *Racing Form* with the other.

"You're in the funny papers, rider."

Under "Official Rulings," he read, with lips moving:

OZARK DOWNS

"Jockey Hollis Floweree has been suspended for one day and fined fifty dollars for entering a frivolous claim against jockey Elisio Casaflores following the eighth race of Thursday night, July third."

"That's Ishop, not Casa," Floweree felt, "I don't blame the Mexican because his boss pushes the stewards around."

"Well?" she wanted to know, "you got fifty dollars for the front office?"

"You take care of *your* end, I'll take care of mine," he told her.

Kate didn't bother pointing out that she'd been keeping up both ends.

"Front office don't get fifty by noon, you don't ride Red tomorrow night," she reminded him, "and I *don't* want your Cajun buddy on him."

"What's the matter with my Cajun buddy?" Floweree asked innocently. "He's got all the class there is to be had around *this* bullring."

"That depends on what you mean by class," Kate decided.

316

"When you get so good you can get on top of a $10,000 horse and lose to a $3,500 horse without the stewards seeing anything wrong, that's *class.*"

"And when you're paying a rider to ride for *you,* and he's riding for people in New Orleans instead, where's the class in *that?*"

Holding one soiled sock in one fist, Floweree kept peering into the depths of various boots; in hope of finding one equally soiled.

"That don't make him a bad guy, does it?" he asked one of the boots. Then looked up at Kate: "That man can whup his own horse 'n flick the nose of the horse behind, all in one motion," Floweree defended the Cajun, "as good as even Don Meade could. 'N that don't make him a bad guy, neither."

"Oh, toss those stinking things away," Kate ordered him; and tossed him a ball of fresh white socks.

"Just because he done a little time—" Floweree began.

"I know, I *know*," Kate interrupted him, "I *know* that don't make him a bad guy. But he got a big mouth and he got bigmouth people behind him. In my book *that* makes him a bad guy."

"A person don't have to come from Louisiana to have a big mouth," Floweree observed quietly.

"The Cajun ain't riding Red," Kate ended the argument.

"How about that apprentice kid—Duryea?" Floweree sounded her out.

"Duryea rides with his shoulders instead of his hands," Kate pointed out, "he thinks he's supposed to outstrong his mount. He rides every horse the same. Red takes a long rein. Duryea snugs up."

"Can't you get one of the Mexicans?" he asked her softly.

"No," she took him up quickly, "all the good riders are contracted out around here."

He finished pulling on his socks before he answered. She could tell he was hot.

"Believe me when I tell you," he told her, standing up to his full height of five-foot-one, "I can get a contract with any stable in the country. Believe me when I tell you."

"*Sure* I believe you when you tell me," she agreed easily, "tell me a rooster can plow 'n I'll hitch him up."

She drew a rubber-banded roll from the pocket of her jeans and laid five ten-dollar bills beside his cup.

"I don't want you borrowing off the Cajun, neither," she explained.

"It's *your* horse," he disclaimed his involvement, "you take in the fine."

"The horse belongs to me," she agreed again, "but the phony claim is all yours."

"Them people up there look at me like I smell of the shed," he complained.

"You don't always smell sweet around me neither," she filled him in, "what do *you* care what you smell like to *them*?"

He eyed her steadily across the rim of the cup. "The reason that horse of yours don't win"—he put his cup down carefully—"is he's ashamed to have his picture took with you in them clothes."

"Rider," she responded quickly, "your job is to get me into the winner's circle. How I'm dressed for the occasion is my own affair."

"Alright," he gave in, "I'll take the fine in—only don't get the idea you're doin' me a big favor. I got friends all over the country ready to back me."

"*Sure* you have," she yet agreed, "you got friends from coast to coast. Tell me a duck is carrying a gun 'n I'll stay out of his range of fire." She whipped her GI fatigue cap down over his ears, tugged it tight and hurried through the door. By the time he got it off she was down the shed-row.

Floweree spun the cap against the wall without so much as a glance at the money she'd left. He drew on his boots and stomped his feet to make them tighter. He put on his helmet and let the straps dangle. He flicked his little whip. Then he stomped in his boots once again. And once again flicked his little whip. He put on his riding-goggles. Then he picked up the money and left.

And kept trying to figure out, as he followed Kate's steps between the shed-rows, why, when it had been the Cajun who'd done the provoking, that the Mexican had come at *him*.

"*Hey! Casa!*" the Cajun had started it—"*You make fifty dolla! You have good time at your mama's house now, Casa?*"

Not until the Mexican had been sitting on the floor, cupping his nose with a touch of blood on the white of his silks, had Floweree realized it had been himself who'd knocked the boy down. "You don't get the best of it *all* the time, Mex," he'd heard himself saying.

The Mexican Thief got his nerve, I got to give him *that*, Floweree now had to admit to himself. For, in the next race, he'd driven his mount between Floweree's and Houssayen's and beaten both under the wire. His nose hadn't started to bleed again until he'd climbed down out of the irons.

That *still* didn't make The Cajun a bad guy.

*   *   *

A heat haze was already banking above the ridge. Between the sheds grooms were sponging down horses with names like Flying Indian, Billy V., Flash McBride and Popcorn Bummy.

Two grooms were hauling a horse up a ramp into a coast-to-coast horse van, while another shoved the brute from behind. Six horses, already installed, stretched their necks out of the windows like so many shop stewards, to see how the work was going. The driver leaned idly against the van, holding a bill of lading in his hand and spitting tobacco juice now and then to show *he* didn't have to lift a finger.

The hay, heaped and baled between the barns, lent a yellowish scent to the air. Floor fans, whirring all night and into the breaking day, carried music cool or hot from rooms where hot-walkers drank or dozed.

Owners saved a pretty penny here by permitting hot-walkers to do the work of grooms: A green youth could pick up a lifetime craft here. He could learn how to tape a horse without having galloped one. The trick in bandaging was to keep the tape level, so that cotton tufts showed at either end of the bandage. And if the thermometer he shoved into the animal's rectum read a degree and a half off, and the horse was backing off its feed, he knew that that horse should be scratched.

Yet, as like as not, the horse was led to post all the same. And the rider who refused a mount unfit to race might have a rough go getting another.

The riders, as well as the grooms, knew that things that mattered at other tracks didn't matter all that much here. That's what made it a bull-ring. It was all block-and-tackle around the soybean field; where a rider could make more money by running interference for the horse he'd put his backers on than by winning on his own mount.

The rail was too high and the purses too low. There weren't half a dozen rectal thermometers in the whole stable area. Nobody had heard of a film patrol. Hustlers wearing shades walked in and out of the barns without having to identify themselves. That's what made it a bullring, too.

But there were also, around the same barns, men whose respect for horses was merely part of their respect for men. This old-fashioned kind of Western man wouldn't run a horse that wasn't ready; any more than would the fight-manager who won't throw a fighter into a ring at risk of a bad beating. There were owners of horses here who still considered the chief point of racing horses to be finding out whose animal could run the fastest.

This kind of owner insisted that his grooms, when taping a horse, keep the tape level all up and down the leg. And who, when the rectal thermometer was a degree and a half off, scratched the horse.

A stakes-winning rider earned only $50; and the rider behind him but $30. Third money earned $17 and fourth received $12. Out of which each rider paid a dollar to the Jockey's Club and two dollars to his valet.

Floweree waggled his whip at a couple of exercise boys but didn't stop to exchange stories. When the vasty light of morning struck, tilting the straightaway into day while leaving the backstretch in darkness, the odds for the coming night would start forming. Rumors of evening would shape the rest.

That, and turns so sharp that a rider on a $1,500 horse, who knew the turns, could outrun a $3,500 mount; there wasn't enough of a stretch for the better horse to prove his class. His rider had either to take his mount around the leading horse or bull his way through at risk of being smashed against the rail. For the sake of a $50 purse, only apprentices and younger riders took such a risk.

It was also a track where exercise boys competed with professional riders to make two dollars in breakfast money at 6 A.M. And where you saw horses with such string tails you had to look twice to be sure it wasn't a pony.

Spring harness-racing had left the track surface so hard that owners of thoroughbreds risked laming their horses here. The track's hard spots had soft spots that threw a horse off stride. Owners didn't risk running a horse worth more than a few thousand dollars at Ozark Downs.

One morning the apprentice Duryea had worked Red's Big Red out for five furlongs in fifty-seven seconds. The track record was fifty-eight. That same night, while a groom was giving Duryea a foot up in the paddock, the horse had stretched about and chomped the groom's elbow, sending Duryea skittering down its flank. By the time Duryea had gotten him into the gate the horse was awash with a sweat of anxiety. He'd broken badly and finished dead last.

Catfish had waited for her rider outside the jock's room.

"What happened?" she'd wanted to know.

"Nothing happened," the apprentice assured her, "the horse can't run, that's all."

"He ran this morning."

"If a horse can't run between horses, he can't run."

"And a rider who can't ride between horses can't ride," Kate had judged the apprentice immediately. And hadn't put him on the horse

320

since. Floweree was the only rider whom both Kate and Big Red trusted.

"Move over, you," the groom now ordered the animal as Floweree stood by.

"Don't call him *you*, Mike," Floweree suggested. "This horse was brought up by a fool who hollered *Hey you!* at him so much he wouldn't run. He's tore chunks out of people for *Hey-youing* him."

Floweree stroked the big brute's neck and singsonged softly into his ear, "If you move over, baby, your little daddy'll have more room."

The horse shifted its rump to give people more room; then rolled his neck toward Floweree as if to ask, "Is there room enough back there now, little daddy?"

"He's been kicking at his tail, too," the groom reported sullenly.

"Then take the knot out of it," Floweree advised him.

"If he talked like that to women," Kate observed to nobody in particular, "he wouldn't have to risk breaking his back riding around a soybean field."

"No, I could get it broken for me at home," Floweree informed the horse, "and never have to leave the house."

Cantering onto the track, Floweree held Big Red back until Kate reached the scale at the finishing line; stopwatch in hand. He wheeled the animal into the gate with only his toes in the irons.

Then, leaning far forward, shouted into the horse's ear—"*Get all the money!*"

Kate saw the perfect start, yet lost horse and rider in the shadows. But where the backstretch broke into day she saw a darkness driving across the sun, rider and horse a single creature, neck astretch and tail slowly blowing. At the turn for home its mane caught the sun and she glimpsed light beneath all four hooves at once: then it loomed like an oncoming express and she shielded her eyes against a showering dust.

And heard the dying thunder of its hooves.

When she looked up she saw Floweree easing the horse down the far side of the track. *Why don't you run like that at night you sonofabitch?* Kate asked Red's Big Red and God.

Floweree wheeled about and gave her a confirming nod as he passed her on the trot.

Had she seen the horse try to bolt? Floweree wondered. That flash of silvered light, across its hooves, was what had caused it. The clubhouse light, at the first turn—that was it. Now he knew what was frightening the horse at night.

He knew something nobody else knew. If Kate hadn't caught it.

She came up with a scatter of dust across her forehead and the stop-watch still in her hand.

"How'd he make it?" Floweree tried her out.

"One forty-one flat."

"It felt even faster," he risked suggesting.

"The watch don't lie."

It don't tell the truth all the time neither, the rider reflected.

When she led the horse off, to cool it, Floweree pushed his helmet back on his head and lifted his goggles to his forehead. The workout had presented him with a gift package that he didn't want to unwrap quite yet.

The gift was information. And information used too soon could kick back in your teeth; used too late, it lost its value. Used at the right moment, it could bring him the stake he needed to get away from Kate.

He never could admit to himself that it wasn't losing photofinishes to Casaflores that was rankling in him. Not even to himself could he admit that, sleeping with Kate, he was second again to the Mexican.

"He gets the best of it every time," Floweree thought—thinking only of photofinishes.

He and Kate would be better friends, he assured himself benignly now, if he had his own digs.

Information, however, had to be *worked* before it could be used. He lowered his goggles against the sun and cracked his little whip just once. Then set off for the Riders' Café.

He was going to need help.

The clipclop clattering of horses at a walk or a canter, cries of rider to rider and the swift swing of cars off the highway to the barns, carried a clamor of preparation across the hurrying air. In which the faintly bitter scent of leaves parching on the bluffs mixed with the odor of horses awash with sweat. The heat was already building.

In the Riders' Café the horse-and-woodleaf scent was lost in the greasified pall of hamfat frying, bacon sizzling and beef stewing while toast was crisping in the ovens and eggs were burning in the pans.

Great floor fans blew the ovens' heat across the Negro muckers and walkers lounging in the café's back room. For the boys who earned a dollar for walking a horse half an hour, the big rainbow-colored juke played Caterina Valente singing—

*　　*　　*

Chinatown my Chinatown
Where the lights are low
Dreamy dreamy Chinatown
Hearts seem light and life seems bright
In dreamy Chinatown—

while they ate fried chicken and gnawed on the bones. They accommodated themselves to the heat and the noise more easily, it appeared, than did the white owners and riders who ate, with their wives and kids, in the front room.

There helmeted farmboys from Kentucky took off their helmets while jiving teen-age girls off Canadian farms. And high school dropouts from New York, New York, kept their helmets on, while jiving the same girls, so their straps could dangle. Why the girls had left their farms, only in order to muck out stables, nobody understood; least of all the girls.

But they preferred listening to Kentucky farm boys, and New York City dropouts, to listening to some ancient railroad pensioner recalling what it had been like as a brakeman on the Nickel Plate. There were too many drifters of no trade here, parolee-breakers, hiders-by-day and flyers-by-night; smalltime bookmakers gone on the arfy-darfy; too many I-Wonder-Who-Shot-Johns; who *knew* who'd shot John.

Off in a corner, the always-by-himself loner—ex-salesman, ex-insurance agent, ex-teacher, ex-lawyer, ex-husband, ex-father, ex-barber, ex-clergyman, ex-whatever—was making his last stand for survival with the *Racing Form*.

The loner didn't drink any more. He didn't date women. He never went to a movie. He read nothing but yesterday's charts and today's overnight sheet. He spoke of nothing but last night's results and today's entries. He lived as close to the mutuel windows as he could find a bed.

The sure-losing-loner rose early to watch the horses work out. Then sat about the Riders' Café figuring, figuring; until the toteboard lit up.

When all he had was daily-double money, he couldn't risk it on food. Because that two dollars was going to pay him, come evening, $51.50. Thus enabling him to put twenty and twenty on something that was going to pay $11.20 and $6.80; giving him a bankroll of a hundred and eighty-four dollars. Enough to sit at a clubhouse table with fifty dollars going for him on the nose of an 11-1 shot. Which would bring him $596.80; thus permitting him to put a hundred across on a sure thing off at 9-2. Then he'd move into a hotel until the meet closed. Whereupon he'd fly to Hialeah and win the grandstand. Then he'd return triumphantly, in a new car, to his wife.

All this between the peeling of the paper off a chocolate bar and the final bite; that would have to last him until night. It never occurred to him that his wife wouldn't have him back.

Yet the people who really made the show go had no such fantasies. Now and again they'd make a small bet—but not at the price of a night on the town or of going without supper.

They were the muckers and haulers and walkers and washers; who slept in shacks between the barns. Spongers and brushers and combers and cleaners: starters of the gate and jockey's valets, saddlers and scrapers of hooves and manes; of hides and great white horse-teeth. They knew how to file a horse's teeth so its lips wouldn't tear when it was reined sharply. They were the ones who could calm a horse in the paddock; then whip him across the finishing line whether he wanted to run or not.

Riders, trainers, grooms and traders chunked the ice in their glasses; and talked of their horses more like farmers than bettors. The rider turned agent, the carnie turned hot-walker, the agent turned tout; and the exercise boy who'd gotten his start in life by contracting rickets at the age of three.

Beside the ex-pro football coach now running a stable for a Chicago outfit, still wearing a whistle around his neck, sat the ravaged owner of three horses (two of them sick and one of them crippled) in hope of getaway money back to New Iberia, Louisiana.

"Good morning, horsemen!" The PA system exclaimed above the metallic voices and the aluminum trays, "here's how it looks: Thursday morning, July 10th: first race didn't fill. Out. Sixth race goes as she stands. Seventh race goes. Third substitute race out. Scratch Terry's June in the fifth. Scratch Flash McBride in the eighth. Attention! Mr. Jack Coleman the tattoo man is here! Please pay Mr. Coleman five dollars. All horses must be tattooed within the week. Thank you, Mr. Coleman."

This was the place where the rider who weighed 104 found out what had happened to the rider who now weighed 133. This was where the rider, whose riding days had been shortened by whiskey, asked the young rider to lend him ten dollars until he got a mount. It was where the rider who had never taken a fall heard out the rider who'd taken one fall too many—and resolved to sleep alone, stay sober, save his money; never take a fall and avoid bad dreams.

This was the long morning before the night's swift show and these were the ones who made the show go. The grooms who rubbed the soreness out of the horses' legs with ice and Absorbine; scraped the hooves and taped the legs; or held the brute still by a nose-twitch to permit the vet to wrench out an abcessed tooth with a pliers.

These were the ones of whom it could be said: To him who hath shall be given; and him who hath not even that which he hath not shall be taken away. For it was the owner of seventy horses, such as Everett Ishop, who claimed the one sound horse left in the stable of an owner of only four: one crippled, one sick and one bowed. When photofinishes came up it was the bigger owner who got the break; his horses being essential to making up the programs.

"Attention, Stewards!" the PA system demanded, "nominations for the Western Missouri Juvenile Stakes, five thousand dollars added, two-year-olds Missouri bred, to be run Saturday, August 2nd, will close Monday, July 28th."

Clarence Houssayen's career had been unique. Not because he'd come up fast, from the bullrings to The Big A, and then had gone back down to the bullrings. But because he'd come up a second time.

Flimflam men and smalltown sports followed him. He was trusted by such birds of prey as those whose prey was other smalltown sports and other flimflam men. Past-posters, coneroos, double-crossers and informers believed in him. Because when he gave his word that a short-price horse would run out of the money, and he was on it, it ran out of the money.

He never talked face to face with this little group. There were only one or two, among them all, whose faces he'd ever seen. He made his deals by telephone from a house-trailer a few furlongs down the highway.

Somebody had put concrete blocks under a trailer, hooked it up to electric power sufficient to keep a dozen twenty-watt bug-bulbs flickering weakly around a hand-painted invitation over the trailer's entrance:

EXOTIC TOPLESS DANCERS

Whether the other exotics had left, or had not yet arrived, nobody troubled to ask. There was only Wilma-Mae, a lank and freckled barmaid with teeth so bucked she could eat an apple through a snow fence. And a pair of breasts so lactated Houssayen would shake his head sadly, when Wilma-Mae served him a beer, and reproach her gently.

"Wilma-Mae, you ought to wear a bra just to *protect* yourself. Some guy loses control of hisself in here, it'll be purely your fault." Then he'd flick a few fingers of beer foam at those piteous dugs.

He used the bar, in the long afternoons, to take long-distance calls

325

from New Orleans. When the phone rang a man's voice identified itself: "Atchafalaya here."

"Off," Houssayen would answer. Meaning all bets off; no fix. But if things looked right he'd answer "Suffolk. Five. Six."

"Suffolk" meant put your money down. "Five" meant five hundred dollars to win on himself. "Six" meant the sixth race at Ozark Downs. Whether or not he won, his backers stayed behind him. They knew that, once Houssayen gave his word, he'd do all in his power to keep it. Houssayen was trusted by the sure-thing boys.

In order to remain free to choose his own mounts, he never signed a contract with any stable. He had to stay free to choose his own. There were mounts nobody could win on. And there were mounts that it would be particularly risky, for a man on track parole, to lose on.

Houssayen was not only trusted by the gamblers who backed him: he was respected.

The apprentice rider, Troy Duryea, sharing the common disdain of the native-born riders toward the Mexicans, brought a story on Hector Vaes to Houssayen. Houssayen got tight-up.

"Ah take mens as ah *finds* mens," he advised the apprentice coldly, "Ah don't traffic in second-hand info'mation on a man's cha'acta." And had kept a cold distance between himself and the apprentice ever since.

Now he sat, in the Rider's Café, with his unclean underwear turned about so that its red label looked like a spot of congealed blood in the dark hollow of his throat. The tiny patch of dead-white skin, beneath his right eye, made him look even more leathery. It was a hoofmark from a bad fall he'd taken at Evangeline Park. Clarence Houssayen, under his faded helmet, looked like a cross between a bad-tempered rooster and a worn razor-strop.

When you were told he'd been up to the Big A twice, you could believe it. As you knew, just as certainly, that he wasn't going up there again.

The second time he'd gone down he'd gone down all the way to the Louisiana State Pen for armed robbery. This had solved the problem of keeping his weight down for so long that weight was no longer a problem to him.

Making his way through the heat and the chatter, to where Vaes and Casaflores were chatting it up, side by side, with Houssayen on the other side of their table, Floweree thought: it looks like bygones are bygones.

Hector Vaes was a picture rider. He sat a saddle like a man born to ride. Yet his ambition, aboard a horse, was limited to staying on top of it all around the course; then to get into his civvies and get to the Highway Bar before they ran out of whiskey.

Vaes had so many fourths that, when parading a mount assigned to the Number Four gate, some railbird was sure to shout across the rail, "You got your own number today, Hector!"

"Vaes knows all the moves," bettors agreed, "but I'd never buy a ticket on the bum."

For fifty dollars wasn't too much to sacrifice, it was Vaes' thinking, to avoid a broken back. And he conveyed his caution to the animal under him.

When pressed to the rail with room—*just* room—to get through, Vaes would falter and get blocked off. When the apprentice, Duryea, had once charged him coming out of the gate, Vaes had pulled up so hard the horse had swerved, and it had taken him an eighth of a mile to catch the pack. That day he ran fifth.

He'd ridden at Santa Anita. But his conviction, that it was better to give ground than to run into a crush at the wire, made it increasingly difficult for his California agent to get mounts for him. He wouldn't ride at Santa Anita again.

Yet once Vaes and Casaflores had dismounted, all the caution belonged to Casaflores. Vaes went for the girls. He went for the whiskey. He went for the dice. He went for the cards.

The women and the whiskey and the dice and the cards liked Hector Vaes, too. So did the bartenders and the sharpie crapshooters and the stud-poker mechanics and the blackjack cheaters. If nobody cheated him out of his money he'd find a hooker willing to hold it for him. There wasn't a horse stabled at Ozark Downs for which Vaes cared anything.

Although he was six years younger than Vaes, Casaflores nonetheless cast himself in the role of an older brother. All Hector required, it seemed to Casaflores, was edification. He never ceased, therefore, to point out bad examples to his friend.

There was no lack of bad examples.

"Look now Floweree"—he indicated the rider sitting with Troy Duryea in the Highway Bar—"*he* do the whiskey, long time, *he* do the girl. Now he sleep with a lady because she feel sorry."

"Then I got nothing to worry, Indian," Vaes assured Casaflores cheerfully, "I go broke, lady take me in, too."

Casaflores looked disappointed in his friend.

Vaes caught it. "I only want to be happy, Elisio," he tried to explain.

327

"What has *that* got to do with it?" Casaflores asked.

Vaes called Casaflores "Indian" because Casa mounted a horse from its right side, Indian-fashion.

"He could mount from the left," the apprentice Duryea confided Houssayen, "that *still* wouldn't make him a white man. But *imagine*—a Mexican calling *another* Mexican an *Indian*!"

"That's nothing," Houssayen informed the younger man, smiling faintly, "I've heard a *Cuban* call a Mexican a *Mexican*!"

The Spanish riders fought like women. D'Arcia and Josohino had gotten into it because D'Arcia had hooked Josohino's stirrup coming out of the gate. Josohino threw a rock through the window of D'Arcia's car. The next day D'Arcia cut up Josohino's clothes with a letter-opener.

Mounting from the wrong side was only the first thing Casaflores did wrong. Everything he did after that looked even worse. In the saddle he moved in every direction except off. When he should have been pressing himself flat against a horse's neck, he sat up and began pumping, waving his whip across the horse's mane and looking like he was about to leap off and drag the horse across the line by its tail.

"If my mount ain't giving me everything he got," he confided in Kate, "I *scare* that sonabitch till he give it."

Casaflores cared everything for horses and nothing for cabereting. When he had to sit out a race he paced, half-dressed and helmeted, up and down the color-room floor, popping his whip against his boots: that same left-handed whip that flicked chalk-bettors with fear when he began popping it, coming down off the crown of the track on a horse so frightened it looked blind. He'd gotten so many wins by coming down off the crown that bettors had named it "Mexican Alley."

Why the Mexican Thief would take a bad mount, rather than no mount at all, caused other riders to wonder. Yet up he'd go into the irons of some crow-hopping fourteen-year-old mare that hadn't won in seven years, yammer into her ears and keep yammering around the turn for home although the whole field was already passing the toteboard.

"*Money?*" he answered when asked whether he liked it, "O *yes*—I like *that*." Yet other riders suspected that he rode for the joy of winning as well as for the love of money. The truth was that, though he needed neither a woman nor whiskey in order to get him through the night, Casaflores had trouble getting through a day without driving a horse toward a finishing line.

And this flatnosed little man whose eyes were Asian and who wore his hair too long, could drive a horse five furlongs in one minute flat by the clock in his head.

328

A clock that had never failed him until he'd come to Kate's trailer, on her invitation to share a Mexican dinner. "Made with my own hands," she'd assured him.

The Mexican dinner had been bought frozen. He'd taken it outside and dumped it in the garbage can. But had come back inside himself.

In the twenty months since he'd seen his wife, it had been his single transgression.

When he put down forty cents for a beer, that was forty cents worth of bread he was snatching from the mouths of his four children. Yet he'd been known to spend as much as six dollars in a single evening simply to keep a protective eye on Hector Vaes at the Highway Bar. In return, Vaes read books, newspapers and magazines to Casaflores; in English as well as in Spanish.

Houssayen found it incomprehensible that a rider who'd brought in sixty-six winners, and the meet only half over, could be illiterate.

"Read what it tell here," he was now demanding of Casaflores, handing him the sports section of the *Post-Dispatch*.

"How this man goin' read *your* paper," Vaes laughed lightly, "when he cannot read even his own?"

Immediately, Casaflores put a finger on the previous night's results.

"It tell here Lee K. pay fourteen-forty with Casaflor' up," he reported thoughtfully, "Here it tell Mickey's Miki pay twelve dolla straight, Casaflor' up." He handed the results to Vaes—"How many Houssayen win last night? Tell me where it say. *That* boy make money like crazy I hear."

"Ah made more money in one month in the port of N'Awlins than you've made your whole life," Houssayen let Casaflores know.

"I never make one damned dime in *that* port," the Mexican conceded. Then, seeing Floweree, confided aloud to Vaes, "Watch out now—here that man pop people in the nose. He gonna pop you too!"

Floweree nodded to Houssayen and turned toward the back room; Houssayen followed.

"Big Red tied the track record out there this morning, Dad," he told the Cajun the moment they were seated. Houssayen, in his mid-thirties, didn't appreciate being called "Dad" by a rider himself old enough to be killing the grass.

"What has running in the morning got to do with running under lights?"

"That's *just* what it got to do with, old buddy—the light at the clubhouse turn. *That's* the shadow Red been jumpin'. Can I but get him to the rail before he hits the turn, the Mexican Thief will look like he's standing still—and Red is going to be the price horse in the field. Old buddy."

"Tell the Racing Commission. Maybe they'll turn off the power when you get a mount that's scared of electricity."

Floweree placed his helmet carefully on the table before him.

"Catfish just clocked the horse in one-forty-one," he explained, "but she didn't allow for his shadow-jump: I figure him one-thirty-nine tomorrow night."

"Why not just use a one-eyed blinker and a shadow-roll?" Houssayen suggested.

"The horse won't run with equipment. Besides, I couldn't put extra gear on him without that woman wising up. If she sniffs something up, the word'll be out."

For the first time Houssayen regarded him seriously. Then shook his head, No.

"Caint afford to get into no more of your jock-room brawls, Flower. I'm on track parole."

An apparition, gaunt, lean and unshaven, held out a handful of programs to them.

Houssayen paid The Apparition a quarter, the standard price, for one of the programs. Yet the Apparition waited.

"It's how much I pay for them myself," he explained, looking sorrowfully down at the coin in his palm, "certain folks give me a nickel extry for bringing them in early."

"Let's go to my place," Houssayen suggested, adding a dime to The Apparition's palm.

Floweree rose to go. Yet now it was Houssayen who stood waiting.

"You want *change?*" The Apparition asked at last.

When he'd found a nickel, Houssayen accepted it and they left.

The morning workouts were done now. All that was running the track, as they walked past the soybean field behind the toteboard, were tiny tornadoes made of chaff, dust and rumor: that wheeled in pursuit where horse and rider had lately run. That scattered sparrows under the rail then began making up ground. That circled the winner's circle triumphantly as if mocking that nightly ritual. And at last blew across last night's crushed lily cups, dead tickets and such.

Into the vasty hollows beneath the stands.

A green haze of heat, so heavy it looked like a wall, kept building higher and higher above the bluffs. Then a flash of heat-lightning cracked it and the whole green wall came tumbling down.

Yet there was no thunder.

Down the shadowed shed-rows the horses hung their great sad heads. The water in the big orange buckets was already turning brackish. Above the piled hay-bales a small chaff blew.

Houssayen sniffed the air: "Somebody's using cane," he sensed, picking the scent of sugar out of the scent of hay.

Between the bales, in small stone rooms crowded with tack, exercise boy and mucker, rider and groom, all slept. Only the faint insistent tapping, of a hammer against a hoof, and a transistor murmuring near at hand, broke the stilly heat.

"Get out your mud-silks, old buddy," Floweree warned Houssayen, "when them clouds bust, she'll pour for days."

"Pretty-day colors will do for tonight," Houssayen judged.

His room was an army cot surrounded by coffee-stained plastic cups, empty Coke bottles, riding boots, socks drying on a line, a calendar whose pages fluttered when he switched on his small floor-fan; and flies that buzzed contentedly. Never having known any other home.

"Ah can git you a hundred across the board in N'Awlins," Houssayen came directly to the point, "if your information works—But only Gawd can git you to the rail."

"If you're in the One Gate I won't need God," Floweree assured Houssayen.

"Ah won't be posted on the rail. If the Mexican Thief don't git it, Josohino or D'Arcia will—'n that comes to the same thing."

"Or Vaes," Floweree suggested.

"Even worse," Houssayen warned Floweree, "the sonofabitch caint ride a lick any more—but he'll bump you over the rail to let his buddy git it."

"Why, that's where *you* come in, old buddy"—Floweree brightened—"it don't matter whether it's Casa or D'Arcia or Vaes or Josohino—you thwack the first cat out of that gate—*thwack!*—like *that*"—Floweree smacked his right fist into his left palm—"all I got to do is to get *inside* before we hit the clubhouse light. When I let him out—we'll leave that field tied to the rail."

"What the hell you think ah *am*, Flower?" Houssayen demanded, "the Confederate cavalry? How many them damn horses you think ah can cut out for God's sake? Ah don't even know what the Mexican Thief is riding."

"Moon River."

"Ain't *nobody* can hook Moon River," Houssayen now feigned inexhaustible patience—"ah *know*, buddy—ah've *rode* that horse. He runs from behind or he don't run at all. Now how you goin' to hook a horse that won't try until he got the pack in *front* of him? *Wait* for him? You hook a horse *between* horses, when he try to git out front *early*. By the time the Mexican let Moon River make his run, whole field be strung out.''

But Floweree began scratching an overnight sheet with a pencil stub. Flies buzzed against the screen. The floor fan rattled as if ready to quit. The light was hot yet the shadows were chill. The scent of instant coffee dried in old cups mixed with the choking odor of manure. Floweree handed his sketch to Houssayen.

Houssayen saw starting gates numbered 4 and 6, with a diagonal line from 6 to the rail; and a crude representation of a clubhouse light purporting to be an eighth of a mile away.

"That simplifies *your* work,'' Floweree decided, "if Casa breaks slow all you have to do is drive *at* Vaes.''

"*Have* to?'' Houssayen glanced up quickly from the sketch, "*Have* to? All ah *have* to do is drive at Vaes? If ah jist grabbed his tail 'n waved to you to come on ahead would that be alright with you?''

"All I meant was that if you drove at him, he'd give ground,'' Floweree apologized, "you *know* all Vaes wants to do is stay on top of a horse until it slows down enough to let him get off.''

"That's only how he's riding this meet,'' Houssayen recalled, "he didn't use to ride like that. If Vaes *wants* to ride, he'll leave you thinking *you're* tied to the rail. What's his mount?''

"Fleur Rouge.''

"What's the class of the race?''

"Port-O-Pogo.''

Houssayen shook his head.

"No. Fleur Rouge.''

Then he tore Floweree's sketch in two and the halves raced, in the floor-fan's windstream, head-and-head to the open door and out into the haze of day.

Houssayen went to the door, bolted it, and drew a riding crop and two batteries from a drawer. Sitting opposite Floweree, he unscrewed the top of the whip, exposing a hollowed center. He inserted the batteries. Then, turning the cap of the whip to Floweree, revealed a small coil. He drew a half a dozen small pins from his pocket, inserted them in the handle of the ship, screwed the top back on; then touched Floweree's forearm lightly. Floweree drew back as if he'd touched an exposed light bulb.

"Ah paid six hundred bucks for this small goading device, Flower,'' he assured Floweree, "if ah wasn't on track parole ah'd use it m'self. Ah caint take the risk."

The penalty for using a buzzer, as Floweree was well aware, was to be ruled off Canadian as well as American tracks for five years. And though other riders had used buzzers here, only one (a Chicago rider) had been caught and ruled off.

Floweree began laughing, he didn't know why. Houssayen's small pillified face looked out at him from under his helmet, like the face of a dog in a kennel's dark. Then he began making the kind of dry clicking, deep in his throat; that passed, with Clarence Houssayen, for rollicking merriment.

"Now you're putting me on, Dad," Floweree decided—"every steward in the tower would spot a move like *that*."

Houssayen rose and stood in the middle of the room, studying Floweree. "You don't buzz him on the track, Flower," he explained, "work it in the areaway under the stands. You wave it in front of the horse. Then you get a strong double-grip in the reins. Then you give him a touch—*just* a touch. You'll have to hold him *hard*—because that sonofabitch is going to stand up on his hind legs and holler. Can you hold Big Red?"

"I can hold him," Floweree felt certain.

"Then, after you've made the turn for home—ah said *after*—you let him see it again and he won't *run* for that wire—he'll *fly* under it."

Houssayen waited for Floweree to ask him something. But Floweree merely studied the device.

"Well," Houssayen asked the question himself—"how are you going to get rid of it?"

Floweree hadn't thought of that.

"You toss it to Drumgo. Drumgo'll know what to do with it. You know Drumgo?"

Drumgo was Houssayen's Negro groom.

"I know Drumgo."

"Then be sure nobody but Drumgo gets it. *Damned* sure."

A flash of heat lightning turned the room pale green for a split second. In that green moment, two small gaunt men, one helmeted and one unhelmeted, leaned rigidly toward one another.

Floweree closed his eyes at that flash and kept them shut when the flash was done. In the darkness that followed he heard Houssayen's voice.

"You're a mean little bastard, aren't you?"

The rider opened his eyes.

"I have my reasons," he replied.

Red's Big Red swung his great sad head across the stall's webbing, forth and back, forth and back, lifting his left foreleg an inch then the right; in a slow immemorial dance. A small floor-fan, at the rear of the stall, whispered a changeless rhythm; that ruffled the feathers of the rust-colored rooster that was Big Red's best friend.

Were it not for her horse's attachment to this mangy old bird, Kate would have wrung its neck and fried it. The stupid rooster was forever underfoot. But when you're the owner of a one-horse stable, your horse is an only child that always has its own way.

"Hold *still,* you long-striding sonofabitch," Kate scolded Red when he shied, pretending to be frightened by the brush against his flanks; yet he didn't shy too much. Red's Big Red was a nervous stud who wasn't against cow-kicking her if he'd dared. But whenever that impulse entered his mind she'd show him the broad white flat of her palm; and he'd decide against cow-kicking. Because with a single smack of the flat of that palm against his belly she'd bring him whinnying to his knees.

This afternoon he was sassier than usual because he knew she never knocked the wind out of him on a day he was going to the paddock. Red always sensed when she was getting him ready to run.

Kate Mulconnery might have spent her days teaching disturbed children. Her own need was to minister to beings less endowed than herself in flesh, spirit and wit. But as her own education had never gone beyond the barnyard, she ministered instead to the spiritual and emotional needs of a great inbred four-legged neurotic; slightly retarded and perpetually disturbed.

Warming, cooling, calming, currying, combing, feeding, coaxing, cleaning, Mercurochroming, bandaging, iodining and soothing this creature lent Kate the feeling that she was of some small use in the world.

"Hold *still* I said," she commanded Big Red now, "if you want to be a horse *act* like a horse."

Why all her horses had been losers and all her lovers had just missed being dwarfs, Kate needed no shrink to explain. When you're a single woman cutting toward forty you don't need to have a witch-doctor to advise you to take what's at hand. Nor that, if you're a woman weighing 189 pounds who likes men, your chances of getting cow-kicked by a jockey are greater than those of getting cow-kicked by a horse.

A hint of rain in the air, however distant, had always had a calming

334

effect on Red's Big Red. Now he permitted her to pick his hooves with no more than an occasional twitch of his hide. He was feeling well despite the heat. Kate could tell.

"Looking for rain, Red?" she asked him, tying small red and green ribbons into his mane. "You want mud again, Stud? Like the time we won in Ohio?"

Red's Big Red nodded: nothing he'd like better than rain bringing mud enough to send him splashing past all those horses that had been running away from him on these nights of fast tracks and dry going. Red snorted.

She patted his neck. "Get all the money, Red," she blessed him. Then kicked his rooster.

"Frivolous claim" kept going through her mind all the way back to her trailer with the U-Haul behind it. Her life, recollected, seemed a sequence of frivolous claims: all put in by riders whose saddles she'd gotten out of hock. Now she'd paid out her last fifty dollars to reinstate a man she wished to trust; yet could not because he didn't trust himself. That's about as frivolous as a woman can get, Kate Mulconnery reflected, and began humming to herself.

> *Your cheating heart*
> *Will tell on you*

Their bed was unmade; the floor unswept. Pots, pans and dishes stank in the sink and beer cans rusted below. *Forms,* overnight sheets and copies of *Sports Illustrated* littered the table and the single overstuffed chair. A week of Floweree's dungarees, shirts and muddied boots cluttered the trailer.

Kate kicked a sweatshirt aside, unhooked a black satin gown that had the sheen of age upon it, and slipped her feet into a pair of red slippers. She slapped on a floppy, flowered hat and took a swig from a half-pint of Old Overholt. Then she sank into the overstuffed chair with the bottle in her lap.

And there Kate Mulconnery sat in her foolish hat; in the slow soft darkening of day. Watching where headlights, beyond the woods, showed the night's first bettors making their ways.

Now in the early-bettor's hour, when the toteboard's two hundred shuttered eyes light neither WIN nor PLACE nor SHOW; nor whether a track is fast or slow. In the hay-smelling evening light, among the litter of her days, she took another swig.

Till lamps, and leaves and damps and glooms, of times and homes that once were hers, and now were gone, returned like the twilit glimmerings of the headlights approaching; then receding beyond the ominous wood.

One October had come down the Mississippi like a cloud returning home to rest. Waters had followed through the woods. When the waters had ebbed, every tree had stood stripped of its April finery; bare, dark, and separated on a sea of sour mud.

There, in the sinking ruins of somebody's kitchen, the handle of an iron frying pan had loomed like a lopsided gravemarker; above the grave of someone who'd lived a lopsided life. Yet the very thing, the girl had decided, to pry a rusted lock off some long-lost river-pilot's sea-trunk stuffed with treasure.

Plodding barefoot through the stinking gullies, she'd searched, among drowned roosters and cats the blueflies were already at, for the magic sea-trunk of her child's fancy. If the watches and bracelets and rings and brooches in it weren't pure gold, silver would do. If there was no silver, she'd be grateful for copper. If the dresses weren't silk she'd be content with cotton. If they didn't fit she'd cut them down.

Rye was for remembrance. Kate took another swig.

Thirty years now since those waters had ebbed. And all there had been, in the sea-trunk of all her days, was a U-Haul on which payment was overdue. And a four-legged brute she'd have to enter in a claiming race if he didn't get into the winner's circle this same night.

She'd had other horses before Red's Big Red. As she'd had other men before Hollis Floweree. Some of the horses had pulled a tendon; some had lost speed. Some had looked good when she bought them but had later gone bad; and all the men had turned mean. Horses or men, whether paid for or gotten in trade, had sooner or later been claimed. The difference was that losing a horse didn't wound her pride.

She drifted off into the kind of woman's dream where one sees herself acting out some fantasy; yet knows she is only dreaming.

Kate saw herself leading a horse to paddock whose name she could not recall. Yet she'd run him once—just once—at Waterford Park. A stallion.

A horseman, wearing a Westerner's hat, was leaning against an old-fashioned railroad bell and smiling at her as she approached. Then she saw that the smile was mocking, and turning about, saw that all she was leading was a small, pinkish penis. It was alive and had a rope-twitch about its head. In a surge of shame she tried to rid herself of the end of the rope in her hand. It coiled itself about her wrist as if it were part of the creature she led, and she wakened.

The room had grown dark. She lit the lamp above her dresser.

She slipped a gown over her head, then let down her bright hair; itself as tawny as a mane. There was always a bit of chaff in it; she brushed it now till it shone in the light. Then she braided it, as she'd once seen Ann Harding do in some forgotten film, about her head.

"Not bad," she decided, checking her reflection in the mirror, "I look strong enough to braid trees."

She clasped a string of imitation pearls about her throat, clipped on a pair of imitation jade earrings and smiled for the track photographer.

Dressed for the winner's circle if not for a ball, Catfish Kate went to lead her horse to paddock.

Now the horses had been tried too often against the same horses. Moon River had outlasted Flying Indian, Lord Wingding had easily outrun Moon River; Port-O-Pogo had overtaken Lord Wingding in a rush, Djeddah's Folly had nipped Port-O-Pogo at the wire. Then Moon River had beaten Djeddah's Folly and Flying Indian had outlasted Moon River.

The riders had been tried too often against the same riders. The Mexican Thief had ridden the daily-double twice around this bullring of the summer night. Then Houssayen had begun getting the jump on everybody especially Casaflores. So Vaes had held Houssayen's saddlecloth, coming out of the gate, long enough to get Casaflores the rail and bring in a route horse at 35-1. So Houssayen had told Floweree That Mexican Thief Gets The Best Of It Every Time.

Then the apprentice Duryea, D'Arcia and Josohino had come down the stretch stride for stride until Casaflores came down off the crown again, picking up speed as he came and got under the wire before all three stride-for-striders.

The red INQUIRY sign went up. While the crowd grew still in order to hear whether the protest, entered by Duryea against Casaflores, would be sustained.

The toteboard kept flashing—1-7-7-1-1-7 off and on and off and on until the PA system cried out most pitifully: Owner of red Corvair Illinois license DJ 5485 Come To Your Car Motor Is Running Doors Are Locked. And an old sad scuffler, car-less all his days, thought with relief, "I'm glad that ain't *me*."

The Mexican Thief won the photo. "Nine claims of foul against him since the meet began," Duryea complained, "and not one sustained."

"Mexicans get the best of it every time," Floweree agreed.

So Floweree broke the Mexican's nose in the jock-room brawl, Vaes accused Houssayen of having pinned Casaflores' arms, a jockey's valet swore the Mexican had swung first, Josohino accused Vaes of having no guts because he'd stood by and watched his best friend slugged, The Clerk of Scales said "I didn't see anything," D'Arcia said, "Leave me out of this," and The Popcorn Woman under the grandstand said, "I never seen such a bunch of popcorn-eating motherfuckers my whole born days."

"It's one time the Mexican Thief didn't get the best of it," Duryea congratulated Floweree.

"Keep your saddlecloth tucked in," Floweree had cautioned the apprentice.

But Djeddah's Folly is moving up in class, an old sad scuffler quickly explained, while Port-O-Pogo is moving down: First bet the breeding then bet the speed. Speed up when you're winning, slow down when you're losing. In a claiming race look for condition and forget class. Never bet on the rider—bet the horse. Your strongest bet isn't on a horse but against it.

"I *know*, I *know*," another scuffler cut in, "but if a route horse is wearing bar-plates in a short event when the track looks fast but is actually *still* sloppy, do I *still* bet the breeding? When a horse is clearly the class of a race, what do I do if I know he's just a good old sport? Do I still bet the breeding? Do I *still* bet the class?"

"When a track is sloppy watch out for any two-year-old filly wearing smooth-plates in case of a change of riders, in event the moon is full and the slop turns to mud—she might just *roll* in. But never let anyone put the touch on you standing next to the fifty-dollar window. Tell him you'll meet him in the hotel lobby and he'll settle for ten."

"But what do I do if my horse lugs in? And what do I do if my horse lugs out?"

"If your horse lugs in, *you* lug out. If he lugs out, *you* lug in. And never date a girl vocalist whose favorite song is *Somewhere Over the Rainbow*—there'll always be a dude in the lobby wearing long sideburns and green eyeshades waiting to take over her check."

"And what do I do if I don't do what I *ought* to do? What do I do *then?*"

"Just watch out for those sheenies D'Arcia and Josohino. Watch out for that hillbilly Duryea. Watch out for that ex-con Houssayen. If he don't ride as he's told to ride those New Orleans dagoes'll bury him in the Old French Cemetery. But mostly watch out for that Mexican Thief. He'll bury you under the grandstand."

Watch out don't forget, pay no heed don't look now, keep in mind, get on, lay off, here he comes, there he goes—O *Boy* am I glad *he* ain't *me*.

Now the night's earliest tipsheet-shouter began hawking *Father Duffy's Hotshots*—"Nine straight winners today, folks—*nine!*"

How this clown got two dollars a sheet just by turning his collar around, when the red-sheet, green-sheet and yellow-sheet touts were getting only a dollar, could be explained only upon the premise that Catholic bettors paid the extra dollar because they assumed it was going to the church; or to assuage the pang of guilt some endured in attending a gambling occasion. More likely, they felt they'd have a better day with The Virgin going for them.

"Father Duffy"—a renegade Jew—suffered no pangs when his clients (or were they his parishioners?)—went home with nine straight losers. There would be no lack of believers whose faith in The Virgin would remain unshaken.

Nor was he troubled by the Protestant loser who snarled at the holy father every night when he came in; and snarled again when he left —"*Why don't you turn that collar around and go to work, you bum?*"

The holy father only smiled benignly; as much as to say "I forgive you, my son."

He knew the Protestant loser. The PL materialized on TV, just before the evening news, five nights a week, offering financial advice. For fifteen minutes he offered consistently conservative counsel on investment. Then the camera-eye blinked out and he drew his *Racing Form* from his desk and raced to the clubhouse at Ozark Downs.

Six races later he'd be standing before the shoeboard, his jacket wrinkled by sweat and tie askew; the very image of a man in desperate need of a 35-1 on-the-nose shot to get him even for the night.

"No matter how much a man makes in his own business," Father Duffy explained, "so long as he's playing the horses he's working for me. The dollar-bettor will stay with you longer, and pay you off sooner, than the thousand-dollar bettor. The higher the fee you charge for information, the more horse-players will believe in it. And when you're hustling tip-sheets it don't matter whether you're giving out winners or losers, so long as you holler *loud*. The louder you holler the more they'll buy. Here, I'll show you."

"Nine straight losers yesterday, folks!" Father Duffy shouted, "nine straight losers again today! Get your losers here, folks!"

Three bettors hurried up; each with two dollars in hand.

Chicago money is coming in on Good Old Ed, the word got out, *but it won't go down till the flag is up.* So the old sad scufflers scuffled about till the flag went up before they put their money down. But Good Old Ed never got a call, because the Chicago money had gone down on Helen's Peach; which was why the rumor had gone out to bet Good Old Ed. And each old sad scuffler, rebuffed once again, went milling around with a dead ticket in his hand.

Watch out for Duryea, he'll drive through any hole he can get a horse's nose through—watch out for Houssayen, he picks his own mounts —watch out for D'Arcia and Josohino, they work together. Watch out for Floweree unless he's lost his nerve. But mostly watch out for The Mexican Thief when his horse begins switching his tail. Are they going to take a urine test on the Mexican's $82.80 win? Did you know that Mexicans ride with only one toe in the irons? Why don't they take a test on the Mexican?

Every night, as the small amber lamps of the paddock came up, the same word went out: Watch out for Duryea, Watch out for Padagua, Watch out for McLennon, Watch out for Anson, Watch out for Di Stefani. But mostly watch out for the Mexican Thief.

But not even old sad scufflers said Watch out for Hector Vaes.

The beardmen moved big bets away from the track while screening their action with small throwaways on other horses. They padded the machines with other peoples' money to bring the price up on off-track wagers. While security men moved among the bettors looking for faces of short-wave past-posters; whose photographs they kept, for matching purposes, in pockets made to hold dossiers.

Anytime a face appeared in the local press, captioned *Known Hoodlum*, that face was officially barred from the clubhouse, grandstand and stable area of Ozark Downs.

Any person who had served time, regardless of the offense, was categorically refused employment on the premises of Ozark Downs.

Any employee discovered making a wager, while in the employ of Ozark Downs, was dismissed.

Consequently the waitresses brought in a whole tribe of unemployable touts to run their bets for them as well as for their customers. The bartenders watered the whiskey to make up their losses at the daily-double windows. And the women who grilled hamburgers and hot dogs brought in their own rolls so they wouldn't have to account for hot dogs and hamburgers sold on the company's rolls.

Therefore the front office had to hire people-watchers who were paid better than the people they watched.

One people-watcher caught a waitress coming out of the gate carrying stolen cocktail glasses. All she had to do, to keep her job, was to go to bed with him. But, after she'd slept with him, he had her fired anyhow. The consequence of this was that two weekend bartenders, one of whom had once been married to the waitress, beat up the people-watcher.

It wasn't until the people-watcher fingered them that it was discovered that both bartenders were Known Hoodlums and that the people-watcher himself had served time. Everyone involved, excepting the waitress, lost their jobs. She was able to keep hers by going to bed with the Chief of Security.

Didn't you see my rider stand up in the irons to let that Mexican Thief pass him? Could anything like that happen at Ak-Sar-Ben? Do you know that Barnett has only one eye? What became of Don Meade have you heard? Do you know that a hog can out-run a horse—for the first hundred feet? Didn't Red's Big Red quit at Miles Park?

That wasn't Red's Big Red it was Good Old Ed and he didn't quit he throwed a shoe—I'll see you at the fifteen-dollar combination unless a Chinaman wearing a blue beret crosses my path—everything else is superstition.

Some depended upon a sudden gust from the northwest to propel their selection across the finishing line; while others banked upon the wind to stop the favorite at the head of the stretch. Others prayed, as the flag went up, that all the winds of the earth would stop blowing for one minute and fifty seconds.

Some hung around the sellers' windows, cash in hand, before the windows opened, fearing to be shut out. Others never bet till the horses were in their gates and there could be no further fluctuation of the odds.

Some balanced barometric readings against post positions; others rested their hopes upon drought or depth of dust.

And though some figured results by the changeful skies and others by the shoeboard, nobody asked how much either shoes or skies would count if a groom pried a calk just loose enough for a horse to throw it. Or how much speed would count if a rider took his mount wide simply by slacking his left rein at the turn.

And if a rider were bought and the owner didn't know and the trainer didn't care and the paddock judge wasn't quite sure, how could the bettor be sure that the rider might not lose his nerve a furlong from the finishing line and fling his electrified whip into the soybean field just when he needed it most?

As no offtrack bettor could be certain, when he went to collect on a long-priced horse, that he might not find his bookie gone.

Gone on the arfy-darfy saying: "I wish this wasn't me."

The biggest larks were the photograph finishes. For the darkroom at Ozark Downs was very dark indeed. Anything could be accomplished up there short of inciting a riot: the horse that had won by half a head could be made to appear to have lost by that margin, simply by giving the finishing line an imperceptible slant; or by retouching the nose of one horse to make it appear to be touching the wire. The track itself, of course, gained nothing by this. But to the member of the camera patrol who had a five-hundred-dollar bet going, it afforded innocent merriment.

Till the big field lights came on in a blue-green glare and everybody warned everybody to bear in mind that a short-legged horse could out-run a long-striding one in the stretch if the long-legged one's hooves had been weighted.

And don't you know, they warned one another, that a sponge up a nostril can hamper a favorite's breathing?

Don't you *know* that a battery can be fitted into a whip? That a fistful of bennies up a plater's behind will make him pass up Damascus?

A skinny old man and a stout middle-aged one were in a hassle among the seats beside the paddock.

"These seats aren't reserved," Fats, who was sitting, reminded Old Skinny; who was standing.

"I left my program on that seat," Old Skinny complained—"*that* reserved it."

"There's no program on *this* seat, old man," Fats contended.

"Stand up 'n let's see," Old Skinny challenged him.

"Give the old man his seat," someone behind Fats intervened.

"Mind your own business," Fats put the voice down without turning around.

"I want my program," Old Skinny persisted.

"Don't get arrogant, old man," Fats warned him, "I'm a *doctor!*"

This threat, implying not only that an M.D. was beyond ethics when it came to usurping a seat, but that he might see to it that anyone denying him a seat of his choice might be denied medical attention for the rest of his life, troubled the bettors about the pair. If an M.D. was immune to racetrack ethics, didn't that also allow dentists to evict other bettors from seats they'd come early to get? And interns? And nurses? And gynecologists? And psychiatrists? And once the psychiatrists were in, how were you going to keep out pharmacists and mailmen? The prospect of chaos was imminent.

Fortunately the crisis was resolved by the announcer's cry, *"They're off!"*

342

And so they were, going six and a half furlongs on the other side of the track. They disappeared behind the toteboard a moment, then emerged with Rain Swamp, off at 11-1, neck and neck with GoGoGo, off at 5-2; until Popcorn Bummy, off at even money, charged down off the crown at the track and under the wire by a length and a half.

When the big shout had died the players looked around. Sure enough, there was Old Skinny still waiting for his seat. And Fats still sitting on his program.

"Two-year-old Anthony is in the Security Office," the PA system announced, "he is waiting for his mother."

Some bet the stable and some bet the rider; some bet the trainer and some bet the program selection. Some stayed at home if the day was clear and sulked, having put all their hopes upon a steady all-day drizzle turning the track from dust to slop; from slop to mud and from mud to a sinkhole and rising tides.

Watch out for a horse coming out of the paddock taped to its rump —they warned one another—it might be taped that high to keep the odds up against it. Look out for a horse on the outside post if he's wearing one-eyed blinkers. Look out for a horse on the inside post if he's wearing a shadow-roll. Look out for a rider who's been flown in to ride just one race. Look out when there's a last minute change of rider. But ignore the mud-bettor who keeps samples of mud, in Mason jars, from Santa Anita, the Big A and Hialeah: he may sell you one of his jars.

Then here comes the clown with yet one more system: all you have to do is add the selections at the foot of your program. "What does it say here?" "Nine, five, and six." "Okay, how much is that?" "Twenty." "Okay, now look at the second race—add *them* up." "Eight, two and one makes eleven." "Alright, how much is eleven deducted from twenty?" "Nine." "Okay—number nine is the winner of the third race. It *never* fails." And he walks off, program in hand; looking as though he were actually in his right mind.

While small whirlwinds made of soybean chaff, pursued one another tirelessly, out of the chute and into the backstretch, around and around, hugging the rail then going wide; sometimes lugging in then lugging out, in a race that had no starting gate nor even a finishing line; that yet made perpetual mimicry of riders forever driving.

Upon horses forever dumbly driven.

Bearing hopes of bettors who first lost their cars and later their crafts; later their homes and at last their wives. Yet went on discerning quinellas, exactas and daily-doubles by a fickle shoeboard, a changeful earth; and certain treacherous stars.

Don't bet a race with a horse in it whose odds are even money or less, they warned one another. Don't bet to place or show: one way to lose a bet is enough. Don't bet jump races or races for two-year-old maidens. Don't tout anyone else onto a horse. Don't listen to anyone touting you. Bet when the odds are 4-1 or better—and if two horses in the same race look good, bet both to win. Don't fight your losers. Remember there's always another race.

But not one said Look out for Vaes.

No other woman would have risked making a public fool of herself, by dressing up for the winner's circle, while leading a 23-1 shot to the paddock, except Catfish Kate. Yet, after the grooms in broken straw hats and manured boots, here she comes in her black satin party gown, her flowered and floppy hat with the pink ribbon about its crown, stepping lightly in red-tasseled slippers. Leading a big tawny ridgeling with red and green ribbons braided into his mane.

Helmeted riders were crowding the paddock bench. Casaflores, Houssayen, D'Arcia, Duryea and Vaes; but she didn't see Floweree. It went across her mind that he'd taken off with the fifty instead of paying the fine. Was he stupid enough to pull something like that? She wondered. "Almost," she decided.

Then she saw him leaning against the paddock in his silks. Just as Red's Big Red decided to go back to the barn.

"Hold him, Catfish!" Vaes called out.

"He's worried about his rooster is all," she called back, laughing; and got Red moving back toward the paddock.

"He'll be alright in the gate," the Paddock Judge assured her, "we had a mare once who got so hooked on her goat that we couldn't get her saddled less'n the goat came along and stood by."

"The only kind of goat I'd keep would be a nanny," Kate went along, "I wouldn't have a billy. You know why their whiskers are stained yellow?"

The Paddock Judge expressed no interest; but Kate told him anyhow. "Because they piss their whiskers. *Deliberately*. To keep people away. You get a horse who doesn't like people either 'n he'll really appreciate sharing his stall with a stinking yellow-beard billy."

The Paddock Judge cupped his palms and gave that big barnyard shout—"Last bus for the Sunday School picnic! Everybody up!" to summon the riders.

The little men in their bright silks sauntered to their saddlings. And every time a horse kicked the boards of its stall, an old sad scuffler

344

peered through the webbing and thought, "I'm glad that ain't *me* in there!"

Kate gave Floweree a leg up and Red's Big Red wanted to leave right then. But Kate held him long enough to give Floweree final instructions.

"Take him back off the lead and lay about third or fourth going down the back side. Let him move on the elbow. If you can't get through on the rail at the head of the stretch, circle the others—he'll have plenty left."

"I'll try not to fall off," Floweree replied; and flicked his little whip. Yet held Red's Big Red tight until Moon River, Casaflores up, then Port-O-Pogo, D'Arcia up, passed his stall.

Then he swung Big Red in front of Lady Night, Houssayen in the irons. Kate kept her hand on Red's bridle until Floweree swung the horse into the narrow brick-walled areaway between paddock and track. He glanced back to make sure that Drumgo, Houssayen's groom, was giving Big Red plenty of kicking room. He pulled Red in a half-turn away from the wall, showed the horse the whip, took a double-grip on the reins, flicked on the current and touched Red under his tail.

Floweree felt the shock of terror flash through the horse and hauled hard on its head, talking low and reassuringly into the animal's ear—*"I see you, little bay horse, I see you."*

Big Red quieted and Floweree swung him out onto the track. It had taken him less than ten seconds to throw fear into Red; then to quiet him. yet the horse had come asweat.

Floweree cantered past the toteboard lights, keeping Red's head averted. The on-and-off flashes of the board increased Red's nervousness. By the time Floweree had gotten past the lights, the horse's neck was shining with sweat.

Floweree leaned forward toward the horse's ear, kneading the great neck with his free hand and asking softly, "You think it'll rain, old buddy? How would you like mud, old buddy?" Then patted the horse reassuringly. Mud would never come in time now.

A wind came drifting down from the heights and moved across the soybean field behind the toteboard. The whole field stirred.

And old sad scufflers, lifting their eyes, saw a full moon barely risen, looking down in mild surprise; on grandstand and clubhouse alike.

A moon that appeared to know, somehow before the toteboard itself knew, all possible daily-double payoffs.

Yet could not remember the last time it had rained.

ALLOWANCES

One Mile and 70 Yards

Track record: Ski's Lee 108 lbs. May 8, 1969—1:41

		Owner	Trainer	Jockey	Odds	Ask for Horse by This Number
Green, white circles, white sleeves	A	E. Ishop **Moon River**	J. Hightower 117	Elisio Casaflores	2	1
Green, gold diamond on back, green cuffs on red sleeves	A1	E. Ishop **Port-O-Pogo**	J. Hightower 120	Gabriel D'Arcia	2	1
White, red "J" on back, red bars and cuffs and sleeves	2	D. Vanenberg **Lady Night**	N. Nichols 113	Clarence Houssayen	13	2
White, red ball, black circle	3	K. Mulconnery **Red's Big Red**	M. Gibbons 116	Hollis Floweree	23	3
Red, white "H" on back, blue collar	4	C. Anastas **Djeddah's Folly**	J. Anastas 113	Julio Josohino	8	4
Orange on back, blue sleeves	5	V. Leone **Fleur Rouge**	H. Sierra 117	Hector Vaes	11	5
Yellow, royal blue diagonal stripes	6	S. Horowitz **Flying Indian**	H.L. Nieh 114	Troy Duryea	3	6
Black, orange diagonal stripes	7	C. Mathias **Flash Mc Bride**	I. Mais 115	Chas. Haerr	6	7

Quiniela   Windows   for   the   Fifth   Race   Will   Open   Immediately   After   This   Race
Becomes Official

JOCKEY STANDINGS

Jockey	1st	2nd	3rd
E. Casaflores	66	42	30
J. Josohino	31	14	34
C. Houssayen	30	14	32
G. D'Arcia	29	22	22
T. Duryea	26	22	32

Port-O-Pogo delayed the start of the third race by backing out of his gate every time D'Arcia had him halfway in. Two starters, in yellow raincoats against the imminent threat of rain, hauled at the horse, rump and mane, until they got its big rump locked in at last.

Sensing the tension building in Big Red since he'd gotten the electric touch, Floweree murmured, this time softly, into the horse's ear until the flag went up. Then he split the ear with a sudden shout—*"Get all the money!"* The affrighted horse leaped out a full jump ahead of the field, with Casaflores, D'Arcia and Houssayen on his tail neck and neck. Floweree cut to the rail.

Houssayen cut into Lady Night, veering her into Moon River's flank and Moon River went off stride. Floweree got the rail and Houssayen got it right behind him half a length ahead of D'Arcia. Houssayen kept the half length to the first turn then took his horse wide in order to draw D'Arcia wide—the whole field might follow wide.

It didn't work. D'Arcia let Houssayen go wide. Then got to the rail behind Floweree and began making up ground.

"Spinning out of the turn," the caller made it, "on the rail Red's Big Red by a half, Port-O-Pogo by two on the rail Djeddah's Folly, Flying Indian in the middle of the track by three Fleur Rouge by one Flash McBride Lady Night by four trailing the field Moon River."

Fearing to spend Red's strength too soon, Floweree wasn't letting him have full rein. The horse was running well. Houssayen, now far back, saw Big Red's tail begin to blow and knew he'd done his own job well: all Flower would have to do now would be to hold the horse to the rail until he made the turn for home; then let him out.

He'll make it by three, Houssayen judged the pace—nothing but Port-O-Pogo could catch him now. He saw Big Red beginning to draw away and instructed Floweree in his mind: "Not too soon, Flower; not too soon."

"Red's Big Red showing the way by two—two and a half—" the caller made it, "Port-O-Pogo on the rail in the middle of the track Djeddah's Folly and Flying Indian head and head by two and a half on the outside Fleur Rouge by four Flash McBride by three Lady Night"—then he got a laugh by adding, "the distant trailer Moon River with his tongue hanging out."

Now he ought to make it by four, Houssayen judged the final turn —then caught a flash of orange emerging from Port-O-Pogo's outside flank against D'Arcia's green—*"Look behind you, Flower!"*

He warned the rider in his mind. And as if Floweree had heard him he glanced back and saw Vaes coming.

Floweree stood in the irons, doubling the reins in his left hand and flashed the whip before Red's eyes—the horse took off as though freshly shocked. The big lights flashed like an explosion above the line, Big Red swerved and Vaes drove Fleur Rouge straight up onto Red's heels.

Fleur Rouge propped. Propelling a blue-orange streak over her head head-on against the rail. And raced on riderless.

Vaes lay face down with one boot hooked by the rail and his fingers spreading to get hold of earth. Then heard horses coming and put both hands to his ears.

Duryea stood in the irons to clear the fallen rider and the horse appeared to clear; its hind legs kicking dust against Vaes' goggles.

"Loose horse on the track," the caller appealed to the crowd, "please try to make as little noise as possible, ladies and gentlemen, so as not to frighten the animal"—as the great shout slowly died.

And a stillness came down upon grandstand and clubhouse like a great dark hand. Then a wind went about tossing drifts of rain into faces of all who were listening there: who didn't know what they were listening for; losers and winners alike. Yet all moved back, murmuring, to the sheltering stands.

"Ambulance to the finishing line," the caller added like a sorrowing afterthought.

Two groundkeepers raced to Vaes. One jumped the fence. But the other, a stout Negro wearing a red cap, tried to go under the rail and knocked the cap off. He bent to pick up the cap, appeared to falter; then picked up something else that he put in his raincoat pocket. He stood watching his colleague prying at Vaes' left boot to get it loose from the rail. He'd forgotten his cap.

"Take the boot *off*, dummy!" some railbird shouted.

"Don't move him!" a woman's voice cried warning. And her voice, so querulous and thin, brought troubled laughter; almost like derision, from the crowd.

The *Inquiry* lights began burning an angry red while the yellow figures blinked beneath:

3-5-5-3-3-5-5-3

The ambulance, blocked by horses being led to paddock for the fourth race, got onto the track at last. By the time the stretcher-bearers bore Vaes into the ambulance, the pony riders had reined Fleur Rouge.

"One thousand pairs of panty hose to the first thousand ladies through the gate next Thursday,'' the PA system reminded all bettors, ''make your wagers early.''

''A rider fell,'' a customer informed The Popcorn Woman, ''his haid hit the rail.''

''If his head hit the rail he'll lie still quite a spell,'' The Popcorn Woman decided with finality.

''The boys were riding rough right out of the gate,'' he added—''put some more butter on this stuff.''

''I don't care whether that bunch kills theirselfs off one by one or in a group,'' The Popcorn Woman assured him; adding a shot of oleo.

''He kept trying to raise his haid,'' the customer recalled.

''I can always tell a killer,'' The Popcorn Woman filled the customer in, ''because he don't have a sense of humor. And, if he does, he laughs all the time.''

The vasty hollows beneath the stands began ringing again with the cries of tipsheet-shouters. Paddock lamps burned in the heavy air like stars trying to burn themselves out.

''It must be an arfy-moon,'' the Popcorn Woman thought to herself, ''the outpatients are out in force.''

The ambulance siren had long faded before the toteboard lights at last stopped blinking. And the red OFFICIAL came on at last.

		Win	Place	Show
1.	1	$6.60	$4.00	$2.80
2.	4		$8.80	$4.80
3.	3			$8.80

Floweree dressed slowly. While D'Arcia was being photographed with Port-O-Pogo, he'd seen the Chief Starter handing a whip-handle to one of the stewards. ''I didn't even feel it leave my hand,'' he remembered. ''It must have bust against the rail.''

They'd let Kate pick up the purse for show money, anyhow. But there was no need, now, of hurrying about anything.

Framed photographs of forgotten riders, that lined the color-room walls, looked down at him. And though he'd always felt that he knew them all, they looked like total strangers now.

Walking, bareheaded, back to the barn area in the warm drizzling rain, the small lamps of the shed-rows shone like harbor lights in a fog. In the off-and-on drizzle he took shelter under a shed. Knowing that Kate would pass, cooling Big Red.

He heard the horse's hooves before he could make the animal out. They were almost up to him before he could make out Kate, in her flowered hat now sodden. He knew her slippers must be muddied. The horse was shining with rain or sweat. He stood under a lamp so she couldn't miss him; then he had nothing to say.

"Pay your own fine this time, rider," she let him know as she passed. And led the horse around the shed-row's corner.

"Kate!" he called after her. She stopped and turned about, waiting for him to speak.

"I'm glad Red didn't get hurt!" was all he could think to say. He felt her studying him in the dark.

"You'd fuck up a one-car funeral, mister," she told him at last. Then turned and led Red's Big Red away.

She'd be walking the horse for twenty minutes more, at least. That would give him time to get his clothes out of the trailer and be gone before she returned. If he didn't get his things on the sneak, he'd have to face her in the morning. Best to sneak it, he felt.

The naked light above the trailer was burning and she'd left the door unlocked. But when he entered all he saw, that was really his own, was a pair of rider's boots so down-at-heel they weren't worth toting around the country any longer.

He shut the door and turned back toward the stands. Headlights were swinging out of the parking lot. Bettors were already leaving.

He stood at the rail while the riders paraded the horses, for the final event, past the toteboard. Their silks were already darkened by the rain; as if the color of every stable was black against darkening grey against black. The course had changed from dust to slop; from fast to slow; slop was turning to mud.

It was a mile and sixteenth event. And when they came into the turn for home the lead horse was already splattering mud against the goggles of the rider behind him.

Had Big Red entered in the ninth, instead of the third event, he considered ruefully, he would have had no need of all that block-and-tackle work. There would have had to be no inquiry. Like everything else, mud came too late.

Then a visual image of himself came to him: He was standing, in his civvies, before a small table on which lay the broken half of an electrified whip. Faceless men stood around him. He forced the image out of his mind: that was one scene he'd never make. And turned from the rail as the riders, their pretty-day silks muddied, began returning to the jockey's room. He waited, in the shelter of the paddock, until they began coming out in their civvies, heading for the bars. He let them all pass, in the dark where he stood, until Troy Duryea came out; and called to him.

The boy peered into the dark to see who'd called to him.

"Hi, Dad," he recognized Floweree, "What's your story?"

"What's the word on Vaes?"

"Bad, Dad. Bad. Broke his back."

Duryea turned away—then swung suddenly about—"*My* horse cleared him," he absolved himself. A light high in the stands went out as he turned away. Others followed, as the apprentice moved toward the gate; one by one.

When the crowd is gone and lights go down—how strange a change! How ghostly a toteboard, where payoffs flashed past like boxcar numbers, when the board is shuttered, dark and still.

When no lights were left except those of the barn area, burning like lights in a shifting mist, Floweree stood at the rail and looked at the shuttered toteboard. The moon was a wan dying light. Behind it he heard the soybean field whisper faintly; as the rain began slanting across it. A line of horses, each one black and bearing a rider in black silks, began parading before the darkened board.

He counted eight horses, one by one. He looked for their numbers; but they wore none. He heard no sound of hooves; though he listened.

The lead rider broke into a canter straight into the soybean field. Behind him the others spurred their mounts to a canter and followed. Then the dim shrouding light went out. Darkness surged back across the moon.

The lights of the barn area, he saw, were the lights of a far-off country.

One he would never see again.

MOON OF THE ARFY DARFY

THE 9th race prices flash once and out: first SHOW; then PLACE; then WIN. the red OFFICIAL blinks once and goes dark. Winners and losers alike have left. Tipsheet-shouters and shoeboard watchers, touts and sellers, railbirds as well as the clubhouse cocktail set: all will be back at window and shoeboard, lounge and paddock, rail and boxes, when odds for the first race light up tomorrow.

Only the sweepers high in the seats remain in the vaulted, echoing stands.

Then along the rail, one eye cocked for security men, one man moves alone through the windy glooms.

He comes in a curious shuffle-and-pause through a litter of crushed lily cups. Comes kicking dead tickets, bad guesses and such, through the ruin of the day's million-dollar defeat: seeking a five-dollar victory to last him through the night.

"Hey you!"

He doesn't turn to see who's summoning him. Instead he scoops up a handful of tickets and hurries through the gate.

Where he leans one moment against the iron to take a whittled toothpick out of his shoe. Then moves on, without shuffle or kick, to wherever toothpick-shod men go.

The day's last stooper has finished his day. Whether he's made it or whether he hasn't, they'll run again tomorrow.

And a moon of the backstretch, still and white, peers around a corner of the stables; like a moon with a ruled-off rider's eyes.

A moon of the arfy-darfy.

Never to return.

I slipped the quarter into the box before the conductor could say "Hey! *You!*" How was it that, the time I beat Shoemaker, nobody said "Hey! *You!*"?

It wasn't Hey-You when I brought in Jealous Widow at 44-1. It was roses for The Widow and roses for me too. It was "Mr. Cannon's having a little party tonight, he'd like you to come." It was "Meet Mr. Cannon.

Mr. Cannon, meet Hollis Floweree." It was "Why couldn't you win on The Widow at Waterford but you bring her in in Evangeline Park, Mr. Floweree?"

"Because of the longer straightaway, sir," I answered Mr. Cannon.

I sat in the back of the bus running through a last handful of dead tickets. Bettors overlook winners. Nobody had missed a good thing in the handful I was holding. Yet I didn't throw one of them away.

It's a big comedown, from parading in front of the clubhouse in your pretty-day silks, to stooping for tickets people throw away by mistake. But I never stooped until the stands were empty. And nobody I used to know—at Waterford and Evangeline and Ozark Downs—had any idea that Sportsman's was my playground now.

Sometimes I'd spot somebody I used to know—but I'd keep on moving past and wait to see whether I looked familiar to *him*. The way I was dressed, and wearing shades, he'd need a closer look to be certain. *Much* closer.

And why should anyone want to look twice? I'd had my picture in *The Form* once—but who remembers *that?* I didn't really care any more, one way or another. When you come to the end it's the end, that's all.

And there were greater comedowns than my own. Like coming down from mounting favorites to wheeling yourself about in a hospital chair. *If* Vaes could afford a chair. On fifty bucks a month from the jockey's fund you don't get a name as a wild spender even in Mexico. It was time Vaes cut down on the whiskey and women anyhow.

How a Mexican jock was making it was the least of my troubles now. Had he fallen because I'd cut into him, or blocked him, it might have troubled me—I don't know. But trying to climb over me as he had, when I'd had that horse out front by a good length and a half, he'd brought his own fall on himself. Had he let me go under that wire I'd still be riding and so would he.

Can the front office suspend a rider who doesn't show up to get suspended? I suppose they can. They can do whatever they want. But there hadn't been any mention in the papers about it. Wouldn't they have to publish it in *The Form*? Maybe they had. If they had, Catfish would know.

The day I'd go looking up Catfish would be the same day I'd show up in front of the stewards. What *for?* I wasn't going to ride any-more—and that was a mortal deadlock for certain. I went up the aisle dropping tickets on empty seats one by one. I got off where Ogden crosses Fifth Avenue.

Six streets go six different ways at that intersection; with a bar every other door. One route, it looked like, had nothing *but* bar doors. The very route I was needing.

I saw the bums and I saw the nabs. I saw the hustlers and old-time scuffs. I saw people light as feathers. I saw people heavy as lead. I saw some made of water and some held by wires. One walked with a pocket full of fishhooks. Another had never had pockets at all. I saw those struggling to reach the top of some hill—and those trying to keep from reaching the bottom of a hill they'd come over too fast. Fireships, finks and coneroos; and an old-time hooker with her own ghost following. I saw round-the-block cruisers and hide-by-day-fly-by-nighties. It must be a full moon on the rise, I thought, the way the bings are coming out.

Two blind cane-bummies were taking up the middle of the walk in an argument. One jerked off his shades so he could see better who he was arguing with. "You've led five runs running," he accused the other bummy. "Yes—and I'll lead the next five, too!" the other told him who was the boss of the outfit—and the other went right for him with his cane. The boss-bummy slapped the cane flying and the other ran into the street to pick it up before it got run over; then put his shades back on. It looked like a Japanese movie.

"O *hell*," he came back complaining, "you lead *all* the time."

Who got to lead for the next five runs I didn't tarry to learn. Everyone in Chicago wants to be the front man. I walked on.

An oversized bison in a red turtleneck sweater, and his cap shading his eyes, rattled a collection box and tried to pin a paper heart on me— "Have a heart for little kiddies, buddy," he told me. What little kiddie did you slug to get that box, I wondered. Then he forgot the paper heart and played it straight:

"The price of one beer may save a life," he blocked my way to let me know; in a voice like a rowboat being dragged across pebbles.

"It'll take the price of six whiskies to save mine," I filled him in; and he saw my condition was worse than his own. He let me by.

When I glanced back he was looking after me. All I had to do was turn around and put out my hand and he would have put two bits into it. I walked on hoping he wasn't following.

"Hey soldier!"—I looked around to see who was calling on the military. It was a wino-broad in a doorway, and she was signaling *me*. "Hey soldier" was such an improvement over "Hey-*you*" that I threw back my shoulders and walked up to her.

"Drag my old man out of here," she gave me the orders of the day.

"Can't you do it yourself?"

"Ram declared me out of bounds."

"Who's Ram?"

She pointed one finger, sticking out of a torn glove, at a hand-lettered sign swinging between flowerpots, just overhead. Something that looked like it had once been a palm frond was stuck in one of the pots. Between the pots it said:

SOUTHSEA ISLE

R. Enright. Prop.

"I'll do what I can, Sis," I told her as an excuse to go inside.

Inside I saw that what Sis meant, when she'd said her old man was inside but she was out of bounds, was that he hadn't escaped. It was the people inside who were out of bounds. It looked like the place people come to when they want to go somewhere they never have to leave. I'd seen some caves in my day. But no cave like *this*.

The front bar was just one long narrow aisle that would have passed as the side-door to hell if it had ever been swept. The front bar was so dark all you could see was the bar mirror—and the back bar was darker than that.

Someone began banging a piano even farther back, accompanying himself. I felt my way, taking care not to brush against anyone on the stools —a light push against any one of them would roll him onto the floor on his head. And there he'd lay, just lay. I made it all the way to a bead-string portiere and then I stepped through the beads.

Everyone in that room looked at me as if I'd been sent for. Especially the piano-man.

Wanted man in California

he was singing. Then he nodded at me like he wondered why I'd kept him waiting so long. I looked down to see if I were standing on somebody who'd just been killed. I'd never seen the cat in my life before.

Outside the circle of blue-green light around the piano-man, was nothing but a sinking gloom. Where little white faces rose real slow then sank back into the gloom.

All I could smell was a pit where tigers lived without room to pace. All I could hear, beneath the piano's beat, was a breathing—breathing.

Like every breath was the last.

I began to distinguish figures. Cats who couldn't stay on the front-bar stools any longer had been assigned to lean on walls back here—

Wanted man in old Cheyenne—

he stopped playing yet the voice went on—

Wherever you might look tonight
You might see The Wanted Man—

A record-mimic no less. I'd been listening to Johnny Cash. This time when he nodded I went over: he *couldn't* be anyone I'd ever met.

"It's all too easy now," he told me like he knew all about me. He read me right. For I knew the feeling he had in mind.

I know how it feels, when things have come so hard, to have them come so easy for those who come later. We mucked out stalls, hauled water, walked hots and cooled horses and calmed horses until we smelled of horse ourselves. It was three years before I got to gallop one. I knew how *that* felt, that first gallop. I'd earned it. Now it's a couple months and they give a kid a contract. He sits on top and thinks he's race-riding and don't even rate the horse. Rides him like his contract is for one race, so he got to be first out of the gate. I've even seen them whip a horse coming out of the gate. All he knows is to make his horse run faster than the others so they'll put a wreath around the horse and maybe one around him too. It *is* all too easy now.

Don't breathe it to nobody
'Cause you know I'm on the lam—
The lam-the lam-the lam-the lam—

the needle had hit a crack yet he kept grimacing with the crack. Then he took off his shades, bent down and switched the record off.

"That's *my* trade, friend," he told me. "What's yours?"

"I see what you mean," I told him.

Suddenly squatting, eyes shut tight, he began a rocking on his toes in that misty green light, clasping his knees, making some sort of old-time singsong deep in his throat in time with his rocking. He leaped up. "Now I got to get to *work*!"

Just like that. Crooks a finger at me, tells me what it used to be like, makes like Johnny Cash, gives an impersonation of a Chinaman kicking cold turkey; then blows me off. I stood around to see what he meant by going to work. But he didn't start the record-mimic routine again.

He had a tambourine on that box and just pounded away on things like *Blue Moon* and *Cocktails for Two* and *Chinatown*. Until a woman came walking like she was held together by Band-Aids, dropped a dime in the tambourine and went back to where she'd been hiding before the Band-Aids had come loose.

"If I put down a dime for *that* kind of banging," I let him know between productions, "I'd never be able to face my friends again."

Then I walked away.

"How are they?" he called after me.

I turned around and asked, "How are who?"

"Your friends," he told me and began singing in his own frog-croak.

Somebody had just fallen off a stool at the front bar. He was lying on the floor. I stepped over him and sat down.

Two of the bartenders' aprons were dirty. Neither stopped rushing whiskey and beer. The third fellow's apron was stainless. He stood to one side and counted the house. If somebody who was lying on the floor didn't get up inside half an hour, he pointed the body out to the bartenders; who then got it to its feet and out the back door. When somebody got thrown out the back door three times in one night, he was barred from coming in the front door for a week.

The fellow with the clean apron, it was easy to see, was the one who decided "Out you go" or "Have one on the house." There was no trouble spotting R. Enright, Proprietor.

I didn't bang the bar for service. I just sat and waited. Finally Enright strolled over, took off my shades and handed them back to me. I didn't put them back on. I didn't ask for an explanation.

"I've seen you before," he told me, "but I don't quite make you."

"I've seen you before too," I told him, "and I'd rather not make you."

He put a bottle of Cutty on the bar in front of me, washed a glass with his own hands, iced it and put it down beside the bottle.

"On the house," he told me; and walked away.

A country-type girl, wearing a green babushka, two bar stools away, observed Enright's move and studied me in the bar mirror. She began beefing to Enright while looking at me.

"These Chicago broads," she told him, "you know what one of them *Fireball* fools tried to tell me—'*I* started the babushka fad around here' she tried to tell me."

Enright looked like he'd heard all this before.

"The very *nerve! I* was wearing a babushka two years ago in L.A.

357

I was the one brought it around here and *they* think wearing a babushka gives them *class*. Honest to God, broads like *that* must drink out of their old man's shaving cup."

Enright wasn't listening. He'd tuned her out. But he was still tuned in on me. Seeing I wasn't using his bottle, he came over and pushed it toward me. That was when I began to gather that he had something in mind; something into which I fitted.

I could have knocked that bottle off without setting it down. I hadn't been on a drunk since the night I'd left Ozark Downs. But I let it stand. I wasn't going to drink the man's whiskey until I knew what he had in mind. The one thing I learned from riding horses was control; and control is all I've kept.

I caught Green Babushka's eye. "Can I offer you a drink?" I asked her.

"I buy my own drinks," she told me. "Do you want to say hello?"

I couldn't remember ever having been brushed off faster. A hooker who knows her lines that well has a pretty solid pimp behind her.

"That finky cop," she began again on Enright—"you know that one directs Saturday morning traffic on Warren and California? I was carrying my old man's pants to the cleaners 'n you know what that clown asked me?"

Enright didn't know and cared less.

"He asked me 'Baby, is them *my* size?' Just like that."

"What'd you tell him?" Enright went along.

" 'They're too small for you,' was all I could think to say. It was just the way he *said* it—like he *knew* me—that burned me."

"He does know you," I filled her in, "he was giving you a pass."

"Go ride your horse," she told me.

I knew then Enright had made me. There was no other way of Green Babushka knowing I was a rider unless Enright had filled somebody in. I had the feeling I wanted to move on; but not to leave. So I moseyed on toward the back bar and stood next to a hooker about twice the age of the country-type at the front bar. That was why she was at the back bar. All I could make out of her face, in the dimness, was that it was squarish; and that her hair had been tinted gray to cover up that underneath it was gray.

"I'm Zaza," she told me without being asked, "if you don't want to say hello, it's alright with me. If you don't want to buy me a drink, that's alright, too. But if you do want to buy me one I won't stop you."

"What kind of accent is that?" I asked her—"Or are you putting it on?"

"French-Canadian," she told me, "or rather, *Canadienne*."

The way sounds carry in Enright's Southsea Isle is something I've yet to understand. Although the woman was talking in a whiskey-whisper, Enright was right there with the bottle I'd left on the front bar.

"On the house, Rider," he told me as if he thought I might have misunderstood him the first time.

"I've never seen Ram chase a customer from bar to bar with a house bottle before," Zaza told me—"What are you—a VIP or something?"

"I think the man has me mixed with somebody else," I told her, "I've never even been in this cave before. Well, drink up." I poured her a double-shot and a single for myself.

"Is he a horse degenerate?" I asked her.

"Not hardly. He wouldn't bet on a one-horse race, not Ram. But he books them."

The record-mimic in the back room started up again.

"Well," I decided, looking around, "I suppose now and then a loser does come in here by mistake."

She laughed in her throat.

"These cats weren't victims of circumstance, if that's what you mean," she told me, "bad luck is what they *live* for. They couldn't *bear* being a winner."

"Include me out," I straightened her out, "I'm a loser but not because I *like* it."

"What difference does that make?"

"I'll tell you what difference it makes," I told her, "it means that, the next time you see me, I'll be a winner."

"Then you won't come in here," she told me, "you'll look up other winners. If you come in here it'll mean you can't stand being a winner neither."

"This is where the record hits the crack," I let her know what was coming—

> *Don't breathe it to nobody*
> *'Cause you know I'm on the lam*
> *The lam-the lam-the lam-the lam—*

"I think that fool has hit a crack himself," I told Zaza.

"I know," she agreed, "he's my old man."

I poured her another but not any for myself. I kept myself from asking her "What *for?*" But I wasn't about to take back calling that fool a fool.

"He only plays the fool around the piano," she took me up, "that don't mean he's a *real* fool."

"He's chained," I explained, "somebody has him chained. That makes him a *real* fool."

"We're all chained to something," she told me, studying her glass, "he's chained to the piano and I'm chained to him. What are *you* chained to?"

"The piano isn't all he's chained to," I had to point out. I had the feeling that something was starting here that I could do without. I decided to put it in the open and then clear out. "Are you on, too?"

She didn't even get mad.

"No," she told me, "as a matter of fact I'm not even chained to *this*—" she nodded toward the bottle.

"Then you're *both* real fools," I made up my mind. And put on my cap.

She looked me up and down from my scuffed shoes to my jacket out under the arms. She even looked at my little wool seaman's cap.

"It's plain to be seen you're not a man who makes mistakes himself." She'd figured that out by herself.

Enright tried to pour me another but I kept my hand across the glass.

"I've got something for you, Rider," he told me at last.

"Tell me about it tomorrow," I told him. And left feeling sure I'd never be back.

I bought a chickenwire cubbyhole at the Hotel McCoy for fifty cents that night. But thinking about the way that old hooker had looked me up and down kept me tossing.

I felt a change in luck coming at the combination window, the next day, just before the fourth race was off. The dude in front of me said "two dollars on number eight three times." The seller punched him a combination and the beef began. The dude didn't want Place or Show. He just wanted Win. The seller pointed to the sign: *Combination*. The dude walked off not knowing what he was holding. I kept him in view.

Number Eight ran second. The dude howled with disappointment, threw his tickets down and went to complain to a bartender. I could have run after him and told him the seller had done him a good turn: that he had Place money as well as Show. By the time I'd picked up his tickets he was gone.

I picked up twenty-one bucks and sat down next to a big old darky gal and asked her how she was doing.

"I dreamed number five last night," she told me, "today I bet four races 'n no number five win yet. Now I know, fifth race *got* to be number five.''

I took her program out of her hand—"That's the very reason number five *can't* win," I told her like I knew something she didn't know. *"There's* your winner—I got to do it with *your* pencil"—and circled Mom's Request. What did I have to lose?

Mom's Request broke in front, drew away and was home free: eighteen dollars straight.

I didn't ask the old girl for anything. And all she said was "Mind my seat." Like she was sure I would.

When she came back she handed me a five-dollar ticket, on number five, Ilo-Ilo, to win. I was sorry she hadn't just handed me the fiver. I never would have bet it on Ilo-Ilo. I excused myself and moved down to the far end of the bleachers, at the turn for home. We'd done all we could for one another.

Ilo-Ilo, Skoronski up, broke behind the pack, made up ground at the far turn and began moving up. Skoronski let him out right in front of me. I picked up $32.80. I spent a buck for a *Form* and huddled with it next to the paddock.

The next couple races were maiden races; which I never bet. But the seventh had what I was looking for. *Popcorn Bummy*, a mile and a sixteenth, Troy Duryea up. That was the one horse Duryea knew how to handle. I went down to the saddling to get a peek at both Popcorn and Duryea.

Popcorn looked fit and Duryea looked taller, somehow, than he used to be. Maybe because he wasn't an apprentice anymore. The horse was on the board at 11-1 and it didn't drop. I waited until Duryea had him in the gate. Then I put twenty on the nose.

Duryea didn't try to take him out front, as he used to do at Ozark. He laid back fourth and laid back so long I thought he might be waiting *too* long. Then he began inching up, had him neck and neck at the turn, and let him out at the eight-pole. Under by two full lengths. A beautiful ride. Troy Duryea had become a real race-rider. I wasn't about to wait around the jock's room to shake his hand. I picked up $268.00 and headed for the gate. I'd be sleeping in a bed without chickenwire overhead this night.

I was back in business.

"You're looking sharp, Floweree," Enright spoke up the minute he spotted me.

"Why not?"

In sports slacks, a zippy sports jacket, new half-boots and a shave and a haircut, why not admit I was sharp?

Green Babushka was in some sort of hassle with a pimpy-looking character who came on like he thought he looked like Steve Lawrence but he looked more like Spike Jones to me. I heard her call him Daddy but I didn't ask her to introduce me. Then I leaned on the backbar, two stools away from Zaza, just to let her get a full view of the new me. She didn't register amazement and delight. In fact she didn't even look as though it made any difference to her how I was dressed.

Whatever Enright had for me, he'd have to come to me. I made no move, except to lean on the bar behind my shades, until he came up. He didn't bring the house-bottle. He knew now I wasn't going to drink his whiskey without knowing what he wanted from me.

"You're looking better than when you hit here, Floweree," he told me. I just looked at him from behind the shades.

"Can we talk?" he wanted to know. I nodded. He could start talking whenever he wanted. I was ready to listen. He motioned me to the corner of the bar and talked with his head turned away from the barflies. But I think Zaza was listening.

"You know that thing Skoronski been riding?" he wanted to know.

"Skoronski been riding lots of things. He brought in a 11-1 shot today."

"Flamisan."

"It don't matter who's riding *that*," I knew, "the horse is part eagle. There's nothing stabled out there can run with him. They'll put 136 pounds on him the next time out and that still won't get anybody in his right mind to bet against him. He'll be off at 3-5 is my guess."

"I got a party will put up five bills to have Flamisan run no worse than second."

"Second to *what?*"

"Second to *anything*. That's *his* business. Look—"Enright looked ready to scold me for not taking him seriously—"he's been in here every night for a week. I been holding him for you."

"Does he know me?" I asked Enright.

"He don't know you from Ezra Taft Benson."

"Who's Ezra Taft Benson?"

"No matter. What I'm driving at is he don't know you, he don't know Skoronski either. Does anyone around the paddock know you?"

"I rode with some of those people."

"Good. Then they won't bother you."

362

"I don't get your drift, Enright," I told him; although I *was* beginning to get it.

Enright drew back as if to study me from a distance. I let him study away. Zaza was studying both of us.

"*You're* Skoronski," Enright finally let me have it.

"Okay," I went along, "I'm Skoronski. And you're Ezra Taft Benson. What do we do now—play unnatural games?"

Enright shrugged. He'd said all he had to say. It was my move.

The impersonation bit has been worked around stables since people began to bet on horses. But there's always somebody who hasn't heard of it. Usually from Omaha.

"I'll think it over and let you know," I told Enright. Then I slid off the stool and went to see what the piano-fool was up to.

He was *still* doing Johnny Cash.

When Enright took me to him I was wearing my pretty-day silks, shades, and a whip tied to my hand. We met him behind Skoronski's barn.

He was a big-hand, big-belly, big-laugh old boy full of the jollies, on the surface. Underneath he never stopped counting the house. The ten-gallon hat, the shirt covered with rose-petals and the badge I'M FROM OMAHA was all part of his act. He was probably from The Bronx. He was Omaha all the same. He was *all* Omaha.

He was so hungry to make a killing that I *had* to be Skoronski. I gave him the Skoronski shake—as cold a piece of skin as he'd ever felt.

"Yew knaow what kin run fastern's a horse?" was his idea of opening a conversation about fixing a horse-race.

"What runs faster than a horse, Amos?" Enright humored him.

"A pig!" Amos let us know.

"A *pig?*" Enright asked, feigning astonishment.

"*Shor!* For the first thutty feet! Yak!Yak!"

Enright pretended to laugh. I didn't even try. I tipped Enright the wink to let me handle Amos. I don't think he went far.

"Was there something you wanted to see me about?" I asked Amos, flicking my little whip.

Amos dropped the jolly-boy routine and got into it.

"I think something is going to outrun that thing you're riding," he told me.

"Then you better bet against me," I suggested.

"It's what I *want* to do. But a man wants to be *shor.*"

"Nothing's sure in a horse race, mister."

"Step over here, son," he asked me. We went over to a shadow of the stable.

"I can't hang around here long, mister," I told him, "I'm supposed to be up in the color-room right now. My mount is even money and dropping."

"If your mount should lose stride—" he faltered.

"He won't, mister," I told him.

"*You're* on his back," he reminded me—and he had it ready. Five C-notes. I didn't touch it.

"It's worth eight."

"What it's worth 'n what I got are two different things, son." Now he was begging. But I knew there was more where that came from. I turned to go.

"Six is high as I can go," he called me back.

"Six-fifty."

He counted out six-fifty but he must have palmed the fifty. Because when I found Enright six bills was all I had. I felt better that Amos had held back on me. I showed Enright the six and handed him three.

"You were great in there," Enright told me.

"You think the guy will lay for Skoronski?" I wondered; though I didn't really care.

"He won't lay for Skoronski. He'll lay for me," Enright told me. "Give him a couple of days to get back to Omaha before you come in again. He might put it together if he sees you again." But I could see Enright liked the idea of the mark making a beef on his own territory.

I wondered how much the mark had bet against Flamisan.

Flamisan, the *Form* described the race, *in hand while placed on the inside, was forced to come out and circle the field on completing the first mile, continuing gamely to take a commanding lead through the upper stretch. Won driving.*

It looked like a rainy day in Omaha.

When toteboard lights go blind with dusk
And other losers have gone home
Above the grandstand's damps and glooms
A moon of the backstretch on the wane
Sees a rider whose silks are long outworn.

Whose hands once guided whose wrists once eased
Whose fingers could gentle or warn or praise

Whose hands that commanded have nothing to do
But riffle dead tickets like bad guesses through.

A moon with a ruled-off rider's eyes
Lights his way to those rain-caves and night-blue dives
Nine steps under the traffic's cries
Where raggified ruins and draggified queers
Emerge from The-Street-Where-Nobody-Cares:
Begoggled young bandrats with boozified squares
Do-Wrongies, Do-Righties with coppers turned kuke
Mascaraed martyrs with maybellined spooks
To a furlong of stiffs in a swizzlestick cave
Where triumphs don't matter just losses remain
Left at the starting gate all's one and the same
For it isn't cats who kill and drag out
Who are ever in charge on the Kiss-And-Claw Route.
Virgin or viper, thistle or flower
Who come at the close to the same night-blue hour
Where fists count the most but money counts more.

> *Can't you tell by the breathing breathing*
> *And the smiles that drain through gin*
> *Can't you tell by the smell*
> *Of this swizzlestick hell*
> *The name of the place you're in?*

Whose gains are on paper whose losses are cash
To fevered informers or pandering cats
Where whiskey is free to all who've just died
(Others pay double though barely alive)
Teatalking strippers with compulsive old lechers
(The stick and the raging arrive in all weathers)
Keybroad and callbroad, cruiser or tout
Careless or wary, shut in or shut out
Straightbroad, boothbroad, headbroad and plain whore:
Each waits where she's caught on the Kiss-And-Claw tour.
Where fists count the most but money counts more.

Yet not one knows the name of this understair dive
Where none are seen leaving yet new ones arrive
Where each stirs his bourbon yet none chunk the ice

Each pays his money yet none ask the price
Some made of water and some held by wire
Some with their green years yet afire
Each dressed for a ball though draped for the grave
None speak the name of this night-blue cave.

> *Through sunlight bright as seconal*
> *Through twilights swept by snow—*
> *Can't you see by the gloom*
> *Of a blue paper moon*
> *These are Christ's poor damned cats*
> *Who'll never see home?*

On a stretch stretching back into dreams now done
The old jock hears the hooves of races long run
Here among cats of various stripe
Some on the heavy and some on the hype
He beats the bar with a swizzlestick click—
"Bartender! Booze! And fetch it damned quick!"
Then takes it straight till he's stoned to the bricks.
When you come to the end it's the end that's all
Where fists count the most but money counts all—
Don't you know that the cats who kill and drag out
Are never in charge of the Kiss-And-Claw Route?

WATCH OUT FOR DADDY

1. *That day so still so burning*

By the brought-down look of that gas-plate trap you'd scarcely have guessed it was the best deal we'd had yet. Everybody in L.A. was driving convertibles and us two fools thinking if a place had a rag carpet it had true class. This place had a carpet and cups, too. I was glad not to have to drink out of that shaving mug any more.

I got a job car-hopping but Daddy is too hard of hearing to do much along those lines himself. His right ear is as good as anyone's, but the left is the one the guard at Industrial bust. What Daddy is best at is just hanging around the house in his tattery shorts with a stick of tea in his teeth.

Now and then he'd make a deal with a Mexican for half a can of backyard tea, double-wrap it and sell it to some other hill-billy as the pure Panama. That way we'd catch up on the rent and have enough left for a bottle of gin.

Other times people paid Daddy off in a pair of two-tone shoes the wrong size or a wristwatch with a home-made hairspring for me. "Daddy," I told him at last, "this stuff is nowhere. Why take just *anything?*"

"For that grade of pot you're lucky to get just anything."

"But all you get is junk. Sheer junk."

"I'll take that too if I can get my hooks into it," he told me.

I was still that simple I didn't know what he meant.

I found out in due course. In that same room right under the roof where you had to battle for every breath.

On that day so still so burning.

I woke up with a lawnmower that had one blade missing ricketing around the room, cutting corners and coming back. It took me a full minute to realize the racket was all inside my head. I was face-down on the sofa with a hangover like a cliff.

I could feel my arm just hanging. And the watch with the homemade hairspring, that hadn't run for days, hanging onto my wrist. Everything in that room was just hanging on. Everything in the world needed fixing.

"If I'm going to wake up feeling like this," I told him, "I might as well drink whiskey."

"You start on that again, Little Baby, you'll be drunk again before night."

"What makes me sick will cure me," I told him. It was what he'd so often told me.

"There's better cures than whiskey, Beth-Mary," he pulled a switch on me.

"If submitting to that spike in your pocket is what you're driving at, forget it," I told him, "I'd sooner do without care."

"I'm not asking you to undergo anything at my hands I'm not willing to undergo at yours."

"I don't want you to undergo a thing at my hands," I told him, "I don't want to punch holes in your hide—why punch holes in mine?"

He come to sit beside me on the horsehair sofa and took my hand in his own.

"Baby," he told me, "Little Baby. Once we agreed that I was to take care of you in the big things and you were to take care of me in the little ones."

"But why begin with the *big* ones, Little Daddy?" I asked. For at sight of that needle my strength simply drained.

"What kind of man do you think I am? You think I want to see my little wife go to work sick? Don't she deserve my care?"

"Daddy," I told him with what strength I had, "you'll be more sorry than you now know if you do me this way. For your own heart's sake, don't do me this way."

"Baby," he told me, "a fact is a fact. And today's fact is, are you going to work sick or well?"

There wasn't any question of not going to work at all. I'd already missed one day's car-hopping. When you missed two they automatically de-hopped you.

"Fair is only fair, Beth-Mary," he told me," so hold out your pretty arm."

Fair *is* fair. And a fact *is* a fact. Yet I didn't hold out my arm. I just let him have it, he took it so gentle. He hadn't been gentle in so long. He began stroking the down, up and down. Watch out for Christian Kindred when he starts being gentle.

"Don't jerk, Little Baby," he told me so soft—and no sooner had he said it than my arm jerked of itself and jerked the whole outfit clean out of his hand and left the needle shivering in my hide. I hadn't got Drop the First.

"Blowing a whole sixteenth! Fool! After what I distinctly *told* you"—Daddy went into a simply terrible huff—"you realize you just cost us two-seventy-five?" How that child did huff and puff about my spendthrift ways.

In that room so close so burning.

We couldn't afford to blow another two-seventy-five, that was plain. So I looked the other way for the sake of thrift. And felt a gentle *whoof*, like someone had touched my heart. And felt the gentlest tingle; like someone saying "Darling."

That was all. But Daddy felt much better.

"Was that the real thing, Daddy?" I asked. For somehow I'd expected something far greater.

"It's the real thing alright, Little Baby."

Us two fools. We didn't either us know what the real thing was. "Lucky for you we had a sixteenth-grain left in the paper," Daddy told me, "lucky for you that needle didn't snap when you blew the shot. God must have his arms around you, girl, that's the only way I can figure it."

Somebody got his arms around me alright but I'd hate to think it's the party he claims. The minute I got my blouse off that night he banged me again. "That one is history, Baby"—like that he said it. As if he'd been lying in wait all day just to bang me.

"That one is history"—I didn't know what he meant till it brought me up deathly sick over the wash basin.

"Why, it wasn't no bigger shot than the first," he pretended he couldn't for the life of him figure that one out—"it was only a sixteenth-grain, Little Baby."

"It may have been only a sixteenth, Little Daddy, but it was into the vein and the first was just into the skin." I let him know I was on. "A fact is a fact," I reminded him.

"What makes you sick will cure you," *he* reminded *me*. And grinned. Just *grinned*.

The way that boy makes history on my hide since, he ought to be a professor in a school. What if that vein collapses? Will History collapse, too? O, I forgive him for the money he threw away like it was afire! the clothes he hocked to get more money that were my clothes. I can forgive him for making me do time for him.

After all, if he made a whore out of me, I made a pimp out of him.

If I did time for him, he done time for me. If he hocked *my* clothes to support his habit, I've hocked his to support mine.

For Little Daddy, much as he likes to dig, never digs too deep. He never fools with that one spot in my heart where I'll never forgive him ever. For all his brags he has never yet said to me, "Baby, who took you from your baby?"

Little Daddy, the day you say that to me will be the day I'll take my turn on you. And I won't stop with banging you. I'll bone you like a fish.

Little Daddy wants someone to give him credit for something so bad, but I don't give him Credit the First. Why make things easy for him? Since when did he ever make things easy for me?

"You were a hare on the mountain," he'll brag right to my face, "when I fired your way you were done for."

"I was done for before ever you took aim, Little Daddy," I have to remind him, "every sport in town was firing my way two years before you came calling, bringing me caramel candy like I'd never seen the back room of a bar. Little Daddy, I felt sorry for you with your haircut out of Boys' Industrial and the town sports laughing because you thought nothing had changed since you'd gone. You made it so *plain*, Little Daddy.

"But I weren't no hare on the mountain. I'd been pigmeat two whole years."

"Who made a *whoor* out of you? Who turned you out?"

O, it goes right through me when he says *whoor* like that. And well he knows it. "Little Daddy," I tell him sweet as sugar candy, "don't trouble your poor heart so. I did it to send money back for the baby's care, nothing more. All you done was tell me what a fair price was for the product I was marketing. For that I'm still grateful to you."

"You were against working with a sponge when your time came around," he keeps trying, "but I made you work with one all the same. Who ever treated his old lady harder than *that*?"

"If I hadn't worked through how would I have made enough money to keep my Little Daddy knocked out?" I ask him. And pat his little cheek.

He slaps down my hand, peevey boy—"Baby, who made a dope fiend out of you?"

He'll get that needle under my hide in more senses than one.

"I don't consider myself a fiend about dope or anything else," I'm

370

forced to point out to him. "I've taken a little liking to the stuff and don't know how to quit, that's all."

"Then you're not actually *against* it, Baby?" And grins. Just *grins*.

"I'm against it in my heart, Little Daddy. Right there's the difference between me and you."

"That's what I like so much about you, Beth-Mary," he tells me, "your mind is so weak."

"I know I can't ever be so strong as *you*, Little Daddy," I have to admit to him, "for I'm not so weak to begin."

"Then take your own chances and suffer the consequences," he says.

I'm suffering the consequences every hour since that day on South San P. Street.

That day so still so burning.

2. Watch Out for Daddy

"Stuff is making a regular little go-getter out of you, Baby," my Daddy begun getting proud of me the hour we got off San P. Street, "now all you need to get is a little know-how."

"Daddy, I already know how," I told him.

"You know how all right but you don't know with who. Your small-town ways don't fit out here. Don't *ever* tell a trick you're married and have a baby daughter. You don't ask him to buy you a drink. You don't drink with him at all. You ask him does he want to play house or not? Buy your own drink, Baby. Don't you want to be real great? Don't you want to keep your Daddy knocked out?"

We got so great, shortly thereafter, that we were both kept knocked out. Every time we walked into a joint someone was sure to holler, "Look who's here!" Usually the bartender. Everybody with class was hollering hello. I got over being bashful and advanced clear to the Anxious-to-Please stage. "Are you satisfied, Mister? You're not disappointed?"

And Daddy got even more anxious than me. "Are you *alright*, Baby?" He'd sneak me a fast whisper from behind a potted palm in the lobby where he had no right whatsoever to be—"You want to go home and rest now? You tired, Baby?"

You call *that* a pimp?

"Baby, did that cat act married-like? Does he want to see you again? How did he come on, Baby? Fairly great or so?"

"Not too bad," I answered offhanded one time—"as a matter of fact, not bad at all."

"Why don't you marry the man for God's sake then?" he turned on me—"*I* won't stand in your way! *Imagine* it—a hustler falling in love with one of her own tricks! And you can call yourself a *whore?* Why, I think you *like* this trade."

He'd never said a thing that hard to me before.

"I'll go back to car-hopping tomorrow," I told him. "I think I make as sorry a whore as you make a macker."

That hurt *his* feelings.

"No wife of mine is going to be seen hustling hamburgers," he got real stern to make himself out the real thing in mackers.

And I never answered him so offhand again. "Daddy, that fellow was just no good whatsoever," I'd report, "if he got an old lady I'm sorry for her."

After a spell Daddy just stopped asking. And I just minded my own peace and didn't use so much platinum nail polish.

L.A. people like a young country-looking couple. There were gifts almost every day. Ankle-bracelets and earrings and perfume for me and nylon shorts for my Daddy. Right up to the end, everyone tried to help. Even the old clerk at the desk tried to warn us the night Daddy came into the lobby with an envelope in his topcoat pocket.

"A message for you," he told Daddy—and scribbled *nabs* on a phone slip. Daddy folded the slip without looking at it. It was still in his hand when I opened for him and they followed in like I'd opened for them.

One on each side, patting Daddy all over, and Daddy giving them the wrong pocket every time he turned. I set tight as a little gray mouse. You do yourself nothing but harm to ask, "Where's your warrant?" They'll tell you, "We don't need one for a rooming house." You can tell them, "This ain't no rooming house this is a hotel" then if you want. But one will wait while the other fetches and they'll make the warrant stick then if they have to plant something to do it. Well, you asked for it.

"Everything us two kids own in this world is right in that there grip, mister," Daddy told them and got rid of his coat on the bed.

There wasn't anything but old clothes in the grip, and that was right when Daddy got his real good chance. He had two C-notes in his fly and one of the nabs went into the bedroom. All daddy had to do then was pick that envelope out of the coat pocket, hand the nabber left alone with us one of the C's and flush the tea down the toilet. Only the other came back just then and he was the one found the right pocket at last. He tried a seed on the very tip of his big cow-tongue—"What's this?" he asked the other clown.

"I'm sure I don't know," Daddy told him, "I never seen it before."
But he looked just *so* all in.

All we could hope for was the stop-warrant from Kentucky wouldn't show up in court.

I remember His Honor putting his glasses on to see how come Daddy done two years so young. They were the rimless kind. "Two murderous fights in two years," His Honor told himself, out loud.

If he had just asked *me* what had happened, I would of told him. Then he wouldn't have had to read all that paper.

When my Daddy came out of Boys' Industrial and began courting me, how he battled everyone he thought had courted me before! Even though all I was was the first sight he saw wearing a dress. Yet them evil town-boys had only to name some country boy like he'd had a roll-in-the-meadow with me and Daddy would whup that boy, no questions asked. But the kids he whupped were the ones who'd had no more fun with me than that of walking me home from vesper services. All I hoped was one of them boys wouldn't be so mean as to bring up the name of the Morganfield boy.

He was the one I started to lewdlin' with and it got out of hand—yet I hadn't set eye on him since Christian had begun courtin' me. Fact is it wasn't but a bare ten days between that last night with the Morganfield boy and my first all-night night with Christian. Seven months after, it wasn't a certainty in my mind to which one of them boys I owed my condition. But of course I chose Daddy. I've *always* had good taste.

When I seen Daddy waiting by the pinball machines I tried to get him out of the bar. But he lit up the machine and paid me no mind. No mind at all. When the Morganfield boy came in and seen Daddy, he knew who Daddy was waiting for, too.

I asked the bartender to help me get Daddy out. Or the Morganfield boy either one. And the Morganfield boy would have been more than happy to leave; but for the way he'd look in the eyes of others. "Leave them have it out," the bartender told me.

"I recommend *you* to leave," Daddy gave me orders. But I got no farther than to go through that bar door. Something held me outside. I knew what was going to happen in there.

Daddy has his own ways. He didn't so much as reproach that boy. He simply invited him to a game of pinball.

They played several games, so I was later told, with the Morganfield boy playing to lose, until Daddy accused him of tilting. The Morganfield boy just shook his head knowing it was no use denying anything.

"You ain't by way of being much a man, are you?" Daddy then put it to him; and that the boy was forced to deny. I was standing outside the door when I heard the bartender turn the key in the lock.

The Morganfield boy must have heard it turn, too. It was the last key he ever heard turn. He lingered a week after that beating then died in the night.

A week after, I had my girl-baby. The very spitting image of Christian.

Christian won a plea of self-defense in the same courtroom; the same week I gave the baby up for adoption.

Ten days later we were riding a moving van into L.A.

His Honor didn't have to keep his specs on any longer. He'd read enough for a spell. "Young man, I think you're a Menace to Society," and by the way he snapped that glass case shut I knew that was what he'd really been wanting to say all along. He had his excuse.

"I think society is a menace to my Daddy"—it was out before I could bite my tongue. Because that was what *I'd* been wanting to say all along.

"Prisoner remanded in lieu of bail. Cash bond set at five hundred dollars. Case continued till Thursday at nine." He was really going to give it to my Daddy Thursday at nine.

Forty-eight hours to raise half a grand. It could never be done by turning tricks even at the outrageous prices I charged.

"If you tell me to go for the sodium amytal, I'll go," I told him, for I'd worked with knockout drops when we were hard pressed once before. It isn't my line. But when it comes down to a matter of Daddy's freedom I can do anything.

Daddy forbade me. "Forget the rough stuff, Baby. If you slipped we'd both be busted. Just get what you can on your coat. Then what you can on your watch. You don't actually *need* that Japanese kimono. If there ain't half a grand hanging in your closet I miss my guess. Only don't dump it all in one joint," he warned me. "Spread it around so it don't look like we're thinking of blowing town or nothing like that."

My coat. *My* watch. *My* kimono. Not one word about *his* coat, *his* watch, *his* raw silk pajamas or *his* red silk foulard robe. That child is so jealous of his clothes he can scarcely bear to part with a button if it's pearl.

I spread the stuff around like he told me. Half a bill for his topcoat. Another for his watch and ring. I only got twenty for the foulard robe. I didn't begin to spread my own things till his were gone. I got the half a grand up without losing either my Longine or my chubby. Daddy got to sign his bond just before midnight Wednesday.

But O that long walk down the courthouse corridor, with an eyedropper hype in one cup of my bra and a bottle of dolaphine with a five-spot wrapped around it in the other before we made the open street.

As soon as we made it he wants to grab a cab back to the hotel for his clothes. My own coat was hanging over my arm.

"I got a sneak-hunch somebody's waitin' for us there," I lied. Because I know how he respects my sneak-hunches.

"Why?"

"I don't know. But I won't go back."

"I take your word only because I *have* to," Daddy gave in with doubt.

Then that big cold lonesome lights-out bus. Without a driver, without a rider. Waiting just for us.

The aisle had just been swept and a little wind kept snooping under the seats to see was it clean there, too. We sat in the back seat, us two fools, and Daddy turned his collar up against me. He was still trying to figure whether I'd hocked his clothes ahead of my own. The question was only technical, of course; but it was important for him to know all the same. I'd never gone against orders before, and he had no way of knowing if I had or not. I scarcely could blame him for feeling brought down.

After the way he'd come hitchhiking a vegetable truck into L.A. and in two months rose to the top of the heap, from San P. Street to Beverly Hills; after all the class he took on in almost no time at all; after the argyles and the monogrammed shirts, the cordovans and the easy days, till he'd reached a point where people with class invited us both to spend an afternoon on a yacht in The Bay—to be leaving now with no more to show than tracks down both arms and heel-holes in both socks would have brought down an even yet greater Daddy than mine. Except of course there ain't none greater. He may not be the best macker there is. But he is the meanest little old dog of a Daddy in town.

After Vegas the trick would be to see how long we could keep from coming sick in a cornfield. I didn't show him the dolaphine till it was breaking light and I was getting a weak streak through my own middle. Daddy had just rest-stop time enough to fix hisself. There wasn't time for me there and it's a long deal between stops. When I did fix at last I added just a drop of water to replace what I'd used; so Daddy wouldn't fret at sight of the stuff going down too fast in the bottle. Or he might get sick sooner than need be.

Just before Vegas I took a little closer look and seen it was fuller than I'd filled it. I didn't say nothing. I just let him handle the refills and didn't let him know I was on until we got on the highway with a half a bottle of dolaphine-water between us and Chicago. That was when I showed him the fiver.

He laughed then, he was feeling real good. "Everything's going to be perfect, Baby," he told me. Then we both fixed and sure enough it looked like everything would be perfect.

"Baby," he told me, "you're taking care of me in the little things."

"I'm taking care of you in the big ones as well," I told him—"Didn't I tell His Honor where to head in?" I got that in quick because it had to be settled while Daddy was still feeling well.

"You certainly did, Girl-Baby," he come through ever so nice.

Now you see how he is? God help me if ever his eye lit on a pawn ticket for a red silk bathrobe—but when he got a really legit beef on me, like costing us everything we own for the sake of one sassy small-town remark, he just laughs the whole deal off.

"Stay out of sight," I hurried him then, "here comes our transportation."

I'd thumb down a driver and get one foot in the car, then I'd say Wait For My Brother Mister and up would jump Daddy out of the bushes and come just a-trotting. I guess for a short spell there he was the up-jumpinest, very trottinest little Daddy on Route 66. Once he up-jumped and come a-trottin' so fast a lady driver wheeled off with a strip of my skirt in her door handle.

"Daddy," I scolded him, "don't up-jump so fast, else you'll be swinging a one-legged whore."

Comical things like that are what I say every now and then. Not very often. Just from time to time. If I do it oftener Daddy says, "I'll make the jokes in this family."

* * *

Neither of us were making jokes when we stepped down off that Odgen Avenue trolley. Four cross-country days of Wait-For-My-Brother-Mister, four cross-country nights on watery dolaphine. I felt like something that had been on a raft three weeks at sea.

The sidewalks so glarey, so hard. The sky all so bare. The people when they pass looking straight ahead—I wouldn't touch one for fear he'd scream. And how that ass-high Chicago wind comes right at you, so mad, it feels like it wants to cut you a new petoochi right then and there.

We went into a grocery and bought a box of graham crackers just to get out of that wind. A sign said SLEEPING ROOMS. That was for us. I just *leaned*, I was that done in. Christian kept one arm around me. He was trying for something, I couldn't make out just what, with that old doll behind the counter. When his arm went for my wrist I knew what he was trying for. Daddy's been trying for my Longine for some time now.

He could of got maybe twelve dollars for it off the old woman—if he could of got it off me. But he had to settle for six dollars on his own hour-piece. That I'd paid forty dollars for.

And then handed the six right back across the counter for a week's rent sight unseen. How could she afford to make a trade like that? She won't be in business long.

But she threw in the crackers and took us upstairs with her keys in one hand and a quart of milk in the other. The stairs were so dark we would of got lost on the way up but for that bottle. My throat was so parched I could near taste it. If she'd set it down when she opened the door I would of picked it up for her and then let my tongue just hang. But she only needed one hand to open the door.

For that door you didn't even need one hand—it hung so far ajar we could of squeezed in between it and the jamb one by one. Inside the room she looked right into my face and set the bottle down on the dresser.

Then she looked into Daddy's and picked it up again. Daddy got too much pride to ask for things and I was too sick to. She went downstairs taking it with her.

"She needs it to light the way down," I told Daddy.

He pulled up the shade and I seen a square of red brick wall dripping wet though it wasn't raining. I seen a brassy old high-ended bed. I seen a soggy mattress made of great big lumps and tiny burns. I seen four green-paper walls. I seen a holy calendar from what year I couldn't tell but I'd judge it was B.C. This one made the San Pedro trap look sharp.

"I'll see you at the Greyhound Station," I told my Daddy.

"You can't come sick in the open street, Beth-Mary," he told me; and he got to the door before me and locked it so tight all you could see through it was two inches of the hall.

"I'm sick already," I told him though it killed me to admit it. Daddy don't let hisself come sick in his mind, heart and bowels like me. He puts his own sickness down for the sake of mine. That way I get to be sick for both of us.

He put newspapers under me. He made me a little pillow out of his hole-in-heel socks and a hand towel with a red border. He took my shoes and stocking off so's I wouldn't get runs when I started to kick. He put my chubby over me. He called me his Girl-Baby.

That's what he calls me when he loves me the most.

Watch out for Daddy when he loves you the most. You have to come next to deathbed before he lets himself act tender.

"Let me take your Longine, sweetheart," he told me, "else you'll crack the crystal when you start in to swing."

"I'd as soon keep it on," I told Daddy.

For I felt the big fear coming on. It was coming a-slipping, it was coming a-crawl, it was slipping and crawling down that slippery red wall.

"Don't leave me, Christian," I asked him then.

"I've seen you from Shawneetown. I saw you through L.A. I'm here to see you the rest of the way."

"The rest of the way is by the stars," I told him.

"By starlight or no light," he told me, and his voice started going far away then; yet I knew it was telling me I wasn't to have Stuff any more ever. Something got a grip on that red brick wall and wouldn't let go.

"Pull down the shade," I told him, "they've changed their plans."

He pulled down the shade. I could tell by the shadow that fell as it fell. I had a little secret to tell. "Where are you?" I asked him.

"Right beside you, Beth-Mary."

"They're waiting in the hall," I told him my secret: "They've stole the master key."

He put a chair under the doorknob and stuffed the keyhole to humor me. "Daddy is here right beside you."

There was somebody in that hall all the same. And somebody on the rooftop too.

The Federal man was beside the bed pressing my left hand for prints; but I hid the right under the covers because that was the one that really counted. I kept turning the wrong hand like Daddy turning the wrong pocket because it was me wearing that big stop-warrant W and not Daddy at all. That was what I'd been suspecting for some time now. "Beth-Mary," the Fed began to sound like my Daddy, "try to rest till dark."

"Never heard the name till now," I told him, "but the first hustling broad I meet who answers to it, I'll tell her she's suppose to come down-town."

"It's only me, your little Daddy," that Fed tried his best. "*Look* at me, Beth-Mary."

"I *have* seen you somewheres before," I told him. "You're the nigger bellboy tried to pimp me off my little Daddy on San P. Street—remind

378

me to have him cripple you back of the parking lot. It won't take as long this time as before."

Not till that moment did Daddy know I knew about *that* deal.

"Beth-Mary Kindred," he asked me—"*Look* at me. Are you putting it on?"

"Come closer," I told him. For I was much more sly than he ever had supposed.

He came up close. He was all misty-white. "Get out! Get out!" I screamed right out—I wanted to cry, I wanted to laugh, I was freezing cold, I was sweating-wet. I couldn't get up still I couldn't lie still. I wanted to feel of someone's hand. Yet I couldn't bear human touch.

I can hear a country mile off, sick or well. Daddy don't hear a thing till it's next to his ear.

I heard steps in the hall. I said what I heard. Was it really steps or not? He didn't know whether to duck or go blind.

"Hold my hand and be still, you talk too much," I told him—"say something to me—*Hush*! What train is *that*?" It troubled me to hear a passenger train making time and not being able to tell was it going west or coming to run me over.

"That's the New York Central, sweetheart." He thought he could tell *me* just anything.

"Christian Kindred—*finky liar*—you good and well know that ain't no New York Central."

"Maybe it's the Illinois Central then. Maybe it's the Nickel Plate. For all I know, Baby, it could be the Rock Island."

"You lie in your teeth. You know as well as I it's the Southern Pacific."

"That's right, sweetheart," he agreed too soon, "it's the Southern Pacific for sure."

"Wait in the hall!" I hollered right *at* him—"Do as you're told!"

He closed the door quiet to make off like he done as he was told. He didn't dare leave me. Yet feared to come near me. "Little Baby," I heard him ask, "don't battle me so. You're grinding your teeth."

It's the kind of sickness you do well not to grind your teeth. But I wasn't battling him. I was battling *it*. Though it's a sickness it's the purest of follies to battle. Yet you have to battle it all the same. Battle and grind till your strength is spent in hope of one blessed moment of rest.

That moment comes yet it's never blessed. Your nose runs. Your eyes water. Your mouth drools like a possum's in love. "Daddy," I told him, "I don't want you to see me looking this way."

Then it's some sort of fever-doze where you're dreaming by the moment. Yet know right where you are all the while. It's something real wild that can't be endured. You endure it all the same.

It's all misty-white, it's like under water. Yet of a sudden the whole room will come clear and everything in it stands out to the wallpaper's tiniest crack.

It's the sickness that turns you against yourself. You're like two people, a weak cat and a strong, with no use for each other but they can't pull apart. "I don't deserve to be punished like this," you hear the weak cat grieve.

"If you deserved it, it wouldn't be punishment," the tougher party tells.

"Then let me get it all and be done. Let me come to the end of suffering then."

The stronger cat just scorns all that.

It goes and it comes, it creeps or it runs, there is no end and it's never done.

"Then why just *dole* it? Let me have it all at once," the weak cat begs.

"If you could see an end it wouldn't be punishment."

It's all so useless. It's nothing like sleep.

Once my eyes cleared and I saw Daddy plain: he was watching the light beyond the shade, waiting for the dark to come down. "Here I am," I could guess what he was thinking, "without a penny, without a friend. And a W on my forehead. If I get picked up it'll be a long deal before us two fools sleep side by side again. Who would fix a poor broad in a rented bed then?"

"Daddy," I whispered to him, "I got too many worries to go through with this."

He tried to give me something by mouth but my lips felt pebbly. I spit it all out. Daddy ought to have known better than that. Your mouth doesn't want it, it's your vein crying out. You can't ease a vein habit by mouth. Not even with graham crackers.

I felt him unstrapping my Longine. "You're getting it all spittly," he told me. I tried to swing my arm but I was too weak.

I must have dozed, because I heard Daddy's voice near at hand; yet he wasn't talking to me. He was talking on the phone.

"What time can my wife and I catch a bus to Shawneetown, sir? We can't go directly? Nearest stop is Morganfield? But are you certain it won't be overcrowded, sir? I don't mind for myself, but I'm traveling with my wife and little girl. I want them to be rested when we get home.

Yes sir—that's the reason we *prefer* travelling by Greyhound, sir. O no sir, not by far, I should *say* this isn't our first trip by Greyhound. 'We know we'll travel in comfort when we take Greyhound' is how the little woman puts it. Our little girl prefers Greyhound too. 'And leave the driving to *them*, Daddy' is how our little girl puts it."

I opened one eye.

It seemed a peculiar time to be putting me on.

But there he was, making all arrangements.

I was too tired to follow. He just went on and on. I didn't hear him hang up when I came around again he seemed to have cancelled with Greyhound.

"Bluebird Lines? What time is a bus available to Shawneetown, sir? Shawneetown, Illinois, yes sir. No, we don't want to charter it, there are only the three of us—my wife, little girl and myself. I don't mind standing up myself—I'd stand up all the way, it wouldn't bother *me* in the least. But I have to think of my wife and little girl. You're *sure* it won't be overcrowded? Plenty of seats for everybody? I see. Yes, one next to the window—for the little girl, of course." He hung up.

Grey is for Greyhound. Blue is for Bluebird. But what color is a pimp who thinks it's funny to make comical phone calls over a dead telephone when his old lady is preparing to die for lack of a fix?

He came over to the bed. He touched my hair and said "Lay back, Beth-Mary." So I knew he'd give up trying to amuse me. "Just rest. Your Little Daddy's with you."

My Little Daddy's with me alright. The Jesus God, what can be said of a man who can even make a failure of pimping? There we were with movie directors putting hundred-dollar-bills in my hair, so faggy they didn't even mind Daddy coming along, having the both of us out on a yacht in The Bay; him in clothes so classy he called himself a "technical advisor" whatever that may mean. And me so cute they used to brag about me all over the boat.

Then he has to get on Stuff and I have to get on because *he's* on. How do you like *that* for a man who once had good sense? Honest to God, when I think of the silk shirts, the lounging pajamas, the watches I wore and the French-heel shoes, the black lace undies and smoking jackets, the dresses I looked like an actress in—all down the drain like the sixteen-gauge hype you'd fixed with.

All gone. All down.

"You're still my one true tiger, Beth-Mary," he told me with his hand still on my hair.

I felt like his one Old Faithful. I didn't feel like nobody's tiger. I just felt bowed low.

Poor pimp, he does his best.

"Let me take your Longine now, Sweetheart," he told me, "else you'll crack the crystal when you start to swing."

"Put it where I can see it," I asked him and he strapped it onto a handle of the bureau. I could see the shiny golden circle hanging even though I couldn't see the time. At least I knew where time was to be had.

"Baby," he told me, "you got the worst part over."

Then the big sick hit me bigger and sicker than before.

It comes on real quiet, like nabbers at work—the only thing that's something deep inside you and something far outside, too. The only thing that feels so soft that hits so hard. The only thing that's more like nabbers at work than nabbers at work.

Nabs holding both your arms—then letting you pull loose just to see where you'll hide. There's a key in your door but it won't turn. Nabbers coming down both sides trying all doors—Get your back flat against the wall. Maybe they won't try this door at all. Maybe they'll never find you.

They're trying it, they're telling our name doorway to door—"Beth-Mary Kindred. Beth-Mary Kindred. *Beth-Mary*"—I saw my Daddy's face, so dear, so sort of pulled with care—"Beth-Mary, I'm right here beside you."

Then I knew nabbers at work had been just sounds inside my fevery ears.

Spook-docs and croakers, bug-docs and such, meatballs and matrons, nurses and all, there's not one cares whether you live or you die. For not one knows what true suffering is. But Daddy who stayed on my side and beside me that sorriest day of any, *you* know. And you're the onliest one who knows.

People like to say a pimp is a crime and a shame. But who's the one friend a hustling broad's got? Who's the one who cuts in, bold as can be, when Nab comes to take you? Who puts down that real soft rap only you can hear to let you know your time is up and is everything alright in there Baby? And when a trick says, "Where's the twenty I had in my wallet?"—who's the one he got to see? Who's the one don't let you get trapped with the monstering kind?

When ten o'clock in the morning is dead of night, who still keeps watch over you?

"What time is it, Daddy?" I asked him.

"Time to get off the wild side, Beth-Mary," he told me like he'd found out for himself at last. Then just set on. So pale, so wan.

I turned my head toward him so's he'd know I was with him.

"Is it getting a little darker, Christian?"

"It's nigh to dark, Beth-Mary."

All I could do was touch his wan hand. My fingers were too weak to hold it. Yet he took it into mine and pressed my palm to let me know.

"Baby," he told me, "I'm sorry for what I done to you on South San Pedro Street."

And said it so low, poor just-as-if-macker, as though I were part of his very heart still. That I heard it clear as little bells.

I must have slept then for a spell, because I dreamed I was buying seeds for some flower that blooms under water and when I woke it was raining. And someone kept humming from ever so far. When the rain stopped the little hum stopped. And all was wondrous still. When the rain began the hum began, from ever so far I could scarcely hear.

"Is that you humming, Daddy?" I asked.

Nobody answered. Nobody was near. The hum came closer—a little girl's humming. How could such a tiny hum come from so terribly far?

"You need sleep, Mother," she said my name. Sick as I was, my heart sank yet farther.

I lay on my pillow, how long I can't tell. After a time I noticed my Longine was gone. But it was all one by then.

I didn't have to open my eyes to know that Christian was gone too. I didn't care, one way nor another.

I didn't care for anything.

I was the one the law had wanted all along.

Then I heard his step.

My Daddy's step way down. Then the key turned in the lock and his voice came to me—

"Are you going to sleep all day, Little Baby?"

"Not if Little Daddy is going to make me well," went through my mind; but I was too weak to say it. All I knew, by his voice, was that he had scored. I felt myself getting well before I could tell where he was at. Then I felt his arm holding me up and the slow press of the needle—he hardly teased me at all this time—though that's Daddy's pleasure and I don't begrudge him—he hit me then in a way no doctor or nurse on earth ever could. It takes a junkie to fix a junkie. And *nobody* knows how to fix you like your own Little Daddy. Little orange fires began to glow deep inside me. I felt myself getting warm.

"Don't try to sit up yet, Little Baby"—and when he said that I saw him clear. I saw my own Little Daddy's face. My onliest Little Daddy. His face so old so young. So sort of pulled with care. He dried my nose and mouth and patted me with a warm damp rag. Then he dried me ever so gentle. Nobody can gentle me like my Little Daddy.

"You're the best connection a working girl ever had," I told him then.

"Don't try to talk yet, Little Baby," he told me. "We'll have good times again—This is the old Christy talking now."

He didn't look like the old Christy. Not by far. I remembered the old Christy.

Yet I've tried to live without him and it's like living without a heart at all.

How old was I when he came past looking so young yet so old? Seventeen? I was needing someone to lean on.

"I want to get up, Christian," I told him again. He brought me my slip and turned his head while I dressed. When I looked in the bathroom mirror I gave a bit of a jump to see how thin my face had got. Still, it had a bit of color now. I added a little more.

"I'm ready to go to work," I told him when I came out.

"Sit down, Beth-Mary," he told me, "I don't know whether you're ready or not."

I thought he meant I wasn't strong enough yet. But that wasn't it at all.

"We won't make a bankroll tricking bums," he let me know.

I *felt* his drift. Yet I wasn't sure.

"Is there some other kind of trick?"

He got up and walked around. Daddy had something on his mind.

"It's time to go the kayo route, Baby," he told me.

"You didn't want that route in L.A.," I reminded him. "How come you want to go it now?"

"Different circumstances," he told me.

"What different circumstances?" I wanted to know.

"Look around you, Beth-Mary. Just look around you."

I looked around. I looked at the bed still damp with sweat and the walls the brick was showing through; the wash-basin like something stole off a junk-wagon and four inches of alley-window that gave down the last of day.

"I see what you mean, Little Daddy," I told him. "Where you going to get the prescription?"

"A place called the Southsea. A bartender name of Ram."

"You've been covering a lot of ground, Christian," I praised him. "If we score do I get back my Longine?"

I remember a time he would have clobbered me for checking him like that. Now he grinned weak-like.

"Get your handbag," he told me. "I want you to meet some classy people."

"What about my Longine, Daddy?" I made bold to press him harder.

Then he pulled his wallet and flashed me the pawn ticket.

"You keep checking me out," he warned me, "next time I'll hock *you*."

"I just wanted to know whether you'd sold it or hocked it," I let him know.

And out we went, down the stairs and onto the street.

Just two fools leaning on each other.

3. *O Shining City Seen of John*

O Shining City Seen of John I thought, if that country fool of mine has but the country sense to phone Enright, that he can keep the chubby if he'll go our bond and forget who threw the shot-glass, at least one of us can make the street and it had best be me.

If she don't we're both going to get too sick to call for help on anyone but God, and God can't help you from behind a solid door. The solid door is where they lock you when you deny being a user but they know you're one all the same. It's part of the treatment, I've had it before.

That's why I was keeping an eye on that string of light between the floor and the door. Because that time we were busted in L.A. and they wouldn't let Beth see me, she rolled a cigarette under my door to let me know she was making the street. For a country fool to get city-smart takes but five days in Los Angeles.

Poor piece of trade who needed someone strong to lean on—Who'll you lean on now if your Little Daddy gets time? What'll you do when the dolaphine gives out? Ride Trailways to Shawneetown?

Who do you think'll be at the station to meet you? The Shawneetown Parent Teachers Association? I doubt you'll be able to score for your midnight fix at the Shawneetown General Store, Beth-Mary.

Face up to it, Little Baby: you were born unfit to be anybody's mother and you're unfit yet.

Where Can I Get A Good Piece of Tale, some fool had scratched in yellow chalk, on the wall just over my head. I couldn't think of an answer.

I didn't feel good, I didn't feel bad. Just a little low in mind for knowing I was never going to play the clarinet after all.

"But *Daddy*"—the fool complained after I told her I'd *seen* the clarinet, marked down to twenty bucks, in the hockshop window

385

—"Daddy, how do you know that you can play that thing *right off?*"

"How'm I going to *learn* to play the licorice-stick if I don't *have* a licorice-stick, Beth-Mary?" I tried cold reason on her. Then I forgot about the licorice-stick because she started putting on her chubby.

"Hang that right back up," I told her. In no uncertain term.

Right off she has a story—she needs it to keep the wind off her.

"You'll do better to worry about the law than the wind, Little Baby," is what I told her then.

There's no wind blows that that broad fears. All she had in mind was showing the chubby off in front of Enright's other hookers, especially that one calls herself Zaza. Had Beth-Mary had so much as a pearly-grain of sense she'd know that I was only leading the poor broad on.

"*No!*" I told Beth-Mary—"*No*, Little Baby, you don't need a fur-piece to walk half a city block. Now hang it back up like I told you."

"But it's so *cold*, Little Daddy, the way the wind cuts right *at* you I might catch my *death!*"

"You have a greater chance of catching your death setting at a bar with that thing wrapped around you, whisking in and out of the cold," I was forced to point out to her.

"I wouldn't wear it *in* the bar, Little Daddy—I'd take it off till it was time to leave."

Allowances have to be made for persons unsettled in the head. Though just when you think Beth-Mary has surely lost one of her marbles, she'll pull something that makes you think she's got one extra.

"Little Baby," I asked her, getting her down on the bed beside me and one arm around her chubby, "you remember how we agreed your Little Daddy would take care of you in the big things if you took care of Little Daddy in the little ones?"

I worked the chubby off one shoulder.

"*I* never agreed," she told me; hunching her other shoulder.

"I agreed *for* you," I had to remind her.

"But *Daddy*"—she began trying to pull away from me—"all I want is to wear my own very own mink chubby to work. Why can't that be one of the *little* things?"

"Because if you get busted on that mink in Enright's, Enright is in trouble too. And *that* makes it one of the big things."

"But *Daddy*, Enright don't even *know* it's a credit-card chubby."

"And how do you know the next trick sits down beside you in Enright's isn't from the pawnshop detail, looking for that very coat you've just thrown across the bar?"

"I'd put on the coat so's he couldn't see the label."

386

"For God's sake, Beth-Mary, this cop isn't some two-hundred-pound flatfoot wearin' a badge and revolver. He's a long-hair cat wearing glasses, with a book under his arm."

"I'd know he was law all the same, Daddy,"

"*How* would you know?"

"I'd just *know*, Daddy, that's all. I'd just *know*."

"You'd just *know*, would you? And what if you weren't even there but he came in with your description to Enright and was waiting for you with a warrant?"

"Enright wouldn't snitch, Daddy."

"Beth-Mary, why take risks when everything is about to be perfect? As soon as I've mastered the clarinet we'll both get off stuff and send for the baby."

She pitched herself face-down across the bed with her shoulders shaking.

I kicked the mink onto the floor. I never should have mentioned the baby.

I let her sob for a while then pulled her up beside me and dabbed her eyes with Kleenex from her handbag. It wasn't too clean because she'd been carrying her needle in it. She dry-sobbed, then got control.

"What good are things, Daddy?" she asked me then.

"What good are *what* things, Beth-Mary?"

"Having a chubby I don't get to wear even. What good is *that?* Hassling every freaky old man on West Madison. What good is *that?* Just to stay out of jail? What good is staying out of jail? What good is *anything*, Daddy?"

It was getting close to her fix-time that was clear.

"Daddy," she told me after a while, "I need rest," and put her head on my shoulder.

It was getting dark and she hadn't turned a trick for twenty hours. The telephone wires across the window took on light from the arc-lamp and swung a little in the wind. I let her nod off against me for five minutes by her Longine. "Beth-Mary," I told her too low for her to hear, "I'm sorry I made a whore out of you." Then I tied her green Babushka under her chin and got her to her feet. She wasn't yet full awake, fumbling at the bow I'd just made in the babushka and smiling a little just to herself.

Then she was out the door with the chubby under the arm simply clickety-clacking down the hall and me right behind her—but I had to swing back to turn the key in the lock so she had a headstart. But I could take two steps to her one because of her heels and gained almost a flight on her before she hit the second-floor landing. Had it been five flights down, instead of only four, I would have caught her and *dragged* her back upstairs by those same heels; but she hit the lobby clickety-*clacking* so fast the desk-clerk glanced up. I had to slow down to a stroll.

Did you ever, all your born days, hear of a simple-minded whore so purely *determined*, at whatever risk to herself and others, to have her own way?

She was waiting for me, under the marquee, with the chubby tight about her.

"You *are* the most pig-headed country fool ever to walk in shoeleather," I filled her in right off, walking on the outside to cover the coat the best I could—"you *are* the *slyest* country-sneak ever to thrash about the cheapest bar in town"—I kept giving it to her all down Madison, meanwhile keeping on the hawks for the two-man squad that keeps an eye on Enright's—"I've tried reasoning with your childish brain. I've whupped your pitiful hide till my arms ached—and you're still the most calf-brained smalltown *idjit* a man ever got himself chained to."

"Is *that* why you like me so much, Little Daddy?"—she got in just as she swung ahead of me into Enright's—"because my mind is even weaker than your own?"

The lights in the holly-wreaths hanging across Enright's bar mirror had been switched off for a week. He hadn't gotten around to washing off the HAPPY NEW YEAR FOLKS chalked across the mirror.

Beth began taking off the stupid coat, taking her time to make certain that every woman in the joint had a chance to see she wasn't wearing cat-fur, that it was the real thing. I just stood there studying her reflection.

"Just who *do* you think you're showing off *for*, Baby?" I asked her. After all, the only other woman to see her, at the moment, was Lucille, a teen-age lush who never leaves the joint, that Enright uses as a B-broad because the chick drinks hard stuff along with the marks—and that's all she gets out of sitting there, too.

The used-to-be hooker, Zaza, that Enright keeps in the dark at the back bar, still comes on like a hooker. But all she is now is a deadpicker and Enright gets half of what she steals.

"Little Daddy," Beth-Mary told me kind of low, when she finally got the chubby off, "you didn't make a whore out of me. I made a pimp out of you."

388

Then she tossed the coat across the bar and turned her back on me like I didn't exist.

You can always treat a woman too good. But you can never treat one too bad. My mistake had been in giving the broad her leadership. Now she was out of hand.

"Just because you got another beef going with your old lady," Zaza tells me the second I sit down, "don't mean you have to make up to *me*."

It's hard for a hustler to work a joint where she's not on speaking terms with anyone but the bartender. I took note Zaza was glad to have my company even though she wasn't about to admit it.

Zaza must have been goodlooking before she worked lumber camps. Now she was just burned-down timber.

Yet not so burned down but she might not help a trusted friend to get a certain clarinet out of hock. The broad needed someone to talk to so bad I figured she might just come up with twenty. Might just.

"I'm the one to blame for everything," I took full responsibility for my idiot, "she's a wonderful, *wonderj..* child—and that's just where the trouble comes in. Because it's just *what* she is—a mere child. Life can't be just all a matter of getting kicks. Life has its *serious* side."

Zaza looked me down then up from my Keds to my high hairline, then down again.

"Say something serious," she finally asked me.

"Buy me a drink. I'm serious."

"Why should I? Enright don't want you hanging around your old lady when she's working, so you come back here thinkin' I'll be grateful to have your company; only I ain't. You're going to put down the same old story on me, how you're going to swing with another mink chubby any day now just to see how *I* look in mink. Only you aren't. I'd be lucky if you swung with a pair of Goldblatt earrings for me."

"*Earrings?*"—I picked her right up on *that*—"You want *earrings*, baby? Just don't go away."

I took a slow stroll toward the front bar past Lucille. She gave me her baby-lush smile but I didn't even rap to her. Just strolled on by and came up behind Beth-Mary as if I meant to give her a hug. Instead I yanked her earrings off both at once—she yelped and swung about. But I was already strolling back. Now she knew she wasn't the only one who could make a fast move in our family.

Lucille didn't lush-smile me this time by. "*I can get me any pimp in town!*" She let me know how I stood with her now.

"Without an ID card?" I asked her and kept on moving. Yet I took care, when I got to the back bar, to put Zaza between me and the front door. Just in event anyone from the front bar should want to see me about something.

I squirrel-eyed the front bar and, sure enough, I see Beth-Mary coming. But I failed to take note of the shot-glass in her hand.

"Here, honey," Zaza told her, holding out the earrings to Beth, "*I* don't want them. *My* ears are pierced."

Beth-Mary ignored the offer. She purely hates the idea of any other broad buying me *anything*. Especially a clarinet. "Daddy," she asked me, "can I just talk to you?"

Now I knew I had her hanging. I just let her hang.

"What do you think," I asked Zaza, leaning a bit back from the bar to make sure Beth didn't miss a word I was saying, "of a woman who'll use her daughter's education-money for her own midnight-score? What kind of a woman would put her habit ahead of her husband's musical career?"

Zaza lay both earrings down, very carefully, on the bar in front of her. She looked at them like she wanted no part of either one.

"I'm talking about what a *drag* a woman with a habit can be," I kept right on, "what a day-to-day *burden*—"

Had Enright not walked out from behind the bar just as Beth pitched the shot-glass it would have skulled me instead of him. *Zonk!*—he spun half-about right into Zaza, nearly knocking her backward off the stool. She grabbed the bar with her left hand and swung her handbag with her right and *zonk!*—Enright went out cold face-down across the bar with his big behind sticking out.

"Call a priest! Call a holy father!" Lucille began hollering and ran out into the street to get one. Enright started to sag. I caught him around the waist and Zaza and Beth-Mary were helping me to get him up straight when two cops stormed in followed by Lucille. Who did she think *she* was working for?

"Who hit him?" Cop One wanted to know, taking Enright away from me.

"*That* one skulled him with a shot-glass," Lucille got right in there, pointing out Beth-Mary—" and *that* one"—pointing out Zaza—"skulled him with her handbag!"

Enright raised up as though all he'd been doing with his head on the bar was resting it—"I'm not pressing charges!"

I'd never seen a man come around that fast before.

"And I don't blame you," Cop One went along, taking Enright's big moon-face between his hands and studying it like a map. There was a black and blue bruise on one side where the shot-glass had grazed it and a lump, just starting to come up, on the other.

"I fell over a beer bottle," Enright explained everything.

I sat at the back bar looking straight ahead because I felt Cop Two's eyes on me.

"Get the two broads into the wagon," Cop One told Cop Two.

"*Which* two?" Cop Two wanted to know; not taking his eyes off me.

"The one who pitched the shot-glass and the one who swung her hand-bag."

"I'm not pressing charges neither!" Lucille suddenly came back into her right mind; and handed Cop One her ID card.

"Did I ask you to show me that?" he asked her. She put it back in her bag.

"That's right," Cop One congratulated her. "Keep it safe, honey, you're going to need it at the station." Then he turned to Cop Two: "Take all three of them."

"What about *him*?" Cop Two asked.

"Put the broads in the wagon," Cop One decided, "I'll take the pimp in the squad so's they don't fight over him all the way to the station."

The *pimp*? That just *might* be me. Just *might*.

Yet neither one of those stupid bulls so much as noticed a mink chubby lying across the front bar.

Now every few minutes I heard the big door at the block's far end being opened. Yet I never heard it being shut. As if it had opened just far enough to let people with bills in their hands in to squeeze through. If you can't let somebody out for free, I thought, for God's sake let somebody in for nothing.

Then I heard a whole pack coming and got back out of the way in case they came through my door.

"Brideswell! Brideswell!" some kukefied broad was hollering, "*have* consideration!"—but it wasn't Beth-Mary.

Someone was slammed against the door like the mother-cops had backed her up flat against it and were milling around. I could hear them milling: she couldn't get loose. Then all the feet began going away fast way down the line. Till a cell door slammed.

That was when it came to me that Enright might already have bonded out my fool. She might be back at the front bar this very moment, the chubby in front of her, listening to whatever the old man was telling her she ought to do next. Like letting her Little Daddy kick his habit cold turkey in Cook County Jail while she went on feeding her own.

O Shining City Seen of John I thought, if that fool of mine lets that old man talk her into *that*, there'll be no use of her waiting on the courthouse steps when her Little Daddy comes down them; because she won't have a Little Daddy anymore. Because Little Daddy'll be clean, he'll be his old self once more. What need then will he have for a country whore with marks on her arm?

No, Little Baby, there's no hardluck story in the book that'll work *then*. Because Little Daddy won't even rap to you. He'll walk right on by, hop a cab to the Trailways depot and be back in Old Shawneetown, never to leave again, by morning.

And when the baby is big enough to understand, Little Daddy's going to tell her her real mother died young. And never give that piece of trade he left on the courthouse steps further thought.

Yet I really couldn't believe Beth-Mary would come in on me.

On the other hand, there was the time in L.A. when she spent a whole afternoon in a movie with a nab. But maybe that was just because she liked the movie. Besides, that was different. I was setting home in my red foulard robe—the one with the tasselly sash—reading *Mad*. I wasn't setting behind a solid door in blue jeans with a patch in the seat. Little Baby, aren't you *ashamed* to let your Little Daddy walk around in tennis shoes in midwinter? Don't you want your Little Daddy to look *sharp*?

And what does *she* have to show for five years of hustling, except that mink chubby? That, chances are, she's had to forget by now.

The cold began coming up off the floor. But I knew it was from inside myself that it was really coming. I hadn't used anything except paregoric for almost sixty hours; and that had been by mouth.

I got a cigarette out of my pocket and got it lit with one hand. I didn't draw the smoke up my nose because I wasn't sure what happens when nicotine hits paregoric. Hold tight, Little Baby, I told Beth-Mary, Daddy may be about to drowse about.

Way up and far off I heard a church bell inviting everyone to Sunday mass. Everyone except Beth-Mary and me. Us two fools; the only place we get invited is jail. Just jail.

Can we help it if we're cute?

Then all the doors, both sides the other side of the solid door, were standing wide. All the broads had gone home. All the mother-cops had taken them home and not one of them was coming back. I was the only one left locked up.

Then someone pulled the shade.

I was in some kind of old country barn with just one weakass bulb burning high high up and swinging a little. All I was wearing was the red silk foulard robe with the tasselly sash. That I thought Beth-Mary had hocked in L.A. I had nothing on under it. And there was a smell of burning; like in a lion-house.

I saw their shadows moving whenever the bulb swung a little; they were all lionesses. That I had to fight one by one.

That was to be my punishment for not being a broad.

Then the burning smell came stronger and I came to with my cigarette burning out on the floor under my nose.

I'd never had a dream like that before.

I got down off the bunk and put my eye to the string of light beneath the door.

"Beth-Mary!" I called under the door, "are you alright, Little Baby?"

Not a sound, not a whisper the other side of the solid door. If I could only hear her whining, *"Little Daddy, can't we just drowse about?"*

I got back on the bunk and read the question again that that fool had chalked there in yellow chalk, right over my head. And suddenly I had the answer.

"At your mother's house, fool," I told him right out loud.

But I didn't have a piece of chalk, of any color at all, to write my answer down.

Out of the corner of my eye I saw a cigarette come rolling under the door. It came a full two feet into the cell before it stopped rolling.

And heard my fool's high heels go clickety-*clacking* down the corridor.

And keep clickety-clacking away.

You'd think a pimp could do no wrong, for God's sake, the way them two stick up for one another. You know what that old Southsea bartender told me before I come out here at this ungodly hour?—"You been a bad girl, Beth-Mary, you got to make it all up to your Daddy now. You can't spend a whole night turning one trick anymore."

I flew right *at* him—"You take care of *your* customers, old man, 'n I'll take care of *mine*."

For God's sake, just because he goes my bond he thinks he can talk to me like my Little Daddy. *Nobody* talks to me like my Little Daddy. What do *I* care if people say he's no good? Don't I know that? Of *course* he's no good. But he's the best connection a hustling woman ever had 'n I'll go all routes with him.

Don't douse the light yet, mister. Just hang some old tie over it. Else I'll sleep till the buses stop. Then I'll have to hail a cab. One cab less, my Little Daddy's out one day the sooner. I know he's working up a perfect fit at me as it is out there.

He's lucky to have someone outside working to get him out, as *I* see it. How many them locked-up cats got anyone outside hustling for *them?*

And had it not been for me forcing the old man to bond Zaza out with me, he'd have left her set until her day in court. Only I wasn't about to leave her—Why should I? Was it *her* fault he walked into a flying shot-glass? So what if she swung on him with what was nearest to hand? What did he expect after almost knocking her to the floor?

When she opened that handbag at the station we both broke up. But the mother-cop just shook her head 'n asked "What happened *here*, honey?"

The inside of the bag was a mess of cold-cream, broken glass with kleenex and bobbie pins stuck in it. What she'd hit Enright with was a two-pound jar of Pond's cold cream; that she'd swung with on her way to work. Small wonder that old man went out cold.

She didn't even claim the bag when we got sprung. "Nothing in it but a quarter and a few pennies," she told me, "and I'd have to scrape cold-cream off *them*."

Climb into bed any time you feel like, mister. I'll jump in in no time. I just feel like yakking first for a while. Do you mind? It all just strikes me as so comical. I never robbed nobody my whole life. Even that credit-card we got the chubby on was by my Daddy's hand. I couldn't get my own hand in a rain-barrel. But I'm in and out of jail like a fiddler's elbow all the same.

I'll say this for Little Daddy—he never lets me set for long. Even when he had a W on him in L.A., and couldn't show up in the courthouse hisself, he sent a bondman down to spring me. I know he's mad enough at me to eat snake, lettin' him set there a week already. I'm going to have to answer a lot of questions when he comes down those court-house steps.

First thing he'll want to know is how much did Enright put up for the chubby. When I tell him I sold it outright for three hundred to the old man, he won't believe me. Not until I tell him the old man don't know the coat is hot. That'll put him in the switches—especially if Enright has turned it over. We can't go back there if he has.

When he gets around to asking why *three* hundred, when bond is only a hundred-fifty, I'll have to tell him I got Zaza out. He'll find out anyhow.

Enright thinking he got us all three on the hook is the biggest laugh of all time, Zaza thinks. He figures to get five hundred for the coat, tell us all he got is three so we're all square, and make hisself two hundred.

"*Keep* the coat, old man," I told him, "it's *yours*. Just get us out of here." Zaza kept her mouth shut when I told him that. And she was good as gold when we were locked up together, too.

"Please take these stupid earrings back, honey," she asked me, "as a *favor*." I took them back even though they don't mean a thing to me. For a fact I don't even remember who put them on me. It wasn't the earrings, I told Zaza, it was the way Daddy went about getting them that got me burned—"I don't hold *nothing* against *you*," I told her—"if it wasn't for my bad aim you wouldn't even be settin' here."

"I'm just sorry about your having to give up your chubby," she told me, "your old man is going to be hot at you for that."

"Not for long," I told her, "you don't know my Little Daddy."

Nobody knows my Little Daddy. Once in L.A. somebody gave him one of those tennis-bats. Right away he got to be jumping nets all over town. He has the flash notion he's going to be a tennis-player and he don't even know where the places are they play for God's sake. My part is to buy him a box of balls and a pair of white shoes. Then everything's going to be perfect.

"You want to be a tennis-player," I told him, "*be* a tennis player. And I'll get me a pimp who *is* a pimp." I never all my days heard tell of a pimp jumping over a net. Or one tennis player asking another would he like to say hello to the girls.

"I don't need a tennis-bat to swing a smalltown hide like you," he told me—"the flat of my shoe will do." After all the times I put him to bed when he was hitting the bars, and after that the times I scored for him when he was too weak to score for himself, he called me "smalltown hide." What could I *do*? I bought him the box of tennis balls and the white shoes and a T-shirt to match and we march into the bar where we hung out, him holding his stupid bat.

The bartender took one look, hollered, "O look girls" and made swishy moves like a little girl throwing a balloon.

That put an end to Little Daddy's tennis career. He traded off the lot, that had cost me a twenty-dollar trick plus cab-fare, for six sticks of lowgrade pot. Then tells me, "Forget it, Little Baby, let's just go home and drowse about." As if nothing had happened at all.

Now he comes leaping into Enright's—"I'm mastering the licorice-stick!"

He's going to join the musicians' union, he's going to play with a big-name band, we're going to send for the baby, hustling and hypes and shakedowns and busts are just a thing of the past—yet he doesn't even have the stupid flute out of the hockshop window.

"Everything's going to be perfect, Beth-Mary—only we got to get down there before someone else grabs it!"

But I know it's just another just-as-if deal like with the tennis-bat.

"Daddy, couldn't you learn to play a clarinet first, from someone who already owns one?" I asked him—"When you get the hang of it we'll get you one of your own—not a secondhand one—a *new* one, Little Daddy."

"Is that all you think of me and the baby?" he asked me. "Doesn't your husband's career mean *anything* to you? You want your daughter to grow up in *your* footsteps?"

Daddy, I thought, if you weren't so weak inside you wouldn't come on so hard.

"I'll tell you what I've about decided, Joan-of-Arc"—he never calls me *that* unless he's furious with me—"I've decided it's time for you either to get on a bus to Lexington or taper your habit down within reason."

Nothing, not a *word*, about *his* habit of course.

"So's you can build it up higher than before?" I put it to him; which seemed to take him by surprise. "Little Daddy," I went right on, "I'll hustle for you, I'll work for you. I'll go to jail for you. If I have to be sick for two for you I'll do that, too. And, if you want, I'll roll you the biggest stick of tea in town. You're the best connection I ever had and I think you're here to stay."

He doesn't know that, when he took me from my baby, something in my heart shut hard on him.

Poor just-as-if boy, I was sixteen when he came by and became a sickness in my heart. I'm going on twenty-four and he's a sickness to this hour.

I knew something was gnawing him from that first night, down by the river. When he told me he'd just done two real hard years at Boys' Industrial I thought that that was it.

That wasn't it at all. All his mother had had to do to keep him from doing a single day, was to claim him from the court. But she'd tied up to marry some fool who wasn't *about* to let an outlaw boy in *his* house. She had her choice between having a husband or a son. She couldn't have both so she picked the husband. Some husband.

That's what is still gnawing Little Daddy.

Yet Mother always gets a pass: "Mother done what she thought best for both of us." So who's left to blame for what happened *then*? Me! I didn't know he was on earth at the time; yet the whole thing is my fault now. He don't say it in so many words; but it's what he feels all the same.

"You ought to hate your old lady for what she done," I made bold to tell him once, "not *me*."

I'll never make *that* mistake again. He'd never hit me in the face before. It was my first time. Poor just-as-if boy, what's ever to become of him if anything happens to me? I needed someone strong to lean on when he came along 'n now it's just two weak fools leanin' on each other.

Poor useless boy—I'd rather have his hate than some fat square-fig's love. Love or hate, whatever, it don't matter so long as it's real. My daddy's hate is realer than any old squarefig's love. His hate is more beautiful, I think, than love. Because it's what he truly *feels*.

It's why I told him that time, "Little Daddy, I'll hustle for you, I'll work for you, I'll get sick for two for you, I'll go to jail for you, I'll go all routes with you. If you want I'll roll the biggest stick of tea in town for you."

What I've never told him is that, when he took me from my baby, the best part of my heart closed on him.

Mister, I don't think that old tie across the light is working out. I can smell it starting to scorch. Try your cap instead. You only got two caps? In that case hang up the best one.

That's better. Now crawl in here before you set yourself afire. I never chippied yet on my Little Daddy.

So I guess it's time to try.

THE LAST CAROUSEL

I wonder whether there stands yet, on a lonesome stretch of the Mexican border, a green legend welcoming Spanish-speaking motorists to an abandoned gas station:

SINCLAIR se habla español SINCLAIR

A sign I once sat beneath, between a chaparral jungle and a state highway, shelling black-eyed peas. With a burlap sack, a pan and a pocket-size English-Spanish dictionary beside me, I shelled through the searing summer of 1932.

I'd painted that green welcome myself. Above a station that was home, storehouse and operational base for me and a long, lopsided cracker named Luther. I was proud to be his partner and proud that the station was in my name. I'd signed the papers.

We were occupying it, ostensibly, to sell Sinclair gas. What we were actually up to was storing local produce, bought or begged, for resale in the border towns. We had sacks, buckets, pails, pans, Mason jars and crates filled to overflowing with black-eyed peas. When word got around to valley wives that they could now buy black-eyed peas already shelled, they'd be driving up from all over southeast Texas. The Sinclair agent would think we weren't selling them anything but gas. By the time he caught on, we'd be rich.

Sitting bolt upright at the wheel of a 1919 Studebaker, under a straw kelly the hue of an old hound's tooth, Luther turned my memory back to the caption on the frontispiece of *The Motor Boys in Mexico:* "We were bowling along at 15 miles per hour." He lacked only duster and goggles. I feared for the Mexican farmers.

"Protect yourself at all times, son," was Luther's greeting every single morning. "Keep things going *up*."

I hadn't seen a newspaper for weeks. For news of the world beyond the chaparral, I awaited Luther's evening return. I did the shelling and he did the selling.

There were deer in the chaparral, buzzards in the blue and frogs in the ditch. Once a host of butterflies, all white, came out of the sun and settled about me as though they'd been sent. Then they rose and fled as if they'd been commanded to leave. In the big Rio heat I shelled on.

Luther was the man who'd discovered the unexploited shelled-pea market. I'd make him foreman of my ranch in return. The Mexican help would love me, too. "Got the whole plumb load for only two dolla'," Luther announced smugly over his latest outwitting of a Mexican farmer: He'd returned with another carload. We sat down to a supper of cold mush and black-eyed peas; in the kerosene lamp's faltering glow. Our kerosene was running low. We were short of everything but peas.

"Collards 'n black-eyed peas on New Year's Day means silver 'n gold the whole plumb year," Luther assured me. He was full of great information like that.

"They thought they had Clyde, but they didn't." He gave me the big news once the meal had been eaten.

A sheriff had nearly trapped Clyde Barrow and Ray Hamilton in a farmhouse outside Carlsbad, New Mexico. But Bonnie had held the sheriff off long enough for Clyde to come around the side of the house and get the drop on him with a shotgun. New Mexico police had subsequently brought in a body, found in a ditch beside a highway.

No body was ever Clyde Barrow's.

"They'll never take Clyde alive," I prophesied.

The Sinclair agent had let us have a hundred gallons of gas on credit. As well as a high-posted brass bed whose springs bore rust from damp nights at the Alamo. Our chairs were orange crates. I lugged a five-gallon jug of water, pumped from a Mexican farmer's well, two miles down the highway every morning.

When the Sinclair agent had driven up with papers assigning responsibility for payment for the hundred gallons, Luther had claimed illiteracy.

"Mister, Ah cain't but barely handwrite mah own name, far less to read what someone else has print-wrote. But this boy has been to college. He's *right* bright. Got a sight more knowance than Ah'll *evah* git."

The right-bright boy with all the knowance had felt right proud to sign the papers.

"When we git enough ahead to open a packin' shed," Luther assured me after the agent had left, "Ah'm gonna need your services to meet our buyers—Ah'll just see that the fruit gits packed in the back 'n you set at the desk up front. How do *that* suit you, son?'' That suited Son just fine. And if Luther averted his eyes, I realized it was only to conceal gratitude.

Once, at midday, the agent caught me in the middle of my bushels, jars and sacks. "We plan to can them for the winter," was my explanation.

"Well, you'll never get to be a millionaire by askin' for raises," he counseled me.

I already knew that you had to work for nothing or you'd never get rich. Grit counted more than money. All a poor boy had to do to get a foothold on the ladder of success was to climb one rung whenever anyone above him fell off. This made the rise from a filling-station partnership to owning a cattle ranch merely a matter of time and patience. And when the day came that I'd made the top rung, the first thing I'd buy would be a pair of Spanish boots and a John Batterson Stetson hat.

The reason we'd sold only one gallon of gas in that whole autumn season, it looked to me, was that Mexican farmers preferred to buy from Spanish-speaking merchants. *"¿Quiere usted un poco de este asado?"* I would invite myself aloud to dinner while shelling. And, finding the roast beef tasty, would ask for more: *"Dame usted un magro, yo le gusta."* That made a pleasing change from what actually went on in our mush-encrusted pan.

So I'd painted the sign that invited the Spanish-speaking world to our two pumps: with fifty gallons of gas beneath each pump. I'd gotten as far as *"Acérquese usted tengo que decirle una cosa"* when a Mexican drove up, hauling a trailer. I raced to give the crank forty-five or fifty spins. But the bum didn't want gas. He wanted tequila. What were we doing out here in the brush if we weren't selling whiskey? He turned his coat inside out to prove he wasn't a revenue agent. He couldn't believe that we were actually trying to *sell* black-eyed peas. Laughing, he swept his hand toward the chaparral: Black-eyed peas were as common as cactus. We *must* be kidding him.

Still convinced that we had tequila cached somewhere, he showed me a coin, with Franklin D. Roosevelt's head engraved upon it, to prove he could pay. It was smaller than any quarter I'd ever seen. I wouldn't have taken it even if I'd had whiskey to sell. He wheeled away.

One night I woke up because someone kept snorting. "Is that you, Luther?" I asked.

"No," he grunted, "I thought that was you."

The snorting came again. From under the bed. "Who's under there?" Luther asked, leaning far over. For an answer he got another snort.

He got up, dressed in a union suit, though the night was steaming. He probed under the bed and looked in all the corners with the help of our kerosene lamp. Finally, we both got up and played the lamp under the station's floor: A wild pig was rooting under our heads.

"SOOOO-*eeeee*, soooo-*eeeee!* Git out of there, you dern ole hawg!" Luther challenged it. But no amount of soooo*eeeee*ing could get the brute out. Or stop its snorting.

The next morning, I piled into the front seat of the Studebaker beside Luther. I wanted to go to Harlingen, too. "Now, if we had an accident on the way," Luther pointed out, "with both of us settin' up front, both of us'd be kilt. But if one of us was in the back, he'd likely git off just bein' crippled but still able to carry on our work."

I climbed into the back seat. Luther smiled, smugly yet approvingly, into the rearview mirror. "Done forgot what I to'd you about protectin' yourself at all times, didn't you son?"

I picked up a week-old San Antonio paper in town. Four youths had driven up to a dance hall in Atoka, Oklahoma, arguing among themselves. Two officers had come up to pacify them and both had been shot down. Other youths had grabbed the officers' guns and given chase. The outlaws had abandoned their car when it had lost a wheel, had kidnapped a farmer in his car, had set him free at Clayton, had stolen another car at Seminole and then had disappeared themselves. One of the officers had survived.

"That *got* to be Ray Hamilton and Clyde Barrow," I decided.

"*And* Bonnie Parker," Luther was just as certain.

In the window of the jitney jungle in Harlingen, Luther pointed out a Mason jar of black-eyed peas I'd packed for the industry myself. I could hardly have been more proud. "You're practically the black-eyed-pea king of the whole dern Rio Grande Valley awready," Luther congratulated me. I felt the responsibility.

Sheltered from the sun in the station's window, my fingers forgot their cunning in a dream of a Hoover-colored future; wherein I supervised a super Sinclair station wearing a J.B. Stetson hat. Never a yellow kelly.

"I never been North"—Luther came up with more curious news —"but my family been struck by the Lincoln disease all the same."

"What disease is that, Luther?"

"The one that stretches your bones. My Auntie Laverne growed to over six feet before she was fifteen, same as Abe Lincoln. Her shoe was fifteen and five eights inches, it were that long. Same as Lincoln's. It caused her nipples to grow inward. Which made her ashamed. Later she went blind but recovered her sight 'n spent the rest of her days blessing the light God had sent her personally.''

The next night I wakened to hear a motor running that wasn't Luther's Studebaker. Yet I could make out his long lank figure in the dark, bent above the gas tank. I thought he was drunk and trying to vomit, because he had both hands to his mouth. There was someone at the roadster's wheel whose face I couldn't make out. *"Llévame a casa"* had been chalked on one side of its windshield and "Take me home" on the other.

"Feeling badly, Luther?" I called. He made a long, sucking sound for reply. Then he climbed into the roadster and off he wheeled with the mysterious stranger.

He'd siphoned the last drop of gas out of tank number one. I wasn't going to be the black-eyed-pea king of the Rio Grande Valley after all.

So I filled the Studebaker from the other tank. Then I dumped a bushel of peas into that tank, added five cans of Carnation milk, two plates of dried mush and a can of bacon grease. Then went back to bed content. Toward morning I heard the roadster return. I hoped I hadn't flavored the tank too richly. I didn't want Luther to choke on anything. After he'd emptied it he wheeled away once more.

In the forenoon I went bowling along in the Studebaker at fifteen miles per hour. On a day so blue, so clear, it took my breath away to breathe it.

The *Llévama a casa*—Take-Me-Home roadster was parked out on a shoulder of the road on the last curve into Harlingen. Luther came out of it wigwagging. I pushed my speed to eighteen miles per hour and he had to jump for it. In the rearview mirror I saw him standing with his hands hanging at his sides like a disappointed undertaker's.

Now he'd walk into town to save a nickel phone call. And report to the agent that I'd absconded with a hundred gallons of Sinclair gas in a stolen Studebaker. Would the agent telephone Dallas to alert the Rangers? Would I have to run a roadblock at Texarkana? Would my picture be posted in every P.O. in Texas: WANTED DEAD OR ALIVE?

Clyde, Bonnie, Ray Hamilton and I were at large. I'd never felt so elated in my life.

I sold the heap to a garage in McAllen for $11 without being recognized. I treated myself to *tortillas* and chili in a Mexican woman's lunch counter that leaned toward the Southern Pacific tracks. She didn't recognize me either.

402

I took cover behind a water tower until a northbound freight came clanking. I climbed into a boxcar, slid the big door shut and fell asleep in a corner. I slept for a long time; waking only to hum contentedly:

Dead or alive, boys, dead or alive
How do I look, boys, dead or alive?

Until in sleep I heard a music, like children calling; between the beating of the wheels. Little lights were pursuing one another under the boxcar door. A calliope's high cry came clearly. I slid the big door open just an inch. Great silver-circling lights were mounting like steps into a Ferris-wheeling sky. A city of pennoned tents was stretching under those mounting lights. Then a tumult of merry-go-rounding children came on a wind that blew the pennons all one way.

I hit the dirt on a run, leaped a ditch, jumped a fence, fell into a bush, crept under a billboard, straddled a low brick wall and followed a throng of Mexicans under a papier-mâché arch into the Jim Hogg County Fair. And the name of that carnival town was Hebbronville.

A banner, strung between two poles in front of a tent and lit by carbon lights, showed two boxers squaring off. Someone began banging on an iron ring. A big woman, tawny as a gypsy, with a yellow bandana binding her hair, mounted a bally and began barking: "¡Avanza! ¡Avanza! ¡Avanza! Hurry! Hurry! Hurry! See the two strongest men on earth battle to the death! See Hannah the Half-Girl Mystery! See the Human Pincushion!"

A dozen rubes were already gaping. A skinny boy, wearing white boxing trunks and muddy tennis shoes, climbed up the bally beside her. "Say hello to the folks, Melvin," the gypsy instructed the boy. The boy grinned stupidly.

"I never saw anything like it!" a roughneck in farmer's jeans exclaimed beside me.

I didn't see anything that remarkable. The boy looked to be about fifteen, thin as a long-starved hound, with legs that had little more than knobs for knees. His shoulders were so narrow there was just room for his goiterish neck between them. His chin receded so far an ice-cream cone would have had to be inserted beneath his upper lip before he'd be able to lick it. The Human Pincushion looked as if a pin stuck into his egg-shaped skull could cause him no pain; while his hair had the look of bitten-off pink threads.

Two young huskies, one in a tattered red bathrobe and the other in a faded blue one, trotted from opposite sides of the tent and climbed onto the bally, one beside the boy and the other beside the woman. "The Birmingham Strong Boy!" the woman held up the hand of the red-robed terror, who merely looked sullenly out toward the midway. "The Okefenokee Grizzly!" she held up blue-robe's arm. Grizzly merely frowned. Both men were high-cheekboned blonds, unshaven; and looking enough alike to be brothers.

The Mexican sheriff came down the midway, checking the joints.

"Keep movin', tin-can cop!" Strong Boy challenged him. "Keep movin' or I'll come down there 'n whup you!" Grizzly, the woman and the Pincushion grappled with him to keep him from assaulting the officer. The sheriff kept on walking, smiling faintly. The rubes grinned knowingly.

"The man is an *animal*," the roughie whispered to me confidentially.

"You must have seen the show before," I took a guess.

Grizzly threw off his robe, began pounding his chest with his fists and roaring. Strong Boy immediately threw off *his* robe, pounded his chest and roared back. They created such an uproar that one Mexican came on the run, leaving his wife and two children standing on the midway. Melvin and the woman got between the two monsters and the roughie jumped up onto the bally to keep them from tearing each other to bloody shreds publicly.

"The boys are going to settle their differences inside!" the woman announced after the two had been cooled momentarily. "Mountain style! No holds barred!"

"I don't want to miss *this!*" Roughie chortled at the crowd and headed for the tent, with the rubes following him like sheep following a bell ram. Melvin jumped and began taking dimes. His chest, I noticed as I paid him mine, appeared to be mosquito bitten.

Someone had painted both sides of the tent with figures intended to be those of seductive women; but had succeeded only in creating two lines of whorish dwarfs. The angle at which the tent was pitched amplified the breasts and foreshortened the legs; so that each grotesque leaned forward as if she'd been impaled at her ankles. The artist had used too much red. Some whores.

Roughie, standing in front of a curtained closet no higher than himself, announced, "Hannah the Half-Girl Mystery!"—and opened the curtain. Swinging gently there on a child's swing, against a background of velvety black, a girl in a purple-and-cream-colored sweater looked down upon us with long, dark, indolent Indian eyes. Her body apparently ended at her waist.

"As you see," she explained in a voice as low and husky as a child's,

"I have no visible means of support and still I don't run around nights. Thank you thank you thank you, ladies and gentlemen. Thank you one and all. *Señoras y señores, gracias.*" The crowd sighed, as one man, with pity and love.

"She tires easily," Roughie explained and drew the curtain.

"You *believe* that?" a simple-looking fellow, in need of confirming his own doubt, asked me.

"Might be she got run over by a train," I took another guess.

He looked at me with the indignation a simple mind feels when confronted with a mind even simpler. "You dern *fool,*" he accused me. "Couldn't you even tell that girl was a-layin' on her belly?"

"Step this way, gentlemen," Roughie commanded us and nodded to the mosquito-bitten boy. "*Melvin the Human Pincushion!*"

Melvin shuffled onto the bally with a sheepish look and began pinning red-white-and-blue campaign buttons into his skin. Some were for William Gibbs McAdoo. When he used a Hoover button I thought he'd surely bleed. He didn't bleed for either McAdoo or Hoover. He was a bipartisan pincushion.

Then he jabbed a huge horse blanket pin into his shoulder and Roughie went face forward in a dead faint. Strong Boy and Grizzly, both in their fighting robes, carried him off. I was glad to see they'd made up their differences in this emergency.

The dark woman handed Melvin a small blackboard and a piece of chalk. He drew a line beside three lines already drawn and held the board up for us all to see. " 'N that's the number of people has fainted during my performance just today!" he announced triumphantly and jumped off the bally without waiting for applause. That was a good idea; because there wasn't any applause.

"In this cawneh!"—and here came Roughie again, now in white referee's trousers, into the center of the makeshift ring—"in this cawneh, at two hundred and fifty-two pounds, the champion of the Florida Coast Guard—*the Okefenokee Grizzly!*" Pause for scattered applause. " 'N in this cawneh, the champion of the Panama Canal Zone—*the Birmin'ham Strong Boy!*" Scattered applause by the same hands. "These boys are about to settle a long-standin' grudge, so any of you men who faint easy, kindly leave now. No money refunded once the battle has begun!"

"How about yerself?" someone had to remind Roughie; but he paid no heed. "Now, this event is presented at no extra cost and no hat passing, because you men are all lovers of good clean sport, auspices of the Rio Grande Valley Wrestlin' Association." He turned to the wrestlers. "Boys, remember you're professional athletes at the top of your class, representin' the honor of the Florida Coast Guard and the American fleet in Panama, respectively, and I'm here to enforce the rules. Now, shake hands, return to your corners, come out fighting and may the best man win!''

Grizzly put out his paw, but Strong Boy, hateful fellow, struck it down. Then he turned on his heel back to his corner, handed his robe to the dark woman and flexed his thighs while holding the ropes.

"You'll pay dearly for *that*, Strong Boy!" The Human Pincushion threatened him from Grizzly's corner.

"Watch your mouth or I'll whup *both* of you!" the dark woman answered. Strong Boy, still grasping the ropes, spat across the ring directly at the opposing corner. The yokels loved it.

Strong Boy and Grizzly began circling each other, both frowning, yet not closing. Somebody booed. Grizzly went to the ropes, scanned the faces looking up through a haze made of tobacco and heat.

"What do you want for a dime?" he challenged the whole tent. "Blood?"

"*Look out!*" Pincushion warned him too late.

Strong Boy leaped on Grizzly from behind and they went to the canvas, rolling over and under from rope to rope in a roaring fury. The canvas shook, the tent poles trembled and the carbon lamps swung. Strong Boy clamped a headlock on Grizzly that nothing human could break. But Grizzly—being subhuman—broke it, sending Strong Boy staggering, his hands waving before his eyes in the throes of blinding shock. Grizzly backed against the ropes to gain leverage, then propelled himself half across the ring. Strong Boy stepped lightly aside, grabbed Grizzly's ankles as he flew past and brought him crashing down on his face. Strong Boy had only been *pretending* to be hurt! Swiftly applying a double scissors, a toe hold, a half-nelson and a Gilligan guzzler with one hand, he began poking his opponent's eyes out with the other.

"*Give* it to him, Strong Boy!" the crowd came on in full cry, uncaring which of the two brutes got it, as long as one of them was punished murderously. "*Wreck* him, Birmingham!"

The blood-lusters hadn't reckoned on the Human Pincushion. Melvin slipped through the ropes carrying a length of hose and now it was the dark woman who cried warning—"*Watch out, Strong Boy!*"—just as Melvin conked him behind the ear and knocked him flat on his face.

The referee snatched the hose length from the boy's hand and began loping about the ring, holding it aloft and crying, "*I'm here to enforce the rules! Here to enforce the rules!*" as if waving a hose length proved that that was what he was doing; while Strong Boy still lay stretched defenselessly with Melvin kneeling in the small of his back. Grizzly, instead of helping Melvin, merely loped after the referee with his fists clasped in the victory sign. A bear's head was tattoed on his right biceps: a grizzly with small red eyes.

Then Strong Boy lurched to his knees, sending Melvin spinning, got to his feet and went loping counterclockwise to Grizzly, holding *his* fists aloft in victory. They passed each other twice making the same claim. Then both climbed out of the ring, followed by Melvin. Roughie paused to announce the results, *"Draw! Draw! Two falls out of three for the world's free-style championship! Final fall in one hour!"* Then he climbed out, too.

"That were the worst fake fight I ever seen my whole born days." A voice behind me drawled its disappointment.

"The holler 'n uproar was pretty fair," a woman observed. Fake fight or real, the holler 'n uproar had been fair enough to fill the tent with marks; some of whom had now brought women.

"And now, if the ladies will allow, I'll talk to the gentlemen *privately,"* the dark woman said; then waited. The half-dozen women in the crowd retreated, huddled and sheepish, as their fine bold fellows inched forward. "And I know you *are* gentlemen," she resumed, using a more intimate tone. "Do you see this little bell I hold in my hand?" raising a small tin bell and holding it high until every gentleman had seen it. "Now, I know what you men are here to see. I was young once myself—ha-ha-ha—and although you're gentlemen, you're still hot-blooded Americans." Her eyes scanned their ashen and chinless faces in which most of the teeth were missing. "But there's a city ord'nance against presenting young women in the ex-*treem nood* within forty feet of the midway—but back *there*, gentlemen, back *there* our young women are only waitin' for me to tinkle this bell so's they can start *goin' the whole hawg!"*

One tinkle and we'd be off! The men craned their necks like trackmen; but she lowered the bell as if having second thoughts. Then suddenly threw up her hands as if pleading. "For God's sake, men, don't go tellin' total strangers what you're about to see! You'll spoil it for your friends!" She waited to assure herself nobody was going to tell. Several more marks joined us from the midway while she still held the bell aloft.

"Gentlemen! If there's anyone here who can't control his passions when we get back there, I'll have to ask him to step forward and have his money refunded at the box office! No money refunded once the performance has begun! Nobody stepped forward. She tinkled the bell at last.

407

"Awful sex acts goin' on right this way, gentlemen," the Roughie-referee directed us. "Step this way, gentlemen, for *awful* sex acts!" He was holding a sombrero into which we each dropped a dime as we passed into the partitioned rear of the tent.

"You handle quite a few jobs around here," I observed as I paid him.

"Why not?" he remarked cheerfully. "It's my tent."

A crude wooden cubicle, octagonal, with shutters at the height of a man's eyes, waited in the flickering gloom. We stood around it while crickets began choiring to a generator's beat. The Roughie came in, wearing a coin bag around his neck. "Get your nickels here, boys," he advised us, "two for a dime and five for a quarter, see the little ladies shiver and shake. You pay for the ridin' but the rockin' is free!" I had to wait in line to get change for a dime. A gramophone began playing inside the cubicle:

> *Ain't she sweet?*
> *See her coming down the street!*

I put in a nickel, the shutter lifted and Hannah-the-Half-Girl-Mystery's long, indolent eyes looked straight into mine. She was wearing a red veil tied in a great bow about her hips and a green veil about her breasts. She moved her hips and breasts gently as the the gramophone droned on:

> *Now I ask you very confidentially*
> *Ain't she sweet?*

The shutter closed. I put in my other nickel hurriedly. This time she had closed her eyes and was smiling faintly. The gramophone began another inquiry:

> *How come you do me like you do? . . .*
> *I ain't done nuth-in' to you.*

And *click*. Another nickel shot.

"Mighty short nickel's worth," I complained to the ex-referee.

"Ain't *nothin'* to what's comin' next son," he assured me, "and no charge *whatsoever* for this next show—just keep your voice and your head down, right this way." I stooped to keep from bumping my head as he raised the next flap and then stepped into the ultimate mystery of a wide and stilly night. A full moon was just starting to rise. I stumbled across tent stakes until I'd regained the midway.

Under the new moon's coppery light, the fair seemed strangely changed. The dust that rose down its long midway, catching that light, looked like metallic flecks restlessly drifting. A glow, like beaten bronze, burnished the sides of tents that by day had been mottled gray. And the faces of the men and women behind the wheels and the stands and the galleries looked out more ominously than before.

The dark woman's plea of "¡Avanza! ¡Avanza!" sounded more pleading and the calliope cried *La Paloma* more urgently now. An air of haste stirred the dark pennons as if to hurry the tempo of pleasure along. Everyone began moving a little faster as though time were running out: All lights might darken at the same moment and never come on again.

"Spin 'er, mister!" Someone was challenging the wheel in a wheel-of-fortune tent. "Doublin' up! Let 'er spin! This is *my* night! Cash on the barrel!" A clinking of silver dollars followed and I hurried over to watch.

If the aging man in the paint-stained cap was having a winning night, he looked to me it must be the first winning night of his life. "Takin' the six!" he announced like an auctioneer. "*And* the nine!"

"Only one number to a player," said the wheelman, refusing the Cap's double bet. He looked worried.

"Afeerd I'll beat you *both* numbers, mister?" the Cap taunted the wheelman; yet the wheelman still refused him. I felt the Cap slipping a silver dollar into my hand as he whispered, *"Put this on the nine for me, son."* I liked his plan of putting something over on the wheelman. Immediately.

The wheel clicked fast, slowed at 5-6-7-8, then nudged onto 9 and stopped. All the poor wheelman could do was shake his head ruefully and complain, "This is the worst streak of bad luck I've *ever* run into," while he paid me twelve silver dollars. When I slipped them to my backer, he returned one as a token of his appreciation, whispering, "Play this for yourself, son."

I was careful to wait until the wheelman stepped back from the wheel before I put it down. Nobody was working monkey business on *me*.

I put the dollar on 7. The wheel almost stopped on 6, then nudged over onto 7!

"We're killing him!" the Cap cried joyously.

The wheelman stacked the $12 I'd won just out of my reach. Then stacked twenty of his own beside them and asked me casually, "Try for the jackpot, son?"

"*Take him up,*" the Cap urged me in the same hoarse whisper.

"*I don't know how it works,*" I confessed in a whisper almost as hoarse.

"You get the chance at the twenty-dollar jackpot because you won twice in a row, son. You don't have to bet on a number, you can bet on color 'n that gives you a fifty-fifty instead of just a thirteen-one chance, 'n if you bet on both color and number 'n you hit both, you get paid double on top of thirteen-one, making twenty-six-one 'n a chance at the twenty-dollar gold piece—"

"*Red!*" I shouted. But the wheelman just stood waiting.

"*It costs a dollar to bet on the color, because the fifty-fifty pay-off gives you too big an edge over the house—that's the rules of the game, son.*" I put a dollar of my own down and the wheel, sure enough, stopped on the red 5.

"*Hit again!* I never seen anything like it!" the Cap exulted and I wished he weren't so loud about it. He was attracting the attention of people on the midway. "Whoo-*eee! This kid is a gambler! Pay the kid off, mister!*" he threatened the wheelman loudly enough for the whole fair to hear. I didn't see any need for threats; because the man was already stacking my winnings in three neat piles.

I decided not to press my luck. "I'll just take my thirty-two," I told him.

"*Play,*" the Cap hissed in my ear, "*you can't quit now.*" Only this time he wasn't advising. Now he was *telling*. I felt someone standing right behind me; but I didn't turn to see if it was anyone I knew. I just gave the Cap a fixed smile and then turned it on the wheelman so he wouldn't think I liked the Cap more than I liked him.

"Try for sixty, sport?" he asked.

"Sure thing," Sport agreed, "make it or break it on the black."

"It costs five dollars to try for sixty," the Cap informed me. "Rules of the game." Could he be making those rules up as he went along?

"I don't have five, I have only two," I lied; because I didn't want to go into my right shoe.

"Let him try for two," a voice behind me commanded. The wheelman spun for two. If I won again, I'd have to make a run for it—but it stopped on red zero. The house had recovered its losses; plus three dollars of my own. I turned to go. Nobody was standing behind me.

"Sport!" the wheelman called me back and handed me two quarters, "get yourself something to eat at the grabstand and come back if you want to go to work."

I went wandering down the thronging midway, clicking my two consolation coins. One was smaller than the other. Why was it somebody was always trying to slip me phony money? I turned it over and saw it had Roosevelt's head upon it. I gave it to a woman selling *tacos* just to try it out. She gave me 15 cents change. Well I be dawg. That Mexican had been on the up-and-up, after all. With the ten-dollar bill in my shoe and 40 cents in my hand, I had enough to go courting! I worked my way through the throng toward Hannah-the Half-Girl's tent.

The ex-referee was sitting on the bally stand chewing a blade of grass; looking as if he'd been put together with wire; then sprayed with sand. A sinewy, freckled, sandy-haired, pointy-nosed little terrier of a fellow of any age between thirty and fifty.

"Stick around for the girlie show, son," he hustled me the moment he saw me, "you never seen anything like it."

"I've already seen the show, sir," I let him know. "May I ask you something?"

"Ask away."

"Is that wheel down the midway on the up-and-up?"

"Every show on the grounds is honest, son," he assured me; looking me straight in the eye.

"Reason I ask is that I lost three dollars playing it and that gave rise to some doubt," I explained.

"Nobody wins *all* the time, son."

"I feel better about it now."

The dark woman came up, walking as though she were wearied out. Behind her the Half-Girl put her head and torso out of the tent. I hoped that that *really* wasn't *all* there was to her. Then the rest of her emerged on two sturdy legs and began moving toward us. I kept my eyes on the man and the woman. When she came up I caught a faint scent of clove and lavender.

"Oh, they're nice enough," I hastened to assure the tent people, "one of them loaned me half a dollar and told me to come back if I wanted to go to work. It's the wheel with the Navaho blanket nailed up in back."

"That's Denver Dixon's," the man informed me. "You're in good hands, son." He added, to the girl, "Dixon has offered this young man a position." All three then looked me up and down; as though one thought were in all their minds.

"I can see how he'd prove useful," the woman decided for them all.

"We take care of Dixon's boarding-house," the girl put in. "It's where you'll stay if you work for him. If you come back here at closing, we'll drive you out."

"I appreciate your hospitality, miss," I assured her.

The man put out his hand. "Name of Bryan Tolliver," he told me. "My wife Jessie. My daughter Hannah."

"That's spelled T-a-l-i-a-f-e-r-r-o," the girl explained. Now, how had a sandy little man held together by wire, and a woman as weary and heavy as that, gotten themselves a girl so lovely?

*   *   *

WELCOME TO
DIXON'S SHOWFOLKS BOARDING HOME
SPANISH COUSINE A SPECIALTY

Everything was settled, yet nothing was settled. Hard times had taken the people apart and hard times had put them back together: some with parts missing; some with parts belonging to others; some with parts askew; yet others with extra parts they hadn't learned to handle. The times themselves had come apart and been put together askew.

Doggy Hooper, the shill in the paint-stained cup, had been a railroad clerk on the Atchison, Topeka & Santa Fe for twenty years. Now he showed me how he'd made Denver Dixon's wheel stop at 9 by a wire attached to his shoe; how he'd stopped it at 7; and then how he'd stopped on red zero when I'd bet on the black 11. Doggy replayed such small triumphs with the air of a man who'd made a killing on Wall Street.

"'N that's the way we flap the jays!" he grinned up at me; but a bit to the side because his right eye was slightly turned out. "It's how we move the minches 'n give the rubes dry shaves"—and he did a bit of a jig.

We moved the minches and flapped the jays every night. Doggy was the reach-over man; Dixon was the cool-off man and I was the stick. Anyone we hooked between us was a mark. When we got two or three more Dixon pulled the sticks.

Then Doggy and I would be free to take a turn of the midway, past the stand that sold what I called cotton candy but Doggy called sweetened air. Past the flavored drinks that I called pop but Doggy called flukem. Past what I called a ferris-wheel but Doggy called the chump-heister. Past what I called the merry-go-round; but Doggy called the razzle-dazzle.

"Son," Doggy asked me seriously, "do you have so much as a flash

412

notion of how much people will pay for the chance of losing their shirts?''

I didn't have a flash notion. He showed me a pair of dice; which I had only to weigh in my palm to tell were loaded.

"I wouldn't play against you with these," I told him.

"Even if I told you *beforehand* they were loaded, that what I had in mind was to cheat you?''

"Surely not.''

He stuck a finger at my chest. "You wouldn't *now*. But you will, son. You will." And he walked away.

Doggy was right.

Born on the hooks and looking for prey they were all fly-by-nighters and hustling rogues, hip to the lay and the holdout box: accomplices in putting the bends or playing the humps. They'd caught early-on to the Gypsy switch. Yet when hit with the swag when the hooks were out, they could take a drop without hollering cop. They were no whit less honest for all of that.

Though the ducks in the shooting galleries had lead in their tails and the blackjack decks had a missing six; though the wheels were wired and the dice were rolled, the men and women who cast the dice and spun the wheels were no whit less honest. For all of that.

And though they pitched their tents on the very same lots where, but a year before, they'd sheared the rubes and flapped the jays, flimflammed them at the jam auctions and suckered them at three-card monte, yet their tents were hardly pitched before the rubes were jostling each other to try again: crawling under the flaps for the chance of being sheared, suckered, conned, hooked, fleeced and flimflammed one more time.

The Atchison, Topeka & Santa Fe had made a good move in getting Doggy away from their rolling stock, I concluded. He'd sprung a coupling and been left on a spur.

Doggy Hooper's parts didn't match. But then, nothing else around that old strange house matched. Upstairs or down. There were hens in the yard; but when you looked for a rooster here came a capon.

Denver Dixon himself belonged somewhere else. Six-feet-one and slim in the hips, wearing a dark suit sharply pressed, walking so lightly in his Spanish boots with the yellow string of his Bull Durham pouch dangling from his lapel pocket, keeping his face half-shadowed by his Stetson and his drawl pitched to the Pecos, nothing he wore or said would indicate that he'd been born and brought up in Port Halibut, Massachusetts.

Had his big red-white-and-blue boardinghouse sign stood near the state highway, instead of being smeared across the side of a dilapidated stable, that would have seemed less fanciful. Chicken wire, nailed across the stable to prevent horses from leaping its half door, would have made sense had there been a horse inside. But all the stable held was a domino table teetering on a scatter of straw. Where harness and saddles should have been, fishing tackle hung. Kewpies of another day, that once had smiled on crowds tossing colored confetti, smiled on; though their smiles were now cracked and all the confetti had long been thrown. Along shelves were ducks of wood and cats of tin remembering, among paint cans in which the paint had dried, their shooting-gallery days. An umbrella hung above the Kewpies—what was *that* doing here? A burlap sack marked FEED held nothing but dusty joint-togs discarded by belly dancers; whose bellies by now had turned to dust.

The deep-sea tackle belonged to Doggy; who'd never come closer to a creature of the deep than to a crawfish in a backwater creek. Yet nobody considered the man strange because he practiced casting, with rod and reel, in ranching country. Once, showing me how to reel in bass, he hooked his line into a bristlecone pine. Then stood purely dumb-founded that anything like that could happen to a man in a country of cactus and bristlecone pine. If a blue whale could have been hooked in alfalfa, Doggy Hopper was the man with the bait, sinker and line to haul the awful brute in.

Doggy *liked* beating marks. He liked beating *me*. He beat me at dominoes and he beat me pitching horseshoes—and every time he beat me, he called me Sport. But he never beat me for money again.

One forenoon I found him crouching before an orange crate half-covered with tar paper. Chicken bones, recently gnawed, littered the crate's uncovered side. A hole, sufficiently large for a small animal to enter, had been cut into the top of the covered section. I thought I heard a faint scurrying in there.

"What is it, Doggy?" I asked. He was too preoccupied with what was going on inside that crate to reply. He drew back without taking his eyes off that hole.

"Did you catch something, Doggy?" I asked. Doggy nodded as much as to say he'd caught something but wasn't too pleased about it.

"What did you catch, Doggy?" I asked after another minute. "What's in there?"

"What's in there? What's in there?" he mocked me. "The Thing That Fights Snakes, fool! Now, stand back while I rile it up a little." I backed off.

He drew on a pair of canvas gloves, lowered his cap to protect his eyes and bent to the box once more. He appeared puzzled about something. "Damned little bugger just et 'n now he's hongry again," he reported, shaking his head reflectively.

"It *is* a pure wonder to me, though," he reflected, turning back to his captive, "that it'd want *another* rattler so *soon*. Barely had time to digest *that* one. Where *am* I to find *another'n?*" he asked himself, then answered, "I just plain don't *know*." He stood up, appearing relieved. "Sleeping," he confided to me in a whisper. I bent down over the crate with utmost caution.

The top sprang open and a silver-streaking fury, all fur and fangs, flew at my face. I stumbled backward, wigwagging frantically to protect my eyes; then recovered myself and peered down through my fingers. An eviscerated squirrel, its fur painted silver, lay coiled at my feet. A spring had been wired to its tail and a set of old dentures joined to its jaws.

Doggy began leaping about the yard, his laughter breaking like crockery cracking on stone, holding his stomach for sheer joy of his prank. One can't expect too much of a semiliterate booze-fighter, I thought, walking to the house and registering contempt with every step.

Jessie was in her rocker on the porch with a copy of the *Valley Morning Star* on her lap. I took the rocker beside her. A column of coal smoke kept rising from a Southern Pacific switch engine directly across the rutted road into a cloudless and windless sky. Voices, from the *Iglesia Metodista* just down the road, rose in praise of that same sky.

"En la cruz, en la cruz
Yo primera vi la luz
Y las manchas de mi alma yo lavé
Fue allí por fe yo vi a Jesús
Y siempre feliz con él seré.

"The papers keep puttin' every killing in Texas on Clyde and Bonnie," Jessie complained, "I know for a fact that Bonnie was in jail at Kaufman when them gas stations at Lufkin was robbed. 'N it wasn't them that shot down the grocerman at Sherman. That was Hollis Hale 'n Frank Hardy. Clyde 'n Bonnie was up in Kansas gettin' married by razzle-dazzle."

"By what?" I asked politely.

"By razzle-dazzle. Flat-ride. Carousel."

"Merry-go-round?"

"No. A merry-go-round is the gambling wheel you're working with

Doggy. Could a couple fixing to get married ride *that?*" As a victim of one practical joke that day, and the day still short of noon, I thought it best not to pursue the matter.

"Just one of Mother's pipe dreams," Hannah advised me from the door. She was wearing some kind of hand-me-down burlesque gown, ripped under one arm, to which a few silver sequins still clung. The sun glinted on them so sharply that she canted one arm to shield her eyes; exposing a dark tangle of hair in the pit of the arm. Again I caught that faint scent of lavender or clove; touched now by perspiration.

"If you think me and your pa got married in church," Jessie reminded her sharply, "you'd do well to check with Bill Venable's steam razzle-dazzle in Joplin—'cause it was on that your pa and me got bound in wedlock, holy or no. 'N don't you go forgettin' it."

And here came Doggy shuffling along with his cap pulled too low over his eyes. Well, let the poor geek tell his sorry joke, I thought; I'll go along with the laugh.

Yet the old man spoke not a word. Simply braced his back against the sun-striped wall with his cap low over his eyes. But when he glanced up, blinking toward the light, I saw his eyes looking inward and his cheeks pale as ash. Jessie gave me a flicker; as if to say she understood something I did not.

"I wasn't *disputing* you, Mother," the girl explained, "I just purely doubt that Bonnie Parker and Clyde Barrow married that way. After all, they're *not* carnies."

"They wouldn't be the first outlaws rode the flat-ride because they couldn't risk walkin' through a JP's door," Jessie suspected.

"*I'm* not an outlaw, Mother," the girl caught Jessie up.

"And not much of a carny neither," Jessie put her down quite as fast.

"All the more reason for me to be married in church instead of on a merry-go-round."

"*We* don't call it a merry-go-round," I put in authoritatively, "*we* call it a flat-ride or razzle-dazzle. Merry-go-round is a gambling wheel. Or a lay-down."

"*Now,*" Jessie exulted at Hannah's expense, "you hear *that?* Here's an eye-tinerant college boy turned carny bare a week 'n he talks better carny than you who was born 'n bred to tent-life."

"*I* didn't attend college," Hannah explained, taking the rocker beside her mother's. "I want a *church* marriage. By a *preacher.* I'm just not goin' to set on top of some dumb wood brewery horse with a calliope blowing 'n call *that* a marriage."

416

"Your pa and me rode wood horses driven by steam 'n *we* called it marriage," Jessie said reproachfully, " 'N the flat-ride *we* rode we could have set atop a zebra or a lion if we'd wanted—*that* razzle-dazzle had a whole *jungle* on it. If we find you a steam-driven ride with a zebra, will you like that better, honey?"

"Mother, *try* to be serious."

I had the impression that this fanciful debate had been fought, uphill and down, numerous times before. Always about whether it would be a carny or a church wedding; and never a reference to a groom.

It had, of course, to be one of the half brothers who alternated nightly in the roles of the Strong Boy and the Grizzly. Lon Bethea, at 233 pounds, outweighed Vinnie by less than four pounds. Yet their combined 462 pounds of sinew, with the sheen of youth and the shine of health and the poise of power upon it, could hardly have left Hannah Taliaferro less impressed.

When they took her into their Model A in a kind of protective custody each evening, she sat in the back seat flipping the pages of a magazine; while they sat up front matching her indifference with their own.

"It's up to Vinnie and Hannah," Lon would say, resigning himself too easily to losing Hannah.

"If Hannah 'n Lon make the ride, I'll be their best man." Vinnie was equally gallant, "I'm not a-going to stand in my own brother's way."

"It's awright with me if you marry 'em *both*, Sis," Melvin came to his own decision—for which he caught a fast clap on his ear from her.

The Bethea boys hurled themselves into battle night after night, applying airplane spins and turnover scissors, hammer-locking each other, then butting like bulls; stomping each other's feet, barking each other's shins, then choking each other purple with Gilligan guzzlers; yet they breathed nothing but good will toward men by day.

The S.P. engine shunted a boxcar onto a siding, then raced backward, tootling all the way. "What's *that* fool got to toot about?" Jessie feigned indignation at the engineer, "because he's driving a yard pig?"

"Goin' backwards is when folks blows their whistles loudest," Doggy decided, "or when they got no mail whatsoever to pick up. Don't I do a lot of tootlin' myself?" he asked. "And what have *I* got to tootle about? Ain't I been tootlin' backwards ever since I was born?" he asked in a voice prepared to grieve the whole bright day away.

"I cheated on my folks by playin' hooky," Doggy mourned on, unheeding. "I cheated on my wife with other women. I cheated on my kids by hittin' the bottle. I even cheated countin' boxcar numbers for the Atchison, Topeka 'n Santa Fe.'' He paused for dramatic effect. "What else *could* I do? I were only a child.

"Giving the Atchison, Topeka 'n Santa Fe a wrong count on boxcar numbers wasn't cheating,'' he explained to clear that point up, "it was a subconscious matter I haven't to this day been able to understand myself.'' He waited to see if we were interested in this mystery. Nobody was.

"I couldn't report a three if I was counting *inside*,'' he recalled. "I had to go outside to do it. I could *not* form that number within walls. Inside, my fingers simply would not *do* it. Had to write another number or go out in the rain.''

The little engine raced all the way back toward us, as if the engineer had been listening to our conversation and wanted to put in a word himself. Surely our voices, in that clear bright air, carried far down the tracks. Then he raced back down the roundhouse and out of sight. Jessie turned toward Hannah.

"And if you're making plans to sew that seam under your arm before it's ripped to your belly button, young woman, I'll loan *you* a proper needle.''

Doggy poked his ferrety face out from under his cap. "Aren't no proper thread.'' Then he pulled his head back under his cap and began singing challengingly:

> *If he's good enough for Lindy*
> *He's good enough for me*
> *Herbert Hoover is the only man*
> *To keep our country free!*

"Good enough for Lindbergh ain't good enough for me,'' Jessie derided the President, the pilot, Doggy and the song. "Franklin D. Roosevelt is the man to set *this* country free.''

"I'll tell you about Roosevelt,'' Doggy offered: "He's like the bottom part of a double boiler—gets all worked up but don't know what's cookin.' 'N I'll tell *you* something, Sport.'' He turned to me. "Any time you get into a town where the cops don't have uniforms, you can be sure the chow is going to be lousy.''

Doggy seemed to be coming out of his mood nicely.

"Is Mr. Dixon up yet, Mother?'' Hannah asked.

"Gone to town bright 'n early to pick up the Jew fella,'' Jessie reported. "Took them two fool wrasslers along.'' The "Jew fella'' was Dixon's wheelman, Little British.

418

Although Hannah Taliaferro was a sturdy girl, she gave an impression of fragility. She was quick in mind and movement; but, even more, the impression came from that strange personal scent that seemed to mingle clove and lavender with perspiration. Men who fixed their eyes on a distant point, when she stood directly before them, looked perfect fools to me. I avoided looking the fool simply by shutting my eyes until her mother called her away.

The true mystery about Hannah the Half-Girl Mystery was not how her lower body disappeared at tent time, then reappeared as she swept floors, made beds and turned hot cakes the next morning. It was how, whether bending, walking, turning, resting, stretching itself or just standing still, it became more voluptuous at every reincarnation.

Her carelessness toward her own charms was not the least of her charm. She went about barefoot, wearing nothing but that hand- me-down burlesque gown, once red, now faded to brown. Her nipples, always pointing as if forever taut, stretched the dress's thin fabric. When she bent down over the table to serve a dish, I saw a skin so tawny that the circles about the nipples were only a hue darker than the breasts themselves.

After that I'd go upstairs to rest.

Doggy got so drunk, between the stable and the town, that he lay all day Sunday on his garret cot, paralyzed by exhaustion. By Monday noon, however, he'd recuperated sufficiently to go about consumed with remorse: "No, you don't get a cigarette," I heard him pronouncing various penances upon himself—*"you* had *yours* Saturday. No, you don't get any lunch today. *You* had *yours* Saturday." All day Monday he denied himself; and part of Tuesday, too. Thursday evening he began letting up a bit on himself. By Saturday he'd be ready for an all-night bender once again.

A carnie named Hawks owned the ferris-wheel and the wild-man concession as well. Neither concession was drawing. He came to Dixon's Showfolks Boarding Home, one Sunday forenoon, seeking Dixon's advice.

Hawks was having touble with Leroy, his wild man. Leroy was a country boy who'd joined the show in Texarkana. Hawks gave him his meals, a bed, and a couple of dollars every Sunday morning. All Leroy had to do was to sit in a cage, wearing flannel underwear dyed black, a frightwig, a mouthpiece that lent him the appearance of being fanged; with a dog-collar and chain around his neck. Sometimes Hawk tossed chicken-bones onto the straw at Leroy's feet. If the tip was good Leroy would gnaw them.

It wasn't hard work. The boy didn't even have to howl unless he felt like it.

The yokels paid a dime to stare at FANG THE SAVAGE SOLOMON-ISLANDER. But Leroy was bored. He bought a small radio to pass the hours while the yokels paused, looked, and passed on. The sight of a wild man from the Solomons listening to square-dances disappointed many. Leroy was turning Hawks' show into a farce. So he'd forbidden the boy to take the radio into his cage.

Leroy sulked. Then he wrote a note to the sheriff, saying he was being held against his will in a cage at the Hogg County Fair. The sheriff dispatched a constable to investigate.

Hawks was so annoyed with the boy, for bringing law onto the grounds, that he fired him on the spot. But the constable wouldn't permit Hawks to fire Leroy. Not in Texas.

"If you're going to fire him you have to fire him in the state you hired him," the constable decided, "you can't fire this fool in *my* state."

Hawks had had to drive Leroy the entire length of Texas in order to fire him in Texarkana.

"I wouldn't have made an issue of the radio," he assured Dixon and Doggy now, "if the kid had had any talent. But he wasn't paying his way even without a radio."

"Don't blame *him*," Doggy reproved Hawks, "it's *your* show. You can't expect people to pay just to see somebody sitting in his underwear in a cage. You have to give them a *story*."

Doggy and Hawks retired to the front porch for a story conference. I wasn't surprised when Dixon replaced Doggy at our wheel that night. Dixon didn't trust me to work the gaff by myself.

Doggy was sitting in a cage across the midway, wearing flannel underwear dyed black; a frightwig; with a dog-collar and chain around his neck. He claimed *he* didn't need fangs.

Toward ten o'clock, the hour when the tip begins milling from bally to bally, trying to see everything before midnight, I heard a scream, high-pitched as a tom-cat's in heat, across the midway. The tip began milling wildly, hoping somebody was getting killed.

In that cat-scream I'd heard Melvin's voice.

And here he comes staggering side to side, bespattered with what surely looked to be blood—and the wild man in wild pursuit.

"The wild man has broken loose!"—I heard Jessie shouting.

Women fled. Men backed away. Children stood quietly observing. Every time Melvin screamed, the wild man roared and lunged for him.

420

Every time he barely missed. Once the boy fell prone and the wild man nearly had him—but the boy staggered to his feet and shook off the wild man's grip on his shirt. A woman began shouting "Help him! Help him!" Yet not a man dared get near the wild man.

They made a complete lap of the midway before Melvin collapsed—conveniently—in front of his own tent. There the Bethea boys grabbed the wild man and dragged him, struggling wildly, back into his cage. Jessie and Bryan came rushing to minister to the wounded youth.

The crowd gathered around Melvin. Lon and Vinnie carried him into the tent and the crowd tried following.

Jessie barred the way.

"Ladies and gentlemen!" she commanded them, "your kind attention please! The management has asked me to express its deep regret—and that of everyone in this show—for the tragedy you have just witnessed. But we can assure you that the young man who has been mauled by FANG THE SAVAGE SOLOMON-ISLANDER will get the best attention medical science can offer! At the moment his condition is critical! Nobody will be allowed to enter the tent! Unless he or she is associated with the medical profession!"

"I'm a practical nurse!" a big redheaded woman announced, and began pushing her way through the crowd; followed by a redheaded man and two redheaded teen-age girls. Bryan, standing at the entrance, let the practical nurse and her family in; but another woman tried to follow—"My husband is a doctor," was her claim; but it didn't work.

"Those related to members of the medical profession cannot enter unless *accompanied* by their relatives in the profession," Bryan announced firmly—"or by payment of a small contribution to our medical aid fund!"

When the contribution was understood to be only a dime, the whole crowd surged forward, holding dimes. Jessie moved inside the tent to keep the crowd moving past Melvin, bandaged and prone.

The ketchup on his chest already beginning to dry.

*   *   *

On September 1, 1932, the moon moved across the face of the sun and I heard an owl hoot in Dixon's stable just before noon. It was lighter than night yet darker than day. I'd never seen an owl.

So I went searching the stable's shadows, with a flashlight, in hope of seeing that curious bird. All I saw was Doggy Hooper huddled in a corner, his eyes staring at me so fixedly I wondered whether it might have been himself who'd hooted. "You playing owl on us, Doggy?" I asked, playing the flashlight on his face.

"Gonna be a shakedown an' a shake*up!*" he cried without blinking right into the flashlight's beam. "Union's gonna throw old Doggy out! Roman black snakes after old Doggy!"

An uncorked pint lay on its side, seeping darkly onto the straw. "You're losing good whiskey, Doggy," I told him. His head wobbled, trying to focus on the figure behind the flashlight.

"Awright, Dixon," he muttered, "you come to collect"—he struggled to his feet, holding the wall of the stall for support—"this is the showdown! Show*down*, Show*up. Shakedown! Shakeup!*" I had to support him into the yard. Hannah came out to help. Between us, we got him up the narrow stairs to the room above the stable.

A Navaho blanket, torn and stained by tobacco juice and whiskey, covered Doggy's cot. A cheap alarm clock ticked on the floor. But Doggy wouldn't lie down. He sat stubbornly on the cot's edge and began croaking lonesomely—

> *Mother's voice is gone from the kitchen.*
> *She's teaching the angels to sing—*

"Try to sleep it off, Doggy, dear," Hannah pleaded with him, spoon-feeding hot black coffee into him.

"I'll do anything you fellows can force me to do," he finally conceded. "I'll take anything you can give me so long as I don't have to like it." He took a few spoonfuls of coffee from the girl, then looked at her drowsily. "If you don't behave yourself," he warned her, "I'll stop taking your money." And with that threat he fell back, rolled onto his face and sank into a snoring sleep.

Later I wandered down the road paralleling the S.P. tracks, up to the *Iglesia Metodista.* The doors were open, though no service was being held. Candles burned in the church's dusty gloom. I sat on the steps and waited for a train to pass in either direction. There was no train nor a rumor of one down the bright rails.

I wandered back to the house and around to the stable, wondering vaguely whether there might be anything left in the bottle Doggy had abandoned. There were half a dozen drops, no more. I drank them and pitched the bottle into a corner. Then saw, in the shadow, the crate that held The Thing That Fights Snakes. The Thing still lay coiled inside. I fooled around with its spring until I got it to leap. Then I put the cage in full view of the kitchen window.

"How was the tip Saturday night, Sport?" Hannah put her head out the window to ask.

My back toward her, I contemplated the cage and made no reply.

"Did you have a good tip Saturday night, Sport?" she repeated a bit louder. I held my silence and my pose. Her bare feet came padding up behind me. "Something happening?" I heard her ask softly.

"*Shhh,*" I shushed her, "it's not finished eating."

"*What's* not eating *what?*" She came up right beside the box. Doggy's contraption was new to her. "What's not finished eating what?"

"Shhh, I might have to rile it up a bit."

"Rile *what* up, for God's sake? What *have* you got in there?"

She reached for the box, but I held her back with my hand and shouted, "The Thing That Fights Snakes, fool! *Back!* Stand *back!*"

That girl wouldn't back for tigers. Hannah put her eye to the opening. I sprang the catch. The Thing flew, claws, fur and silvered teeth, into her face. She fell back, waving her hands before her eyes, yet made no outcry. For a moment she stood looking down; until the crazed look in her eyes subsided.

She turned The Thing over with her bare foot. As she turned it onto its back once more, a smile too sly formed on her lips.

Then she came right at me.

Around and around the stable I fled her rage. I had to keep running until she ran out of rage or breath, or stepped on a nail; or all three. Her fingers closed on my shirt, but I ripped away, feinted as if to double back and leaped again, gaining enough yardage to make me halfway around the stable once more. Then I stopped short and wheeled about. She barreled head down right into me, spinning me backward into the stable, crashing me against the domino table as she bore her whole weight down on me. The table collapsed above us in a cascade of dominoes. I clapped my hands about her buttocks, arching myself against her. She broke my hold by straddling me and we both lay a long minute then, struggling for breath. She recovered hers first, because I had her weight on my chest. I tried to push her off with my hands against her shoulders, but she pinned both my arms and slipped her tongue deep into my mouth. That kiss drained my remaining strength.

"Your buckle is hurting me," she complained, and released my arms to unbuckle it. Instead, I got my hands around her buttocks again. They were round and firm as new melons. I hauled her panties down nearly to her knees. She slipped half on her side to kick them off; when they caught on her ankles, she gave a wild kick and sent them flying toward the stable wall. That gave me my chance to roll out from under. I got halfway out and pressed her back with all the strength I had.

She was nearly pinned before she gathered her own strength and I felt myself being forced back inch by inch. In a flash it came to me why she was evading those heavy brothers. This girl wasn't going to be pinned under *anybody*: she could not bear it. Either *she* did the pinning or nothing was going to happen. She entwined her thighs about mine. I thrust upward at the same moment that she thrust down. She gasped with the pain that turns so quickly to pleasure. There was a fast flash of light behind her shoulders and I knew the stable door was standing wide. Then I heard a hoarse cry from far away. I blacked out.

I came to hearing my own cry dying hoarsely in my throat. A moment later, utterly spent, eyes closed, I felt her weight leaving me at last. When I opened my eyes I saw Hannah, silhouetted against the light, scuffling through the straw of the stable floor.

"Lose something?" I asked her.

"My underpants."

"What color were they?"

She glanced over at me. "What kind of question is *that?*"

"Because if they were pink, it must be somebody else's white pair hangin' over that paint can over your head."

I'd caught the sun's glint on the panties' white fringe, draped across the can out of which a brush was still sticking. It stood on a shelf behind and above her head. She snatched the panties down. Then, half rueful and half laughing, she held them up for me to see.

"Now, look what that Doggy Hooper done!"

The panties were dripping with silver hoof paint. It seemed that Doggy had half roused himself from sleep and had come down to do some redecorating. He was gone now; but he had daubed everything within reach. This brought a heavy worry to my mind.

"Give me a couple minutes to get to the house," I asked her. "I don't want to spoil your marriage plans."

"Those boys wouldn't hurt you even if they did find out," she assured me. I wasn't that sure. I took a long swing around the house, so that I could approach from the front.

424

Jessie and Lon were taking their ease in the front-porch rockers. The rocker holding Lon looked ready to crumble beneath all that brawn. He was shirtless. That bear's head, tattooed on his right biceps, began studying me with its two small red eyes.

"I suppose Doggy went and told you of the practical joke he pulled on me," I asked as soon as I reached the step, my plan being to start asking questions before anyone started asking me anything.

"He jumped a dead squirrel out of a box on me once," Lon recalled. "I hit him with the box. He ain't tried it again."

But where was Vinnie? Had he been watching the acrobatics in the stable from his upstairs room? Had he come down the back stairs softly to see what was going on? Had he then conferred with Lon? Had they already set up a plan to catch me that night on the carny grounds? Had they taken Jessie and Bryan in on it? If they consulted Denver Dixon, would *he* speak a word in my defense?

"Clyde Barrow 'n Bonnie Parker kidnapped an officer of the law," Jessie said, "drove him around New Mexico all day before letting him go."

I couldn't have cared less that the law had been outwitted again. "I reckon I'll ride out tonight with Mr. Dixon," I said, forestalling Lon's usual offer.

"Suit yourself, Sport," he said cheerfully.

"There won't be much of a tip tonight," Jessie guessed, "the sand is starting to blow."

I went up the footworn stairs to the little room beneath the eaves. Heat was piling up between the walls. A small clock was making a muted ticking; like news of some lost time too dear for losing.

Fifty-odd years from the bourn of his mother, $22 in debt to Dixon, face down on the cot where he always fell, one palm outflung as if to say *"Spent it all!"* Doggy Hooper was sleeping it off fully clothed.

I stretched out on my cot, hearing voices mingling on the porch below. I fell asleep thinking I'd heard Lon speaking my name to Vinnie. Or was it Vinnie to Lon?

In sleep I felt something near and endangering. I struggled to waken. And quite clearly, though framed by a bluish mist, two massive dogs, sitting their haunches, waited for me to waken.

When I woke at last, Doggy was gone. Sand was tapping the eaves. I listened for something else but heard nothing. The small clock had stopped ticking and the wind was blowing up.

The carny folks were gathered about Dixon's board; but I passed the door as if I had somewhere else to go. I went out onto the porch and watched the wind swirling sand between the S.P. ties.

Dixon and Little British drove up, British at the wheel. I climbed into the rear seat.

"I think Doggy's off to town to get the hair of the dog," I explained Doggy's absence.

"No," Dixon corrected me, "Hawks picked him up to sober him up so he can work tonight."

"He'll never get him sober enough to make that midway run," I was certain.

"The sheriff don't like that act," Dixon filled me in. "He spoke to Hawks about it. What he wants Doggy for tonight is just to ride the ferris-wheel. When people see nobody riding the wheel, they don't want to be the first to get on."

"He better strap Doggy in real tight," I suggested.

As Little British straightened the car out toward the state highway I glanced back and saw, briefly yet clearly, a pair of silver-colored panties hanging above the stable-door like a challenge.

Challenge? A challenge to Jessie and Bryan maybe; but a downright threat to *me*. That child was going to bring on a family row *deliberately*.

To get out of marrying either of the brothers? Or to get out of her role as the Half-Girl? It had to be one or both. Because Hannah wasn't so thoughtless as to hang her silver-colored panties up to dry on a chicken wire in full view of the kitchen. There simply was no way of explaining away that garment, shining with silver hoof paint. She was going to blow up the family circle. And whether I got my neck broken in the ensuing row was, it was plain enough, a matter of no concern at all to Hannah.

My heart didn't spin with the wheel that night. Everything, it seemed, had stopped with Doggy Hooper's clock. Something had ended; yet nothing new had begun. And, in that interval, I had to be more alert than usual; because I was working with Dixon instead of Doggy. In Doggy's absence, Dixon had wired the gaff to his own shoe; while I fronted the marks for him one by one.

"Don't let your luck get away, mister," I encouraged a Mexican old enough to know better. "All you have to do is hit the red to get the thirty-dollar jackpot!"

It cost that one two dollars to try for the $30 jackpot, while signals went flying between Dixon and British. When they had eight dollars of the man's money, British wanted to get rid of him; but Dixon felt he'd stand more gaffing. They built the fool up to a $100 jackpot, and I helped by confusing and encouraging him at the same time; until the man had gone for $30 out of his own pocket. Then he turned back to the midway with his collar awry, sweat on his forehead and a dazed look in his eye.

As Jessie had foreseen, the tip was thin that evening. Some of the tent flaps were already down; though it was still two hours until closing. Only the flat-ride seemed to be doing normal business, I judged, by its calliope crying *La Paloma* without ceasing. When I told Dixon I wanted to walk down to a grabstand because I'd missed supper he gave me the nod to leave.

I made the rounds of the joints chewing a taco. The sand was whirling, in mounting spirals, around the base of the ferris-wheel; but the wheel was still turning. Some fool must still be riding, I figured. Either that or Hawks has walked off, on some business or other, and left his generator running.

I'd known, as soon as I'd seen that girl's panties above the stable door, that this was my last night at the Jim Hogg County Fair. But my mind was so dull from the heat and the heavy day, I couldn't think clearly about a means of getting away.

When I went back to Dixon's wheel, there was an old woman in a black-lace mantilla waving her arms at Dixon and British. That is, her tears and Spanish cries made her seem old; but when I went up I saw she was hardly thirty. I hung back, trying to understand a few words of her Spanish rage.

All I caught was "thieves" and "husband." That cleared matters up. She was, most likely, the wife of the Mexican we'd just sheared.

By rights, as one of the hands in the shearing, I ought to be right up there taking some of the fire. On the other hand, what was *I* doing flapping the jays, anyhow? I didn't belong on any midway.

She was pointing a finger directly at Little British, feeling that *he* was the villain of the plot. Then Dixon put one hand on her shoulder and I saw him reaching for his wallet with the other. He wasn't going to risk having the sheriff shut his wheel down. And possibly the whole fair.

I took two steps backward, turned slowly away and began walking through the dust storm like a man walking through rising waters. I put a bandanna to my mouth and nose, as if to keep out sand. But it was also, I felt, a disguise. I held it there while moving against the crowd of marks coming in, despite the dust, under the papier-mâché arch with its legend: JIM HOGG COUNTY FAIR.

Then I ran for it.

I got over the same fence I'd scaled a week before and mounted the embankment before I looked back. In those few moments of flight, the whole sky had darkened. A swirling darkness was enwrapping the tents. Yet the calliope went on crying.

And the merry-go-round kept circling, circling, though its red, yellow, blue and green lights were blind with dust. Finally, the calliope began to subside. The merry-go-round was going around for the last time.

Then the music stopped and pennons and tents, grabstands and galleries, kewpies and carnies and gaff wheels and all, were lost in a rising dust wind.

Only the ferris-wheel's empty seats rose and fell above the storm. And as I watched, I saw a small dark figure, its head buried in its hands, rise for a moment at the wheel's utmost height.

Then sank, like a sinking hope: forever downward into dust.

TRICKS OUT OF
TIMES LONG GONE

Again that hour when taxies start deadheading home
Before the trolley-buses start to run
And snowdreams in a lace of mist drift down
When from asylum, barrack, cell and cheap hotel
All those whose lives 'vere lived by someone else
Come once again with palms outstretched to claim
What never rightly was their own.

Boothbroad, bluemoon cruiser, coneroo
Drifters of no trade whose voices, unremembered
Complain continually among the cables overhead
Hepghosts made of rain still on the hawks
Tarts out of times long gone who softly try old doors
Or search for long-lost dimes down broken walks
Where spears of summer grass once thrust their green ways up
Through iron and cement.
All green thrusts fade where rainmade hepghosts go:
These grasses have turned white; are shaken to their roots
Between dark cracks in winter's measured stone.

Tonight when chimneys race against the cold
And cats are freezing fast to fire-escapes
I hear them tapping back-doors of old books
And think they must be ghosts of hookers who died broke
Still seeking chances lost and long-missed scores.
Their shadows rise in paving-flares against old walls
Then fall
Then hurry off with some last souvenir to pawn—
This is the victims' hour where they go

Where winos used to drink themselves to death
Or merely slept away their 29-cent woes.
For no ghost follows where a square has gone.

"Chicago pimps just have no class
"No class at all"—
You told me in that long-gone dusk.
Beyond our pane electric forests came magically alight
El cried to El across the city's height.
"Why, when me 'n Little Daddy went into an L.A. bar
"Everyone in the cave would holler, 'Hello cats!'
"Especially the bartender.
"Chicago hookers got less class than their daddies—
"I couldn't stand myself if I came on like *them*—
"You know what one of them fools told me just today?—
" '*I* started the babushka fad around here,' she tells me—
"Imagine the class of people you have to deal with
"Who think that wearin' a babushka gives them class!
"For God's sake I think them broads drink
"Out of their old man's shaving cup is what *I* think—
"'n anyhow I was wearing a babushka two years in L.A.
"So it was me who started *that* style around here.
"Baby, will you put that Earl Bostic on?"

So I listened to Earl Bostic and yourself
Going on and on—
" 'n that old bartender at the *Fireball*
"Telling me my Daddy is no good—
"Don't he think *I* know?
"Didn't Little Daddy come to me himself saying
" 'Little Baby, when I made a *who*-oor out of you
" 'I didn't mean for you to be a junkie too—'
" 'n his face so sort of drawn 'n pulled with care
" 'Daddy,' I asked him then, 'Remember how I needed someone strong
" 'To lean on when you come past?
" 'Well, how was either us to know *then*
" 'It would turn out to be just two fools leanin' on each other?'
"People don't *know* my Little Daddy.
"When Little Daddy says he's going to *do* a thing
"He'll do it if it kills him. He ain't afraid of *anything*.
"If he tells me he'll go away

430

" 'n I won't see my Little Daddy anymore
"He'll go away. 'N I won't see him
"Never anymore.
"And then he'll never know what's in my heart for him."
A tattered yellow kite, caught upon a cable
Tightened its tether to the evening air.

"I'd rather have my Little Daddy's hate
"Than any square-fig's type of square-fig love.
"Who lights my cigarettes 'n says 'I love you'—
"All of *that*. My Little Daddy's hate
"Is more beautiful I think
"Than any square-fig's love.
"Because what my Daddy feels for me he feels it in his heart
"It's *how* a person feels, not *what*, that matters.
"Saying 'I love you' when he don't feel a thing
"Love or hate or anything in his heart
"Don't do a thing for me."

—Da-aa-dee
Da-aa-dee

A smiling child moving her fingers
Through the dark smoke-tangle of her hair
Who owned one record all her own—*Rock Love*—
But no record-player.
Whose clothes her little daddy hocked but not his own
(And once, in lieu of clothes, deposited her
One whole hockshop morning; for collateral.)
"My little Daddy likes to make his brag to me:
" 'Little Baby, I made a who-oor out of you
" 'You ought to hate me something terrible for that.'
"I've never let him know he never made no *who*-oor out of *me*—
"It was me made a pimp of my Little Daddy—"

—Da-aa-dee
Da-aa-dee

One-stocking-on-one-stocking-off country-talking whore
Poor piece of trade whose home was any numbered door
Whose Daddy never learned what was in her heart for him—

431

Thank God for country pimps who go from town to town
Who when they say they'll do a thing
They'll do it if it kills them.
Who aren't afraid of County Sheriffs or State Police
Or soft clothes dicks or Justices of the Peace
Who aren't afraid of *anything*.
Except at night with Little Baby lying by
And whisper then:
"I made a *who*-oor out of you, Little Baby."
Thank God as well for Little Babies who whisper back:
"You're the best connection a hustling woman ever had
"And I'll go all routes with you.
"I might have married some old square-fig type,
"Little Daddy, had it not been for you
" 'n never even got to know I was alive."—

Da-aa-dee
Da-aa-dee

"Don't douse the light," you told me
"Just hang some old tie over it
"Else I'll sleep till day
"Daddy says I got to be back home
"Before the trolleys stop
"So's I don't spend his good money riding cabs—
"I take care of Daddy in the little things
"So's he'll take care of me in the big ones
" 'n if I'm not a good girl he'll stop taking money off me."
If Little Daddy missed his morning fix
It would be all your fault again of course—
Piteous girl who owned a wristwatch with one hand
Its hours as unreal as her own
Who took such care of Daddy in The Little Things
Asking from hour to hour, "What time it is?
"What time it *really* is?"
Then warned me dreamily going on the nod:
"Baby, don't let my monkey in."

Your hair flowed dark across the pillow's white
Your heroin-colored throat at last breathed peace
I kissed your hair yet dared not breathe your breath

"Babytalking whore," I said, "Goodnight.
"Goodnight."

That night the chimney-stars wept ice
Wind tossed light from lamp to lamp
Black trolley-buses raced the moon.
I heard your monkey scratching; but I never let him in.
I never let him in.

Tonight the proud new thruway forged of iron, steel and stone
Courses without a stoplight state to state
Above the rails of trolleys we once rode—
Iron that now lies twisted under stone.
These paving-flares that burn so separately tonight
Burned each to each where once we went
Along old walks that led us always home.

And sleep, that lifted me so light along your side
Now toils with labored breath behind me all night long
Until between two walls of billboards
That many washday rains have lashed to hangnail tatters
Dream upon dream of the same cheap street appears:
Whereon the same dark peddler waits; his cap across his eyes
Hawking a single tie.
All pass and not one buys.
"What time it is?" he whispers as I pass—
And winks too knowingly—
"What time it *really* is?"
It was that time we kissed
Where pigeons made a city skyline strut
It was that hour of waiting for a green-eyed El
Made out of dusk.
It was that moment when your high-heeled step
Down an uncarpeted hall
Made arc-lamps burn more bright all over town.
"I never chippied on my Daddy until now," you said.
We were kind to one another before love
And kind again after.

" 'You were a hare on the mountain'—
"Daddy tried to put me down one time—

" 'When I fired your way you were done for.'
" 'I was done for before ever you took aim, Little Daddy,'
"I filled him in,
" 'Every sport in town was firing my way two full years
" 'Before ever you came calling
" 'Bringing me caramel candy as if I'd never seen the back room of
    a bar.
" 'Little Daddy, I felt sorry for you
" 'With your haircut out of Boys' Industrial
" 'And all the town sports laughing because you thought
" 'Nothing had changed since you'd been gone.
" 'I wasn't no hare on the mountain when you fired, Little Daddy.
" 'I was pigmeat. 'N you were the only one who didn't know.' "

The old connection of the wind knocks once, then leaves
To go on blowing snow from roof to roof.
Along a hallway strangely like a street
I hear again your swift heel-tapping step.
I never guessed how far the boundaries of night could reach
How very dark how very wide how very cold
Beyond the country where old tie-vendors sell.
In a skirt too short and heels too high
You left in a boiling rain.
The coldest that ever fell.

Upon the just-before-day bus I saw a woman
The only one who rode
Look wanly out at streets she used to know
"And there I went": "And there I slept": "And there I rose."
She came forever toward me walking slow
Saying *zaza-za-zaza-za-zaza*.
Walking slow.

The bells of St. John Cantius ring out midnight mass
An unprotected night-bulb casts refracted light.
The El moves overhead on wheels that have no rails.
My babytalking whore: Goodnight.
Goodnight.

All day today old dreams like snowdreams drifting down
Faces once dear now nameless in a mist

434

Return from hospital, prison or parole
Mouths that once the mouth of summer sweetly pressed
Saying *zaza-za-zaza-za-zaza*

Within a rain that lightly rains regret.